Turn the page for

D1019893

"*Keepsake* is a deeply emotional tale of love and life in a small New England town—with all of its secrets, prejudices, unforgettable characters, and charm—interwoven with a murder mystery that has a surprising solution. A fine offering from an author worthy of keeping an eye on."
—Lois Faye Dyer, Amazon.com reviewer

"By now the secret is out that Antoinette Stockenberg is one heck of a writer. *Keepsake* lives up to its name as well as the previous works of the author by being a keeper."
—Harriet Klausner, *Painted Rock Reviews*

A CHARMED PLACE

"Ms. Stockenberg writes with the wisdom and grace of the ageless to create a beautiful story in this intricately woven suspense. I love everything she creates."
—*Bell, Book and Candle*

"Award-winning author Antoinette Stockenberg takes a dramatic turn in her new mainstream release. Passion, love, hatred and deceit all collide with unexpected force in the powerful and expressive A CHARMED PLACE."
—*Romantic Times*

"Well written . . . Every sentence builds the tension as the protagonists try to find their way back to each other and Maddie tries to protect her daughter. Ms. Stockenberg's passion for writing pulses through this superb story."
—*Rendezvous*

"Ms. Stockenberg has a very witty writing style and wonderfully drawn characters."
—*Old Book Barn Gazette*

DREAM A LITTLE DREAM

NIGHT has a terrific plot, a wicked villain and a sexy hero. But the novel ventures beyond sheer entertainment and it is easy to see why Stockenberg's work has won such acclaim."
—*Milwaukee Journal Sentinel*

"Full of charm and wit, Stockenberg's latest paranormal romance is truly enthralling."
—*Publishers Weekly*

"Antoinette Stockenberg creates another winner with this fast-paced and lively contemporary romance with a touch of the supernatural. A definite award-winner . . . contemporary romance at its best!"
—*Affaire de Coeur*

BELOVED

"BELOVED has charm, romance and a delicious hint of the supernatural. If you loved the film *Somewhere in Time*, don't miss this book."
—La Vyrle Spencer

"A delightfully different romance with a ghost story—a great combination that was impossible to put down."
—Johanna Lindsey

"BELOVED is great . . A lively, engaging, thoroughly enchanting tale . . . I savored every morsel of BELOVED."
—Jayne Ann Krentz

EMILY'S GHOST

"A witty, entertaining romantic read that has everything—a lively ghost, an old murder mystery and a charming romance."
—Jayne Ann Krentz

"I loved EMILY'S GHOST. It's an exciting story with a surprise plot twist."
—Jude Devereaux

ST. MARTIN'S PAPERBACKS TITLES
BY ANTOINETTE STOCKENBERG

BEYOND MIDNIGHT

DREAM A LITTLE DREAM

A CHARMED PLACE

KEEPSAKE

SAFE HARBOR

SAFE HARBOR

ANTOINETTE STOCKENBERG

St. Martin's Paperbacks

SAFE HARBOR

Copyright © 2000 by Antoinette Stockenberg.

ISBN: 0-312-97306-3

Printed in the United States of America

St. Martin's Paperbacks edition / April 2000

St. Martin's Paperbacks are published by St. Martin's Press, 175 Fifth Avenue, New York, N.Y. 10010.

10 9 8 7 6 5 4 3 2 1

For Gene

SAFE HARBOR

1

Holly Anderson's birthday surprise turned out to be a two-by-four over the head.

She had been expecting, oh, a cake and candles in her studio; maybe a singing telegram; possibly to be dragged out to dinner at one of the island's fancier restaurants. She had not expected to spend the last half of the first day of her thirty-first year at the bottom, emotionally speaking, of a ditch.

Her summer birthday had begun routinely enough, with Holly devoting the morning to cleaning and sanding the wide drawerfronts of a sweet old pine dresser that she'd snatched up at a yard sale on the Vineyard just two days earlier. Then came the fun part, sketching a whimsical farmstead across the faces of the three drawers. After erasing a cow and two geese and adding more chickens, Holly was ready to mix her paints and make folk art magic.

She loved what she was doing, loved the way she was connecting in some mystical way with the generations before her who had used and loved and worn out the workaday set of drawers. She would have loved it even without being paid; but her folk art was in wild demand, and that continued to amaze her.

Holly had filled in a few brushstrokes of sky when her mother's white Volvo pulled up in front of the red-shingled barn that was serving so well as a summer studio. Good: all signs pointed to a quiet dinner with her parents at the Black Dog this year, with maybe some cake and hopefully no telegram.

"Hi, Mom," she called over her shoulder through the clutter of broken furniture, handmade birdhouses, and charming whirligigs that filled the ground floor of the building. She laid down another stroke of impossible blue. "Come see my latest."

The hum of her creativity was so strong that it drowned out the sound of her mother's silence. It took a moment for Holly to emerge from her trance and turn around.

"He's having an affair with Eden," said Charlotte Anderson, skipping right past any birthday greeting. Her lip began to quiver. Tears welled but did not fall.

"Who is?"

"Who do you *think*?" Outrage boiled, not quite over.

"I'm sorry," said Holly, forcing herself to abandon her work. "I wasn't paying attention. Who's having an affair with Eden?" She began wiping her paint-stained fingers on a soft cloth. Her mother could have been talking about almost any male on the island. Eden was gorgeous, twenty-nine, not shy. Eden was an enchantress.

Charlotte Anderson closed her eyes and bit her lip, then gave up the struggle. Her face contorted with pain, and then she broke down. "Your father . . . your father . . . your *father*, damn him to hell," she moaned between racking sobs.

Holly simply stared. "Are you crazy? *Dad*? Are you crazy?"

"My God—would I make it up?" her mother cried. Suddenly she turned all of her pain and fury on Holly. "Take *his* side, why don't you!" she said, and she staggered, newly wounded, to a rickety Windsor chair that was awaiting glue and a folk art treatment.

"Not that one, Mom; it won't hold you," Holly warned. She rushed to get another.

Her mother said mordantly, "Now I'm *fat* besides being old?" More tears, bitter streams of them, from sixty-year-old-and-no-longer-thin Charlotte Anderson.

"Mom! You *know* I didn't mean it that way."

Holly tried to embrace her hysterical mother, but she was shrugged off violently.

"Mom, you're wrong, you're just wrong," she insisted through her mother's sobs, trying to soothe, though she was reeling herself. "This is a bizarre mistake. Someone misinterpreted. It's so easy to do that with Eden. You know how she is."

"Yes—thanks to you! You *had* to sublet to the woman, didn't you," Charlotte said, casting a hateful look at the ceiling above them.

"That's not fair! Eden worked at the gallery and she needed a place to stay. She was a big fan of my work; I couldn't let her sleep on the beach. Even you admitted early on that she was the perfect tenant: cheerful, conscientious, hardly ever around to disturb m—oh."

"Exactly."

"But, Mom—*Eden*. Think about it: she's half Dad's age!"

"Which makes her half *my* age. Oh, God . . . I can't bear this. I really can't," Charlotte moaned. She slumped into a nearby rocker instead of Holly's armchair and wrapped her arms around her stomach as she rocked disconsolately; and, yes, the years did show.

"What will our family say?" she wailed in misery.

"Your brother, your sister? This will tear us apart. This will destroy us. How could he do this to me? How could he? Oh, God . . . how *could* he?" she kept repeating, sobbing throughout the mantra of her despair.

Still shocked, Holly said, "Mom, Mom . . . how can you not trust Dad? Why are you so convinced he did anything?"

Charlotte Anderson lifted her head. Her face was puffy, her hair a mess. The light had gone out completely from her gentle and trusting gaze. In a flat, dull voice she said, "Because he told me so. Because he's gone off on the boat with her. Because he wants a divorce."

Holly had seen the two-by-four coming, but she was way too stupefied to duck. She gasped from the shock of the blow and fell back into the armchair she'd dragged over.

"When did he tell you this?"

"This morning."

"That's what he said? He wants a divorce?"

"Not for his sake. For mine," her mother said, trying for a trenchant smile but failing. "He says he doesn't want to put me through the prolonged agony of his affair."

"I can't believe this. We may as well be talking about two different men. Dad hasn't had an unfaithful thought in his life!"

"You're so sure of that," her mother said through her sniffles as she searched her bag for something to blow her nose on.

"Well, has he?" Holly demanded. She held out a box of Kleenex. "Before this, has he ever had an unfaithful thought that you know of?"

Her mother's grudging lift of a shoulder told Holly that as far as she knew, Eric Anderson had not.

"I mean, really. The man is sixty-two years old. He's quiet, reserved, you could say prudish. His work is his life. He doesn't get risqué jokes; I've seen the blank look on his face when someone tells one. He's . . . he's a probate lawyer, for Pete's sake, not a rock star or a politician. It doesn't get any less charismatic than a sixty-two-year old Scandinavian probate lawyer. Good grief. Who would want him?"

Charlotte's face crumpled in another wave of misery. "Me-e-e," she said in the forlorn wail of an abandoned child, and she began to cry again.

Holly felt more wretched than outraged; it broke her heart to see such pain. Soothing and coaxing, she managed to get her mother out of the rocker and onto her feet. "Come to the house," she murmured. "We'll have tea."

They walked in miserable silence across a path that meandered through a thicket of trees between the barn and the back door of Holly's rented Cape. Small, cozy and peeling, The Cape was the house of her dreams. She hoped to buy it by the end of her lease and lavish both love and paint on it and make it all better. It was her way.

Holly avoided glances at her mother as she filled the copper teapot from the old cast-iron sink, but her mind was racing. Probably it was foolish to bring it up, but: "Are you sure they've sailed off the island?" she asked.

Her mother was blowing her nose into a wad of fresh Kleenex. "Does it matter?"

"He could have had second thoughts."

"Second thoughts? What kind of second thoughts?" Charlotte asked, looking up from her tissues.

There was such hopefulness in her face that Holly immediately back-pedalled and changed the subject. "Nuts, I left my brand-new brush out," she said, making a dash for the kitchen door. "I'll just go dump it in some turp. Be right back."

Holly wasn't merely being cowardly; she wanted to see for herself if Eden had gone. Safely out of her mother's view, she headed for the stairs that climbed alongside the barn and led to the apartment that once had been a hayloft.

The last tenant there had been an antiques dealer who had planned to sell his treasures from the wide-planked barn beneath. But the business had folded by November, and the dealer had moved back to the mainland. His desperate landlord offered Holly both the house and the barn on a long-term lease; she snapped it up even before subletting her own condo and studio in Providence.

Holly had always wanted a place on Martha's Vineyard, close—but not too close—to her parents' summer home in Vineyard Haven. Now she had it, and she would someday marry a quiet, faithful, honest man like her father, and she would have children and run them over often to her parents to babysit, because that's what doting grandparents loved to do.

She slid her key into the door of Eden's apartment and swung it wide. Immediately her hopes, all of her hopes, were crushed. Eden had flown. The small closet that yawned at Holly held nothing but a few bare hangers. The drawers that she had lined with rose-patterned giftwrap were ajar and empty. The sink was clean, the bed was made, the newspapers were stacked neatly in a pile. Holly was impressed; Eden was quite the tidy fugitive.

The little shit.

Holly went back reluctantly to the kitchen, where her mother sat shivering in the warm July sun and warming her hands on her mug of tea as she sifted through the emotional wreckage of her life.

"It's because of the boat," Charlotte said numbly. "You know how he loves the *Vixen*."

"So?"

Charlotte sighed and shrugged. "I get seasick. Eden doesn't. Remember how much fun she had on that day-sail we all took to Nantucket? *I* spent the whole time belowdecks, sick to my stomach as usual."

"And you think that's why Dad's left? For someone with a stronger stomach?"

"Essentially, yes."

"If I weren't so depressed I'd laugh out loud," Holly said, managing a smile. "I'm amazed at how your mind works."

Her mother's look was almost pitying. "You truly don't get it, do you? But then, you're young; you take youth for granted. How can I explain this in terms you can understand?"

Her gaze became unfocussed, and Holly knew that she was replaying something awful in the videoscreen of her mind, trying to come to terms with it. Groping for words, her mother finally said, "The day that Eden first stepped aboard the *Vixen*: it was as if your father had been sunning on a rock like some sleepy toad, and a beautiful fairy princess had come up to him, and, completely unexpectedly, leaned down and kissed him on the cheek."

"Oh, Mom, don't," Holly begged. "Don't do this to yourself."

"Your father was a frog, and now he's not," her mother said in a quavering voice. She bowed her head and broke down again in soft, pitiable sobs. "And there's nothing . . . absolutely nothing . . . anyone can do about it."

The hell there isn't, thought Holly, and she dialed her sister's number.

She had given her mother plenty of time to call Ivy with the devastating news, and she was surprised that Ivy hadn't called the instant she'd gotten off the phone. Since Ivy was having work done on the house, it was possible that she had been off with the kids for the day.

So, fine. I'll be the one to tell.

Because time was of the essence. If their mother was right and their father was under a spell, then it was up to his family to knock some sense into him before it was too late.

"And how, precisely, do you suggest we do that?" Ivy wanted to know after having been brought up to date on the mind-boggling event. "Brass knuckles? Baseball bat?"

"Why are you sounding so resigned to this?" asked Holly, dismayed by her older sister's cynicism. "What's the matter with you? I was counting on you to lead the charge."

Her sister's voice was calm to the point of sounding grim. "Holly, you are so clueless. How could you not see this coming? Dad's done raising his kids. His career has peaked. He's tired. He's bored. He obviously feels taken for granted—"

"*I* don't take him for granted."

"Oh? When's the last time you paid him a compliment?"

"The last time I saw him. I said I liked his tie."

"Whereas Eden probably looked into his blue eyes later that night and murmured something about still waters running deep. Men love to think they're deep."

"That's ridiculous! Dad's not deep. He's just . . . Dad."

"Cloooo-lesss."

Annoyed, Holly said, "Just because I'm not married doesn't mean I don't understand men. I know when a man is being dishonest, and Dad is too honest to be dishonest. I'm telling you: he's under a spell."

"Maybe we should have him exorcized," Ivy said dryly.

"No, but I was thinking, an intervention. We all confront him when you come out to the Vineyard next week. We tell him—"

"I'm not coming out next week."

"What? Since when? You're bringing the girls to spend August here, just the way you do every year."

"Except this one. I won't be out until the last part of the month, if at all."

"Is something wrong?"

"No."

"Ivy—is something wrong?"

"I'm just very busy," she said, sounding vague.

"Busy doing what? You're a stay-at-home mom," Holly blurted.

It was a running stream that divided them, that issue of mom versus career. Most of the time the stream was a dried-up trickle, easily crossed, but sometimes it ran over its banks. This was one of those times. "The kitchen makeover is behind schedule, as you know," Ivy said in her supercilious older-sister voice. "I can't be everywhere at once."

"Well, this *stinks*. The family is in crisis, and you're worried about paint chips and cabinet knobs? Why can't Jack oversee the work? He only comes out here for a few days at the end, anyway."

"Jack? Please. Holly, honestly, I can't do it now," Ivy insisted, sounding harried.

"All right, fine. Then I'll just confront Dad on my own."

"And say what? That he's killing Mom? Do you suppose he doesn't know that?"

"I'll tell him that he's infatuated; that it will pass."

"Based on what? Your own experience?"

"I'll tell him what you just said: that he's bored; that he feels taken for granted."

"And he'll agree. Then what?"

"I'll tell him what a conniving, lying bitch Eden is!"

"Again, based on what?"

"Based on . . . based on . . . She vacated the apartment without giving notice."

Her sister didn't bother to respond to that. "The most obvious thing you could say is what we all think: that Eden is using her body to go after Dad's money. But so what? A lot of his friends have made the exact same deal, and it seems to suit them just fine."

"But Dad's not like that!"

"Holly," her sister said softly, "we don't know what Dad is like, deep down. No one does. Except Dad."

Deflated, Holly answered, "You're right. I guess. But I still have to try."

2

Sam Steadman was struggling through his third piece of lemon meringue pie, wondering what the hell was up. All evening long, his mother and his father had been exchanging dire glances across the dining room table of their New Bedford bungalow. Something was obviously on their minds, but every time that Sam asked what, his mother jumped up and said, "More pie!"

Finally, too stuffed to move, Sam pushed his brown vinyl chair back on its casters and said, "Okay, you two: what's going on?"

His mother smiled nervously. "Oh, it's nothin' that can't wait. It's late. You'll be wanting to get back home to Westport."

"Is it money, ma?" he asked her bluntly. "Can you use some cash?" He hadn't been home in nearly a month; the medical bills must be getting away from them again.

"Don't be silly," said his mother, reddening. She began to clear the table of cups and plates. "We don't want you to give us no money. It's not about money. It's about—"

"Money," his father said flatly.

Millie Steadman gave her husband a look that would have quelled a lesser man; but stroke or no stroke, big Jim Steadman was not about to be silenced. "Sooner or later, he has to know," he muttered to his wife. "We already waited too long as it is."

Alarmed now, Sam said, "Ma, I'm *beggin'* you—"

"Well, all right," Millie conceded, brushing crumbs into the palm of her hand. Without looking at Sam, she said, "It's about Eden."

"Eden!" Sam's chest constricted, the way it always did on those rare occasions when her name was mentioned. "What about her?"

"We don't like to bring her up, you being split up for so long now." She shook her head and gave him a look more sympathetic than critical, then took off on her favorite tangent.

"I just can't understand why your marriage couldn't work. Eden adored you; anyone could see that. And you were so proud of her. It seemed like the perfect match. You're both so good-looking, you're both so smart. Your children, oh, my goodness, what children you could have had—"

"Ma, *don't.* Don't, or I swear . . ."

"I know, I know," Millie said hastily, her dark eyes welling with tears. "You've told me many times. All right. I won't dwell."

She sat back down in the chair at her husband's side. After his stroke, she had switched to that seat so that she could handfeed him during the devastating paralysis he had suffered. As he regained mobility, she had held his hand and helped him lift the forkful of potatoes, the spoonful of custard. Big Jim could feed himself now; but Millie still stayed close with a napkin.

"Every once in a while," she said to Sam, "Eden drops by."

"*What*? You've never said boo about this!"

"Because look how you react. You get all squirrely. Anyway," she said, before Sam could respond to that, "Eden has been dropping by a couple of times a year just to say hi-how-are-you, and we always thought that was very nice of her. Sometimes, it's true, she was tight for cash. You know how it is when you're young and have car payments and rent and such. It's a tough situation."

Sam groaned and said, "You didn't give her *money*, Ma. Tell me you didn't give her money."

"Well, what if we did?" his mother answered defensively. "She used to be your wife. That made her our kin. You don't have to be blood relations to care about someone."

Sam didn't dare ride roughshod over that argument. Millie and Jim Steadman had raised a series of foster kids before they'd taken in and eventually adopted Sam, and they loved every one of them as if they really were kin. They still stuck five bucks in their Christmas cards for each of the kids of those who kept in touch. Eden, however, wasn't a kid. She was a witch and a scam artist in a woman's very desirable body.

He said bitterly, "You know, you may as well have taken that hard-earned dough of yours and thrown it down a toilet."

It infuriated him to think that Eden had borrowed money from folks in need of it themselves. He wondered which of her many get-rich-quick schemes the cash had gone to finance. Maybe an afternoon's thrill at the tables at Foxwoods? The one thing he knew is that it didn't go to pay bills.

"Wasn't much money, Sam," his father said. "Few hundred, here or—"

"Well, there was that one time when she needed more than that," Millie admitted. "But Eden insisted on giving us a, whatddyacallit, a promissory note that time. She wouldn't take no for an answer, wouldn't even hear of it. I can show you the note!"

Sam kept a lid on his anger. He said softly, "Even after Dad's stroke? She took money from you even then?"

Please let the answer to that one be no. For whatever reason, he didn't want to think that Eden was capable of stealing from the infirm.

His mother's answer was to smile lamely. Millie Steadman was a stout woman who, even in her seventies, had a big, life-affirming laugh. The woman never did *anything* lamely, least of all smile. Sam's heart sank.

"It gets a little complicated," she said. "The first thing you do, Sam, is you have to promise not to get mad. Or feel hurt. We couldn't tell you, all this time, because we were sworn to secrecy."

"By Eden?"

"Eden? She wasn't even born!"

"What the hell are you talking about?"

"Start over, Mil," her husband said tiredly.

"You're right, I'm making a mishmash of this," said Millie. "It's just I'm nervous, thinking about the possibilities. Because if it's gone, oh, Lord, if it's gone for good I don't know *what* we'll do."

The panic on her face and in her voice made Sam sit up straight. Throughout the trauma of the stroke and its aftermath, Sam had never seen in his mother anything like panic. Concern, yes; anguish, definitely. But not panic.

His mother took a deep breath, fixed her dark gaze on the *Lady of Fatima* print that hung opposite one of Sam's award-winning photographs, and started over.

"Fifty-two years ago, my Uncle Henry left us an inheritance. I was his only niece," she explained, "and he liked Jim because Jim worked with his hands as a carpenter. Uncle Henry used to say that people who actually made things deserved more than people who made things happen, but that life didn't usually work that way. Anyway, he left us this . . . this . . ."

She turned from the Lady of Fatima to her watchful husband, leaning helplessly, inexorably, to the left. "Is it okay if I say what it was, Jim?"

"We been through all that," he said, nodding permission.

"Okay. This engraving. It was an engraving. It was done by a man called Albrecht Durer. We looked him up. He died in 1528, so you know the engraving was old. It was of Adam and Eve in the Garden of Eden. It wasn't very large, about the size of a sheet of notebook paper, but it had a frame just like the one on your photograph of that fishing boat *Sandra D.* wrecked on a beach—you know, the one in the Whaling Museum that I like so much? That was really nice of you, donating that one to them. The frame must've cost you a pretty penny alone. Whenever we take visitors there, I always—"

"*Ma.*"

"Yes, yes. Anyway, Uncle Henry's will specifically said that we weren't supposed to—let me just get this right—'divulge ownership.' We never did understand why. The lawyer couldn't tell us, and if I'm not mistaken, he wasn't supposed to divulge anything, either. I don't know if he ever did or not. I think he's dead now. We were confused by the whole thing, almost frightened. When we got the engraving home, we didn't know what to do with it. So we hid it in the attic."

"The attic!"

"Well, where did you expect me to keep it? The people in it were practically naked. A couple of leaves— that was it!"

"Ma, they're Adam and Eve. Clothes weren't invented yet."

"I don't care who they are. How would that look, hanging something like that on the wall next to Our Lady? The attic is where we put it, and the attic is where it stayed."

In a softer voice she added, "In his will, Uncle Henry referred to the engraving as our 'nest egg.' That's what we thought it was, all these years."

Sam's knowledge of the sixteenth century artist was marginal, but he knew enough to realize that an engraving by Durer would be worth a considerable sum. He was afraid to pose the next question.

"Where is it now?"

His father grimaced and said, "There's your sixty-four thousand dollar question."

"We were watching *Antiques Roadshow*," Millie went on. "You ever see it? I suppose not; you're not very big on television. My word, the money the stuff in your attic can be worth! They had this chair—it looked like a piece of junk and yet they said it might fetch thirty thousand dollars! You couldn't very well sit on it; it wouldn't hold a ten-pound puppy."

When his mother felt self-conscious, she babbled. Sam knew that, and yet it was all he could do not to scream "*Eden*! For God's sake, tell me about *Eden*!"

Instead he made himself say calmly, "So you saw—something? On the *Antiques Roadshow*?"

"They had another engraving by this same man Durer," his mother said. She covered her face with her hands and said in a muffled voice, "And it was worth more than a hundred thousand dollars."

That should have been good news to them. Great news. *Oh, damn. Oh, hell.*

"What did Eden do with it?" Sam asked in a low and dangerous voice.

His mother shook her head. "We don't know. We don't know. Your pa and I decided it was a sign, Eden popping in like that right after the *Roadshow*. We were still so excited. We told her all about it and showed her *our* Durer. We told her that we were faithful to Uncle Henry's wishes all these years, but that we surely needed to cash in our nest egg now if ever we did. We told her how amazed we were that it might be so valuable, but Eden wasn't surprised at all. She was so nice, so helpful . . . she knows a lot about art, you know. She's a very smart woman."

Sam's nod was grim. "I never said otherwise."

"She offered to take the engraving to New York and have it appraised," Millie continued, wincing from the stress of telling her tale. "She said she knew people. Oh, we said, she shouldn't go to the trouble. We said, maybe Sam would know someone, too. After all, he's a professional photographer, we said. She said, 'If you tell Sam about the Durer, he's bound to insist that you hold on to it and take money from him instead.' Well, we couldn't argue with that, could we?"

"When did she take it?"

"Three weeks ago."

"Three *weeks*—? And you're first telling me now? This is unbelievable," Sam moaned. "*Jesus*." He slammed his hand on the tabletop and stood up so suddenly that the chair fell over backward on the shag carpeting.

"Oh, you're not going to get the way you get, are you, Sam? Oh, please don't. This is hard enough—"

"Jesus!" Sam paced the small room in self-absorbed fury. Of all the low-life scams that Eden had pulled, this had to be the lowest. Eden could spot a mark a mile away, and his parents were as naive and trusting as they came.

Which didn't go far to explain how he, the savvy and

cynical Sam Steadman, could have fallen for her like a clown with big feet. What a fool he'd been! Fool, fool, asshole fool! If it hadn't been for him, his parents wouldn't be sitting at their dining room table in a state of financial terror.

Fool!

He got himself under control enough to ask, "How long had she planned the appraisal to take?"

His mother shrugged. "She said she'd be in touch."

"You don't have an address or phone number, of course."

Both parents shook their heads. Millie said softly, "The number on the card she gave us isn't in service."

"Do you have any idea where she's been living? City? State? *Country*, for chrissake?" He couldn't help it; anger was flowing like hot lava from him, scorching his bystander parents in the process.

Millie bowed her head and murmured, "Jim remembers something about Miami. I thought she said Memphis. Is that any help?"

Sam sighed. "What about her car? What was she driving? Where were the plates from?"

"Jim didn't walk outside at the end, but her car was blue. It had a big carpeted trunk, I know that," said Millie. "I was nervous about the engraving getting damaged or stolen, but it looked real safe there."

Not pausing to observe the irony, Sam asked, "Did you see any evidence of luggage in her car? Trunks, suitcases, clothes on hangers?"

"No, not r—oh, wait. There was a duffel bag on the back seat. You know, like a sailor would use? I thought it looked a little sporty for Eden, because she's so very feminine. Maybe it belonged to someone else."

Just what we need; an accomplice. Sam said, "Did Eden allude to anyone else? Maybe a man she's seeing?"

Surprising, how it smarted to ask that.

His mother said, "No. She didn't talk about anyone. We were commenting on that afterward. We think maybe she still has feelings . . . Well, anyway. No."

"Okay, apparently we're at a dead end, then," Sam decided, disgusted by the realization.

Amazingly, his mother seemed determined to believe the best instead of facing the worst. "It's probably taking longer than she thought to get the appraisal, that's all. She said it was a very important piece of art and that appraisals take a little while, you know. I wouldn't have raised all this hullabaloo at all, except Jim insisted we tell you."

She threw an accusing look at her husband, who said slowly, plaintively, "One of them mortgage people come by yesterday, Sam. How do the bastards know?"

"Dad, don't you dare take out a loan from those shysters," said Sam angrily. "Don't you dare. I'll take care of the bills until this gets cleared up."

"We have enough money," his mother insisted.

Yeah, right.

"I'd like to stay here tonight," he said, surprising his parents. "Maybe you'll remember something."

Sam's plan was to canvas the neighbors the next morning and question them about Eden's car. The working-class neighborhood was fairly close-knit, full of porch-sitters with easy views through chain-link fences. Maybe someone had been sitting on a stoop and had recognized Eden from the old days; maybe they'd be able to recall a license. It was going to be humiliating, going door to door in search of Eden. Sam dreaded it, and yet he was flat out of any other ideas.

Until three A.M. That's when he bolted upright in the spindle bed that his father had painted Superman-blue shortly after they had taken him in.

Phone calls.

He clung to the possibility until he dropped off to

sleep, and in the morning, over waffles and O.J., he said to his parents, "Did Eden make any long-distance phone calls while she was here?"

His mother, misinterpreting, said, "Well, yes. She would have used her calling card, naturally, only there was some kind of problem with it. She said that she'd square up with us after we got the phone bill."

"All *right*," he said, making a victory fist. "Now we're getting somewhere." It wasn't like Eden to be so careless; but then, the risk of a call being remembered was relatively small. "Has the bill come in?"

"Yesterday." Picking up on his enthusiasm, his mother hurried over to the Formica counter and brought the unopened bill to him. "I haven't even—"

Sam took his knife, still all buttery, and slid it under the flap. Heart hammering, he scanned the toll calls on it. There were half a dozen made to the same number— his mother's sister—and one to Martha's Vineyard.

Sam punched in the number and reached someone at a gallery called the Flying Horses.

He hung up. A faint glimmer of a smile, the first in twelve hours or so, hovered at the edges of his lips. He got up from the breakfast table and dropped a kiss on top of his mother's gray hair. "She didn't take off for Germany with it," he said. "That's something, at least."

Next stop: Martha's Vineyard.

3

A fresh southwest wind was kicking up seas and slapping them against the sides of the ferry as it steamed through a fleet of sailboats scattered like daisy petals across the sound. Ahead lay Martha's Vineyard, blue-gray in the summer haze. Sam Steadman leaned on the starboard rail and squinted into the afternoon sun.

Yeah. This is more like it.

He had fled the cabin, which was crammed with August tourists and smelled like cheap food, for the open air of the upper deck. His work as a marine photographer had taken him aboard every conceivable type of vessel, from kayak to freighter, and always it was the same: the scent, the sight, the sound of the sea is what brought out the best in him. He took deep, long breaths of air, filling his lungs with its salty essence, and rued again the time he had to spend on shore.

Sam considered it one of life's great ironies that he wasn't cut out for a full-time job at sea. The long hours, brutal conditions, and sheer terror of a fisherman's life were not for him. Merchant Marine? Too many hours belowdecks. Navy? Coast Guard? Too many times in jail for that. Nope. Chronicler of seamen, that was what suited him.

He still remembered the day he held his first camera, an Instamatic, probably stolen, that at fourteen he'd bought for five bucks from a pal. The local paper had been sponsoring a cat photo contest, and even though Sam didn't have a cat, he knew where to find them: on the wharves, scrounging for rats and fish guts.

The photo he submitted, of a white cat sleeping hammock-style in the folds of a fishing net, took first place. He won a gift certificate for fifty dollars at JCPenney and realized, for the first time, the difference between a job and a career.

Although his record as a human being remained spotty for the next few years, he kept up his interest in photography, and eventually he traded his Instamatic for a Canon, the Canon for a Nikon. Awards followed, and pretty good money, too, and all because Sam liked to hang out by the sea.

The sea. He inhaled deep—for the moment, content.

A pair of lovers strolled by, hand in hand, and that brought Sam to thoughts of Eden. He had first met her on the waterfront. Friends had introduced them at a harbor fair in Boston, and they had hit it off immediately. Both of them, it turned out, liked fried clams, French rum, and calypso. It was only later that he learned that if it suited her purposes, Eden could feign an appetite for a plate of rotting goat innards.

Fool, fool, fool.

The strolling couple stopped a few steps away to embrace; Sam studiously ignored them and tried to concentrate on the task at hand. Eden had stolen his parents' engraving, and he was going to get it back no matter what. It was as simple as that. He turned his back on the lovers, the sun, and the sea and retraced his steps to

the confinement of the cabin, where he had left his duffel. There was a book in his bag on German artists. He
wanted to give it one more look.

The Flying Horses Gallery seemed too upscale for the
honky-tonk atmosphere of Oak Bluffs, the most
souvenir-ridden of the Vineyard's small towns. Sam
stood across the street from the gallery and pondered his
next move as a stream of tourists ebbed and flowed
around him.

He hated the thought of lying—he was as bad at it
as Eden was good—but he had little choice. He needed
an excuse for being on her trail. After shrugging into
the cotton blazer that he'd slung over his shoulders, Sam
snugged his tie and crossed the narrow, car-clogged
street. The window displays that flanked the gallery's
black door were minimal. A seascape in a heavy, gilded
frame was perched on an easel in one of them, and a
grouping of carved, painted whirligigs was sparely arranged in the other.

Sam paused on his way inside to check out the whirligigs: a scarecrow with arms that would circle in the
wind, a seagull with wings that would do the same—
and a winged pig. He read the label in front of the last:
Pigasus. Despite his grim mood, Sam smiled at the
whimsy, then turned to go inside.

He was just in time to see, leaving the gallery in the
other direction, a woman he'd know anywhere on earth.
Her back was to him, but the curve of the hip, the way
her hair bounced as she walked . . .

"Hey! Eden! Hold it," he snarled, grabbing her arm
before she got away again.

He whirled her around and faced, not Eden Walker
Steadman, but—well, not Eden Walker Steadman.

The woman was around Eden's age, but her eyes
were wide with apprehension as she looked, not at Sam,

but desperately around her. Presumably for a cop.

"Oh, geez, I am so *sorry*," Sam said, aghast. "I, ah . . . whoa. Really. I'm sorry. You look just like someone else."

"No, I *don't*," she said with brisk hostility. "Please let go of me. Do I look like a blonde to you?"

"Uh, no. Brunette, washed in shades of auburn. Definitely not a blonde. Sorry. Here. Um . . ." He let her go, then patted smooth the sleeve of her pale blue sundress. He was behaving, of course, like an idiot, but he didn't know how to assuage this innocent victim whose face bore absolutely no resemblance to Eden's.

Her eyes were green, very green, for one thing, whereas Eden's were a startling blue. "I was told that I might find Eden, uh, Walker here, at the gallery," he said, winging it.

"You might have. Once."

Yes!

And her nose had a bridge to it. An interesting nose, a Debra Winger nose, but nothing like Eden's, which was straight and aristocratic. "I don't know what this Eden looks like," he went on, "so naturally I thought—"

"You just said that I looked like her," the woman pointed out.

Not at all. Eden had high, hollow cheekbones; this woman had more rounded ones. "And so you do. Look like her, I mean. From the description of her that I got, I mean."

"I'm a *brunette*."

"Yes. You are."

"Eden's a blonde!"

"No, she's not."

"How do *you* know?"

Shit. Caught. He wriggled free and made a dash for the end zone. "What did you mean, I might *once* have found her here? She isn't here anymore?"

"Who *are* you?"

Leery of what stories Eden might have made up about him, Sam lied and said, "Percy. Percy Billings." God, a Percy, yet. He couldn't have named himself Stone or Cliff or something.

"Look, Mr. Billings—"

"Call me Percy." Hey, what the hell.

"Look . . . Percy . . ." She cocked her head sideways at him. "Percy? Honestly? You don't look like a Percy."

Thank God for that. "Be that as it may . . ." he said with a smile. "I'm an attorney. A probate attorney named Percy Billings."

Up came her left eyebrow. "Really? My father's a probate attorney."

Holy shit. "Small world," he said faintly.

"What firm are you with?"

Holy shit. "None that you'd know. I'm from, uh, Austin."

"You don't sound like a Texan. You sound New England."

"I wasn't born in Austin; I just practice there."

"Are you looking for Eden on business?"

Oh, yeah: she had the Attorney Gene, all right. And yet she looked so fresh, so winsome. "I'm not here to subpoena Eden or anything, if that's what you're worried about," he reassured her.

"Attorneys don't serve subpoenas."

"We can if we want to," he said. He didn't know if they could or not; he was flying blind and getting more disoriented by the minute. Just his rotten luck to stumble onto a probate attorney's daughter who happened to know Eden.

"Look, I appreciate your effort to protect Eden's privacy," he said, "but it's really hot and—"

"Shouldn't you be used to the heat?"

"—I'd like to get on with my mission. Thank you for your time."

He gave her a barely civil smile and turned to head back to the gallery.

"Wait, Percy-if-that's-who-you-are!"

Back around he turned. She looked completely undecided about whether to trust him or not. "Why are you looking for her?" she said in a voice that sounded oddly distressed.

With a softer smile he said, "I'm afraid I can't breech my client's confidentiality."

"Why are you *looking* for her?" she demanded, sounding genuinely anguished now.

"I'm sorry. Really. If you would just tell me where I can find her . . ."

"Find her? Sure. Just—look for the nearest married man!" she said bitterly, after which she suddenly burst into tears, changed her mind, stopped, turned, and ran away.

While Sam, agape, watched her flee, three thoughts went through his mind. One: she was obviously the wife of Eden's latest prey. Two: she didn't look anything like Eden, either from the front *or* the back. And three: Eden was now a blonde.

Oh, and four: it stung like hell to know that Eden was still running around seducing other men.

The only good news, and it was scant good news indeed, was that Sam's hunch had been right. Eden *had* taken off for Martha's Vineyard, and her trip had everything to do with the engraving. Had she brought it here with evil intent? That was a no-brainer. Where was Eden now? He didn't know. Where was the Durer? He didn't know.

He was sure he was about to find out.

Praying that she hadn't already fenced it, Sam stepped inside the quiet, intimate gallery.

*   *   *

Holly Anderson escaped up Circuit Avenue and didn't stop to catch her breath until she reached the main entrance into the Camp Ground, the old revivalist meeting place that was now one of the most charming sites in New England. Ahead of her, in the middle of a large and soothing oasis of grass, stood the historic Tabernacle, a massive whimsy of iron and pipe and rafters holding up a corrugated roof that was topped by a spire, itself topped by a large, plain cross. Rimmed all around by tiny, wildly colorful and extravagantly scrolled gingerbread houses, the plain old Tabernacle beckoned Holly, as it always did, to come sit down and muse a bit.

It was easy to do that in the Camp Ground. Maybe it was the thick canopy of trees, muting the sounds of the cars, mopeds, ferries, sirens, and boom boxes that bounced around the crowded waterfront. Maybe it was the eye-popping colors of the tiny, tent-sized Carpenter Gothic cottages, loud enough to drown out anything short of a nuclear explosion. Whatever the cause, the silence on the often empty green was a delight, one of the best-kept secrets on the island. If Holly needed a quick fix of serenity while she was in Oak Bluffs, this was where she came.

All alone, she took a seat under the cool shade of the Tabernacle and tried to make sense of the mysterious Mr. Billings. He had unnerved her, no doubt about it. When had she last burst into tears in front of a man? Never, to be exact. Her conviction that Percy Billings was not who he seemed was overwhelmed by her mortification that Percy Billings, whoever the hell he was, had seen her cry.

Why is he looking for Eden?

That's what Holly wanted to know. She spent the next hour sitting alone on the bench, with only a handful of wanderers passing in and then out of her view, as she fixated on the edgy-looking male with the sissy-sounding name.

Even if he were a lawyer, which was hard to believe, why would he want or need Eden? Why, why, why?

Eventually Holly came up with what she thought was the only possible explanation: he was there to bring Eden news of someone's death, and maybe an inheritance.

"But lawyers don't do that personally, not unless they're friends of the families," her mother argued over dinner that night. The two women were in constant communication now, comparing every new theory, every sad thought about the crisis that had mowed them down just three days earlier.

Charlotte Anderson reflected for a moment. "Maybe he's a private investigator who was working for a law firm," she threw out. "He sounds a little rough around the edges, despite the jacket and tie."

Holly bobbed her head from one side to the other. "That's slightly more plausible, I guess. But the fire in his eyes when he spun me around—boy, now that *was* personal. He didn't look either like a lawyer *or* a P.I. just then."

"A jealous boyfriend?" her mother suggested, not without a certain amount of hope.

"I don't think so," Holly decided. "He was too flustered when I turned out not to be Eden. And too stunned when I told him my father was a probate attorney. Ha! I got him there."

Charlotte Anderson peeled away a blob of congealed cheese from her slice of cold pizza and laid it aside on the plate. "He and Eden sound like birds of a feather, if you ask me," she muttered, poking at the remains. "Two liars."

For whatever reason, Holly wanted to defend her Mr.

Billings. "We don't know that for sure. We should at least give him the benefit of the doubt."

Her mother lifted her head. Tears, one more rainfall in a record season, began to fall again. "Oh, what's the difference? Eden's gone and Mr. Billings is, too, by now. We'll never know what he wanted." She wiped her eyes rather fiercely with her napkin.

"I suppose you're right," Holly conceded.

It was an oddly disappointing realization. Percy Billings was an intriguing man with a wide range of emotions. Embarrassment, sheepishness, a good-looking guy, bravado, anger, a good-looking guy, arrogance— Holly had seen all of that in the space of five minutes with him.

Too bad he was a liar.

"Do you suppose she really was an orphan?" Charlotte asked out of the blue.

"Hmm? Eden? Hard to say," Holly answered. "The only time I ever ventured a question about her family, she told me it was far too painful a subject to go into. Somehow she made it sound as if they all died on the *Titanic*."

Charlotte smiled wryly. "Yes, she was good at that. Remember when she told us that she had been studying art at the Sorbonne, but that she left to come back and care for her best friend who was dying of cancer?"

"Sure I do. Why?"

"Well, Nancy told me this morning that Eden once mentioned that she'd never been to France," Charlotte said. "I believed Eden. I believed everything she said." She added softly, "And so did your father."

"He'll discover what a fraud she is."

"What if he doesn't?" Charlotte's lip began to tremble and Holly thought, *I have to do something, anything, to stop the flow of this pain.*

She grabbed her mother's hand and began hauling her

up from her chair. "Mom, you are not going to sit in your kitchen and cry anymore—not tonight, anyway. We're going to Mad Martha's for ice cream. It's the only sensible solution to all this."

Her mother smiled haplessly—a pale echo of the warm and winning version that Holly was used to—and dabbed at her gray Katharine Hepburn bun. "My hair's a mess."

"It looks fine," Holly said, tucking in one of the longest loose ends. "You look beautiful."

And she did, too. The lines in her face made her look more kind than old, and those few extra pounds only made her more huggable. Her eyes were far and away the most beautiful that Holly had ever seen: large, green, and luminous, with thick black lashes that had never seen the business end of a mascara brush. Charlotte Anderson's beauty was of the deep-down kind. How could anyone turn his back on it?

"Come on; it's a beautiful evening," Holly coaxed. "Let's not stay inside."

Her mother sighed an acquiescence, but her mind was somewhere else. "We're so convinced that Eden's a gold digger," she mused. "What if your crazy theory is right, and Percy Billings is looking for her to give her a chunk of money? Wouldn't that be something? Do you think . . . do you think she'd dump your dad?"

Holly shrugged philosophically. "Who knows? It would have to be an awful lot of money."

But in the meantime she was thinking, *Eden could rub an inheritance in people's faces as proof that she wasn't after Eric Anderson's money. She'd do that even if she were a gold digger.*

"Maybe she's already dumped him," said Charlotte wistfully. "Maybe he's going to walk through the front door just as soon as we go out the back."

"Then we'll go through the front, just in case." Holly meant it to sound light; it came out grim.

Ignoring it, Charlotte said, "I should wash my face. Would you get me my sunglasses from the upper deck? Lately the sun hurts my eyes when it's low."

And of course your eyes are puffy from crying, thought Holly, but she merely said, "Sure," and took the stairs two at a time to the second floor, then through a sitting room onto a deck outside of it.

The deck had a million-dollar view of Vineyard Haven Harbor. Holly hadn't been on it since her mother opened up the house for the summer; she'd been too busy with her work. She was dismayed to see that the white balusters that surrounded the deck had started to peel. That was inevitable with a house by the sea . . . but still.

She remembered spending what had seemed like an entire summer on that deck when she was ten, painting every single one of those balusters for thirty-five cents apiece.

"You say you want to be an artist when you grow up," her father had said with a twinkle in his eye. "Let's see if you've got the right stuff. Let's see if you've got what it takes to keep going, after it stops being fun."

First Holly had counted all the balusters, and then she had done some multiplication. Seventy dollars! She'd never made that much money at one time in her life. It was going to be the most fun thing she ever did.

But it wasn't. It was hot and boring and endless. After every baluster came another baluster. Holly wanted many times to throw down her brush and run off to play, but she kept at it—not because she wanted the money anymore, but because she wanted to be one of those people who had the Right Stuff. Because she wanted, most of all, not to disappoint her father.

How bitterly ironic.

She couldn't bear to be up there. Her mother's sunglasses were lying on a bistro table in a corner; Holly scooped them up and turned to go back down. She was surprised to see the old telescope, still mounted on its tripod, that her father had liked to use whenever an interesting boat sailed into the harbor. On an impulse, she turned and stooped to squint through the eyepiece. As she suspected, the telescope was focused on the slip where her father kept the *Vixen* tied up.

As she feared, the slip was empty.

4

The Flying Horses Gallery opened at ten A.M. Sixty seconds later, Sam strolled through the door. He had been told the day before by a pretentiously discreet assistant that he'd have to speak about Eden with the gallery owner herself.

The owner, it turned out, was slightly less discreet.

"Ah, yes," said Claire Delaney, sizing him up after sipping from a paper coffee cup. "Eden. She worked here briefly, but you won't find her on the island. I understand that she's off . . . well, let's just say, yachting, at the moment," she explained with a dry smile. "Do you know her?"

"Vaguely. It was many years ago." That was more or less the truth. "We're not exactly pals," he ventured. Also the truth.

The gallery owner was forty, citified, and well turned out—uppity, but nouveau uppity, Sam decided. There was still something a little downtown about her. He could see it in the way she looked him over with interest.

He liked that in a woman; he wasn't much for guessing games.

She said, "Eden took up with one of our more respected summer colonists. Unfortunately, she did it while she was working for me. I didn't like that. This is a small island. When people talk about the Flying Horses Gallery, I'd prefer that it be about an exhibit here—not an exhibition."

"Do you mind if I ask how Eden got the job?"

She shrugged. "My ex-business partner knows her. Jeffrey has an unfortunate—well, it doesn't matter," she said briefly. "He knew her."

"Where can I get in touch with your business partner?"

"Ex. I have no idea. Try Palma de Majorca.

Sam probed her a little more. "When I knew her, Eden used to broker the occasional transaction," he said, keeping it bland. "Does she still?"

Claire Delaney gave him a surprised look. "Buying or selling?"

"Selling."

She said briskly, "Eden *was* a sales clerk, after all. As for what she bought or sold on her own time, I'm afraid I couldn't say."

It was a dismissal. Clearly she wanted Sam out of there. Was that because she was itching to call Jeffrey and give him a heads-up that someone was after Eden?

Sam flashed her a thoughtful smile and said, "Thanks for your help. Do you have any idea where Eden has gone off 'yachting'?"

She shrugged and said, "Eric could have taken the *Vixen* anywhere."

Sam lifted an eyebrow, and she explained. "*Vixen* is the name of Eric's boat. Rich, don't you think?"

Sam's response was a cool look.

Embarrassed, she added quickly, "I do feel badly for Eric's wife, though. Charlotte's a dear."

"I think I ran into her leaving the gallery yesterday," Sam said, calling up an image of the green-eyed brunette with the Debra Winger nose.

"You may have. She's in here fairly often." Suddenly the gallery owner decided to haul out her uppity tone. "And now you really *must* excuse me, Mr. Billings."

He was barely out the door when she picked up the phone and began punching in a number.

An hour later, Sam was still searching for a room for the night. He must have been out of his mind, thinking he could just wing it on the Vineyard in August. He'd spent the previous night sweltering on a cot jammed under the eave of a shabby bed-and-breakfast, and even that miserable hovel was now booked until Labor Day.

He was standing at a pay phone on the street, juggling inn brochures, a pen, and a notepad when he caught a glimpse of the lady with the Debra Winger nose, inching down the main drag in a bright red pickup truck that was carrying a couple of battered bureaus in the back. A FedEx van ahead of the pickup was stopped for a delivery, blocking its lane of traffic. Charlotte apparently ran on island time; she seemed resigned.

Without thinking, Sam hung up in the middle of booking the one and only free room on the Vineyard and ran up to the driver's side of the pickup.

"Hey, Charlotte!" he said, slapping the side of her door in a far too jovial greeting.

She jolted out of her reverie with a confused smile that he somehow liked to see.

"Percy?"

"Who? Oh! Yeah."

"I'm not Charlotte, Percy."

"Yes you are," he told her. "Charlotte Anderson."

"*Holly* Anderson."

"No, I'm sure she said Charlotte."

"Who?"

"Claire Delaney.

"Claire? *She* knows who I am."

"I know. She said."

"My name is Holly Anderson. Once and for all, who are *you*?"

"I'm—hmm." Sam glanced left and right and said in a lower voice, "Can you keep this under your hat? My real name is Sam. Sam Steadman." *Here we go. Take two.* "I'm a private investigator."

She laughed out loud. "Oh, please," she said, more than mildly contemptuous. "First you're Percy Billings, probate attorney. Now you're Sam Steadman, private eye. How corny can you get? Use a little imagination when you choose your names, at least."

Annoyed by her reaction, Sam said, "I'm not here to use my imagination. I'm here to find Eden Walker."

"Best of luck to you."

"Look, Mrs. Anderson, we need to talk," he said, gripping the door frame through the open window. "This is important. I wouldn't—"

A car behind them barked furiously at the pickup's heels: traffic had begun to crawl again. The woman—Charlotte, Holly, whoever—began rolling up her window. "I'm not a missus, and I don't want anything to do with Eden or her lying cronies. Go away!"

The pickup took off with a squeal, and the guy in the Jeep behind it tried his best to run Sam down for good riddance. Sam jumped back on the curb and began jogging behind the moving traffic, waiting for the FedEx wagon to block the flow again. When it stopped in front of an insurance agency, he grabbed his chance. Opening the door of her truck, he scrambled onto the passenger seat.

"Oh, for Pete's sake," she said. "Out, before I call a cop."

"If you're not a missus, who are you?"

"*Ms.* Anderson, to you. I'd make you call me miss if it didn't sound so damned virginal," she added with a defiant look.

Compared to Eden—compared to most women—Sam thought she sounded pretty damned virginal indeed, but he declined to offer an opinion about that. "Well, who's Eric Anderson, if he's not your husband? Your brother?"

"He's my father, if you must know," she said, staring straight ahead and shifting back in gear. "Now get out of the car." She grabbed her purse from between them and put it behind her seat.

"Your *father*! Good God. How old is he?"

She scowled. "Sixty-two."

"Sixty-two! Eden's thirty!"

"No shit, Sherlock."

"So . . . Charlotte's your mother."

"You're quick."

"I'm sorry it had to happen to your mother," he said, as if she'd been struck by terminal disease. "I've heard she was a good woman."

"She's not dead, you know. Thank you for your concern. Get out of the car."

"Look, we really are getting off on the wrong foot here. Can we just begin over again?"

Traffic stopped. Holly turned a blazing green gaze on him and said, "No beginning, no middle, no end. What has happened to me and my family is an intensely personal affair. I'm not interested in sharing our heartbreak with a lawyer, a private eye, a jealous boyfriend, a psychopathic liar, or . . . or whoever you are," she said, sputtering to a halt.

She leaned over his lap, setting his nerve endings

humming with her pleasing scent, and unlatched his door. "Go."

Not because you tell me to, no matter how good you smell, he thought. "All right, it's true. I'm not a private investigator," he said by way of a peace offering. He closed the door again. "So you can take 'psychopathic liar' off your list."

"Really," she said with droll surprise. "Since I've already crossed off lawyer and investigator, that leaves you a—what? Jealous boyfriend?" She looked at him intently, as if that were a real possibility.

As if. "I'm not her boyfriend, and I'm definitely not jealous. I'll swear on a bible," he added with a fervor that sounded shrill, even to him.

A timorous toot-toot behind them had Holly stepping on the gas again. "Well, you've got me stumped," she admitted.

She seemed oddly mollified. Sam laid another offering at her feet, hoping to lure her into eventually confiding what she knew about Eden to him. "I'm actually a marine photographer," he said. "And my name truly is Sam Steadman. And I really would like you to keep that under your hat. If you'll have lunch with me, I'll tell you why."

She glanced at him with interest. "Marine photographer. Not bad. After all, you're on an island. You have the hands of an artist—although who knows about the soul—and you did have a camera pack on you yesterday when you accosted me. I have to admit, the story fits you fairly well. On the other hand," she said slyly, "if I said my brother was a marine photographer—would something like that scare you?"

"Not in the least," he answered, fairly bursting his shirt buttons. *The hands of an artist.* He liked that. Women had always told him he was good with his hands. He was pleased that this woman was able to see it before and not after.

Whoa. Before and after what? *Keep focused, pal.*

"You know what?" she said, swerving into a parking spot that had just been vacated. "I don't believe you. Out of the car."

"Oh, for—this is nuts. I'm Sam Steadman. I shoot fishermen. With a camera. I've won awards. I have a book out, for chrissake."

"Well, goody for you." Again she leaned over and unlatched his door.

She smelled just as good this time. Only this time, he didn't press back in his seat to give her room. Her hair brushed against his cheek and a strand caught on his lip as he murmured in her ear, "What's the matter? Are you afraid of me?"

She jerked back into position behind the wheel and said stiffly, "I'm not afraid; I just don't believe you. Why should I?"

"Well, I guess I'll just have to prove I'm telling the truth," he drawled. "There's a bookstore across the street."

"The Book Box? It's a tiny store. Who do you think you are—Stephen King?"

In fact Sam had visited the store and been pleasantly amazed to find a copy of his book there. "Not King— Steadman. Under 'S.' "

She threw up her hands and said, "All right. Anything to get rid of you."

Without waiting for him, she scrambled out of the car and ducked across the creepalong traffic, then charged into the store and went directly to the art and photography shelf. She scanned it quickly, then turned to Sam in triumph. "Nothing there, Percy."

"Oversized. Bottom shelf."

Her brow twitched uncertainly. She dropped down,

scanned the shelf, and pulled out the single copy of *Men at Sea*. Flipping through the pages of black-and-white photographs without pausing to look at any of them, she closed the book with a snap and handed it to him. "So you saw the book and stole the name," she said cooly. "So what."

He turned it over and held it up. A publicity photo of him, looking suitably nautical in a dark wool sweater, stared back at her.

Her expression didn't change, but he saw her shoulders droop a little. "So you're Sam Steadman," she conceded at last. "So what."

"Have lunch with me," he begged, one more time. "We'll talk about Eden. Not about your dad, not about ... about all the others she's hurt, but about Eden. I promise I won't pry into your personal feelings. But I absolutely have to find her—quickly—and I need your help to do it."

Holly looked him up and looked him down and thought, *What's in it for us?*

Because that was how her mind worked nowadays. Her first instinct was to protect her mother; everything else came a distant second. The man who was standing before her clearly had his own agenda. She already knew that he was capable of lying. Was he capable of worse?

She wanted to believe that the answer to that was no. For one thing, he had come clean—eventually—with her. For another, he was looking straight at her now, not left and right and all around as he had when he was trying to sell her those ludicrous stories.

"All right. But *just* lunch. All I know about Eden won't take any longer than that. We can grab a sandwich around the corner."

"Great," he said. "Let's go."

They were passing the register when Holly suddenly

hooked a thumb at Sam and announced to the clerk, "You have a book of his on your shelves, you know."

Sam shrugged it off, the way men do, and then he said offhandedly, "You want me to sign it for you?"

The young clerk acted as if the two of them were pulling off a scam of some kind. "Sign—? No. I don't think so," he said, lowering his lids in suspicion.

Holly had to suppress a smile on their way outside. "See? He doesn't believe you, either."

"Very funny. Do you enjoy making men squirm?"

"Couldn't say; haven't had any practice at it," she admitted, and meanwhile she decided that she was enjoying it a *lot*. She stole another glance at Sam. He was watching her, too, with a half-smile on his lips that she found both irritating and attractive.

They stepped inside a small, sunny café that was a cut above the usual tourist affair. It was early, so tables were still free. They chose a bistro-sized one over in a corner where they wouldn't easily be overheard by those still lingering over coffee. Sam pulled out a chair for her, a gesture that for some reason surprised Holly. He sat down opposite her and a waitress immediately dropped off two menus.

"This was a good idea, carjacking you," he said matter-of-factly.

"You sound as if you do it often."

He gave her a cryptic smile and turned his attention to the menu, which gave Holly a chance to study him a little more. He had a scar—a nasty one about two inches long—on the side of his neck. Holly wanted to ask about it, but it would have been the worst possible form.

No matter. He caught her staring. "Fight," he said simply, and went back to his menu.

The thought of a knife slicing into the side of his neck, her neck, any neck, sent a shiver of fear through

Holly. "I hope it was in self-defense from a mugging," she said faintly.

He looked up again. "Not exactly."

"Oh. Well! The grilled turkey breast looks good."

"Yeah." He flipped the menu over. "No red meat, of course," he said in mild disapproval.

He probably liked it raw. What was she *doing* there?

"You know, I have a really full day planned," she said with carefully feigned friendliness. "So your questions would be—?

"They don't serve alcohol, either? I could use a beer."

Holly glanced at the watch on his wrist. "It's ten forty-five."

"Aren't you the kind who like their elevenses?" he asked, lifting an eyebrow.

"I'm not the kind who likes being asked if I'm the kind," she shot back. "So suppose we get on with this . . . this inquisition." By now her mood was as edgy as his.

"All right," he agreed. He folded his arms across the green, metal tabletop and leaned his chiseled features half a foot closer to her face. "How did you meet her?"

Wanting only to to get the interview over with, Holly said, "She took a job at one of the galleries that carries my work. I'm a folk artist."

"Whirligigs?"

"Among other things. One evening the gallery hosted a charity event, and my parents came. Eden was there, all . . . bubbling and all," Holly said in distressed recollection.

She could still picture Eden so well, a dazzling straight-haired blonde in a short red dress who had stolen the show. Afterward, Holly and her mother had talked about how quick Eden was, how knowledgeable about how many things. How friendly. How gracious. How flattering and self-effacing at the same time, what a killer combination that was. Neither she nor her mother had been able to believe that Eden was unclaimed.

Holly's father, as was his habit, had said little—a soft grunt here, an easy shrug there. It wasn't surprising. Eric Anderson always seemed to be a million miles away. A boundary dispute, an important closing, a zoning snafu: those were the thoughts that generally occupied his mind.

But not on the night of that show.

"That first night, Eden told us she was staying with a friend and looking for a place on the island to live. I remember how charmingly desperate she was, even offering to rent one of the bunks on my father's boat. I remember how we all laughed."

Holly wasn't laughing now. "I have a long-term lease on a house and a barn on Lake Tashmoo," she continued. "A few days after the show, the tenant who was subletting an apartment above the barn from me suddenly moved off the island. I offered the place to Eden. It seemed so reasonable at the time, but it turned out to be the worst mistake I've ever made."

"If that's the worst thing . . ." Sam murmured.

She shook off his sympathy and went rushing on. Her need to tell him her trauma ran deep.

"Eden took me up on my offer. For the first week or so she spent a lot of time with me, showing up with takeout, watching me work, tagging along on yard sales. My parents liked her; they invited her over for a cookout one evening and took her sailing with us. Then suddenly she was never around. I used to wish—I actually used to *wish*—that I could see more of her. I actually missed her.

"There were a couple of nights when I worked really late in the barn—until three, four in the morning," Holly went on. "I knew Eden wasn't upstairs. I knew the island's nightspots were shut down for the night. I knew she didn't have a boyfriend. I knew my father was spending more overnighters on the boat than usual. And I knew that my mother was becoming tense and on edge.

"I just didn't know," Holly said with a long, mournful sigh, "how to put all of those pieces together. In my wildest dreams . . ."

She couldn't go on; it was too painful to think of the havoc that Eden had wreaked on her family.

A waitress came and took their orders, which allowed Holly to pull herself back from the brink of tears. So much, she thought, for keeping their heartbreak private. She resolved to stick to the facts.

Sam waited until the help was well away before asking his next question. "Did Eden have any visitors?"

"Just people I know, a couple of waitresses from town. Eden worked at the Café Latté for two or three days before landing the job at the Flying Horses."

"Did she get any mail?"

"I don't think so; it would have been in my box. Why do you ask? What are you after?"

"What about phone calls? Did she have a phone put in?"

Holly shook her head. "She had a cell phone; I never needed to know the number. What did she do, Sam? You can't just ask questions without offering answers." She watched him closely, this brown-eyed, brown-haired man who had breezed into her life without so much as a how-do-you-do.

Sam had propped his elbows on the table and was tapping his clenched hands against his lips as he stared at the perforated design in the metal tabletop. If he was waiting for Holly to go pouring out her heart about Eden again, he was sadly mistaken. She had said all that she was going to say until he told her why, exactly, he was in such hot pursuit of the woman.

"Are you a secret admirer?" she asked out of the blue.

"Is that what this is about? Is she some mystery woman that you saw from afar and simply have to have?"

He looked up from his revery. "Are you nuts?"

Holly slumped back in her chair. "It was just a thought."

And a crummy one at that. She realized that she didn't want him to be smitten. It would reinforce the notion that Eden was a *femme fatale*—and *femmes fatales*, Holly knew, never surrendered their victims in one piece. Ever the optimist, she still had hope that her father would emerge from the episode sadder and wiser—but in one piece.

"Eden has something that doesn't belong to her," Sam said at last.

"Yeah. My father."

"Something else. It has great value."

"Sentimental, or monetary?" Holly asked, sitting up with interest.

He shrugged. "Both once, but monetary now."

It was a confusing answer, but at least the man was talking. She said, "Is this thing yours?"

He shook his head.

"But Eden did steal it?"

He shrugged. "*I'm* convinced."

"Are you going to tell me what it is?"

"Nope."

"Are you going to tell me who it belongs to?"

"Nope."

"Well, then I'm wasting my time here, aren't I?"

She stood up to leave, but he caught her wrist.

"Sit down, please. You promised to help."

It wasn't exactly a request. Holly found herself sliding back down onto her chair and wishing she had her Mace. "Fine," she said warily. "But that Jack Webb routine isn't going to get you very far in your inquiries."

"Let me worry about that. I need to know where your father would be likely to sail the *Vixen*."

Holly tossed her hair back and said, "With Eden aboard? The China Sea, for all I know. Obviously he's going to want to cruise somewhere off the beaten path."

"And if he were staying *on* the beaten path?"

She let out a bored sigh—a teenager being grounded would let out just such a sigh—and said, "The Cape. The Elizabeth Islands. He might go through the canal and Down East; he loves Maine, and it *is* August, after all."

"Does he have a favorite harbor?"

"The same as everyone else," Holly said, watching their food arrive. "Hadley."

"Which you can only get to by boat, if I'm not mistaken."

Holly pulled her hands back daintily to give the waitress room. "Isn't that usually the point? To get away from the maddening crowd?"

She stared at her chicken salad with real confusion. It was eleven in the morning, for pity's sake. She'd just got up from breakfast. She gave Sam a look shot with frustration and renewed hostility, then said, "Are we done here?"

"Not quite," he said, returning the look exactly. "Tell me where I can charter a boat."

"Excuse me? You're going to pursue them by *boat*?" She laughed at the sheer absurdity of it.

Sam ignored her reaction and asked another question: "Did Eden clear out of the apartment completely?"

By now Holly more or less hated the man. "She cleared out, all right. Just as I'm about to do." She stood up and unhooked her bag from the back of the chair.

"Hey," he said, much more mildly this time. "Aren't you going to eat that?"

"I am *not* hungry," she said through gritted teeth.

"Well, I am," he answered, slicing through his turkey breast.

"Are you?" Holly picked up her knife and picked up her plate, then scraped the contents of hers onto his. "*Bon appetit*, in that case," she said, and she spun on her heel and walked out.

5

Under a moody gray sky, Holly bicycled past blue-petalled chickory and green blades of dune grass, searching for her mother's car.

She had headed out early for her parents' big, white house, intending to bring her mother up to date over breakfast about Sam Steadman and his mysterious mission. But she arrived to find the white picket gates flung open and her mother's Volvo gone.

It wasn't unusual. Charlotte Anderson was an early riser and walked all over the island for exercise. It wasn't unusual—but for days now, Holly had been watching with dread as her mother sank like a water-logged hat into a sea of deepening despair. Instead of pedalling back to her barn, Holly decided on the spot to track down her missing mother.

Her search took her out of Vineyard Haven and onto Beach Road, which she followed at a fairly fast clip right through Oak Bluffs. She zipped past the town beach with hardly a glance: her mother preferred the more desolate stretches. Once outside of Oak Bluffs, Holly jogged onto the bicycle path that ran side by side with Beach Road down the eastern end of the island, scanning constantly for her mother's car.

She was halfway to Edgartown before she discovered the white Volvo that so clearly was her mother's. (It was the only car on the island with an angel whirligig suction-cupped to its roof, ready to spin its wings if the car ever got up to a speed of, say, a hundred miles an hour. The guardian angel—a disastrous design—had been a welcome-summer gift from Holly to her mother. The most successful thing about it was that in over two months it hadn't been pinched.)

Holly streaked across the road and dumped her bike alongside the car, then peered up and down the long, narrow expanse of white sand being wetted by a gray and sullen sea. The beach was still deserted. She saw a couple with two young children who, sun or no sun, had set up camp on a blanket, and another couple deep in conversation as they walked along the water's edge— but there was no sign of a sixty-year old woman walking along with arms folded and head bowed, wondering what had become of her world.

Holly's heart, which had slowed after the ride, began to pound all over again. How long had the Volvo been abandoned there? She stared left, stared right, strained to see . . .

"Holly! Where did *you* come from?"

She whirled around to see her mother crossing the road from the bicycle path. She was dressed in khaki shorts and a pink cotton shirt and she didn't look desperate at all.

Relieved, Holly said, "I went to the house; you weren't there."

"So you tracked me all the way out here?"

"Well, what did you expect? I'm worried about you."

. "You should be," her mother said bluntly. "I've had another premonition."

The admission sent a wave of cold across Holly's consciousness. She had learned, over the years, not to take her mother's premonitions lightly.

They fell in together and began walking along the beach. "What was this one?" Holly asked, but she knew the answer beforehand.

"Same thing: Eden, dying. The terrible thing is that this time she was dying in my arms. I was holding her; we were near water, just as you and I are now. I could have saved her—the feeling was very strong that I could have saved her—but I was choosing not to. And then I woke up. I don't know whether I woke myself up to stop myself from letting her die, or to stop myself from saving her life."

"Mom, it was just a dream," Holly said. She tried to laugh off her fears. "Don't be so Freudian. How are you feeling, by the way?" she asked, concerned at the furrows in her mother's brow. "Is your migraine gone?"

"It lurks at the edges," her mother said grimly.

"I'm amazed you're out, then. Shouldn't you be lying down?"

"Come home with me. There's something I want you to see."

Charlotte refused to say more than that, so Holly loaded her bike into the back of the car and they drove home with Holly doing the talking. She related word-for-word and look-for-look all that had happened between her and Sam Steadman on the preceding day, but all she got from her mother was the occasional nod.

The sun had begun to burn away the night's rain and the morning's gray haze; by the time they pulled into the grassy drive, the flattened daisies that lined the walk were starting to lift their heads again. Holly fell in behind her mother on the curving brick path and followed her through the side French doors into the kitchen.

Dumping her straw carryall on the marble countertop, Charlotte marched down the hall over an Oriental hall runner worn thin from generations of sandy shoes.

She stopped at the white-panelled door that led to her husband's study. "Look what I've done," she said simply.

Holly stepped inside and stared in shock at the panelled and shuttered room.

Chaos. Her father's "nautical" shelves had been cleared of all of their books, whose ripped-out pages lay strewn about like torn-away leaves from a hurricane. His beloved, antique sextant had been used as a blunt weapon to smash everything of his that was breakable, including the crystal golfing trophy that lay in pieces under its twisted arc. The wedding photo of a smiling Eric and a radiant Charlotte had been smashed in—not a disaster, because everyone had copies—but the World's Greatest Father mug, that was gone forever, and so was the collection of children's mementos that Holly, her brother, and her sister had presented to their father over the years.

Holly stepped over the wreckage with far more apprehension than when, at the innocent age of seven, she had stepped over the mess in her parents' ransacked, burglarized house in Providence. Her fear this time was not of evil forces without, but of terrible forces within.

"Mom," she whispered, stunned into speechlessness.

Her mother was standing stiff as a flagpole. Her arms were folded across her chest and a look of burning defiance glittered in her green eyes: there were no tears there, none that Holly could see.

"I burned all of his Admiralty charts, too," said Charlotte. "He had charts for the entire Bahamas chain, and the Caribbean, and God knows what else. Look over there. In the fireplace. I burned them all. They cost him forty to sixty dollars apiece. I remember how he muttered about the cost every time he invested in one. Now they're ashes. What do you think about *that*?" she asked Holly in a brittle, high-pitched voice.

She went on. "He told me he'd be back for all of this stuff, you know. I can hardly wait. He said he didn't want anything out of this marriage except his boat things." She looked around her and let out a short shrill laugh. "Really: I can hardly *wait*."

Holly picked up a recent photograph, also smashed in, of her brother and sister and her sitting on the bow of the *Vixen*. It occurred to her for the first time that the three of them—but especially her blond, blue-eyed brother and sister—were walking, breathing reminders of Eric Anderson.

She laid the frame gently down on the desk, hoping that it was the boat and not the children that had been the butt of her mother's fury.

"When did you do this?" she murmured.

"Late last night, after you phoned. It's Marjory Betson's fault," her mother explained with a lift of her chin. "She called about an hour before you did to tell me— she was *so* concerned; she would be, the bitch—she called to tell me that when she and Mark sailed into Onset, they saw the *Vixen*, all snugged down at anchor. Eric and Eden were in the cockpit, carrying on. Naturally, Marjory had pretended not to see the boat.

"I lay in bed, thinking about that—it was so easy for me to picture them, you know?—and then sometime after midnight, I came in here and started . . . just started . . . smashing things. It felt, I don't know—good. I was sure it would get rid of the migraine," she added with a sudden, pitiable smile. She took the lone book that remained on the built-in shelves that flanked the fireplace and stood it carefully on end again, as if to prove how reasonable she really had been.

"And did it get rid of the migraine?" Holly asked.

"I told you," her mother said, turning to face her. "It lurks at the edges."

"So then . . . how do you feel about—" Holly lifted her arms, palms up, and gestured around her.

This time her mother's smile was no more than a small, pained twitch at the corners of her mouth. "You want me to admit how sorry I feel; how I came to my senses and was horrified when I walked in here this morning," she said.

Holly sighed and nodded hopefully.

Charlotte turned back to the bookshelves and took down the book she had just propped up, a paperback cruising guide that looked brand-new. She opened it wide over her knee and bent its halves over her thighs until the spine let out a fatal, cracking sound. Without a glance at Holly, she walked over to the fireplace and tossed the fractured book on the grate.

"I feel no more regret than *he* does," she muttered, and she walked out of the room.

In the hallway she stopped and turned back to her daughter. "You're a naive little fool, Holly," she said bitterly. "Grow up."

Holly tried to work that morning, but it wasn't easy; her brain was far too addled after being knocked around by so many different emotions.

Dominant among them was fear for her mother. Depression was one thing, dementia another: the image of a scarily boastful Charlotte Anderson standing in the middle of her husband's demolished study was one that Holly would never forget.

She had offered right away to clean up the mess, but her mother wouldn't let her. "Let it be," she had insisted. "I want him to feel this when he comes back, and he will. I want him to feel every last cut, every last blow."

After that there wasn't much that Holly could do or say, so she left, telling herself that time would make things better. The problem was, who had time to wait for time? Her mother's state was incredibly fragile. It was like watching a child playing with a loaded gun.

Holly's apprehension permeated every brushstroke that she tried to lay down, and the result, after a morning of work, was something that looked like scrambled eggs.

Some sunset, she thought in disgust. She dumped her paintbrushes into a can of turpentine and wiped off the botched drawer with a solvent-soaked rag. It would take a while to dry, she knew. Best to start on something else.

But what? She looked around with no enthusiasm. That big new bedroom suite taking up half of the barn—she could clear it out simply by painting the damn border on the bed and chests to match the wallpaper sample, just as she'd been commissioned to do. It was a mindless if lucrative job, but . . . nah. The client was a pain and her kid was a brat.

She looked for something else to do.

The birdhouses? Half a dozen new ones sat naked in a row, waiting for shingles and picket fences and hollyhocks and little windows with shutters to be painted on them. They would sell like hotcakes. Once she painted them.

Nah.

Her design portfolio of country accessories for the home—what about that? It was an ambitious, ongoing project, and Holly had neglected it lately, which was stupid. She had every intention of shopping it around to a variety of furniture manufacturers. The problem was, she wanted it to look overflowing with ideas, and so far it didn't.

She could just do something simple for it: a design for a dishtowel, maybe, or a working sketch for a canister set. Any little thing, as long it was movement forward. Anything to bring her out of her paralysis.

Nope. Not today. Can't.

She chewed on a fingertip as she roamed the barn, looking for something to start that she could finish. She found a forgotten bag of chocolate chips on one of the easels. There was a job she could start and finish. Holly emptied the bag into the palm of her hand and munched the morsels one by one, stuck in a listless trance.

All the while, at the edges of her vision, ghostly images lurked: her mother, looking devastated. Her mother, looking righteous. Her mother, looking murderous. Those were the faces in Holly's imagination now, not cherry-cheeked kids and slant-eyed cats and sleepy dogs and grazing cows.

I know what I'll do. I'll shampoo my hair. I'll use that five-minute conditioner, that's what I'll do.

Whenever Holly felt really drained of inspiration, she hopped into the shower. There was something about standing there under a steady flow, with pencil and sketch pad unavailable, that let ideas break free and run wild.

She stripped off her shorts and tank top and stepped into her sun-filled shower stall, letting the water run cool and then hot. After shampooing twice, she worked the packet of conditioning oil through her shoulder-length hair and then stood with eyes closed and neck arched, breathing the steamy air. August or no August, she enjoyed the hot flow of water over her body; it melted away the tension, and with it, those appalling images of her mother's agony.

She tried to free her mind for bright ideas and pretty colors, but inspiration wouldn't come. The best she could do was a sudden, unwanted image of Sam Steadman. She saw him with maddening clarity: brown eyes, brown hair, chipped tooth, full lips, washed-out shirt, khaki pants, sockless in his deck shoes and oh-h-h, so not for her. Cocky, yes, that's what he looked. Like someone with a past who couldn't care less about it.

Holly shook her head, less willing to face the memory of him than the one of her mother. No, no, no. Think about something else. Someone else. *Anyone* else.

But distracting thoughts wouldn't come. Instead, Sam Steadman held full sway over her considerable powers of imagination. Where had he come from? How had he got there? Holly groaned and shut her eyes tight, trying to squeeze out his image. She realized for the first time that she had been fighting thoughts of him for the last twenty-four hours straight. It occurred to her—now, finally, duh—that she'd had dreams of him that night, blushable dreams. Suddenly she remembered them well ... remembered his hands, those well-formed, capable hands ... roaming her body, pausing to cup and tease ... and caress ... roaming everywhere. ...

Her own fingers slid down across her soapy skin, on their way to re-capturing the intense pleasure of those dreams. Yes ... yes ... yes yes yes. ...

No! Good grief, no no no! Not him! What on earth are you thinking?

She pulled her hand away from herself, fearful of connecting Sam with conscious pleasure. The thought of *that* was strictly taboo. Sam had something do with Eden, and Eden had everything to do with her mother's pain. It was as simple, and as complicated, as that.

Holly sighed in massive frustration. Then she took the loofah brush from its hook and scrubbed her back until it hurt.

6

After learning from the assistant dockmaster at Vineyard Haven that the *Vixen* was a forty-four-foot Roamer sloop, Sam hauled his ass off to the library on Main Street to see what a Roamer 44 looked like. In half an hour, he had his answer: it looked like any other forty-four-foot fiberglass sailboat, only a little fancier. How the hell he was going to pick one out from among an anchored fleet—or worse, a sailing fleet—he had no idea.

Shit. Holly Anderson was right: if this didn't qualify as a search for a needle in a haystack, nothing did. Sam's mood was completely frustrated and equally foul as he considered his next move.

Holly. Yep, it all came back to her. Holly Anderson knew Eden, knew the boat, and knew the situation as well as anyone. Whatever facts she didn't possess, Sam did; between them, they could surely recover the etching. He wasn't crazy about dragging her into an unholy alliance—she seemed like a sweet enough kid—but catching Eden would take all the forces that he could muster.

He got into his rental Corolla (slated to do double duty as a room that night) and drove out Main Street, headed for the Lake Tashmoo area on the north side of the island. He knew from their brief encounter that Holly had a house there with a barn out back. How hard could it be to find?

Pretty damned hard, it turned out. Sam drove from Main to Daggett to the end of Herring Creek Road, where he found a nice little beach but no house with a barn. He had to backtrack to town for better directions, and after one or two false turns down dirt lanes that led either to nowhere or to other dirt lanes, he finally found what he hoped was Holly's place, at the end of an overgrown drive.

He parked his car and looked around. The Cape Cod house, white and cozy, was surprisingly isolated. Sam could just barely see its red barn behind high scrub and thick trees. Rubbing the bloody scratch he'd got from a branch through the driver's window, Sam made his way to the front door, knocked hard, and waited.

Holly wasn't home.

By then Sam was mad and sweaty and deep in the grip of caffeine withdrawal. He let loose with a round of curses at the whole dumb mission. He considered leaving her a note, then nixed the idea. What would he say? Come fly with me after Eden?

He dropped sullenly back into the seat of his rented Corolla and threw the car into reverse, backing down the scrub-lined drive. He was steering by mirror and was into the second blind curve when he heard and felt it: the sickening crunch of someone's bumper locking with his.

Son of a bitch.

He swung his head around in time to see Holly hanging halfway out of her truck's window and yelling at him.

Perfect.

He climbed back out of his car, tearing more skin on yet another bush, and eased his way between the brush and the vehicles, stopping to check the damage on the way. His rental had taken a bigger hit than her old but higher Ford.

Perfect.

He saw that she stayed put in her seat, opening and closing her fists around the steering wheel in an apparent attempt to stay calm. What nerve.

"I wasn't going very fast," he felt obliged to point out.

"You were going *backwards*. How smart was *that*?"

He went on the offensive. "There's hardly room to swing a cat in front of your house. Why don't you clear out some room there?"

"Why? So people like you can stop by?"

"Yeah, well, never mind me; what about your patrons? How the hell do you expect them to find this place?"

"I don't expect them. This is my home. Clients go directly to the studio in the barn," she said, hanging out the window again. She hooked a thumb over the roof of her truck. "They use the drive over that way, the one that leads to the barn? That's why there's a sign over there and not over here?"

Ah, those question marks; those hints of contempt. It fueled Sam's growing conviction that despite her sweet face, Holly Anderson was just another garden-variety socialite—this one, a subsidized *artiste* killing time until the right rich man came along to lift her out of her genteel struggle and drop her into a beachfront house. Which was one thing you had to admit about Eden: she didn't expect anything; she always went out and fought for it.

"Well? Now what?" he asked, just for the pleasure

of sounding dumb. Let *her* get off her duff and do something.

She rolled her eyes. "Is there any actual damage?" she asked as she would a child.

"Come out and see," he said calmly.

"Not here. There's too much brush. Drive back to the house, please, so that I can assess."

"Your wish is my command," he said in response to her command. What the hell, it was one way to get inside her place.

Self-conscious now, he drove too fast, hit a pothole, and knocked his head against the roof of the Corolla. He swore again; it was all her fault. And what wasn't her fault was Eden's. Women! He should've gone to sea when he'd had the chance back when.

He got out of the car, and so did Holly. It struck him again how truly guileless and innocent she looked. There was something about her face, maybe in those green eyes. Inexperience? If so, she was being brought up to speed the hard way. Eden's way.

Damn it, Eden. Why'd you walk out on me?

The thought vaporized almost as quickly as it formed, replaced by a rush of frustration over his ridiculously complicated pursuit of her. Her escape on a boat was bad enough. But a fender bender in the middle of a dirt drive—could it get any more stupid than that?

"That's a nasty scratch," said Holly, pointing to his right arm.

But it was his left arm that stung. Confused, Sam twisted his right one for a better look and was amazed to see a trickle of blood wending its way down the back of his forearm. He felt like a flunkout in an Outward Bound program.

"I bleed easily," he said with an embarrassed smile.

He'd found it out years ago after he came home one day to a cleared-out house.

"Come inside," she said, surprising him. "You can put something on that before it gets bad."

She breezed right past their beat-up bumpers without bothering to look at the damage. It gave Sam hope. She seemed to be a soft-hearted type; he'd be able to bend her to his needs.

He followed her inside through a short center hall into a humble kitchen with a linoleum floor, a sink on legs, and a stove from the fifties.

"Clean yourself up with soap and wet paper towels," Holly ordered as she tore off some sheets from a roll near the sink. "I'll get the iodine." She gave him a look that said, "And don't you dare try anything funny," then blew off his thanks on her way out of the kitchen.

Sam dabbed at the scratches gingerly, trying not to make them bleed. The odd thing was, it wasn't an heiress's kind of kitchen at all. And yet Holly certainly came from money. Her parents had a million-dollar antique house in Vineyard Haven; he'd seen it himself. *Obviously* there was money in the family. Eden would never go after anyone poor.

Except, he thought dryly, for that one time in her life eight years earlier at a waterfront festival. He remembered it well.

Holly showed back up with antiseptic, Band-Aids, cotton balls—the works. Sam smiled and said, "I don't think it's all that bad, Miss Nightingale; but I appreciate it."

She shrugged. "You never know."

She lifted his left sleeve and peeked underneath, then decided to push the fabric up over his shoulder to clear the area. He heard a funny little half-sigh, and after that she became very businesslike as she swabbed his cuts with iodine-soaked cotton.

"Does it hurt?"

"Nope." *Aagh.*

"I guess I ought to cut those shrubs back."

"A guy could sue," he agreed.

Her reaction was to rub in the iodine just a little bit harder. "But you're not that guy—right?"

"We could work something out," he suggested over his shoulder.

She stopped mid-cottonball. "Like *what?*"

"Well . . . like I was thinking you could show me the area," he said with a disarming smile.

"Oh!" She became all business again, burying her nose in her work. "I suppose that would be all right."

"Great. How about tomorrow at, say, six?"

"Six would be fine," she said almost shyly as she dumped the last cottonball into a swing-top can. She turned to him with a surprisingly warm smile and said, "The sunsets Up-Island are really spectacular."

Her face was a radiant sunset itself. He smiled in the sheer pleasure of seeing it and then said, "But I was thinking more along the lines of sunrise than sunset."

"Sunrise?" She sucked in her breath. "I knew it! I was right the first time! Listen, mister, just because I let you in my kitchen, it doesn't mean you can assume you're spending the night. Who do you think you are? If that doesn't—"

"Hold it, hold it—I meant, I'll pick you *up* at six. I won't even come in if that makes you feel better. I'll wait outside and blow the horn," he added, not without his own hint of contempt.

"Oh! Oh. I misunderstood. Sorry."

Slow, deep color flooded her cheeks. For some reason, Sam thought instantly of Eden, of how he'd never once seen her blush—not involuntarily, anyway. Some actors could cry on demand; Eden could blush on demand. She could cry, too, needless to say. She'd given Sam some Oscar-caliber performances in that regard.

"Why are you looking at me like that, Sam? I said I was sorry."

It took a second for him to refocus on the woman before him. "Uh, I know that. I was thinking of something else, that's all."

Holly was watching him through an appraising squint now. "Why six in the morning? Isn't that a little early?"

He smiled reassuringly. "Not for the grand tour. There's a lot around here I'd like to see." *Rhode Island, Connecticut, New Hampshire . . .*

"I have to warn you, Mr. Steadman, that I'm not very bright-eyed at that hour," she said as she washed up, then tore off more paper towels. She leaned back on a wainscotted cupboard and dried her hands, and her smile seemed as genuine as his had been calculating.

"One reason I became an artist," she admitted, "was that I could set my own hours. Not a very lofty motive, is it?"

He shrugged and said, "Who knows why people feel the need to create?" And then he added in all honesty, "I liked your whirligigs. They made me smile."

"Maybe, but your photographs make me *think*," she said in a hopelessly earnest way. "They're intense, they're real—they make me see fishermen for the first time, somehow. I can't tell you how moving they are to me."

How the hell old *was* she? Her gallery bio said thirty-one, but just then she looked like a freshman sitting in the front row of Photography 101, the kind of student who waved her hand frenetically at the professor with an *I*-know! expression on her face.

"You didn't seem to be paying much attention to my photographs when you flipped through the book at the bookstore," he pointed out, doing a little fishing of his own.

She turned away to toss the towels. "I went back and bought the book," she murmured.

"*Did* you."

"Yes, I did." She turned back to him and said with silly cheer, "So you're one royalty richer than you used to be!"

He grinned and said, "Super. Now you can have orange juice with your breakfast tomorrow."

The laugh they shared sprang from common ground: the struggle of every artist, everywhere, to pay his own way through his work. The difference between them was that her parents could afford to bail her out if she failed, and Sam's could not. Which brought him full circle back to the reason why he was standing in the kitchen of this gentle, whimsical stranger who had smacked up his rental and bound up his wounds: Eden had absconded with his parents' old age.

Eden. Eden. Here he was, seven years later, and she was still leading him on a merry chase.

"So . . . then . . . you'll come by to pick me up at six?" Holly said, poking gently at his revery.

He tried to shake himself free of the vision of Eden, smiling her come-hither smile. "Uh . . . yeah! Sure will! And then we'll see some sights."

From a quarter-mile up, he should have mentioned, but that was tomorrow's problem.

"Oh, my God—I almost forgot about your car!"

Sam waved away her concern. "I'll just say someone hit me in a parking lot."

Her eyes got wide. "Sam! You *wouldn't* do that."

Not only was she scandalized, but Sam could see that he'd lost credibility with her again. Shit: all his fence-mending, wasted. The fact that he had planned to pay for the damage out of his own pocket was irrelevant now; she'd never believe him. Shit.

He decided to throw himself at her mercy. "You're

right. That was dumb. I wasn't thinking it through. That's what happens when you've never been in an accident."

"You've never been?"

"Never." Not unless you counted the speedboat he stole and ran up on the rocks in Woods Hole. Since the owner had never bothered to file a report—the man was a drug dealer—Sam hadn't had to worry about an insurance hassle. (The Coast Guard, now they were a different story.) As for the stolen Corvette, Sam had driven it around for less than a day, and when he dumped it near its owner's house, it didn't have a single scratch on it.

"Are you going to forgive me?" he asked with a pleading look.

Holly seemed mollified by the display of repentance. She even offered an apology of her own: "I'm sorry if I seem testy," she said on their way to the door. "It's—well, you can guess. My father. Eden. This has been so devastating. I'm worried sick about my mother. She's coming apart at the seams."

"I understand," he said softly. Oh, and he did. "Completely."

She took his hand in hers, surprising him again, and turned his arm gently. "Keep an eye on those scratches," she said as she looked them over. "It's so easy to become infected."

He reassured her that he would and then he left, feeling oddly soothed when it really should have been him doing the soothing. It was only later, when he was sitting alone with a roast beef sandwich in a crowd of happy, sunburned tourists, that it hit him: without wearing gloves, Holly Anderson had cleaned up the blood of a total stranger.

He shook his head and stabbed at his fries in a state of vague pique. The woman clearly had a lot to teach him about trust—and a hell of a lot more to learn.

7

Holly Anderson woke up at four-thirty, too excited to sleep. The thought of going with Sam on a sunrise sightseeing tour (she wasn't—quite—willing to call it a date) struck her as wonderfully romantic, much more so than some routine candlelight dinner. Granted, the offer was a little goofy; but when was the last time a man she knew had acted goofy? Okay, there was her father. But Sam's idea to go sightseeing was a charming kind of goofy, and God knew, her life had been a little scant on charm lately.

Sam was changing all that. Whatever his reasons for chasing after Eden, he had laid them aside and had made a decision to stick around. *With me, on my enchanted island.* Holly gave her bare body a squeeze of sheer happiness, and then she added a few more rose-scented crystals to the water in her big clawfoot tub.

Sam Steadman woke up well before sunrise, thanks to a diligent cop who caught him sleeping in his rented Corolla. Bleary-eyed and dry-mouthed, he drove the Corolla to a new parking area at another beach before instantly being discovered there as well. What were the odds? Disgusted with the way he felt and smelled, and furious with the island for not having enough rooms on it and for closing its showers for the night, Sam gave up his struggle to sleep, stripped to his shorts, and waded into the sea. He had to get cleaned up somehow.

Charlotte Anderson lay in her king-sized bed, lost and alone and waiting for the sun to come up so that she could fall asleep. She was afraid to close her eyes at night anymore; it was a little too much like death. Mere weeks ago, her husband had been lying in bed with his arm thrown around her, and she had eased it away because it had been too hot. But now she was cold at night, colder than she'd ever been.

She pulled up the covers and shivered in wait for the sun.

Eric Anderson zipped up his windbreaker, turned off the autopilot, and took over the wheel of the *Vixen* himself. They were in the last hour of an overnight sail, and every one of his senses was on alert. He knew that sailors made their most serious mistakes at the end of a passage with land in plain sight. The thought of making a navigational blunder and then having to call for a rescue made him positively cringe.

But it was going well, this trip. He'd never known such exhilaration in his life. He loved the anonymity of being on a boat—loved the idea that he could go where he wanted, do what he wanted, see what he wanted, be what he wanted. Finally.

He leaned to port and peered through the companionway into the cabin below. The red light over the nav station threw a warm glow on Eden, asleep in the quarter berth without a care in the world. It took Eric's breath

away, the way she trusted that he could handle the boat
and keep her safe. Not once had he heard her say, "Are
you sure?" More than anything else—more than the sex,
more than the laughter, more than her willingness to hide
out on the boat with him—that's what Eric Anderson
loved: the fact that Eden Walker made him feel like a
man.

He felt the boat lift and fall underneath him in a
smooth rhythm not unlike a second round of lovemaking. Patting the boat's starboard flank, he whispered,
"Easy does it, girl; we have all the time in the world."

His thoughts drifted inevitably to the confrontation
he'd had days before at the office. He would not be
coming back, he'd said. Duncan was incredulous, Jack,
furious. It was annoying. He had warned his partners
before that he was planning to throttle back. They *knew*
he wanted to go off voyaging—and that was before he'd
met Eden. When did they think he'd do it? When he
was seventy-five?

They didn't understand. How could they? Duncan
had been married even longer than he was, and Jack was
an old fart of a bachelor. In any case, with them, the
firm came first. Eric had felt that way, too, once upon a
time.

He leaned to port for another view into the cabin and
marvelled that the lithe, fair creature sleeping below had
ever deigned to look twice at him.

Let them find me, he thought, enthralled by his good
fortune. *Let them try.*

8

Sam heard the seaplane before he saw it, swooping down to the water as nimbly as a cormorant after a fish. The pilot was Sam's oldest friend, a New Bedford wharf rat like him, but one who'd somehow managed to stay out of jail and then get a pilot's license. Billy and seaplanes: they went together like cormorants and fish.

Sam grinned and gave his pal an overhead wave, sniffing his shirtpit tentatively in the process. The scent of Mennen overwhelmed, thank God. He didn't want to offend the sensibilities of the freshly scrubbed, sweet-smelling woman who was his one and only link to Eden and the engraving.

He turned to her and said, "Ever flown in a seaplane?"

"No, never," Holly answered, oblivious to the fact that she was about to board one. Still, she seemed as intrigued by the pontooned flying machine as the two kids who were fishing on the dock beside them.

"Well, here's your chance," Sam said. "That's our tour bus."

Don't get mad, lady, please don't get mad.

"*What?*"

He shrugged his most boyish shrug and smiled sheepishly. "I'm not presuming, am I?"

She rounded on him and said, "You certainly are, Sam! I can't let you spend that kind of money taking me around. It wouldn't be right."

"Sure it would," he argued, knocked off balance by her reaction. "The pilot's an old friend of mine; he's doing it for gas money."

"Well, that's not right, either. You're taking advantage of him!"

"Look, it's no big deal—honest. Guys do this for guys. I've given Billy plugs in my books. It comes out even."

"No, really," she said, crossing her arms. "The gesture is too extravagant. I can't accept it."

And meanwhile Billy was threading through the moored boats with a shit-eating grin under his handlebar mustache. Perfect. Somehow Sam had thought that he'd be able to explain the point of the plane over breakfast. Didn't happen. Then he tried broaching the subject of Eden en route. No dice. Then the damn kids on the dock struck up an unlikely conversation with them, and now here's Billy, fifteen minutes early, and to top it off she thinks it's, of all things, a little too romantic. How the hell—when the hell—was he going to explain?

The seaplane glug-glugged its way to a halt alongside the dock, and Billy threw open the door to the passenger seats. "Hop in! Let's go, for chrissake, before the dockmaster gets on my tail! C'mon, c'mon!"

So that was simple enough. In they hopped, with Holly alternating between mutters of dismay and disapproval. After hurried introductions, Billy spun the plane neatly around and reversed his winding route, dodging an anchored catamaran that was drifting back and forth across a wide swath of harbor.

Billy's language, never bland, became even more exuberant than usual. "Jesus Christ, will you lookit the size of that thing? If I had my way, I'd blow that frigging catamaran right out of the water! There's no room in this harbor for a cat that size. Look at that frigging thing roam! Who the hell let that monster in here, anyway? Where am I supposed to go? I'm gonna write the FAA about this for sure. Damn frigging cats!"

"It's a boat, Billy, which gives it more right to be in the harbor than a plane, so cool it, wouldja?" said Sam, taking little comfort from the look on Holly's face. She was rigid. Whether she was more afraid of Billy or of the seaplane, Sam couldn't say, but she was holding on with white-knuckled zeal.

"You'll want to belt up, Holly," he said gently.

"No, I don't think so," she responded, staring grimly ahead. "You can turn the plane around now, please."

The waves were a little choppy outside of the harbor. The seaplane began to bobble and tip from side to side, like the cork on the water it was. With every plop of its pontoons, Holly let out a little gasp. "Back, please. Now, please."

Billy gave her a wink and said, "First time?"

"Yeah-h-h . . ."

"Best time," he said, snugging his baseball cap over his head. "Where you wanna look first?"

"Look?"

"He means, 'sightsee,' " said Sam, pinching his pal's shoulder in warning. "Do the closest harbors first—Hadley; the rest of the Elizabeths. Then swing up to Padanarum and follow the south shore, and after that, move on to the Cape."

"But not the Canal?"

"Yeah, that, too. You're gonna have to backtrack, I

guess. There's no point to following the outer Cape to Provincetown; no one sails that route."

"What *is* this? What's going on?" said Holly, obviously catching on to the point of the plan.

"Here we go," Billy said cheerfully.

"Belt, will you?" Sam repeated. Over Holly's protests that she wasn't going *anywhere*, he reached over and did the job for her.

The seaplane accelerated with an earsplitting but somehow jaunty din, and then with a mighty lift, the little craft became airborne. Up, up, and away they went, leaving the island curled below like a sun-drenched cat. Ahead and to port lay a bracelet of fuzzy green, sheep-grazing lumps: the unspoiled chain of Elizabeth Islands, nailed down at the western end by the quaint community of Cutty Hunk. To starboard lay the channel that led to Woods Hole and the mainland, plied just then by a ferry and a smattering of early sailors.

"Now this is more like it," Sam said, happy despite his misgivings about Holly. He loved being away from it all. A sailboat knifing silently through the water was his first preference; but the seaplane, despite its noisy drone, wasn't a bad way to get around, either. "Nice, huh?" he offered hopefully.

He saw high color in her cheeks; he chalked it off to excitement.

Wrong.

"What the *hell* do you think you're doing?" she said with not-so-repressed fury. "This is an abduction! And you!" she said, poking Billy in the back. "You're going to lose your license over this!"

"Oh, hey, now, lady, I haven't abducted *nobody*. You climbed aboard of your own free will."

"My father is an *attorney*, I hope you're aware of that!"

"Probate, Billy; no big deal," Sam interjected.

That made her, if possible, even more pissed. "This is all about finding my father, isn't it? You actually think I'm going to sit here and hunt him down with you two morons?"

Sam shrugged and said, "Unless you're planning to jump out of the plane—yeah. I do."

"You outrageous, godforsaken liar! I *will* have you arrested. The instant we touch down! This is a kidnapping, pure and simple!"

Now that she put it that way, Sam could see how some law-minded person might jump to that conclusion. It didn't help his case that he had a history of kidnapping things that he wanted or needed: that go-fast boat; the red Corvette. Still, he knew that he'd left his life of crime behind him, so if the morning's otherwise perfectly normal situation had an awkward side to it, it wasn't because of him, but her.

"What do we do, Sam?" asked Billy.

"Keep going."

"Turn *around*!"

"You make things hard on a guy, you know that?" Sam said, getting a little testy himself. "I mean, here's Billy, taking time out of his charter business just to do us a favor—"

"*Us* a favor? *I* don't care where Eden is!"

"But you care where your father is. You have to care," he said simply. "He's your father."

Sam, who didn't have a clue who or where his own biological father was, had cared about that for a long, long time.

"You're wrong," Holly said with icy disdain. "I don't want to have anything to do with my father ever again."

"You say that now. But eventually—in a month, a season, a year—you'll want to have something to do with him again. So the sooner you see him and confront him about this, the better off you'll be. You have issues to work through."

"Issues!" She laughed scornfully at that one and said, "And how do you propose I deal with them? By swooping low over the *Vixen* and pelting it with propoganda leaflets?"

God, no, Sam thought. The last thing he wanted was to tip Eden off. He said, "The way I look at it, if they're still around here it means that your father isn't as committed to this wild affair as you think. He's sticking close to home, at least subconsciously; you can assume that he'll come to his senses soon."

"Why? Because he hasn't sailed off with Eden to Raratonga yet? He couldn't if he wanted to," Holly muttered as she stared out the window at the water below. "My mother burned all his charts."

Whoa. All that stuff about a woman scorned was true.

"Please, Holly," Sam murmured, sensing that she, at least, was softening. "I need your help. I know we got off on the wrong foot. I wish I had been more candid with you from the start. I . . . I've never in my life had to ask a woman to help me out, but I'm doing it now. Please, Holly. I need to find Eden."

Her expression was extraordinarily grave as she studied his face while she considered his plea. Sam had the uncanny sense that she was looking into his soul. While he felt confident that he had God on his side in this one, he wasn't nearly as sure that God approved of the way he was going about His business.

Apparently Holly didn't, either. She whacked Billy on the shoulder again. "Take me back to the dock."

"Hey! Geez! With pleasure," the pilot said, annoyed, and he began banking the seaplane to starboard.

"Hold a turn, Billy," Sam ordered. He took hold of Holly's arm—why, he had no idea; it wasn't as if she was going anywhere—and said, "Would you recognize your father's boat from up here? Yes or no."

She glanced scathingly at their point of contact and said, "Probably. My father has had the boat customized. And he flies an owner's ensign from the port spreader. It's an unusual color—magenta; I think it would show from up here."

"Help me find them," Sam said bluntly, "and I'll have Eden behind bars in no time."

"Oh, good; you can share a cell together," said Holly, yanking her arm free of his grip.

Ignoring the snotty response, he spun a scenario that would help them both. "Eden has stolen an extremely valuable engraving," he admitted for the first time. "It belongs to people I care about deeply. Once I get it back, once Eden is out of the picture, your father will see her for what she is. It's happened before."

"How would you know?" Holly said, surprised.

"No—you misunderstand," Sam said quickly. No way was he going to admit that *he* was the one who'd had a rude awakening after Eden took off. "I meant, Eden has taken things before that she shouldn't have." His heart being one of them.

"Really, Sam? She's a proven thief? And you think my father will reject her once he becomes aware of that?"

Her eyes were wide and green and hopeful and Sam felt like a lying shit. Well, it had to be done. God worked in mysterious ways. "Let's take it one step at a time," he suggested. "First we have to find them."

She nodded. Whatever Sam had said, however he had said it, it seemed to have worked. Holly did a complete one-eighty.

"We can find them," she said, pressing her nose to the window in her sudden determination to locate the boat. "I know all my father's favorite harbors. Billy, don't bother with Quisset; he doesn't go there. But, yes, check out Hadley . . . and Quick's Hole . . . definitely Cutty Hunk. That's one place where he'd actually pay for a mooring if there weren't any room to anchor."

Billy said, "Now yer talkin'," and began a sharp bank to port. Holly didn't think much of the sudden maneuver. She tensed and grabbed Sam's arm reflexively, which he had to admit, he liked: it gave him the feeling that he was back in control of a hideously slippery mission. Smiling, he said, "Billy's just showing off, that's all."

"Billy's just in a hurry," the pilot shot back. "Billy has to be in Marblehead for a two-thirty wedding in the air."

Sam rolled his eyes at Holly. "Good grief. How corny can you get?"

"Really? I think it sounds kind of romantic," Holly ventured.

Ah, shit. "Oh, the general *idea*—definitely," Sam agreed, tap-dancing through his *faux pas*. "I meant, it's doing it over Marblehead that's corny. *I* would get married over Martha's Vineyard. Because the Vineyard—now *that's* romantic."

Holly broke into one of her sunshine grins and he thought, here's a girl who should smile more often. Too bad Eden had tossed that grenade in her lap. Their laps, in fact—her mother sounded like a basket case as well. He had to wonder about the father. How the hell did a probate lawyer ever find the nerve or, depending how you looked at it, become so witless that he was willing to drop a family on its collective head in a willy-nilly chase after a hot piece of ass?

Eden. That's how. Eden. Sam remembered well how she would bat those long-lashed blue eyes at him and then walk away, implying that maybe he'd get some and maybe he wouldn't. She'd driven him crazy, driven every man she'd ever wanted to, completely crazy. *Eden.* He could almost taste the sweet honey of her kiss. He definitely could see the soft sway of her hips. Seven years, and he could still see those hips.

Nosirree. Eric Anderson wouldn't have stood a snowball's chance in hell.

"Oh, my God, I think that's—! No," Holly decided, disappointed. She shaded her eyes with her hands against the window. "It's a Roamer 44, but it's not my dad's. Here, Sam, look. Down there. See the boat with the teak decks? The *Vixen* looks like that, except that all her wood trim is varnished to a perfect gloss. The varnish would be dazzling in the sun right now."

Sam craned to look over her shoulder. Caught off guard, Holly pulled away from him the few short inches she could. She seemed uncomfortably aware of him, which wasn't surprising: he was still very near indeed, near enough to see the fine gold fuzz on her cheeks. He smiled sheepishly and said softly, "You smell good," and then he sat up straight in his seat again.

He, of course, smelled like Mennen, laid on thick. But that aura of hygiene could easily dissipate, and he was pretty sure that the sweet young thing beside him wouldn't survive long with a very raw male. Best to leave her some space, physically and psychologically.

She sighed—with relief, pretty obviously—and went back to searching the waters below them. Up and down the little plane flew, winging over some of the most charming anchorages in New England, dipping low for better views, circling back for second looks, and always, to Sam's bitter disappointment, coming up empty.

The sun rose higher, the water got bluer. Still no boat. It wasn't like looking for a needle in the haystack at all, Sam muttered to the others. It was like looking for a long blond hair in a haystack.

"Correction," said Billy, who clearly was watching

the clock. "Make that a long, blond, wandering hair in a haystack."

"Boy, when the boats are sailing to windward and are on their ears, you really can't identify them at all from up here," Holly confessed. She sounded apologetic, as if it were her fault.

Someone's stomach growled loud enough to be heard over the engine. No one acknowledged it. Foodwise, it was true, they were in bad shape. The Black Dog doughnuts were long gone, and Billy's giant coffee thermos had been drained of its last drop. After a night spent as a vagrant, Sam longed for a steak sandwich, a hot shower, and clean sheets, in that order. It didn't help his mood that he was going to have to throw himself at the mercy of the Chamber of Commerce yet again that night. He settled into a sullen, dogged scan of the water below until Billy eventually broke the weariness of the spell that had them in its grip.

"Okay, folks, that's gonna have to do it for today. I'm low on gas and I got a wedding to get to. Brides get nervous when the chapel doesn't show up on time."

"Are you married, Billy?" Holly asked.

"Nah. Who's got time for that shit, huh, Sam?"

Sam had warned Billy about mentioning his marriage to Eden—but then, he'd warned Billy about lots of things over the years. It hadn't made Billy a lick more discreet.

Sam had to settle for smacking his old friend on the back of his balding head. "Watch how you talk," he said cryptically.

"*Ow*! Geez, you two are lethal. Next time we go up, I lash you to the wings."

They were circling Point Judith in Rhode Island, but all they saw were three yachts anchored behind the stone breakwater, and a handful of boats from the fishing fleet tied up to the docks inside the main harbor. Holly was right: the weather was too fine not to be out and about.

The seaplane banked gracefully and turned away from the sun and back toward the Vineyard. If the *Vixen* was still out there in plain sight, no one seemed to want to know about it: Billy speeded up the plane and Holly sat back in her seat with her eyes shut. Even Sam sat back for a breather; his neck was killing him.

"They could be in Maine," Holly murmured without opening her eyes. "My dad likes Maine."

"Mmm."

"We shouldn't have wasted time searching the Cape. The water there is really too shoal for the *Vixen*."

"Oh, well. We were in the area."

"What will you do now, Sam?" she asked, rolling her head tiredly in his direction.

"Keep lookin', I guess. She's got to be out there somewhere."

After a time of quiet, Holly sighed and said, "She's kind of a Siren in reverse, isn't she? She leads men away from the island and out to sea, instead of the other way around."

If only you knew.

Sam smiled wearily and said, "One of these days you'll turn her into a whirligig."

"Never. Please don't joke about that, Sam," she said almost wistfully. "My art is supposed to bring joy."

"Joy?" Sam locked his hands and stretched his arms through the gap between his knees. "Joy would be a two-pound steak and a baked potato. Ecstasy would be a topping of sour cream."

"Make that two," Billy chimed in over his shoulder.

"Come back to the island tonight, then, bro. My treat."

"Not a chance. Tonight is all Shirley, all night."

"Ah. Thank you for sharing that with us," said Sam

with a glance of apology at Holly—who so clearly was *not* an all-night woman.

Billy's raunchy explanation brought predictable color to her cheeks. She studied a rip in the liner of the overhead for a moment and then turned to Sam and said, "Tell me about the stolen engraving."

Sam grinned. All in all, she was being a pretty good sport about having been kidnapped by two guys in a seaplane.

"The engraving was done by Albrecht Durer and is known sometimes as 'The Fall of Man,' more often as 'Adam and Eve.' It was made in 1504, and if you're really curious to see what it looks like, you can find another print in Boston's Museum of Fine Arts."

"Another one!" Billy took offense at that. "How the hell can it be worth anything if there's more than one of it? It's like he was forging his own stuff."

"Believe it or not, you've got a point there, good buddy. Durer, no snob, had a tendency to make a lot of prints available to the *hoi polloi*. He made a lot of money that way."

"Tell us about the engraving, Sam," said Holly, deeply interested in what he had to say. It made Sam feel good, the way she was hanging on his every word. He was mildly surprised at how good.

Puffed up with recent knowledge, he said, "Durer was fast, good, and cosmopolitan; he went to Italy, soaked up their ideas about Renaissance art, and after a few tries, came up with Adam and Eve, a trailblazing effort in Germany at the time. His Adam is muscular and idealized, but his Eve is a little on the fleshy side, more matron than maiden."

He shrugged and added, "Whether the stylistic treatments complement or conflict with one another is up to the critics to decide. Me, I just want to know where the hell my parents' copy is."

"Sam? How much do you think the engraving is worth?" Holly blurted.

She looked embarrassed about posing the question; but then, her kind never talked about either money or sex, Sam figured. He tried to sound matter-of-fact about the value, but it was a staggering sum to him.

"I'd say, considering the importance of the piece, somewhere in the mid-six figures. It depends how crazy the market is."

Even Holly gasped. "If Eden stole it, wouldn't she run right out and sell it?"

"It's my great fear," Sam admitted.

"But then why stay with my dad and run the risk of being caught? What can she want with *him*? Is it possible that she really loves him?"

"I dunno," said Sam, slumping tiredly in his seat. "What's your father like? What would a woman see in him?"

"He—well, that's not an easy question. I mean, he's my father." She scrunched her face into a thoughtful and slightly freckled frown. "He's . . . well, he's really loyal. Usually. You can always count on him. Usually." After a moment she gave up trying to come up with a decent answer and simply sighed. "My mother still loves him, I think."

"Your dad must be some hot ticket," Sam muttered. It surprised him, how much he personally hated the guy. Sixty-two! A man that age was supposed to be hauling his grandkids off to a waterslide park, not waltzing around the Cape and islands on a yacht with a babe. No wonder bitter women formed first-wives' clubs. Hell, Sam felt like starting one up for first husbands.

Holly had an inspiration. "You know what? We don't actually know if Eden is with him. Maybe she's run off to fence the engraving and she's left him behind. Maybe my dad is alone on the *Vixen* right now, licking his wounds. He'd be too humiliated to come home, at least not any time soon."

She didn't—quite—look gleeful, but she didn't look broken up over the possibility, either. Sam, on the other hand, felt screwed either way. If Eden was staying with Eric Anderson for love, that would hurt; but if she'd already dumped him and had sold the engraving, that would be worse.

Damn you, Eden. I'll find you if I have to track you down to the ends of the earth.

Of course, that determination, and a buck, would get him a cup of coffee on the Vineyard. He ran his hands through his unwashed hair and winced. Too bad it wouldn't get him a room.

"Hey—a Coast Guard chopper," Billy announced. He dipped his wings in salute, and the seaplane banked and began its descent toward the Vineyard.

9

The afternoon sea breeze had kicked in right on time, cooling Holly and Sam as they trekked under a bright sun from the seaplane to Sam's latest Corolla, parked on a side street well away from the docks.

Sam seemed subdued, which wasn't surprising. But he turned down Holly's suggestion that they grab some lunch, and that did surprise her. The two of them had spent the morning in a small plane searching for a fugitive on a boat. Shouldn't that be a little like sharing a foxhole or something?

Disappointment must have shown in her face, because Sam said quickly, "I have to find a room for tonight or leave the island altogether. Call me crazy, but I'd much rather wash with water that doesn't have salt in it."

"Salt . . . ? Where have you been staying?"

Sam smiled grimly and pointed his car key ahead of them. "Chez Toyota."

He may as well have said in a refrigerator box. Holly was shocked. "But . . . you have a *book* out. You're a

celebrity! Don't you know anyone here who can offer
you a guest bedroom?"

"Sadly, no—although one of the ladies working the
desk at the Chamber of Commerce did offer to let me
sleep in a tent in her backyard. That, however, depends
on her grandson's sleepover, which itself depends on the
weather. I get the tent if it pours," he said with a wink
and a wry smile.

Was it the wink or was it the smile? Something
snagged on Holly's heart, her first real hint that she
might be in trouble. So far the man had evoked reactions
in her that ranged from annoyance to real annoyance.
But this was new, this snagging of the heart. The pain
felt oddly pleasurable. Baffled by her response, Holly
decided to tuck it quietly out of view and then examine
it more carefully when she got home. Without Sam
around, she'd be able to think more clearly.

Or not.

"You could stay in the apartment above the barn,"
she was astonished to hear herself say. "As we know,
it's currently empty."

"Eden's place? You're offering me Eden's place?"

She gave him a breathless nod. "Mm-hmm."

Big mouth, big mouth—what're you doing?

He nodded warily in return. "Okay-y-y. That, uh, that
would be nice. I'd appreciate it."

"Good. Yes. Well then. Do you have to retrieve your
bags? Oh! Obviously you have your bags. In—"

"The lobby of Chez Toyota," he said, breaking into
a sudden, wonderfully good-natured grin that took what
was left of her breath away. "I'm ready."

"Good! Good. So . . . I guess we can go home. I
mean, to your home. I mean, the barn. I mean, the apartment above the barn. Is what I really mean."

He was watching her the way he would a dancing
bear, undoubtedly waiting to see if she'd fall over from

turning around so many times. Holly wanted to seem urbane and sophisticated—she'd been raised on the East Side of Providence, after all—but urbane and sophisticated had never been her style. It was a real effort just to keep her knees from knocking while she waited for Sam to open the door to the car that would transport them to the vacant loft above the barn behind her house.

Why *was* she feeling so jumpy? It wasn't as if she was hauling him off to her bed.

Still, as they drove along chatting with apparent nonchalance about Albrecht Durer and his art, one thought and one thought only seemed to be consuming her: *would* they end up in bed? Hers, his, who cared, but would they end up together? Once or twice she thought that he had looked at her with a certain . . . look. She wouldn't go so far as to say he'd been coming on to her (not that she was any big expert on the subject), but once or twice she was pretty sure that there had been a certain . . . something.

And then, damn it, a crummy something else. That was the problem with Sam Steadman—that look he would get, just when you were intrigued by the look that he *had*. Suddenly he would become tense . . . distracted . . . almost startled, as if a possum had dropped from a tree onto the middle of their picnic blanket.

And yet at the moment he seemed perfectly normal and entirely at ease. The good news was that he most likely wasn't an ax murderer. The bad news was that he probably wasn't that interested in her.

Holly sucked in a shudder of breath and let it out in a hurried sigh, and the tiny barb that had snagged her heart dug a little more deeply into it.

"Hey, duh, there *was* a sign," Sam said with a laugh, and he threw a sudden, sharp turn onto the drive that led to the barn.

HOLLY'S ARTWORKS featured prominently on a gaily

painted, flower-bedecked board that Holly had designed, nailed to a stake, and driven into the ground herself. She liked that sign, liked the way it fit in with the mood of crushed quahog shells, blinding white in the afternoon sun, that covered the lane. After a turn or two and a bump in the drive, they emerged in front of the old red barn that Holly had come to love and want for her own.

Sam parked the Corolla in front of the big sliding door of Holly's studio, and they went up the steep, open stairs that edged the side of the barn.

"Eden left everything very neat," said Holly, nervously fishing her key ring out of her bag, "but I haven't been in here since I discovered that she'd gone. I hope the bathroom's okay."

"It will be," Sam said in a voice gone suddenly tight. "Eden had a thing for—she was a woman, wasn't she? She'd have a thing for clean bathrooms. In any case, it doesn't matter at all. Thank you."

Holly stopped with the key still in the lock to stare at him. He was doing it again, that Jekyll-Hyde thing.

"Is something wrong?" she asked, trying not to seem nervous. No way was she going to walk into an apartment on a well-hidden property with a relative stranger who looked as if he had blood on his mind.

Sam laughed softly and shook his head. "Nope. Nothing's wrong. Nothing's right. Everything's in god-damned suspension."

She cocked her head in a puzzled squint, trying to understand. He was there to recover an engraving stolen from people he loved. It was a noble mission. She could trust him. She *could* trust him.

"Why do I have the sense that you're afraid to open that door?" he said at last.

"Me, afraid?"

"Holly." He shook his head. "What do you think I'm going to do? Steal the bedspread?"

No, but you might throw me down on it and ravish me.

"That's ridiculous," she murmured. She could feel her cheeks heating up. "Nothing could be further from my mind. It's just that . . . I feel obliged to warn you that . . . this is a very temporary arrangement. I need to rent this apartment out. It's costing me money to have it vacant in high season."

She had just got done telling him that she'd all but abandoned the place, but never mind.

He was leaning his shoulder into the doorjamb and was standing very close as he said in a soft and insinuating voice, "There must be some way I can repay you."

Her lashes fluttered down. She still couldn't make herself turn the key. "Like . . . how?"

"Well, let's see," he said in her ear. "You already have a copy of my book, so what do you say to straight cash? Assuming, of course, you don't take Visa."

Smartass. She unlocked the door and threw it open. "That won't be necessary," she said primly. "Just don't make a mess. I may need to show it."

He dumped his bag inside the door. "You won't even know I'm here," he promised, which wasn't true at all. Holly was exceedingly, preternaturally aware that he was there—all six-feet-and-change of him, standing in the middle of her rental apartment with his hands in his pockets and looking around with his keen photographer's eye. It struck her all over again that she didn't know squat about the man, and yet here she was, making him feel at home.

"The bathroom's through that door; the bed's behind that pair of folding screens. I think Eden left a couple of yogurts in the fridge if you're hungry, but check the dates. Towels and linens are in that armoire."

She strode over to the bed, whipped back the bed-spread—how bold, how brazen she seemed to herself—and lifted a pillow to her nose. "Just what I thought: these haven't been slept on. So you won't even have to change the bedding . . . and that's about it. There's no phone, I believe I once told you."

"No problem," Sam said, slanting a look into the bathroom. "Would it be okay if I used your phone, if need be?"

"I—suppose."

He was scanning the few paperbacks in the narrow, mostly empty bookcase that was squeezed between two windows. She watched as he picked up a book, scanned the floral cover, and slipped it back on the shelf.

For some reason Holly felt obliged to apologize for the reading selection. "I doubt that you'll find anything that interests you. No Clancy, no King, much less Hemingway. The books are mine and my sister's: women's fiction."

"Ah, yes. Relationships—the kind of story where nothing happens."

"Plenty can happen in a relationship."

"Yeah. Two people meet. They marry. They split up," he said caustically.

"That's a lot. Ask my mother."

"Touché. But I'd still rather read King. There's less horror."

What a bitter man he was. Clearly he'd been hurt by someone and was taking it out on the bookcase. "I'm sorry you feel that way," she said, regretting that she brought up the subject. "If you need anything, just yell. And I guess I should give you a key." She began the laborious process of working the key out of its double-circled ring.

"Here, let me," he offered. He held out his hand for the set. Holly was making a mess of it, driving the key right back over the others on the ring, so she gave it up willingly to him. Freed from the odious task, she was able to study his hands.

She found them incredibly attractive. Most of her friends seemed to be fixated on men's buns. Not her. Perhaps because she was an artist, she could appreciate the potential in someone's hands. Or maybe it was something more visceral: the realization that a man's hands were often the first point of contact between him and a woman. A man might shake a woman's hand at an introduction. He might take her by the elbow in a restaurant. He might pick off a blade of grass . . . help her in or out of a seaplane . . . stroke her cheek . . . touch her in ways that would set her nerve-ends humming. A man might do anything, if he were adept enough with his hands.

What possible good were buns?

Pocketing the apartment key, Sam returned the ring to her. "I appreciate this, Holly," he said, flashing a remarkably boyish smile. Suddenly he reached out to her hair. "You're losing a barrette," he said. He slid the tortoiseshell clip free of its tenuous hold and handed it to her. "You wouldn't want to lose this; it's a pretty one."

She was right; she was right. A man with an adept touch might slide a barrette from a woman's hair and in the process snag her heart so well that it would never get free.

"I'll make us something to eat while you shower," she blurted. "You have to eat."

He looked surprised, then pleased. "That'd be great. I can be over in five minutes."

Holly left the apartment in a state of joy, her hair still tingling from his touch. She didn't care if Sam went and emptied the apartment lock, stock, and bedspread. He could do what he wanted with it, just as long as he came over to lunch.

*   *   *

Sam watched through a window as Holly started down the stairs, and then he began a thorough search of the apartment for signs of Eden. He had no real hope of finding any—Eden was far too clever to leave much of a trail—but sometimes people got lucky. He checked out the dresser, the bureau, the bedstand, and every cupboard in the kitchen, looking for—what? A clearly marked key to a safe-deposit box?

Only in a B-movie, pal.

He found no key and certainly no engraving. He lifted each of the throw rugs. Nothing. He looked between the mattresses and under the bed. Nothing.

He got up from his knees, angry and disappointed and above all else, frustrated. Eden was good at this vanishing shit. She was nowhere and yet everywhere. He could feel her presence, smell her allure. Impulsively he lifted the same pillow that Holly had checked and inhaled deep. Holly was wrong: Eden's scent was still there, mixed with the merest molecules of *Joy*, her favorite perfume, and the awareness of it did wrenching things to Sam's heart.

He glanced at his watch: his five minutes were up five minutes ago. He took a shower in less than two more, though he would have liked another twenty. Towelling himself dry, trying not to realize that Eden herself had used the same towels, he let his gaze settle on a stack of newspapers in the corner. He hadn't noticed it during his search, but an ad on the top page was circled. He picked up the section for a closer look.

In the classifieds of the Sunday *Globe* he found what only the desperate might call a clue: a small want ad offering to buy European landscape art. The three-line ad had not only been circled but had a line drawn through it, as though a probe had come up dry.

So: Eden hadn't known where to unload the engrav-

ing. It surprised Sam; he thought she'd be more con-
nected than that. He looked for more clues but realized
with chagrin that a whole page was missing from the
paper. Had it contained a more promising ad? Sam had
to assume that the answer was yes.

It was maddening. His only recourse was to track
down the missing page of the *Globe* and try to second-
guess any promising leads that Eden might have pursued. He checked his ferry schedule and decided that he
could catch a boat to New Bedford, pick up his car, and
drive it to Boston in time to get a room, hopefully with
running water, and hit the library and then the galleries
first thing the next day. He might be too late—but he
might not. For the first time since his parents had revealed the stunning theft, Sam took heart. He was getting closer to Eden.

He threw his clothes back in his duffel bag and
loaded the car again before realizing that he had promised to be somewhere for lunch. He pictured the old-
fashioned kitchen and the old-fashioned girl preparing a
meal for him there, and he felt an immediate surge of
guilt. He hadn't been candid with Holly, and as far as
he could see, that was never going to change.

Hell. He couldn't just leave her waiting for him to
show.

Reluctantly he backtracked to the little Cape and
tapped on the window of the back door before letting
himself in. Holly was all smiles and setting the table.
She had changed from tank top and shorts to a pale
green, jumper-kind-of-sundress thing, and she looked, if
possible, even more old fashioned than the image of her
that he seemed to have filed permanently in his mind.

Only now she wore lipstick. And maybe a little . . .
her eyes looked bigger somehow, even more green than
usual. It was a subtle and yet startling change. He smiled
sheepishly and said, "You look nice."

"Thank you. I've been known to try."

"I didn't mean you didn't look nice before," he amended. "Just that you look—green must suit you." Suddenly he was feeling vastly uncomfortable.

She laughed and said, "I know what you meant, Sam. Now sit down and we can enjoy a delicious lunch. The avocado's ripe, the wine's breathing, and the crab salad is perfection itself—as perfect as yesterday's crab salad can be, anyway. You really lucked out. There are days when I have turkey hot dogs for lunch."

He saw that she had set the table with care. Lattice-patterned dishes shared space on a fancy white tablecloth with a vase of flowers, stemmed glasses, and a gilded wicker basket filled with French bread. The salt and pepper shakers were silver. The atmosphere struck him as less struggling-folk-artist than lunch at the Ritz. Leisurely lunch at the Ritz.

"This is really very nice," he said as he took the chair he was bid. "You went to a lot of trouble, Holly. The only thing is . . . I have to catch a ferry."

"A ferry! When?" she asked, setting a plate with a crab-stuffed avocado before him.

Right after I wolf this down would have been the honest answer. He settled for saying, "I have a little while yet."

"I see." She brought the bottle of wine over and filled his glass. "It's just that you never mentioned it."

"True. I would have, if I'd known about it. Something just came up."

"What could come up? You don't have a phone."

"True." The girl was quick. "It's more something that I remembered." Lies, more lies, more lies. What *was* it about her that made him want to cover his tracks so completely?

"Well, it's a good thing you remembered," she said, stabbing the stuffed avocado hard with her fork. After a minute she looked up at him and said, "Remembered what, exactly?"

Even *he* knew that she was crossing the bounds of good manners. He twitched an eyebrow in the politest possible reprimand. It was enough to send color flooding into her cheeks.

"Well, of course if you'd rather not say, I understand," she said as she concentrated on buttering a slice of bread. "That's absolutely your right." After a short, meditative chew, she lifted her chin. "Why would you rather not say?"

"I thought it was my right," he answered lightly.

She thought about it and apparently decided that it wasn't. Resting her fist ends on the table, she leaned forward and said, "Sam, can we stop playing games? This change of plans has something to do with Eden. If it has to do with Eden, then it has to do with me."

"I'm not sure I see a connection," he ventured.

"Then take off your blindfold! I've told you everything I know about her—and a lot of stuff I shouldn't have said about my parents besides. Whereas you've told me virtually *nothing*," she said, her voice rising with emotion. "I don't even know who owns the damn engraving!"

She was impassioned, and she had a point. With a grudging frown he handed her a cookie of information. "The engraving belongs to my parents."

"Your parents! You said they were dead!"

"My birth mother is, they tell me. Since no one has a clue who my biological father is, I like to think of him that way as well. But my adoptive parents are alive. Alive and ailing and poor as church mice now."

Her full lips parted in an expression of unquestioning—and unwanted—sympathy. "Sam! Oh, that's awful! No *wonder* you're after Eden. Why didn't you tell me?"

So that I wouldn't have to deal with that look on your face, that's why.

All his life Sam had been an emotional loner. Millie and Jim Steadman had done their best, but a loner he had remained—until Eden. The one time he had fully trusted someone . . . the one time he'd given in to what he now saw was a pathetic need to be wanted and needed by someone . . .

"I didn't see the point of mentioning it," he said with a shrug.

Bad answer. Holly didn't like it at all. "Does everything have to have a point?" she said, sitting back in exasperation. "Can't you just confide in someone because it feels good?"

"You've read way too many books in that bookcase," he shot back. There was definitely an edge in his voice. He could feel it coming, that prickly, defensive reaction whenever someone talked psychobabble. He remembered a title on her bookshelf and said acidly, "Men are from Mars, remember?"

She scowled. "That's right. So tell me, why don't you all just go *home*?"

Yep. It was getting down and dirty at the Ritz. Sam decided to back away smiling before the two of them ended up in a food fight. Abandoning his half-eaten crab salad, he glanced at his watch, feigned surprise, and stood up. "Time and tide wait for no man," he said lightly, "and neither does the Vineyard Express."

He laid his napkin neatly on her prettily arranged table. "Thanks for going to all the trouble. As it turns out, I won't be coming back to the apartment."

"You must be psychic," she said in a deadly tone.

He took the hit and turned to leave, then turned around again. She wasn't expecting it; he saw her unguarded look of baffled dismay and pretended not to notice. He was behaving like an ass, but he didn't see what he could do about it.

"Look . . . Holly . . . this has nothing to do with who you are or what I am. I have a lead, okay? A lead that might take me to Eden. That's why I came to the island, that's why I'm leaving it. To find Eden. It's as simple as that."

"You don't have to explain," she said, gathering her dignity around her like a mailed cloak. "You have a boat to catch. I hope you find her."

"If I don't, I may be back," he said with an apologetic smile.

"Then I hope you find her."

Surprising, how soft words could pierce like a hail of bullets. He sighed and said, "I'm sorry, Holly. No kidding."

"Good-bye, Sam."

He took the key from his pocket, laid it on the table, and left.

Holly's hand trembled as she reached for the phone and punched in her mother's number on the speed dial. It rang six times before Charlotte Anderson said hello in a desultory voice.

"Mom? Can I come over later?" Holly asked plaintively. "We have to talk."

10

Boston in August was definitely not the Vineyard in August. Brutally hot pavement sent spirals of heat around Sam as he walked the length of fashionable Newbury Street, dotted with upscale galleries tucked discreetly between high-end salons and clothing shops. Almost at once he eliminated the two galleries whose ads he had hunted down in the Sunday *Boston Globe*. No one claimed to have heard from Eden, and Sam believed them.

Undaunted, he continued to canvas the street of shops, until he stumbled into The Hungary I, a small gallery below street level that specialized in East European art.

At the end of a long wall hung with dozens of obviously mass-produced religious icons, he discovered a wild-haired man in an ill-fitting suit and with a desperately eager smile on his face. The gallery would be closing in a week, the obese shopkeeper told Sam in fractured English, so this was, absolutely, last chance. Half price! For two, take off extra twenty percent!

Sam had to decline a series of increasingly final offers before he got the chance to put forward his own agenda: Had anyone in the last several weeks offered to sell an engraving by Durer?

The dealer thrust out a huge lower lip and pondered. "Durer? You want Durer?"

Sam nodded, unsure whether the guy was getting his implication.

"Tell you where you go: Ironic Curtain, on Huntington Avenue. You know where is Huntington? Other way from Copley Square. My cousin—Stefan Koloman—he will help you." He winked and added, "Say Lajos sent you, okay?"

The Ironic Curtain sat squeezed between a plumber's supply house and a mechanic's garage in a marginal stretch of Huntington Avenue. The cousins were as different as their galleries. Stefan Koloman was thin and dour and eyed Sam suspiciously as he approached in the dark, dingy shop, stacked three and four deep with framed and unframed paintings.

The first words out of his mouth after Sam introduced himself were, "Yeah? What *about* the Durer?"

Sam said, "I'm trying to locate the engraving, and I understand that a woman named Eden Walker was trying to shop it to you."

Then he waited.

The dealer eased onto a high wood stool. "You lookin' for her?"

"Right now I'm more interested in the engraving," Sam said, which was true enough.

"What's your connection to her?"

"None worth mentioning." True as well.

Stefan took a pack of smokes from the pocket of his polo shirt and shook a cigarette free. He tapped it against the box, stuck it in his mouth, lit it, inhaled deeply.

He said through a stream of smoke, "Tell you what; I'm looking for her, too."

"Why is that?"

"She screwed me," he said, flicking an ash into a cheap glass tray. "I got real scrod."

He grinned evilly, and Sam saw that he had a gold tooth. "You wouldn't be the first," he said.

Stefan grunted and took another drag. He studied the shine on his loafers. After another long pause he looked up. "I found her a buyer for the Durer. A collector of German art. A rich fanatic, the kind who have to have it, no questions asked. But the bitch cut me out of the sale."

"She went around you?"

"Yeah. She took the name off my Rolodex, maybe, when I went out to the front of the shop."

Sam grimaced sympathetically. "Would you be willing to tell me the buyer's name?"

Stefan's laugh was low and sneering. "You joking? It'd be the last thing I ever did. No one messes with this guy. What about her?" he added. "She's not still on that island?"

"The V—?" Sam thought better of naming the island in question and settled for saying, "Long gone."

"Bitch. I could kill her. I *will* kill her," he said calmly, as if he expected Sam to relay the message.

Sam said, just as calmly, "I wouldn't go off the deep end just yet." He propped one of his cards against the stub-filled tray. "If you change your mind about naming the buyer, I'll make sure you recover a fee. Think about it."

Stefan snorted and flicked an ash into the tray; some of it settled on Sam's card. "Find her for me, I'll pay *you*."

He took a deep, deep drag and was still smiling malevolently when Sam walked out.

* * *

So where the hell do I go from here?

Sam slugged beer to wash down a heart-killer Reuben
as he sat alone in a dark Boston pub and considered his
options. He was vain enough to feel pleased that he'd
tracked down Eden and the engraving as far as he had.
But it didn't take a rocket scientist to figure out that
Eden had won not only the round, but clearly the match.

She had stolen the engraving from an elderly, naive
couple who had dutifully kept possession of it a secret
for decades. She had sold the painting to some rich maniac who was never going to admit to having bought it.
She had swindled a dealer out of his commission in the
bargain, and since the dealer was a crook, it was safe to
assume that he wouldn't be suing her anytime soon. The
original owner, good old Uncle Henry, was dead and
buried, and so was the attorney who had handled his
will.

It was a situation tailor-made for Eden, who would've
considered it just slightly more challenging than taking
candy from a baby and then pushing the buggy off a
cliff.

Eden, Eden . . . where have you gone?

Why, off on a yacht, to play with a rich man. And
the loot? That could be anywhere, from a bank in the
Caymans to a pocket in her shorts, haaving been bartered
for the moment into uncut diamonds. She'd done it all
before.

Maybe it was the sauerkraut in his Reuben sandwich
that was to blame: out of nowhere, Sam experienced a
vivid flashback to an afternoon seven years earlier, an
afternoon that had knocked his heart into a black, sticky
bog where it remained still.

He and Eden had been living in Westport; they'd
been married for less than a year. Sam had returned
home from a four-day trip aboard a fishing trawler,

where he'd been documenting the abysmal decline of the cod industry. He was tired, salty, dirty, and reasonably drunk after hitting a waterfront bar with some of the crew. When he pulled up to his rented house, he found a squad car parked in front of it.

Forget the fishermen; it was the cops in that squad car who'd truly lifted the scales from Sam's eyes. He learned from them that his wife—his gorgeous, vivacious, sexy, smart, kind-hearted wife—had fleeced an old woman of her life's savings, which the woman had foolishly invested in diamonds that she kept hidden in a can of Gold's Foot Powder. Diamonds in Gold's. Eden had probably got a kick out of that.

Eden had been a great one for volunteering her company to shut-ins. Sam, naive jerk that he was, used to marvel that someone with so many talents could spend long afternoons sitting on dusty sofas in dimly lit parlors, listening to sad and lonely widows repeating their memories.

And widowers, too, of course. Statistically speaking, there were fewer of those, but Eden had been available to all. She gave unstintingly of her time, her charm, and God only knew what else. Sam used to marvel at it, and he loved her the more for it. Until the cops came that afternoon.

After they left, he found the note—in the drawer next to her birth control pills.

I love you, Sam. Please believe that. I'll never love anyone else. I can't stay on to explain; I wish I could. Just know that I love you. Someday we'll meet again.

But not soon. He couldn't find her, and neither could the investigators he'd hired.

Somewhere in his heart of hearts, Sam blamed himself. If he had done a better job of being married to her . . . if he had given her wealth enough so that she hadn't felt obliged to go out and shake every tree for more . . .

if he had—who knows?—*satisfied* her on some level that went deeper than sex, deeper than commitment, deeper than emotion itself. Then maybe she wouldn't be the way she was, and he wouldn't be panting three steps behind her the way he was.

Steadman, you self-centered bastard. You really think that you could've changed Eden?

The answer to that was still yes.

From some peripheral nook in his brain he had a sudden image of Holly Anderson in a pale green sundress, bent over double in stitches over his arrogance. Her good-humored laughter was infectious. Alone at the bar, he found himself joining in with a snort of self-mockery.

The bartender took Sam's grunt as a signal to top off his lager. Sam nodded his thanks, willing and wishing to be carried away on a soft wave of melancholy. He was feeling hollow and empty, and he wasn't sure how to fill the void. For now, beer would have to do.

11

Under a setting sun, Holly and her mother sat in Adirondack chairs on the upper deck, sipping strong rum punches and murmuring melancholy phrases about the frailty of men.

"Look at the harbor. Isn't it lovely tonight?" Charlotte mused. She added with a sigh, "Your father and I bought the house for this view. I always assumed that we would die here. Now I guess I'll be doing that on my own."

Weary of her mother's mood, Holly said, "Oh, Mom, nobody's dying."

Charlotte rubbed her elbow. "Lately, everything hurts," she insisted. "I'm getting old. No wonder he left me."

"No, *he's* getting old, and that's why he left you."

Smiling gratefully, Charlotte said, "Ivy called last night. She's so preoccupied," she added.

"Don't tell me she's not coming," Holly said, offended in advance by her sister's selfishness. "House or no house . . ."

Her mother gave her a look more sharp than confused. "Is that what she told you, that she can't come? And you resent it, is that it?"

"I didn't say that."

"Because you're afraid that you're going to be the one who ends up the caregiver in the family—aren't you," her mother said.

It was true. "No!"

"Holly, you're a wonderful daughter but a terrible liar. Don't worry, honey: I would check myself into a nursing home before I'd move in with you."

"But I'd never let you," Holly said, realizing it for the first time. She smiled and added, "We can be sad and single together."

"*You'll* never have to worry about being single. What about Sam? You sound as if you have a number-one crush on the man."

"Oh—Sam," Holly said, dismissing him. "I'd never elevate the feeling I have for him to the level of crush. He's just a thorn in my side, that's all. It's hard not to think about a thorn in your side. Trust me, there is nothing, absolutely nothing, between us."

Her mother was about to reply to that when she interrupted herself. "That's a car arriving!" She jumped up from her Adirondack chair—with amazing alacrity for an old woman in pain—and peered expectantly over the balustrade.

"Hell. It's Marjory Betson," she whispered, stepping back quickly. "Hide."

"*Mom*. What if she's seen you?"

"Oh, all right," Charlotte muttered. She yelled down, "Yoohoo! Marjory—up here."

Below them, the island gossip stood with her head bent back, an eager expression on her face. "Charlotte! I have hideous news!"

Holly's mother gasped and said, "Oh, no—about what?"

"Eric! Can you let me inside, please?"

*   *   *

They rushed to let her inside and then listened to news more stupefying than drink could ever be: Eden Walker had gone missing, and an all-day search by the Coast Guard had so far failed to recover her body.

"Body! What do you mean, body?" asked Charlotte, clearly in shock.

Marjory Betson—blond, tall, tanned and fit—crossed her legs and leaned forward from the waist for emphasis as she said, "Supposedly Eden was sailboarding while the *Vixen* lay anchored in Lackeys Bay. That in itself was unusual, don't you think?" she added. "Boats never anchor there. The wind was from the southwest as usual and—oh, but you're not that fond of sailing, are you, so perhaps you wouldn't know. But take my word for it: the roll there would be just awful on a weak stomach like yours. And uncomfortable for anyone. I can't imagine why Eric would anchor there. Except that they'd be alone, I suppose."

"What about Eden? Tell us about Eden," said Holly, cutting impatiently through the woman's innuendo.

"I'm getting to that, dear. After a while when Eden didn't return, Eric supposedly got into his inflatable and searched for her. He became alarmed—apparently—after he couldn't find her, and he called the Coast Guard. They sent out one of their big inflatables to search the area, and that's when they found the bloody windsurfer washed up on a beach."

"*Bloody* windsurfer—?"

"Oh-h-h, yes," said Marjory through pruned lips. "They found blood, long strands of hair, and a silver wrist bangle caught in the rigging." She let that sink in for effect while she sipped her Evian.

The three women were seated in the tile-floored conservatory, surrounded by towering houseplants and tender exotics. The room, a favorite, also happened to be the one farthest from Eric Anderson's ransacked study. While her mother waited in horror to hear what Marjory had to say, Holly jumped up and switched on more lamps. She wanted to ward off what she knew was going to be a long, black night.

Marjory set her icy glass carefully on a stone coaster and then continued. "After the beached windsurfer was reported, the Coast Guard sent out one of their utility boats, and then a helicopter," she explained. "How odd that you never heard anything about it all day. The Coast Guard even put out an Urgent Marine Broadcast."

Holly remembered Billy's tip of the wings in salute to the Coast Guard chopper that they passed on their way back to Vineyard Haven. The seaplane must have been flying right over the search area.

Holly said, "I can see how you might have heard the broadcast, Mrs. Betson; you practically live aboard your boat. But how did you know about the blood and the hair and all the rest of it? They don't go into that kind of detail in the broadcast, surely?"

Marjory Betson was making an effort not to be smug. "I know about the Coast Guard involvement because my niece is married to a petty officer. As for the police involvement—"

"The police?" asked Charlotte in a voice too high. "What have the police got to do with an accidental drowning?"

"*Was* it an accidental drowning?" asked Marjory. "That's what they're trying to find out."

God, the woman was insufferable. Holly wanted to grab her by her Ralph Lauren collar and toss her out of the house, but she felt as spellbound as her mother, and just as filled with dread.

"How did you find out that the police are involved?"

It was exactly the question that Marjory Betson had been waiting for them to ask. Her lips flattened in victory. Her look became serene. "They questioned me."

"You! About what?"

"They were poking around the marina a little while ago. Since the *Vixen's* slip is next to ours, and since Mark and I spend every minute we can together aboard our *MarMar*—naturally the police turned to us. They were very polite about it, but you could see that they had an agenda."

"What . . . kind of agenda?" Charlotte asked, her voice faint.

Marjory locked her hands across her tanned, bony knee and stared at the bronze-and-glass table in front of her wicker chair. "At least, I *think* it was an agenda. I could be wrong, of course. But the questions went along the lines of, 'Did you see them together? Were they very demonstrative?' You get the drift. Through it all, they kept coming back to ask things like, 'Did you ever witness an argument between them? Did Eden Walker seem to have a volatile temper? Did Eric Anderson?' That sort of thing."

She took another sip of her water, as if she'd been on the witness stand too long. "I had to tell the truth, of course. There *was* that terrible argument we saw when they were anchored nearby that one time, although I—"

"What argument? You never said anything about an argument. You told me that they were all over one another in the cockpit," Charlotte said angrily. "Those were your exact words."

"And they were—but that was later, after the argument. I told the police how completely out of character both displays of emotion were for Eric. We all know how quiet and discreet he is—or was, up until all this horrible business started."

Holly sat in rigid silence through the insinuating monologue. She saw that her mother was melting in place, like a flickering candle about to go out. She had to do something, so she stood up abruptly and said, "It was *so* kind of you to bring us up to speed. It would have been awful not to have lost sleep over this."

"Well, yes, that's exactly what I—oh! Oh, my, I've gone and done the wrong thing, haven't I?"

What do you think, you silly cow?

Holly turned to her devastated mother and said, "Don't get up, Mom; I'll see Mrs. Betson to the door."

But Charlotte did get up, and let herself be kissed by Marjory, and let herself seem grateful for Marjory's words of comfort: "You're well rid of him, Charlotte, honestly. Get down on your knees and thank God. That woman had him under an evil spell."

Holly's mother turned away and left the room with tears in her eyes, and Holly led cruel Marjory straight to the front door. She swung it open and resisted the urge to shove the harpy through it, confining herself to a simple "Good night."

But Marjory wasn't quite done. "I didn't want to go into too many details with your mother," she whispered in a funereal tone. "But I got the impression that they found evidence of violence on the *Vixen*, too. There was blood. Everywhere."

"Good night," Holly said again, but this time her voice was shaking.

She locked the door and ran back to her mother, expecting to find her in a new round of hysterics, but Charlotte was nowhere to be seen. After a quick circuit of the house, Holly climbed back onto the darkness of the upper deck. All she found were two empty chaises; her mother had vanished as mysteriously as Eden. Alarmed, Holly scrambled back down the attic steps, shouting her mother's name as she descended to the main floor.

She found her in the ransacked study, cleaning up the wreckage. The scene was surreal: Charlotte Anderson clutching a bamboo garden rake, trying to gather torn-apart books into a pile on the varnished floor.

Charlotte looked up at her daughter with a wretched smile. "This isn't working, Holly. Would you please bring up the snow shovel from the basement?"

"Mom, leave it. I'll take care of it," Holly said, taking the rake gently from her.

Her mother surrendered the tool, but after that she walked straight to the desk and began picking up the broken glass that was littered over the desktop, dropping each shard with a thunk into a metal wastebasket.

"Let me clean this up tomorrow," Holly implored. She was completely unnerved by the vacant look in her mother's eyes.

"Don't be silly. You can't just keep coming here day after day. You have work to do, a career to develop. Have you finished painting that dresser set for that little girl what's-her-name?"

"Not yet."

"I had a darling idea for a whirligig, by the way," said Charlotte as she filled the wastebasket thunk by thunk. "How about this: a boat propeller that attaches to the bumper of a car and spins when the car moves. Actually, it's not my idea; I saw one in Newport and forgot to tell you about it."

"It might be hard to park in tight quarters," said Holly, smiling. "Please ... I'll get a dustpan and broom."

"No need ... no need," her mother argued with aching cheer. "But I really could use the snow shovel. Ivy will be here any minute."

"No, she won't, Mom; you told me not until the day after tomorrow."

"Oh, well, if you're going to nitpick."

"Don't you want to talk about this?"

"Why? There's nothing to say," said Charlotte, turning her eerily luminous gaze on her daughter. "Eric didn't do it."

"I didn't say he did, Mom, but the police—"

"Oh, the police. They don't know your father. He wouldn't do a thing like that. How could he? He doesn't know the first thing about murdering someone." She held a pencil by its eraser flat against the desktop and began using it as a sweep to clear the smaller shards of glass.

"No, not murder," said Holly, wincing as she watched her mother court injury. "Of course it wasn't murder. It was something else . . . an argument that went too far, maybe. But anyway, they haven't even found her yet! She could be alive and wandering around dazed on some island."

But how to explain the blood on the boat?

Her mother frowned and said, "We musn't let the girls play in here. There's glass all over. You know why Marjory never told me that Eden and your father had an argument, don't you? It was because she didn't want me to have even that small satisfaction—knowing they weren't getting along. She only told me about the love-play—the part that she knew would hurt. And now the story about the argument brings no relief."

Sweeping the last of the glass bits into the wastebasket, she said forlornly, "I have to stop beating Marjory at bridge. She isn't a very good loser."

"Mom—you're bleeding!"

Charlotte turned up her fingertips and stared at them: they were dripping with blood.

"How did *that* happen?" she asked with weary surprise.

Completely spooked by the hour's events, Holly ran to the kitchen for paper towels and wrapped them around her mother's hand, then got her to the upstairs bathroom where she tweezed out the glass bits and patched up the cuts with gauze and tape.

This time there were no Florence Nightingale jokes,

no thrill of proximity, as there had been when she tended Sam and his scratched-up arms. This time there was only a profound sense of disbelief on Holly's part, and an even profounder one on her mother's. The silence of the younger woman bounced and echoed off the silence of the older until the room fairly screamed with it.

Holly turned down the covers for her mother and helped her into her nightgown. "Don't use that hand for anything more than you have to, or that middle finger's bound to start up again," she cautioned tiredly. "Now try to sleep."

She tucked her mother in as she would a child and turned off the lights. In the hall outside of the bedroom, she heard her mother call out plaintively, "Do you think the police will come here, too?"

Holly stopped and called back, "I don't see why," which was a lie. "But maybe."

"Because I'm not ratting on him."

Despite her weariness, Holly smiled. "Rat, how?"

"You know. By saying that that he was vicious. Because that isn't true. He's only oblivious. And blind. And selfish."

Well, that should reassure anyone who asks.

"I'll be here if you need me, Mom. Just shout."

"If the police come, tell them I'm not home." After a pause her mother let out a little moan and said, "I hate him. I really do."

There wasn't much that Holly could add to that, so she got out the dustpan and brush, a broom, and a couple of boxes and took herself off to her father's study to clean up the mess before her mother made a bigger mess trying to put it right.

The extent of the wreckage was daunting. It had taken her mother a lot of time and energy to rip up so many books so completely. Holly was at the cleanup for more than an hour; glass was everywhere. She cleaned every surface—shelves, desktop, floors, the lot—sweeping the glass and then vacuuming, and after that, going over all the furniture with a dampened cloth and finishing with a spray of polish.

She was about to take the last of the boxes out to the back porch when she heard screams of terror spilling down from the second floor, screams that sent her up the stairs two at a time to wake her mother from her sleep. It wasn't easy; her mother was caught in the bog of her nightmare as surely as any lost soul on a moor.

"Mom, mom . . . it's all right," Holly said, turning on the light. "Wake up, wake up, shh . . . shh," she said over and over. Her mother didn't see her at all. She was sitting bolt upright in bed, shaking her head violently and waving her arms in rejection—but of what, Holly didn't know.

Finally, mercifully, her mother managed to pull herself out of her terror. Teeth chattering, body shaking, she clung to Holly with ice-cold hands and in a broken, shivering voice said, "There was blood . . . oh, God, there was blood . . . everywhere. In the galley . . . in the cockpit . . . on the decks . . . dark, wet blood everywhere . . . I saw a body . . . caught in seaweed . . . her eyes were open, huge, underwater . . . there was a gash across her face . . . horrible . . . horrible . . ."

"You were upset, that's all; Marjory upset you," Holly murmured, holding her mother tight. But she knew that her mother put great store in her dreams. She always had, and now was no exception.

"I have to tell them; I *have* to tell the police. They can't just leave her there!"

Holly, stronger by far, had to restrain her until she calmed down. "We'll go right to the police tomorrow morning," she promised. That, too, was a lie; Holly was becoming quite proficient at it where her mother was concerned. "But for now, just . . . think of happier things. Think of Ivy and Cissy and Sally . . . they'll be here before you know it. Cissy will have two new teeth and Sally will be missing two baby ones. I cleaned up the study, so you don't have to worry . . . shhh . . . shhh. We'll have such fun . . . shh, shhh . . ."

And meanwhile, all Holly could see was an image of Eden's face, gashed and bug-eyed, floating underwater.

12

The next morning, Charlotte Anderson couldn't lift her head, let alone drive to the police and explain her psychic powers. She had a migraine again.

Holly, bleary-eyed herself from a terrible night's sleep, pulled the curtains and then the drapes across the drawn shades in the guest room where her mother now slept, and then she drove back home.

She hadn't expected to spend the night away from home and had left the back door unlocked. Holly was trusting, but mostly she was lazy: the lock had to be jiggled just right to make it work, and sometimes she didn't like to bother. It was a good thing, too, because she had just left her purse and house key at her mother's place. Annoyed at the lapse, she detoured around to the back and let herself in.

First up: a shower. Second: coffee. Holly would have been more than willing to exchange the coffee for a nap, but that didn't seem to be in the cards. She felt obligated to go to the police, if for no other reason than to get the real version of events.

But would they tell her, that was the question. A lot of what Marjory had said—whether or not she had grossly exaggerated it—was insider stuff. Unfortunately Holly wasn't married to a petty officer. She couldn't even claim to be a gossipy, nosy neighbor. She was merely the daughter of a possible suspect. If he was a suspect. If there was a crime!

She tried again to call her father at her parents' year-round house in Providence, but again, all she got was the machine. She left part of a message and then was cut off: the tape was full.

Where was he? More than anything else, that's what hurt the most: Eric Anderson's willingness to abandon all contact with his own flesh and blood. Holly hung up the phone in a state of profound depression. The earthquake that had sent her family into upheaval three weeks earlier had been bad enough. Was it necessary to have a volcano erupt all over them, too? What next? Locusts?

She thought of Eden. Her mother's description of Eden under water had been too vivid, too bone-chillingly horrific for Holly to dismiss it as either a nightmare or even some shocking form of wishful thinking. The frightening truth was that her mother had had premonitions before, mortal ones, and they had come true.

Most horrible of all: what if it wasn't a drowning accident at all, but a killing staged to look like one? If her father and Eden really had had an argument . . . if it had escalated and ended fatally . . . if panic had set in . . .

Holly's thoughts ping-ponged between the two deadly scenarios before bouncing off to her earlier, more optimistic theory: maybe Eden had simply decided that there was no future for her with Eric Anderson and had packed up her engraving and gone on her way.

Why not? Even at her most innocent and adoring, Holly would never have described her father as the charismatic type. Teddy bear, maybe—on a good day. But magnetic? He was far too serious about life. And for all his money, he wasn't exactly a high roller. Eden seemed like the type who'd need more than a quiet anchorage to keep her happy.

If only.

Impulsively, Holly picked up the phone to call her sister—but what was there to relate? Wild gossip. She hung up the phone. Like it or not, she was going to have to go to the police to verify Marjory's story. She considered whether she should tell them about the nightmare as well, then dismissed the idea. They'd think that she was as delusional as her mother. In any case, it wasn't as if her mother could give them the exact latitude and longitude of Eden's body.

Showered but unrefreshed, Holly dragged herself back down the steps, heading for the coffee that had just finished brewing. She was in the middle of pouring that first coveted cup when she heard a loud knock on the door.

Police?

She took a quick sip, then set down the cup and went to let them in. It was better this way; more private. She opened the door and was unsettled to see not a man in blue but a man in brown. His suit, his shirt, his shoes, his tie—all brown. His hair, his eyes, his teeth all brown.

Clearly he wasn't there to buy a whirligig or a painted birdhouse. "Yes?" she said, all too aware that her charming cottage was situated out of view.

"Good morning," he said with a sudden, twisted grin that revealed a big gold tooth. "If you could help me. I'm looking for Eden Walker."

"No, I'm sorry," Holly said quickly. "She doesn't live here anymore. Sorry." She smiled nervously and began closing the door on him.

He tilted his head to peer through the opening. Again the grotesque, ill-timed grin. "But she used to live here, right? That's what they told me." He held up a sheet of notepaper. Holly recognized the logo of the Flying Horses Gallery but not the handwriting.

"No, never. Eden lived in the apartment above the barn next door. But she's moved out. Permanently. Sorry." Her voice was higher-pitched now, with a note of panic in it.

"You're Holly Anderson, right?" he said through a newly venemous squint. "Her friend?"

Holly wouldn't say yes and wouldn't say no. "Eden's dead," she blurted. "Drowned."

"Bullshit, dead!" he snapped. His hand gripped the door as she tried to slam it shut. "Where is she, god-dammit?"

"No one knows; you have to believe me! The Coast Guard are searching for her now, right now," she stammered. "Call them, see for yourself."

"You're her friend, you're in this with her. You think I can't see that?"

He was near enough for her to smell the stench of his breath. She wanted to run, but her instincts told her to stand fast: if she turned away, he'd surely chase after her.

"If she *is* alive," she said in desperation, "I'll let you know right away. I will. Just tell me who you are and where to call."

He snorted, a brutish, animal sound, and said, "Tell her I'll be back."

"How can I, when she's—"

"*Tell her.* Or I'll be back to see why not."

He gave the door a sudden, vindictive push. The bottom stile dug into her bare foot, sending a bolt of agony through her. Holly sucked back a cry of pain, then slammed the door shut and locked it as he turned away. Limping, she ran to the back door and frantically jiggled the doorknob button into its locked position as well. By the time she remembered to race back to the front window and look for a license plate, the car had pulled out of view.

She was shaking, half with fear and half with pain. All this, because of Eden! It didn't seem possible that one woman could blow up that many bridges in such a short time. She was a relationship terrorist, and Holly for one had had enough. Was Eden dead? Good damn riddance!

Go to the police. Tell them everything you know. About Sam Steadman; about the man in brown. Tell them lots of people are after Eden. Let the police figure it out. That's their job.

It was the reasonable thing to do—unless it somehow ended up tightening the noose around her father's neck. Paralyzed by a fear of making a wrong move, Holly held an ice-filled towel on the arch of her foot and tried to think things through. There was absolutely no point in running off half-cocked and endangering her father unnecessarily.

Damn you, Dad. What a fool you've been.

She wanted to call her sister but couldn't. Wanted to call her mother but wouldn't. Didn't even *know* where her brother was—somewhere in the south Pacific on a research vessel. She had friends on the Vineyard, but not the kind you told your deepest, darkest secrets to. There was no one—no one—who could help her through her dilemma.

Except Sam.

Sam was the obvious, miserable, infuriating, appallingly perfect choice. He could keep a confidence. He knew Eden. He was close to other people who had been hurt by her. He was smart and presentable and had a clear notion of justice, and the police would give more credence to him than they would to any daughter of a suspect. Events were swirling around Holly, and she needed to hold onto something: any old flotsam or jet-sam would do.

Even Sam.

Still, there was no point in grieving over his absence, so Holly came up with a plan of her own. One, call the Coast Guard to verify that Eden was indeed the subject of their search. If the answer was yes, then two, call the police and tell them about the visit from the man with the gold tooth whose name she didn't know.

And Sam?

The hell with him; she'd tell the cops about him, too. Of course, Holly couldn't tell them where *he* was, either. How ridiculous. All these men with no addresses. They were like drifting souls on an alien planet. Whatever had happened to the notion of hearth and home? What was it about a sweet and cozy house on land that made men want to run—sail, fly, whatever—away from it as fast as they could? Jerks! They were all jerks.

She went into her sweet and cozy living room with its sweet and cozy hearth and reluctantly closed and locked the oversized windows, stilling the sheer curtains in the middle of their merry waltz. The sheers became sullen; the fun was over.

If I had someone living here, that gold-toothed guy wouldn't dare try anything funny.

If I had a man, that guy wouldn't dare.

If I had Sam . . .

If.

She plucked the insidious thought from her musings the way she would a weed that was hiding under her perennials: ruthlessly. Sam was gone. So what? She didn't need Sam. *Clearly* he didn't need her.

Still resentful, still jumpy, she went around and locked every other window on the first floor—just in case. When she heard a car approach over the noisy crushed shells, her reaction was one of knee-jerk panic.

Snatching her cordless phone as if it were a gun, she ran to the window with it and peeked outside, ready to punch in 911. There sat a Corolla, red this time.

Who would have thought that the sight of a Corolla could launch her on a rocket ride? Holly watched with rising joy as Sam got out, paused to look at her rented-but-someday-mortgaged hearth and home, shook his head, and approached the front door.

She got there before he did, and threw it wide open.

"Well—look who's back," she said, trying to sound the way she did not feel. "Percy Billings."

13

With a wry smile, Sam said, "Hey, kiddo. How's it goin'?"

"Never a dull moment. If you're here for the crab salad, I ate it all."

"That's all right. It would have gone bad."

"Things do, left unattended."

His answer was a puzzled, painfully attractive smile.

So that's what charisma looks like, Holly thought: a loopy smile in a handsome face that made the heart soar and then plunge like an ill-managed kite. Who needed that? All in all, she could do just fine without charisma.

"Are you going to ask me inside?"

"Do you have wounds that need tending?"

"Nope. For the moment I'm shipshape," he said, still smiling.

"Then why *are* you here?" *To see me, to see me. Say it.* The kite began climbing in a dizzying spiral.

"I ran into a brick wall in Boston, so I thought I'd backtrack a little and start from where I left off. Which is to say, here."

Nosedive. "She hasn't come back, if that's what you mean."

"I didn't think she had. Not alone, anyway. But sooner or later your father has to bring the *Vixen* back to his dock. When he does, I'll be there waiting."

"What do you plan to do? Perch on a pole like a seagull?"

Again the smile; up went the kite.

"Not if I can find a place to rent."

Up and up and up. "If you mean the place I think you mean, it's all but spoken for. I showed the apartment to five waitresses last night, and they loved it. They're coming by tonight with a deposit."

He had just one word to say to that. "Five?"

"It's the only way they can afford the rent. They promised to be as quiet as butterflies."

"Did you check out their references?"

"They didn't have any; this is their first place."

He laughed out loud at that. "You're new at this land-lord stuff, I see."

"Not at all," she said dryly. "You'll recall that I rented to Eden. I figure I have nowhere to go but up."

The smile softened into something like commisera-tion. "Don't rent to them."

"I need the money."

"I have the money. Rent to me."

"Sam, I can't," she said in anguish, even as that kite soared ever higher. "Things have happened. You don't know." What was she *doing*, yammering on about the apartment? "Something's happened. Eden is missing. It doesn't look good. My father's being questioned. And a man was here, looking for Eden. He was some kind of thug. I'm just on my way to the police station. You didn't notice the Coast Guard helicopter, either, I'll bet," she said, finishing up on an dizzying note.

Sam blinked and tried to take it all in, then gestured inside. "Do you mind if we sit down?"

Holly suddenly realized that she'd been barring the door to him. "I'm sorry," she said, stepping back to let him. "New force of habit."

She led him into her locked-up living room and opened all the windows again before taking a seat opposite him in front of that brick hearth that she loved so well. The firebox was in hibernation now, hiding behind a copper screen painted over with bright red poppies, deep purple irises, and lacy green ferns. The painted firescreen was Holly's first effort—not as good as some that she had done since then on commission, but much more beloved.

Books and magazines and sketches were heaped in sliding piles on the battered seaman's chest that sat foursquare in front of the slipcovered sofa, confined to shore duty for now. A gust of wind sent some sketches tumbling like rose petals onto the rag rug, adding to the sense of cheery disarray.

Sam seemed to take in the room and then dismiss it, which made Holly wince. One woman's clutter is another man's litter, she supposed. He was probably one of those minimalist types. She hated minimalism.

"From the beginning," he said.

She related the news, if that's what it was, that Marjory had delivered about Eric and Eden—only without the pregnant pauses, raised eyebrows, and cheap dramatic tricks to which her mother's friend had resorted. Holly was entirely adult about it, entirely calm. But when she was done she yielded briefly to a shudder of stressed-out sobs.

"I'm sorry," she said, pulling herself back out of her emotional tailspin. She plucked a tissue from a nearby box and blew her nose. "This is just such an unbelievable, ongoing . . . disaster."

Sam had let her speak, sob, and apologize, all without interruption. It was unnerving. "Aren't you going to say something?" she asked.

"I don't believe it."

"Of course not. None of us does. But that's where all the evidence points—and then there's my mother's dream."

"About?"

"Eden. It was horrible. I've never seen my mother so terrified in my life." Holly described the nightmare in a few terse phrases, then added, "My mother has always had premonitions that way. The night that my uncle in Phoenix died in his sleep, she dreamed that she was packing a suitcase with black clothes, including a hat with a black veil like Jacqueline Kennedy wore. Five years ago, at the exact same moment that my grandmother had a fatal heart attack, my mother started up from a deep sleep during a vacation in California with a melody going through her head: it was the melody from *Doctor Zhivago*, my grandmother's favorite song in the world."

"It means your mother had fears for their health," Sam said quietly. "That's all."

Holly shook her head. "Both deaths were unexpected," she argued. "There have been other dreams, lesser dreams, but they've been just as eerily on the mark. My mother gets devastating migraines afterward. Believe me, this isn't exactly a *gift* that she has."

Sam hardly heard her. For a long moment he sat with a look of intense concentration on his face. And then he jumped—exploded, really—out of his chair.

"No way! No goddamned way! This is too much like Eden. This is exactly the kind of stunt she'd pull."

"Really? She'd do something like that?" He may as well have told Holly that there really was a Santa Claus.

"Absolutely," he said. He grabbed the mantel with

both hands and leaned into it as if he wanted to push it through the wall. "She's not dead," he muttered at the floor. "She's *not* dead! She can't be!"

Holly stared at him. She didn't want Eden to be dead, either, but . . . some of the oppressiveness returned, she didn't know why.

"Tell me about this thug," Sam said without turning around. "Was he tall and thin or short and fat?"

"Tall. He didn't look thin to *me*."

"Did he tell you his name?"

"No. He had a gold tooth."

"Stefan Koloman! Christ, what was he doing here?"

"Well—terrorizing me, for one thing. He was this close to knocking me down and searching the place for Eden," Holly said, pinching her thumb and middle finger together. "He's convinced that I'm her friend and hiding her."

She stood up and went over to the mantel, then propped her hands on her hips in her best I-demand-an-explanation pose. "How do you know this guy, anyway? Please don't tell me he's a golfing buddy."

"He's a dealer," Sam said.

Holly laughed and said, "Of what? Marijuana?"

"I wouldn't be surprised. At the moment, he also has a gallery full of what looks like forged or stolen art. But I'm no authority; I was picking up on the ambiance more than anything else," Sam said dryly. "Anyway, he found a buyer who was willing to buy the engraving no questions asked. Eden—"

"Cut him out of his commission?"

He smiled and said, "You're quick."

"I understand dealers and commissions. You did meet Claire at the Flying Horses Gallery, didn't you? Cut Claire out of a deal, and you wouldn't be left with hands to create *any* art, good, bad, or forged." She added thoughtfully, "But then, Claire's from New York."

Sam laughed and then suddenly they were standing there, in front of Holly's sweet and cozy hearth, with nothing much to say.

It was Sam who broke the awkward silence. "Holly, I'm sorry I dragged you into this. I mean that." To say that he looked sheepish would be grossly overstating it; but he definitely looked sincere.

"Oh, that's all right," she said, feeling a fierce blush overtake her features. She hated that, hated the way her emotions paraded themselves over her face whenever they felt like it. Holly Anderson, daughter of a Dane! Where was the justice? Where were the genes?

He said softly, "No, really. You've been a great sport about everything—"

"Especially the seaplane," she stuck in, harking back to the event fondly now.

Sam grinned and said, "Billy sends his regards, by the way."

"He made the wedding in time?"

"Yep. The bride got airsick. She's suing Billy in small claims court for the cost of the wedding dress."

"Oh, well."

"Holly, I . . ." Sam blew out air and tried again. "I never meant for you to get caught in the crossfire. I came back to the Vineyard for two reasons. One of them was to wait for the *Vixen's* return. The other was to ask for your apology. I haven't exactly been . . . well. Friends?" He offered his hand.

Her kite-heart had been soaring, but that last word sent it plummeting down to earth. *Friends.* The word had such a pre-emptive ring to it. Friends. She didn't want to be his stupid friend.

Whether it showed in her face—safe guess—she never afterward knew, but as soon as Sam had her hand in his, he pulled her gently into his embrace. With a sigh of consent, she let him hold her in his arms. Inhaling deep, she closed her eyes and savored the moment of him. Her joy ran deep; maybe being friends wasn't so awful after all.

Still, it seemed to Holly that the hug went on a little longer than a friendly hug should. It must have seemed that way to Sam, too, because after he separated from her, he held her at arm's length and said gruffly, "Okay, then. That's settled."

Her eyes got wider. "Settled" seemed strong. She tried not to smile and more or less succeeded. Sam looked confused. Good.

She said, "You can have the apartment."

More confusion. Sam glanced off in another direction, then looked back into her eyes—with an effort, she thought. "That wasn't my motive."

"In offering to be friends? Of course not."

"No, seriously, I—" He pulled himself up short after he saw the smile she could no longer hide. Smiling himself, he said, "You're a witchy kind of innocent, you know that?"

"Not me. Everyone says I'm as sweet as scilla in spring."

"They judge you through your art. I'm going by the look in your eyes."

She wanted to hold that look, whatever it was, but she could feel it go. Her lashes fluttered down and she said, "Do you want the key?"

"I do."

"I'll get—oh, nuts. It's in my purse, and I left my purse at my mother's house. She's in bed with another mi—anyway, I don't dare telephone."

The word had barely tumbled from her lips when the phone on her sofa table rang. It was her mother calling, a not uncommon coincidence between the two. "Hi, Mom," she said, purposely cuing Sam in. He wandered over to the French doors that led to a small brick patio and made a pretense of looking at the garden that surrounded it.

"How are you feeling?" she asked, but she could hear by her mother's rapid breathing that it couldn't be very well.

"Holly, Holly," her mother said in a voice of anguish. "I was just out on the deck. It's back. It's back. The *Vixen* is back!"

14

Feeling like a helpless passenger in a runaway stage-coach, Sam watched through half-shut eyes as Holly blasted into and out of the slow-moving cars headed for downtown Vineyard Haven. The wild ride came to a welcome if abrupt halt in the drive of the Andersons' enviably situated house, and Holly jumped out of the truck with Sam hard on her heels.

As they waited for Charlotte Anderson to answer the bell, Sam noted with approval that the house hadn't been tricked out to boring perfection. The weathered shingles were loose in spots, and the trim was peeling here and there. The black, louvered shutters were thick with generations of paint. The brass light fixtures flanking the massive door had not been lacquered into an unnatural state of shine, but over the years had acquired a pleasing patina of verdigris. The overall effect was of a large, genteel house that had been allowed to age with charm and grace.

Too bad that Eric Anderson wasn't letting his wife do the same.

Charlotte Anderson answered the door at last, and Sam was immediately struck with the resemblance between mother and daughter. The same vulnerability in the same deeply luminous green eyes is what hit him first; but he saw that the nose, the chin, the cheekbones were cut from the same cloth as well. Of all things, he saw a spark of Eden in both mother and daughter—a kind of don't-push-me-too-far steeliness that surprised him. Of course, with Eden, you took that as a challenge; it was almost fun to goad her into a reaction. But with these two . . .

He made a mental note never to test them.

"Mom, this is Sam. Obviously."

"*Sam*?" her mother said, turning to him in surprise. "I thought you said he'd—"

"Never mind. It's him. Sam, my mother."

"Pleased to meet you, Mrs. Anderson."

"Uh-huh. How do you do?"

He wanted to say, "Like you: going in goddamned circles," but he settled for some mindless pleasantry, which—considering that they were missing a body and getting ready to descend on the man who might have hidden it—seemed especially surreal just then.

"You're sure it's the *Vixen*?" Holly asked her mother.

"Of course I am. Go up and see for yourself."

"I will," said Holly, and she charged up the curving staircase.

Sam wasn't sure that he ought to charge past the mother after the daughter—what was it about these Anderson women that they enjoyed blocking his way?—so he stood at the threshold and tried not to shuffle his feet.

"This is an awkward business," he offered after futilely wracking his brain for something to say.

"Yes, isn't it?" Charlotte said brightly. "And just when you think it can't get any more awkward, something awkwarder goes and happens. I'm getting quite used to it!" She flashed him a dazzling grin, then turned and hurried up the steps after Holly, leaving Sam to shuffle his feet some more.

Well, hell, speaking of awkward . . .

He waited a moment, then stepped onto one of the wide planks of the spacious entry hall and closed the door gingerly behind him. How long could it take to figure out if a boat was at a goddamned dock or not? For two cents he'd hijack Holly's pickup and drive down to the marina on his own.

Patience. He clamped his jaw down tight and made himself stay where he was.

The more he thought about it, the more he was convinced that Eden was simply up to her old tricks—in which case, the trail was getting colder by the minute. He didn't really know if at this point he was looking for cash, or uncut diamonds, or pre-Columbian art, or a deed to a farm. Eden could have fenced the engraving for just about anything.

He decided arbitrarily to go with the presumption of cash. The question then became, had she taken it in small bills or in large? The first would be easier to use; the second, to carry. She could cram quite a few thousand-dollar bills into a waterproof knapsack, not to mention a drip-dry tunic to get around in, if she really did have a plan to slip away from the windsurfer after faking her death. Why she'd fake that death to look like murder—that was harder to figure out.

One thing at a time, he reminded himself. One thing at a time.

He had called his parents from Boston and had informed them that he was closer than ever to the Durer. In other words, he'd lied. The hope and relief in their voices had made it a foregone conclusion that he would lie again if the need arose.

He had to find Eden. Now. *Now*, goddammit.

Still no women! Wild with impatience, Sam bolted up the stairs, then followed a trail of open doors through a kind of sitting room that led out to a deck. He found mother and daughter huddled over a telescope, taking turns looking through it. At his approach, Holly looked up from the eyepiece.

"What took you so long? Look through here. Tell us what you see."

She stepped aside and he squatted down to see indeed what he could see. Yes, there it was: a graceful sloop bobbing gently in the previously empty slip. Sam couldn't make out the name written in stylized script on the transom, but it looked like about five letters, and it looked like the first one was a *V*. There was no sign of anyone on board. He adjusted the scope some more. Two men were standing on the dock next to some gear and staring at the boat as they conversed. Sam had to assume that neither of them was Eric Anderson.

He stood up and said, "You'd know the boat better than I w—"

He stopped himself, frowned, and hunkered down for a second look. Something wasn't quite right. Yes. There, tied between the dock pilings—a long strip of yellow. Yellow plastic. Crime scene yellow plastic.

Holly said to her mother, "I knew it! He sees it, too. They've cordoned off the boat, haven't they, Sam?"

"Oh, this isn't good," Charlotte said faintly. "This isn't good at all."

"Where's Dad? He can't be on the *Vixen*. Is it possible that he's in jail?"

It sounded so quaint, almost lighthearted, expressed that way—as if she wasn't sure which bed-and-breakfast her father had booked his family at. But when Sam straightened up, he saw looks of genuine agony on both women's faces. It occurred to him with force that neither wife nor daughter was ready to write off Eric Anderson as a lost cause.

Sam had never seen that kind of loyalty up close and personal before—except maybe in Millie Steadman, a kindhearted lady who had taken in an eight-year-old punk and had decided to love him come hell or come high water. Up until now Sam had believed that the Millies of the world were few and far between. These two were making him rethink that.

A thought came from out of nowhere: what about Sam's birth mother? Had she loved Sam's father with a blind and unquestioning love? Would Sam have done it, too, if he had ever been offered the chance?

You don't want to go there, pal.

He forced himself back to the crisis at hand.

"First things first," he told the two. "I presume that you're on friendly terms with the dock help. Let's see if we can get them to talk. After that, we'll go to the police."

"Yes, absolutely," said Charlotte. "I'm ready."

Holly wanted to spare her mother that ordeal. She argued that Charlotte should stay home; that the police would be just as likely to give information to the daughter as they would to the wife—maybe more so, given the circumstances; and that whatever Holly didn't think to ask, Sam most certainly would.

For whatever reason, her vote of confidence in Sam touched him. What an amazingly trusting young woman she was. How amazingly vulnerable.

It was Charlotte who had the last word. "If your father is a suspect, then the police will want to question me eventually. I'd just as soon get it over with."

So off they went, this time, in Charlotte's Volvo with Sam in the back. They could easily have walked down to the dock, just as they could walk to the police station. He had to wonder if Charlotte had a dread of being under public scrutiny. Would her neighbors be watching from behind their lined drapes and white shutters? Probably.

Humiliation: it was one tough emotion to slog through. He'd had to do it himself after Eden skipped town and the police came a-calling.

It may have been the instinct to hide that made Charlotte stay behind the wheel when they reached the marina; or it may have been the simple fact that there was no place convenient to park.

Whatever the cause, Holly ended up being the one who approached the dock master. Muttering something to Sam about him being the mean one, just their luck, she abandoned their agreed-upon plan to sweeten him up and tried crashing the gate instead.

"No dice, Miss Anderson," said the dock official, stopping them when Holly tried to breeze through the gate. "You can't go aboard the *Vixen* until the crime scene guys are done with it. They're off gettin' lunch, but they'll be back."

"Is my father still on the boat?" she wanted to know.

"Nope. He wasn't on it when it got towed in. Don't know where he is."

"All right. We won't go aboard," she promised, but she began heading down the dock anyway.

"Whoa whoa whoa. Where you goin'?"

"To see . . . someone else. To see if Dr. Pell is aboard *Sweet Tooth*."

"He's not."

"May I check?"

"I'll be watching."

"Go ahead," she said, and she took Sam's hand as if they were lovers out on a leisurely stroll.

Bemused, Sam waited until they were out of earshot and then murmured, "And what exactly is it that you hope to accomplish?"

"Number one, to irritate him," muttered Holly. "And number two—I don't know. To irritate him."

She stopped and Sam stopped and both of them seemed to realize at the same time that they were holding one another's hands.

"Well," said Sam with a somewhat perplexed smile. "Here we are."

"Where, Sam?" she said, gazing at him with a sudden shift into gravity. "Where exactly are we?"

"The *Vixen*?" he said, inclining his head toward the boat.

"The—yes, right!"

A deep, wonderful blush spread across her cheeks. She turned away and made a production of looking the yacht over. "I wonder if they left someone aboard," she said, putting one foot on the transom and leaning on the stern rail as she tried to get a look below.

"Hey, hey, get off there!" came the inevitable shout from the end of the pier. "What'd I tell you?"

Holly dropped back down to the dock. "I wasn't going to go aboard!" she yelled back.

And if anyone believed that, Sam had a couple of tickets for a luxury cruise on the *Bounty* that he'd like to sell.

"You know, you can't go tramping all over a crime scene," he said in an undertone. "This isn't an episode of *The Rockford Files*."

He wondered whether Holly might be deliberately trying to contaminate the scene, presumably to insure her father's freedom. But after she rolled her eyes at him like a sulking teenager, Sam decided that such nefarious thoughts had never crossed her mind. If anyone was having nefarious thoughts, in fact, it was Sam: he was judging Holly through his experience of Eden.

And meanwhile, the evil dock master, flanked by two grim-faced men, was bearing down on them fast. Sam had an abhorrence of being grabbed by the collar and tossed off the premises (it had happened to him once too often in the bars of New Bedford) so he said, "Quick! Pretend we're in love!"

He grabbed Holly, swung her around, and kissed her hard on the mouth, catching her so much by surprise that she went limp and he ended up bending her in a backward dip, like the sailor on the famous cover of *Life* magazine.

Holly might have gone limp, but she hadn't gone dead. Sam heard a soft moan from deep in her throat, and suddenly, amazingly, she was returning his kiss. Her tongue met his and his mouth came down harder and he couldn't get enough of her.

Nor would he. Among other considerations, he and Holly were standing on a public dock in the path of approaching police.

"Hey, you two. Get a room!"

Sam broke off the kiss to see the younger of the investigators grinning broadly as he climbed nimbly aboard the *Vixen*. Sam grinned back in a suitably leering way.

The other cop wasn't as good-humored about the show. "Take it somewhere else," he said. "Move away from the boat."

Or I'll shoot seemed to be his unspoken promise. Grateful that the distraction had been a success, Sam began hauling the little vixen away from the big *Vixen*.

"Didn't I tell you? Didn't I?" he said through gritted teeth. "Jesus Christ, you'll get us both thrown in jail."

She had to skip to keep up. "What's the big deal? You told me yourself that you've been there."

"To *scare* you. To put the fear of God in you. To—"

"Impress me, maybe? And what about that kiss?" she said, tacking off in another direction. "Another attempt to impress?"

"Hey, that was *your* idea."

"Holding hands was my idea!"

"And that's what we're doing."

"Is that why my fingers are turning blue?"

Sam held up the hand he was gripping so securely. She was right: he was holding her just a tad too tightly.

"Sorry," he muttered. He let her go. God damn. What a ridiculous distraction she was from the business at hand. She had his emotions bouncing around like a trick rubber ball; he couldn't seem to get himself under control.

Charlotte zipped down the window at their approach. "What was *that* all about?" she asked, but whether she was referring to their inspired performance or their encounter with the investigators, Sam couldn't say.

"It was all Sam's fault," said Holly, distancing herself from him.

"Did you find out anything?"

"Just that Dad wasn't on the boat; it got towed in. They must be dusting it for prints and taking samples of bl—well, whatever it is they do when they investigate."

Charlotte said wearily, "I suppose the police station's next, then."

Wondering now about the wisdom of accompanying them, Sam reclaimed his seat in the back of the car. It gave him a chance to study this mother-and-daughter pair, these key players in the drama that had begun in a New Bedford bungalow over a piece of lemon meringue pie.

The women's conversation ricocheted all over the place, from the mundane to the profound. Sam sat bemused and took it all in; he'd never been privy to women-talk before.

"Oh, look—the Websters have taken out their whole row of forsythia," Charlotte remarked. "What do you suppose they'll plant there instead?"

"Bayberry, hedge roses; anything with thorns. You know how they hate it when the dogs from next door wander through."

"They're such old farts."

"So uptight. It's hard to believe you're the same age."

"I know," said Charlotte dryly. "I feel so much older."

"Very funny. How's your head?"

"Will you stop going on and on about my head? My head is fine."

"You know it isn't."

"Well, it won't be, if you keep it up."

"When are you going to see a doctor about them? They're always making new breakthroughs."

"Quiet and dark, that's all I need."

"Well, here we are on a crowded, sunny afternoon, headed for the police station. That should do the trick."

"Did you lock your back door when you left? I don't want that thug lying in wait for you."

"Sam will take care of him."

"Who? Oh." She cast a brief glance over her shoulder at Sam and then said to her daughter, "You know, it's not *that* much of an effort to turn a lock."

"It doesn't work right."

"You just won't make the effort. I don't know why you're not more determined about things. Have you done anything at all on that home-furnishings proposal?"

"When? In my spare time?"

"You need to shut this out, that's all. Shut this out and get to work."

"*Mother*. This isn't like having a bad hair day. We don't have a clue what Dad's done with Eden or what the police have done with Dad."

"Do what I do. Don't think about it."

"Of course you think about it! That's why you get the damn migraines!"

"Here we are."

"Let me do the talking."

"Absolutely. I wouldn't know what to say. Mr. Stead-man?" Charlotte gave him her wonderfully bright smile. "Will you be joining us?"

15

Inside the recently built station, the three were quickly ushered into the office of Tisbury Police Chief Matthew Cottler, a barrel-chested, middle-aged guy who in another age might have shipped out to sea with Herman Melville under Captain Pease. But the captain was long gone, and so was the one who'd written so eloquently about men, their ships, and the ocean. In their place was someone who pumped iron instead of hauled on halyards and who wouldn't know a gudgeon from a pintle, sitting in an air-conditioned jailhouse quaintly shingled to satisfy a variety of historically minded commissions.

It wasn't the same.

Still, for all his well-educated manner, the chief had enough of a rough edge about him that Sam sat up and took note. Sam knew a townie when he saw one: Matthew Cottler was not the kind of man who would roll over and play dead just because some rich man offered him a biscuit.

"I was about to call you, Mrs. Anderson, to see when it would be convenient to ask you a few questions." The chief glanced at the others, then suggested politely, "Perhaps this would be a good time. I wonder if I could talk to you you alone for a few minutes."

Up in arms went Holly. "I have every right to be in on this, sir. Eric Anderson is my father, after all."

Cottler conceded the point with a nod, then turned to Sam. "And your connection is—?"

"With Eden Walker," said Sam, choosing his preposition carefully. The last thing he wanted was for Holly to discover then and there the true nature of his relationship to Eden. He'd been trying to tell her about it since the day he nearly knocked her down in front of the gallery, of course, but the timing so far had never been right. Then and there seemed spectacularly not right.

He confined himself to stating simply that Eden had had in her possession a valuable piece of art that belonged to his parents, and that his parents had called him to find out when Eden would be returning it, because they were becoming somewhat concerned.

Holly immediately jumped in with the candid version. "Somewhat concerned? *Somewhat*? You told me they were devastated!"

"I don't remember the exact word I used," he said, keeping it carefully nonchalant. It was better to state the facts without the drama and then see where the questioning went; didn't she realize that?

Apparently not.

"Sam! For crying out loud, tell him what you told me! That Eden was up to her old tricks; that she wasn't dead, that she couldn't be dead!"

Shit.

The chief turned to him with interest. "Maybe the best thing would be for you and me to—"

"Just a minute, please," Charlotte interrupted. "I came here to find out about my husband. I think I'm entitled to that information before you go off on a tangent."

Surprisingly, the chief didn't take offense at her imperious tone. He rubbed the back of his ear while he considered her demand. He sighed. He picked up a pencil and tapped its eraser on the sheaf of papers stacked in front of him. He sighed again. He acted in every way like a car dealer who's about to give his last, best offer.

"Mr. Anderson is not under arrest," he said at length. "The investigation is in its preliminary stages and so far we have no direct evidence that a death has occurred."

No body, thought Sam. Naturally. Because Eden wasn't dead. She couldn't be dead. He refused, still, to believe she was dead.

"We've interviewed Mr. Anderson," continued Chief Cottler, "just as we're interviewing anyone who may have information leading to the whereabouts of Eden Walker. That includes the present company."

"Where *is* my father, if he's not under arrest? He's not on his boat."

"That's correct. The yacht has been impounded until the State Police have completed their investigation. Any evidence they collect will be sent to the crime lab for analysis, and sometime after that, depending, the boat will be released."

He hesitated, then added, "As for Mr. Anderson, I believe he's staying with a friend on the island for now."

"Which friend?" Holly wanted to know.

"Ah, sorry. You'll have to ask him."

"How can I ask him if I don't know which friend?" she said in rising frustration.

"The Bouchards have probably taken him in," her mother said.

But Holly, bless her loyal soul, wasn't done defending her father. She glowered at the impassive officer and said, "You're treating him like a criminal!"

"We're treating him like a suspect. There's a difference."

"None that I can see," she countered. "You may as well suspect—*him*," she said, jumping up from her chair and swinging her arm to point at Sam. "He has an excellent motive: he wants his stolen engraving back. It's worth a fortune. Who says he wouldn't kill for it? Why not interrogate *him*?"

Sam smiled wryly and said, "That's exactly what Chief Cottler would like to do, if only you'd give him the chance."

"Holly, you are out of control. Will you *please* sit back down?" her mother said. She turned to the chief and said, "I'm sorry; this miserable affair has us all on edge."

"Don't apologize, Mother. *We're* not the ones conducting the witch hunt."

Cottler declined to rise to the bait, which made him a hell of a better man than Sam.

"Be that as it may," he said calmly, "I really would like to have a few words with Mr. Steadman. I'll tell you what. Suppose I interview him now, and I'll come by your house later this afternoon. How would that be?" he asked, smiling.

He said it as if he was hoping that Holly would find time for a nap in the meantime.

His condescension sent Holly's outrage up another notch. "What do you think I'm going to do? Feed you facts that you can turn around and use against my father? How stupid do you think I am?"

Pretty stupid, thought Sam. The way she was going on, even *he* was beginning to believe that her father was guilty. With someone like Holly rallying to his defense, Eric Anderson was going to end up in a cell on death row in no time flat.

"Okay, young lady," Sam said, getting up from his

chair to show her the door. "No more Lucky Charms for *you*. Sugar-free breakfasts from now on in." Turning his back to the chief, he twisted his features into a warning scowl fierce enough to stop a charging rhino in its tracks.

A rhino, maybe; not Holly. "I can't believe that you people don't have real crooks to catch," she said, turning back to the beleaguered police chief. "A stranger came to my door this morning and all but threatened to kill me. Look at my foot; it's black and blue! Put *him* in your pretty new jail. Leave my father alone. Sam, tell him that Eden is just scamming everyone! Tell him!"

"I never said that," Sam said quickly.

"You implied it!" She threw up her hands. "Oh, what's the use? All you care about is your godforsaken engraving!"

"*Not* true," Sam said in a low growl. It had never been true. Now it was not true for a whole new set of reasons.

Something in the way he said it seemed to calm her down. She faltered in her tirade, then abandoned it altogether. Bringing her chin up, she said regally, "If you want me, Chief Cottler, I shall be in my barn."

"In your—?"

"Holly, I want to get this over with," said Charlotte, annoyed. "I'm not taking you home now."

"I'll walk."

"And what about him?"

Him, of course, being Sam. "No problem," he said immediately. "I'll just—"

"Where are you staying?" Charlotte interrupted.

"Good question." He looked at Holly.

"Oh, all right. I'll meet you back at my mother's house and bring you home."

That got Charlotte's attention. "Home? Whose?"

"He's staying in the apartment over the barn. We just decided."

"Really." Charlotte turned her green gaze on Sam and looked him up, then down, in a whole new way. "I wasn't aware of that."

"We just decided, Mom, I told you."

"So you're staying on the island a while?" she asked Sam with leery interest. "May I ask why?"

Damned if Sam could even remember at that point. "I thought I'd stick around to see if I could learn anything about . . . about the engraving," he said. He sure wasn't going to say, "about Eden."

"See?" Holly said glumly. "He's obsessed with that thing."

"Well, can you blame him? If it's valuable and his parents are worried . . . I think it's commendable that he's concerned about his parents' welfare."

"Are you saying that I'm *not* the type to be concerned?" asked her daughter, bristling.

"I said nothing of the sort! Holly, what has got into you?"

Chief Cottler had lost patience with the lot of them. "Mrs. Anderson, I'll try to be brief, but I really would like to move this along."

"Of course," said Charlotte. She turned to Sam with an apologetic smile that he found oddly touching and said, "I won't be long, Mr. Steadman, I promise; I don't have much to say. And then Chief Cottler can have you all to himself."

As Sam walked out after Holly, Charlotte reached down for her handbag.

"I've never been interrogated before," he heard her say as he left the office. "Will you be needing my driver's license or anything?"

In the hall it was all Holly could do not to take a swing at Sam.

"Lucky Charms? Could you *be* more patronizing?"

Sam shrugged and said, "If the cereal fits . . ."

"Why did you back-pedal from every single statement you made to me about Eden? I felt like an unmatched sock just hanging alone in there to dry," she said angrily. "I just don't see how—"

"Will you hold it *down*?" Sam muttered, grabbing her by the elbow. He began to steer her toward the door. "I didn't leave you hanging out to do anything. You were doing a great job of that all by yourself. The more you shouted your father's innocence, the more Cottler looked convinced that you were hiding his guilt."

"But my father didn't do anything—except, okay, to run off with her. Why should *he* be the prime suspect?"

Sam looked her directly in the eye and said, "Holly. It doesn't take a rocket scientist."

It was the pinprick to Holly's balloon of hot air; she found herself deflating fast. "You don't know him," she said on a sigh. "And neither does Chief Cottler. That's the whole problem."

The shoulder strap of her purse had slipped down over her forearm. Sam lifted the strap and tucked it back in place with a chin-up kind of smile and murmured, "They're not going to put an innocent man behind bars. I have every intention of telling the chief what I know about Eden. It's just that I prefer to do it one-on-one instead of in a group encounter, that's all."

Holly looked deep into his eyes and suddenly remembered why it was she wanted him in the apartment above her studio.

"Okay, that's understandable," she admitted, then added, "I'm sorry for . . . all of that in there. I was going off half-cocked. It was the yellow tape around the boat, I guess. It freaked me out."

Sam said generously, "Let's not forget Stefan."

"Yeah. That, too."

The fake kiss hadn't helped, either, she decided as

they stepped outside. What kind of man grabbed a
woman on a public dock and then kissed the living day-
lights out of her just to create a diversion? What kind
of man could fake a kiss so *well*?

She squinted in the blinding sunshine and said with
a very casual shrug, "Would you rather I waited here
instead of at my mother's house for you? Because,
y'know, it makes no difference to me."

"Absolutely not," Sam said. "Why hang around a police station when you can be somewhere comfortable?
I'll walk back after I'm done here and we can take it
from there."

Take it from there. Take what from where? It was
making her crazy, the way he always seemed to mean
either more—or less—than he was saying. Here was a
man who could keep his own counsel. How did he feel
about her? What did he know about Eden? She opened
her mouth to ask him to explain what he meant, then
shut up again. This was not the place to arm-wrestle him
for answers.

"See you back at the ranch, then," she said, obviously
frustrated. She turned to go.

"You bet. Holly?"

When she turned around again, it was to hear him
say, "I'll get to the bottom of this. Trust me."

He didn't have to offer her that reassurance; he was
under no obligation at all. It made her feel warm inside—almost as warm as during the fake kiss. "All
right," she said with a steady look. "I'll do that."

His own expression was grim as he returned inside
the station to face the officer on the case.

Holly walked back to her mother's house the long way
around, detouring past the docks. The *Vixen* was still
there, taped off from the rest of the world. Don't touch

me, the boat seemed to say, bowing its head in shame. Unclean.

It all looked so strange, so utterly wrong. And yet, what had she expected to see? Her father, hosing off salt from the deck while he chomped on an unlit cigar in tired bliss after a long day's sail?

If only.

Suddenly she was back to feeling furious at him for bringing down suspicion on himself and humiliation on them all. At a minimum there was the scandal of the affair to deal with, and if Eden wasn't found—if she really was alive and clever enough to fade into the crowds with her stolen engraving—there would always be lingering suspicions no matter how innocent Eric Anderson was.

How were they ever going to hold their heads up in a tight-knit community like theirs again? Holly was reasonably well-known on the island; she was a soft touch who could be relied on to donate her work to the nonstop charity events that seemed not only to benefit but to bind the year-rounders, both struggling and fortunate. She loved being able to do her share, loved seeing her whirligigs pop up in yards and gardens all over the island. After years of putting down roots and nurturing them carefully, to have them hacked at so violently was unbearable.

In a deep funk, she walked past Periwinkle, a small dress shop that stayed open year-round, and caught the eye of the owner, who was in the window stealing a straw hat from the head of a mannequin there. Mrs. Fletcher's smile was as tight as it was brief as she turned away quickly to tend to her customer.

She knows. They all do. And they don't, they won't, know what to say.

Holly tried not to wallow in the vat of her misery, but the footing was too slippery to climb out easily. Her life was going to be affected in so many different ways. The Strawberry Festival, the All-Island Art Show, Illumination Night—all of her favorite community gatherings, ruined, possibly forever. Could she ever show up at them again? She couldn't see how.

She stepped up the pace so that she wouldn't have to look through any more windows at any more people she knew. She tried to appear like a Type-A yuppie with lots of Very Important Things to do. What a joke. Holly Anderson—the one who loved to meander through town, and stop and chat, and ooh and ah at the charming window displays, and stick her nose in every flower box she passed—that Holly Anderson was going to have to behave completely out of character now.

I hate him, she decided; *I really do.*

No, that's so selfish. I don't hate him; how can I hate him? He's my father.

She stopped in confusion. *But—oh, I might hate him, I don't know. I might.*

"Holly—"

"Ai!" she said, startled from her revery by the tap on her shoulder.

She swung around to see Louis Bouchard, a retired partner from her father's firm, clutching his cane as he wheezed his way through a heartfelt and awkward expression of sympathy.

"How is your mother holding up, Holly?" the kindly old man said after an endless string of *terribles*. "I've wanted to come by with a bag of sweet millions for her. I know Judy sent a note, but I wanted to bring tomatoes, anyway. The reason I haven't is that I feel as if it's my fault, somehow, and that Charlotte would rather not see me."

"*Your* fault, Mr. Bouchard!"

He nodded and leaned on his cane, looking terribly sad, terribly remorseful. His hazel eyes, rimmed by sagging lids, stared forlornly at her from under a brow that was deeply splotched from years of tending vegetables in the bright island sun.

"Here's the way I see it," he said. "I've been thinking about it a lot. If I hadn't raved about the island all those years ago to your father . . . if I hadn't invited him to bring the family, those first few summers . . . if I hadn't handed him access to the boat that made him fall in love with sailing—if I hadn't done any of those things, your father would not have bought a house on the island. And all of this never would have happened."

"You can't blame yourself, Mr. Bouchard," Holly said, seeing yet another casualty of the sorry affair. How such a sweet, kind old man could feel even remotely responsible . . .

She tried to relieve his guilt. "Every day we make a hundred different choices that affect our destinies. At least! My father's decision to take you up on your invitation was just one of many, many choices he made back then."

The lawyer smiled and said, "That's very wise, Holly. Although I can't help feeling that Eric's decision to pitch his tent on the Vineyard was more significant than whatever car he decided to go with that year."

She laughed. He was right, of course.

He touched a finger to the tip of her nose, as if she were still eight years old. "You remember how you kids used to hunt for worms in the compost pile? Those were good times . . . good times . . . and now . . . it's terrible," he said, coming full circle to his opening speech.

"We'll all get through this, Mr. Bouchard. Somehow."

"*Do* you think your mother'd enjoy the sweet millions?"

"I . . . don't know, to be honest. I haven't seen her make a salad lately."

He made a face. "What, salad. Cut 'em up, that's all. Or don't even bother; just pop 'em in your mouth like strawberries, that's how sweet they are. It's been a hot, dry summer. We've got a bumper crop."

"Yes, all right. That's very thoughtful of you. Well, I guess I—" Not knowing how to ask him tactfully what was really on her mind, she simply blurted it out. "Is my dad staying with you?"

The old man looked surprised. "Of course. You didn't know that?"

She shook her head, embarrassed to be so out of touch. "The *Vixen* returned without him."

"That's why I'm down here. Eric asked me to retrieve his reading glasses from the boat. They're prescription, you know; he can't get another pair very quickly."

"He sent *you* down for that?"

"You can see why he would, child," he said with a note of impatience.

She wanted to scream, "No, I *don't* see! Let him retrieve his own stupid glasses!" But the word "child" smarted. It came too soon after the phrase "Lucky Charms."

"They won't let you aboard," she said, trying to sound very adult and matter-of-fact. "A forensic team is going over the boat right now."

"Oh, well. I'm here. I'll give it a try."

With a hopeful smile he leaned forward as if into the teeth of a gale and soldiered on, an eighty-something litigator who until then had never had to involve himself in anything more violent than an unseemly fight over a property line.

16

Waiting his turn in what was euphemistically called the "library" (there were bookshelves), Sam nursed a cup of coffee until it got cold and he didn't want it anymore. He was bored but not impatient. Being at the beck and call of the justice system was nothing new; as a kid, he'd often sat in a zonal trance in family court while social workers and advocates huddled nearby, trying to decide what the hell to do with him.

He remembered vividly his appearance in court after stealing the drug-dealer's speedboat and wrecking it on the rocks in Woods Hole. Apparently his bold exploits had created a buzz: one of the social workers had come up to him with a wry smile and said, "In all my years at this, I've never seen a ten-year-old hijack a Cigarette before. What's next? The *Queen Mary*?"

Sam smiled in recollection; he liked that guy. A lot. Joe Doxie was one of the reasons that Sam—eventually—turned away from a life of crime. The other reason was Millie Steadman. A wise-guy social worker and a tenacious foster mother—they were the one-two punch of savvy and tough love that a punk like Sam had so desperately needed. Even then, it had taken a life-altering event before Sam was finally ready, at seventeen, to begin turning his life around.

Sam propped his elbows on the long conference table and stared out the windows, musing about criminal minds and psychopaths, con artist and murderous lovers, until he realized that he'd drifted into a dank and dreary place. With a conscious effort he paddled out of the sewer of his thoughts and ended up, surprisingly, in the clear river rapids of the always exciting, much too excitable Holly Anderson.

That kiss! He didn't want to think about it. What *had* he been thinking, pulling an unsuspecting woman into his arms and kissing the breath out of her? Come to think of it, she could easily have him up on assault. He wouldn't half blame her.

That kiss. The way she returned it . . . the way he, hmm, sprang to attention . . . that kiss! Where had it come from? He puzzled over that kiss, fretted over the way his tongue had found Holly's so easily, mulled over how good it had felt, until he found himself paddling furiously out of *those* dangerous waters as well. Nope. He had absolutely no desire to go over the falls in a barrel.

He went back to staring at the swaying trees and concentrated on the upcoming interview. Sam had been through interviews and interrogations more than once before. He knew that an investigating officer could choose to play a good cop or a bad one, depending on the witness. Sam's guess was that with Charlotte, Cottler had been a sympathetic cop who had moved out from behind his desk and had talked to her as any family man would talk to a woman who had been publicly humiliated by her no-good shit of a husband.

But someone as proud as Charlotte Anderson would

never descend to accepting sympathy. She wouldn't admit to humiliation, and certainly not to resentment or vindictiveness. One-word answers and brief phrases, that's all that Cottler was likely to have got out of her, no matter how understanding he seemed.

Which meant that the officer would be waiting with heightened interest and bated breath to hear anything that Sam had to say.

Finally the chief walked in, carrying a laptop and a printout. Sam had little doubt that they held his criminal history, but the look that Cottler gave him was one of pure civility.

"Before we begin—get you some coffee?" he asked, holding up his own mug.

"No, I'm fine, thanks."

"This time of day, I hit a wall unless I have a shot of caffeine." Pulling out a molded chair, he said in an affable tone, "Hey, I understand that you're a pretty well-known marine photographer."

"Marine photographer, yes. Well-known, probably not."

"You have a book. That's impressive. I've never been much with a camera myself. Point 'n' shoot, that's me."

"No pun intended, I hope."

Cottler got it; grinned and said, "I dunno. Don't they say all puns are intentional on some level?"

Sam nodded. First round to the chief.

"As you can imagine, I'm interested in what Miss Anderson had to say earlier about you and Eden Walker," Cottler said, sliding his keyboard into position. "Very interested." He explained that he was going to take a few notes and that he was going ask Sam to read them over afterward and sign them, if that was all right with Sam.

It was all right with Sam.

Cottler slid a pair of reading glasses over his nose

and began to hunt and peck his way through a series of routine biographical questions that Sam dutifully answered. It was all in the computer, anyway.

Furrowing his brow in an apparent hunt for some missing key, the chief said, "Okay, now, let's see . . . have you ever had any previous contact with the law? You know, traffic court, stuff like that, or been arrested for any other offenses?"

Sam squared his shoulders against the back of his chair. His elbows had nowhere to go; his hands gripped the tops of his thighs. Try as he might, he couldn't help tapping the soles of his shoes alternately on the floor: old habits died hard.

"I was what used to be called," he said with a wry smile, "a juvenile delinquent."

"Uh-huh," said Cottler, studiously hunting and pecking. "Mind telling me what sort of offenses?" he asked without looking up.

Sam felt the muscles of his jaw working. "Stealing, mostly."

"Uh-huh. Big stuff? Little stuff?"

"Some of each. A car. A boat. Rosaries."

"No shit," said the chief. He looked up from his keyboard. "Rosaries?"

"They weren't for me. At one point I had foster parents who put me in a Catholic school. I sold the rosaries at half price to the kids in my class. It was a captive market."

Sam was seven when he took the rosary—one rosary. He gave it to a <u>girl</u> he had a crush on. But he felt like being outrageous with Cottler, he didn't know why.

The chief had no intention of yielding authority by giving in to a smile. He said blandly, "Okay, let's move on. I assume you know the situation: Eden Walker was reported missing after going windsurfing off the *Vixen*, Eric Anderson's yacht. Her body has not been recovered, although given the tide and current direction, that isn't surprising. What I want to know from you is—just let me get this question in the computer—do you have any personal knowledge of Eric Anderson?"

"No, not at all."

"Mm-hmm. Ever done business with him or been at the same event as him?"

"Nope."

"All right." Tap, tap, tap went the keys. "Do you have any mutual acquaintances that you know of?"

"Obviously: Eden Walker."

"Right. Okay, then, how do you know her, if not through Eric Anderson?"

Showtime.

"I was married to her for about a year before she split."

The tap-tap-tapping stopped. Cottler lifted his head, and there was nothing even remotely amused in the calm look he bestowed on Sam. "Married, were you? Okay," he said, going back to the keyboard. "How long ago was that?"

"She left about seven years ago."

"And this was after a year of marriage," he said, tapping quickly. "The reason for the breakup, that would be . . . ?"

"She never gave me a reason. She just left."

"And you haven't seen her since then?"

"Nope."

"But somehow she got hold of this, uh, engraving of your parents. How did that happen?"

"About three years ago, Eden started dropping in occasionally to visit my parents, apparently because she needed money—"

"And you approved of this arrangement?"

"I didn't approve or disapprove. I didn't know."

"Ah. Your parents lent her money on the Q.T., is that it?"

"That's it."

"So she took the engraving three years ago?"

"No. She took it a few weeks ago. My parents waited awhile before they called me."

"Miss Anderson mentioned that your parents were devastated by the loss. Is that your recollection?"

"I think they were but tried not to show it."

"These are your adoptive parents?"

"That's correct."

"Their names?"

"James and Mildred Steadman."

"Do you have a good relationship with them?"

"Is that relevant?"

"Do you?" Cottler persisted.

"Yes."

"And yet they didn't tell you about Miss—Mrs.—?"

"She kept her maiden name."

"—Ms. Walker borrowing money from them. Why is that?"

"I don't know."

"Could it be that they thought it would distress you? Anger you?"

"Possibly."

"Because it was adding insult to injury?"

"I don't know what their reasoning might have been for thinking it would distress me."

"Why did Ms. Walker take the engraving?"

"She said, to have it appraised."

"You don't think she had that intention?"

"No."

"You think she took it under false pretenses? You think she stole it?"

"Yes."

"Why do you think that?"

"Because she had stolen from the elderly before. She was accused of taking some diamonds from an elderly shut-in once. The woman died five years ago."

"Let's go back to your involvement with the law. When was the last time you were in court?"

"I was seventeen."

"And the occasion was?"

"I was involved in a fight."

"Was anyone seriously injured?"

"Yes. An eighteen-year-old was killed."

"And you were responsible?"

"Indirectly, yes."

"How do you mean, indirectly?"

"He and two others were attacking a woman. I intervened. I hit him; apparently it caused him to hemorrhage. Before the police arrived, the other gang members carried him away. They didn't take him to a hospital, though, and he died."

"Who was the woman who was being attacked? A girlfriend?"

"No."

"Did you want her to be?"

"No."

Cottler peered over his glasses at Sam. "You took on three gang members who were attacking a girl you didn't want for your own?"

"Strange as it may seem," said Sam.

"Have you done that since—spilled blood over a woman?"

It was luridly put, an attempt to get a rise from Sam.

"No."

"Did you try to find Eden after she split?"

"Yes."

"What did you do?"

"Made calls, the usual thing. I hired an investigator, but the bills ran on."

"I'll need his name."

"I'll have to look it up."

"Have you remarried?"

"No."

"May I ask why?"

"No."

The chief sighed and went back to his keyboard. "Okay. This engraving. Have your parents reported the theft of it to the police?"

"No."

"Because?"

"They're waiting to see what I find out."

"What have you found out?"

"That Eden sold the engraving to someone who wasn't especially interested in its provenance."

"Who would that be?"

"I don't know his name."

"How do you know that it happened at all?"

"I talked to the dealer that Eden cut out of the sale."

"His name?"

Crunch time. Sam didn't want to give his name. If the police followed up and questioned Stefan Koloman, it was Holly who'd bear the brunt of the dealer's rage. Sam could have, maybe should have, lied about what he had found out. But he'd promised Holly that he'd answer truthfully, and this is where it had landed him.

"I can't remember his name." He was going to lie after all.

"Really. Where is his place of business? Can you remember that?"

"Nope."

"If I gave you more time—would you remember it then?"

Sam shrugged. "Probably not."

Cottler leaned forward in his chair and beat a tatoo on each side of his laptop with the palms of his hands.

Eyeing Sam shrewdly, he said, "Miss Anderson's irate visitor wouldn't be the disgruntled art dealer, by any chance?"

"I can't say," Sam offered, which was true.

Cottler scowled and said, "Look, Steadman, I don't have time for bullshit answers. Suppose I give you twenty-four hours to come up with the dealer's name and address. Sleep on it, try hypnosis, do whatever it takes," he said dryly. "If Eden Walker was hanging with some unsavory types, it would be extremely helpful to this investigation to know who they are. You understand that you're not doing Eric Anderson any favors by holding back this kind of information, don't you?"

"Sure." But Sam understood even more clearly that he wouldn't be doing Holly any favors by coming forward with it. He wasn't about to put her in jeopardy just to save her father.

Sooner or later the cops were going to track down Koloman—sooner, if Holly obliged them with a physical description. Forget about names; how many art dealers sporting gold front teeth could there be in the area?

And then Koloman would come after Holly. Which meant that Sam, who had put her in danger in the first place, was going to have to hang around to keep her out of danger. Which meant that finding the engraving— finding the money, finding Eden, finding *anything*—was going to be even trickier.

After scrolling through his computer notes, the chief said, "I'll need the address where you were living with Eden Walker at the time she left."

Sam gave it to him and said edgily, "Are we done here?"

"Yeah, I think for the moment—wait. One more. When were you divorced?"

Ah, hell. Damn. *Shit.*

"We weren't."

The chief pulled his glasses down to the end of his nose and left them there. "You're still married to Eden Walker?"

"As far as I know. I was never served, and I never filed."

"Jesus *Christ*, why didn't you say so in the first place?"

Sam said cooly, "You didn't ask."

And that was how the game was played. Cottler knew it, and now he knew that Sam knew it. In the course of the interview Sam had volunteered just enough information so that the chief would think he was a cooperative witness. That little delusion was now shot officially to hell.

"Do you mind if I ask *why* you never divorced?"

"I do."

"For the record?"

"For the record, I never got around to it."

Cottler blew out a slow, angry exhale through his nostrils and said, "Wait here. I'll clean up what I've got so far and you can read it over."

Sam nodded briefly and sat back in his chair. He was sorry the bookshelves were empty.

17

After ransacking the drawers of her father's desk, Holly found what she was looking for: an old pair of geeky reading glasses that her mother never could stand to see him wear. Her father had refused to throw them out and had saved them for an emergency.

Well, this was that emergency. Holly left the house and used her truck more or less as a battering ram to get herself through the afternoon traffic clogging the town's quaint streets. She thought of Sam and smiled: he'd be curled up in a fetal position under the dashboard right about now. Wasn't that odd, how someone so tough could be so afraid of a woman driver. She wondered whether he'd ever been in jail at all; maybe it was all an act.

She drove to the Bouchards in a state neither of anger nor apprehension, but of relief. Finally she was doing something. Finally. When she saw the house coming up in the distance, she knew she'd made the right decision.

The house was nothing more than a big box with a hipped roof, but it was spectacularly located just a few feet from the beach, facing southwest. Holly used to feel, and still did feel, that it had the best location on the Vineyard. She had spent many wonderful weeks there. The place was too big for the Bouchards, who had no children; but it was just perfect for guests and murder suspects.

Holly could see Mrs. Bouchard in a rocking chair on the leeward side now, reading a book and keeping an eye on her husband who was nearby, working under a big straw hat on his beloved sweet millions.

"Hello, stranger!" she called as Holly climbed down from her truck. "We haven't seen you all summer."

"It's been that kind of year," Holly said, trying not to sound grim. She waved at Louis Bouchard, who held up a garden trug in greeting. Tomatoes, many pounds of them, were on the first leg of their journey cross-island.

Mrs. Bouchard smiled and said, "Remember the last time I saw you in early spring? You were complaining that things were so quiet."

"I know, I know," groaned Holly. "Be careful what you wish for." She lifted the cat that was curled up on the cushion, nuzzled his nose, and eased him on his way.

She dropped tiredly into the chair; the tabby jumped on her lap. Idly stroking the animal's throat, Holly said in a strained, singsong voice, "*So*, how're you?"

"Oh, *I'm* fine," said Mrs. Bouchard. "You know what they say—whatever doesn't kill you makes you stronger."

That's how Judy Bouchard dismissed life's little setbacks, including the heart attack she'd had over a year ago. Holly began to murmur something polite and agreeable, but the older woman interrupted her. Rocking back in her chair, she slanted her head sideways at Holly and said, "More to the point, how are *you* all doing?"

"A bit off balance at the moment," Holly admitted in a deliberate understatement. She didn't dare start weeping and wailing; Mrs. Bouchard would never have stood for it.

"You're here for the tomatoes?" she asked with an innocent look.

Holly smiled grimly. "Not exactly."

"I didn't think so. He's on 'the beach side of the porch," she said with a nod in that direction.

"Thanks, Mrs. B."

Holly had come specifically to tell her father what an unfeeling monster he was, so she straightened her spine and patted the eyeglasses in the pocket of her shorts, and, thus armed, marched off to do battle.

Her father was sitting in a painted Adirondack chair, facing the sea. If he was aware that his hosts had a guest, he didn't show it. If he was aware that the guest was his daughter, he certainly didn't show it. Holly came up to him from behind and on the right and caught the once-sharp edges of his profile, blurred now by time, as he stared serenely at the sea.

He turned when she approached and looked her full in the face—and Holly became instantly, profoundly aware that she had confused the stillness of serenity with the paralysis of agony. The change in him was shocking; he looked as if he'd been thrown into the lowest pit of hell, bounced around for a while, and hauled back up to die.

Her father had always looked strikingly fit and much younger than his years. This was not that man. His face was gaunt and deeply lined, his shoulders stooped; his mouth hung slightly open, as if it was too much effort to close it anymore. His eyebrows were no longer light brown and streaked with gray, but gray, shot through with white.

Holly's instinct was—anyone's instinct would be— to say, "What *happened*?" But she knew too well what had happened. Her father had gone off on a lark with the devil, and the devil had made him play by her rules.

That, at least, is what Holly wanted to believe. And yet she knew full well that older men fell in love with younger women all the time, and that the younger women weren't devils, and that the older men weren't monsters and didn't come out of the affair looking like— well, like the faded wreck who had a hard time rising to his feet before her.

"Hello," she said with neither pity nor censure. Her heart was far too constricted to feel either.

"Holly . . ."

"They didn't let Mr. Bouchard aboard the boat, did they?"

"Holly, I—no. They did not."

"I didn't think they would. Here," she said, fumbling to get the glasses case out of her pocket. She had wanted to be so cool about it! "You left them at home when you . . . left."

He looked baffled, as if she were offering him Styrofoam when he was expecting water. "Those are mine?"

"You kept them in your desk for emergencies—remember?" Here, too, he was failing her. He couldn't even remember that he looked like a geek in them. That his wife was convinced that he looked like a geek. He couldn't even remember his wife.

"Yes . . . all right," he said, accepting them and then absently dropping them on a little wooden table next to the Adirondack chair.

The offhand gesture seemed to diminish her offering, her sacrifice of going there, still more. After she had swallowed her pride and come to see him, he didn't even thank her. He *was* a monster.

"How is your mother?" he asked her mournfully.

"Oh! You remember I have one."

"Don't, Holly."

"Why not? Surely I have your gene for cruelty."

"Is she all right?"

"What do *you* think?"

He wasn't thinking at all; that was obvious in the way he turned away from her and began staring at the sea again. Wasn't thinking, wasn't feeling, wasn't—certainly was not—aware of Holly anymore. She was the favorite of his three children, but she might as well have been one of the potted geraniums on the porch. For the first time, she understood on a brutally visceral level what her mother had been going through. It wasn't easy to cease to exist before your very own eyes.

Her gaze slid past the back of her father's silvered head and out to the whitecapped sea, glorious and fresh and alive and everything that Holly and her father, just then, were not. The wind, boisterous in its joy, whipped her hair across her cheeks and pinned her clothes against her body as she stood unheeding and unresponsive while she waited for her father to explain his mad deed.

Out on the beach she saw a man walking below the high-water mark alongside a small child, who clutched a bucket with both hands as she stumped across the sand, searching for shells. To say that Holly felt more kinship with the stranger and the little girl than she did with her own father would not have been an exaggeration. Immobile as the potted geraniums, she waited a long, long moment for Eric Anderson to break the agonizing silence.

When he didn't, when she decided that he never would, she asked him outright: "Why, Dad? What were you thinking?"

His head turned slightly in her direction: he had heard her, at least. They were not the father and daughter she saw at the water's edge; they never would be again, she supposed. But he had heard her.

"I wanted . . . more," he said at last, and then he let out a shuddering sigh and wrapped his Scandinavian reserve around him as if it were a thick terrycloth robe.

His answer, his demeanor, infuriated her. "More? More what? More than a woman who loves you, a family who cares? More than the freedom to walk among your friends and enjoy the respect of your peers? More than your house, your boat, your place by the sea? What *more* can you *want*? You have health, wealth, people who love you. To want *more* than that strikes me as—obscene!"

He nodded slowly, apparently agreeing.

"That's it? That's your reaction? Can't you at least say you're *sorry*?" she cried, rushing around to face him. She stood with feet apart, her hands thrown up in frustration. "You at least owe us *that*!"

"But . . . I'm not," he said, almost confused about it. "Why do you think I'm here and not home?"

Instinctively, she balled her hands into fists; her mouth fell open but no words came out.

Her father seemed to hear the response that she wasn't able to scream. He propped his elbows on his knees and folded his hands in contemplation, just as he had when she was five and he was trying not to beat her at checkers.

"I'm sixty-two years old, Holly," he said, looking up at her across the bridge of his knuckles. "I've gone into the same suite of offices in the same historic brick building for over thirty years. The work I do there is mind-numbing—drawing up deeds, setting up escrows, sitting at closings. Maybe a title search, if there's a fight and the stakes are high enough. The fact is, the paralegals can do most of what I do, and for a fifth of my earnings."

"So you're bored by your job," Holly said scathingly. "So *what*. Lots of people are bored."

"You're not," he said with a sad smile.

"Of course I'm not. I'm going after my dream. Why shouldn't I? I don't have mouths to feed, tuition to—"

She stopped herself, aware that she was describing a typical parent. That she might well be describing her father.

He thought so, anyway. "I got married when I was still in law school. I'm not blaming anyone, Holly, please understand me—but very quickly there were mouths to feed."

Holly knew that. Her brother was born six months after her parents eloped. Her sister was born a year after that. Holly herself was the coup de grâce: born less than a year after her sister.

She shrugged and said, "Sorry. I didn't ask to be born."

"I told you, I'm not blaming anyone. But I purposely took the least stressful route there was. I wanted no long hours as a criminal lawyer; no iffy income from contingency work. My entering into probate law has worked out well for our family. Real estate has been good to us."

He rubbed his tanned, smooth hands across his jawbone and sighed, apparently struggling in his search for words.

"You know the clock on the bank across the street from my office?" he asked in a wistful tone. "The one with the big gold hands? That's the clock I watch ticking my life away, minute by gold-leafed minute. Almost every day when that clock tolls noon, I'm at my desk, eating a salad. At the stroke of four I'm packing my briefcase. Day in, day out, there we are: me, and the clock with the gold-leafed hands."

"Oh, please. You could have retired by now. Why are you even there?" she said, pitiless for her mother's sake.

"I could have quit," he agreed. "I *should* have quit. It's the damndest thing: it was such a painless life, such an easy one, that I didn't even know I hated it until—"

Eden. If he said the word, she'd slap his face.

But he didn't. "It's only now, in retrospect, that I see how unsatisfied I was," he said. "How unhappy."

She laughed contemptuously at that. "Oh, and now you're satisfied? Now you're happy? What an odd sense of bliss you have."

He bowed his head over his clasped hands, just the way he had at Sunday services when they all went to church together. "I'm dying, Holly," he whispered. "I'm in hell."

Holly wanted to believe her own definition of his hell: that he missed his family, that he was afraid of jail. But she knew from looking at him that hell for him was a life without Eden. Truly, there was no fool like an old fool, she thought. His refusal to repent was making her hard.

"And if you're cleared but Eden *is* dead?" she said. "Will you still be in hell?"

"More than ever."

She sucked in her breath. *That's it*! *I don't have to listen to this*.

She turned to leave, then spun back around for one last shot. "You understand, don't you, that she's trying to frame you for her death? That she's willing to have people think you're a homicidal maniac?"

He heard the words; he didn't understand them.

She waited for a light bulb, any wattage, to go on in the murky, besotted chambers of his brain. Nothing. He remained in the dark. Finally she threw up her hands and said, "Don't you get it? She's *framing* you! You didn't kill her, did you?"

A spark at last: "Of course not!" he said angrily. "What do you take me for?"

"Oh, Dad," she said wearily, "don't ask." She looked away.

She heard his voice slip back into broken musing as he said, "I should've gone looking for her sooner when she didn't come back on the windsurfer . . . but she was so competent . . . an expert . . . it's my fault . . . I shouldn't have waited so long . . . my fault . . ."

In the distance Holly saw the little girl with her bucket of shells fading from view.

She turned back to her father with white-hot resentment.

"Listen to me. *Listen.* I met someone who knows Eden; he came to the island looking for her. Eden is a thief and a con, Dad. She stole a valuable engraving from an elderly couple who were counting on the proceeds to get them through their old age. That's your Eden."

Now she saw real anger.

"That's *outrageous*! Eden would never do something like that!"

He jumped up and Holly actually believed he might knock her down for the blasphemy, but he turned away from her instead. She saw him clutch his thinning hair with both hands, a shockingly melodramatic gesture for him, and then mutter, "*Jesus.*" He planted his splayed hands on his hips and, bowing his head, stared at the gray-painted planks of the porch. Another pause, and then he looked sideways at Holly. She was the enemy now.

"You met someone who's on a vendetta," he said flatly, "that's all. And you're angry enough to believe him."

"Oh, I'm pissed enough, I agree, but—"

"How do you know this man isn't making it all up? How do you know he's not out to punish Eden in some way?"

It was an entirely new thought. "Because I trust him," Holly said at last. And she did.

"Eden is—was—*is*—a stunningly desirable woman.

Don't you think she's left a trail of broken hearts behind her?"

Holly looked at her father and said evenly, "It keeps getting longer all the time."

"Oh, fu—" He stopped himself mid-sneer and wheeled back around to the sea.

There he stood, apparently calm—but she could see the infinitesmal pumping of his shoulders. Her father was in a state of rage, and the worst of it was, it was holy rage. He honestly thought that Eden was suffering from a bum rap.

Infuriating, exasperating, self-deluded man! Where did you take people like him? To a detox clinic?

"Why would she bother staying with me," he said through gritted teeth, "if she had stolen a prized engraving."

Softly, so that she wouldn't alienate him from further dialogue, Holly said, "Your boat was a good place to hide, I imagine."

He shook his head. "She could have walked off the *Vixen* anywhere along the coast; we sailed nearly to Nova Scotia. Why go to the trouble of sailing all the way back with me?"

"I don't know," Holly had to confess. "I don't know why she wanted the police to think you killed her. She must have assumed that sooner or later, Sam would find out about the engraving and come running."

"Sam is the guy you say is after her?"

"Yes, but *not* because she broke his heart. The engraving belonged to his parents. They're not well-off; they have medical bills."

Her father gave Sam the benefit of a grunt.

"Dad—how did blood get all over the boat?" Holly asked bluntly.

He looked both annoyed and embarrassed. "Simple. Eden . . . she hurt herself cutting an orange for breakfast—you know how sharp I keep my knives—and she bled on the butcher block in the galley, and then on the teak sole in the head when we took off the paper towel and were bandaging her finger. It took a couple of tries."

Holly was watching her father carefully. He was nervous, but surely that was a reflex. He'd already given the story to the police; if they treated him as if they thought he was lying, then naturally he was going to worry about how he sounded every time he told his story later. That's how innocent men flunked polygraphs.

"It wasn't anything that needed stitches," he continued, still averting Holly's gaze, "but . . . but it did bleed for a while. And the police, well, they found blood on the port deck, too," he admitted. He cleared his throat and added, "But the bandage probably started leaking again when Eden was rigging the sail on the windsurfer. It definitely must have done that."

Holly listened to her father with growing dismay. He was lying through his teeth.

"It sounds as if it was a bad cut," she said, trying to draw him out. "Why would Eden go windsurfing with an injury like that?"

Her father shot her an angry look: clearly he did not expect skepticism from his own flesh and blood.

"She's *spunky*," he said. "It's part of her appeal."

There was a lull. Her father turned back to the sea.

"I would have made good on the engraving," he said after a moment. "Even if she *had* stolen it. She would have had a reason."

Besotted! "Did you give Eden any reason to believe that you would be capable of something like that? Dad— did you talk of marriage?"

"That's none of your business," said her father without turning around.

She wanted to shout, "Of course it's my business! Whatever affects Mom is my business!" But that was the surest, quickest way to get him to shut down altogether, so she bit back the retort and said instead, "If Eden's alive, then she must have said or done something susp—out of the ordinary during her time on the boat. Can you think of anything? Anything at all?"

Her father had been leaning with both hands on the balustrade. Now he looked almost shyly over his shoulder at her and said, "So you *do* think she's alive?"

Bitterly disappointed by his response, Holly merely repeated the question. "Can you think of anything out of the ordinary?"

Squinting into the sun, he said, "Yes, actually, there was one odd incident. Eden got a call on her cell phone—it was right after we left Portsmouth, where we'd put in for an emergency repair. It was the first call she'd ever received, and I was surprised; she never gave out the number. Anyway, whoever it was made her extremely upset. So upset that after she hung up, she threw the phone in the water—like this," he said, simulating an underhand Frizbee toss. "She was furious for the rest of the day, when she wasn't acting . . . I don't know . . . frightened. She kept bouncing back and forth between the two moods."

"She didn't say why she was so upset?"

Holly's father shook his head. "Not a word. I'd just got my own cell phone by then," he said, nodding over his shoulder to the one on the table next to his eyeglasses. "Eden could still make calls on mine, so that wasn't it. It's hard to say what had her so upset. She's had a painful life, you know. She's learned to keep her own counsel."

Ha. The only counsel that Eden was keeping was Eric Anderson.

"How long did you stay in Portsmouth?" Holly asked her father. She wondered whether it was long enough to fence an engraving.

"Three days. I had to go back to the office anyway, so it worked out. I stayed at the house."

"At the house? Did Eden go with you?" Good grief. This would kill her mother.

Even her father seemed scandalized by the thought of Eden knocking around the family homestead on the toniest street in Providence. "She stayed behind on the boat. Apparently she never once stepped off it. The shipyard had to do some fiberglass repairs, and she told me later that she simply didn't trust the yardhands. As I said, she's had a difficult life—not like the rest of us," he added.

He was daring his daughter to argue with him, but she wouldn't give him the satisfaction of being able to defend Eden. If he was feeling so all-fired chivalrous, he could just find himself a joust somewhere.

"And you never had—you know—any big arguments or anything?"

His smile was rueful, even fond. "Of course we did," he freely confessed. "We argued all the time, about everything. How to anchor, where to anchor, what movie to see ashore, what restaurants to eat at . . ."

His musing look turned suspicious again. "Why? Are you back to thinking I killed her?"

"No, no, it's just that . . . there were stories—"

He scowled. "Marjory Betson," he said flatly. "I saw their boat."

"Yes, of course Marjory. What did you expect? That you'd go unnoticed?"

"I expected," he said, drawing himself up with ludicrous dignity, "that people would mind their own business."

So he wasn't flaunting Eden as some youthful trophy. Even worse. The thought that he was genuinely, truly in love with her—whatever that meant—left Holly even more depressed than before. She shouldn't have come to see him. Deep down she had had some grandiose notion of acting as intermediary between her parents. She had expected to bring her mother at a minimum an apology, and ideally her father himself. Instead, all she would be bringing back were tomatoes.

The conversation was clearly at an end. There would be no tearful hug, no hopeful exchange. Holly muttered something about being due back home.

"Sure; I understand. You really think she's alive, then?" he asked his daughter plaintively.

"Of course she is."

You couldn't kill someone like Eden.

18

Holly returned to her mother's house to find Sam sitting on the front stoop. Her heart did the funny little flip-flop that she associated with routine thoughts of him, and an extra little flip-flop besides: the reality of him was so much better than mere dreams could be.

"Stick a bottle of beer in your hand, and you'd look just like a T.V. commercial," she said, grinning for no other reason than that she was near him. He did have the look: square-jawed, windblown, slightly scruffy— and topping it off, the kind of offbeat, crooked smile that made women glance instinctively at his left ring finger.

It was blessedly bare, as always, and that made her own smile linger. "Did you knock?" she asked, cradling her bag of sweet millions. "Her car's here; she must be home."

Sam stood up and arched his back in a stretch, then said quietly, "When she left the station, she looked as if she could use a little peace and quiet."

The smile faded from Holly's face. She remembered

now: misery was all around them. "What's the chief like?" she asked, instinctively lowering her voice. "Is he a hard man?"

Sam shrugged and said, "He's a cop with a job to do. But if you're asking me, does he feel for your mother—yeah; I think so. It's a small island. He understands that it's rough on her."

"She's cut herself off from all of her friends," Holly admitted. "And she . . . boy . . . she didn't used to like wine with meals so much, Sam. I'm worried."

"Don't be," he said, slipping his arm around her and squeezing her lightly. "Your mother's a strong woman; she'll get through this."

The simple gesture of comfort was incredibly welcome, more so because it wasn't faked for the sake of some troopers. Holly felt a catch in her throat; not altogether sure of her voice, she merely smiled and said, "Mm-hmm."

She glanced up at the window of the guest bedroom in which her mother now slept. The drapes were closed, but the shades weren't pulled; that could mean anything. She looked at Sam with his reassuring smile. She looked up at the window again. She looked at Sam.

"I think," she whispered, "that I'll leave her be for now. Let's go home."

Let's go home. The words sounded so right. If Holly were to step inside to see how the interview had gone, she was bound to blurt out that she'd just seen her father. Did she have a single iota of good news to deliver? Not an iota. Best to leave the bag of tomatoes on the doorstep and tiptoe away.

Still . . .

She couldn't do it; couldn't leave without checking, however briefly, on her mother. Just to be sure.

"I'll just run in for a second," she told Sam, who was

headed for the truck. She fished out her key and let herself into the house.

"Mom?" she called out softly from the bottom of the steps. "Are you around?"

"I'm up here, honey, lying down. I feel one of my headaches coming on, and I'm trying to beat it off. It's not too bad."

"Oh, good," said Holly. She meant it in so many ways. "I'll check in with you later."

"Okay, sweetie. Thanks."

Holly set the bag of cherry tomatoes on the hall table and ran like hell.

Let's go home.

Almost shyly, she threw the truck in gear and started them on their way. Sam could have walked; it wasn't much more than a mile between the station and her place. She liked—she loved—that he had chosen to wait and go back with her.

"That sure was a lot of tomatoes," he said. "Your mother must be extremely fond of salads."

Holly laughed and said, "Those are from Mr. Bouchard, my father's old mentor. His plants runneth over."

"Ah."

She took a turn possibly a little too sharply, sending Sam groping for his seatbelt. "As it turns out, my mother was right," she said, feeling obliged to confess what Sam probably had guessed. "My dad *is* hiding out at the Bouchards."

All she got in response was a noncommittal nod.

"The Bouchards are incredibly nice people," she went on, suddenly ill at ease. "*Mi casa es su casa*, and all that. Really, their doors are always open. I practically grew up there before we got our own house. Nice, nice people. You'd like them if you ever—well, they're nice. Really nice."

No use. Something had changed. Sam's mouth was

set in a flat line of resolve, his gaze fixed straight ahead. It wasn't her driving, she knew, so it must have to do with her father. Sam's antipathy to him seemed to emanate from every pore.

And yet she had to talk about her father with someone, and Sam was the obvious choice: he wasn't emotionally involved. "Aren't you going to ask me how it went?" she asked, exasperated.

"You're here; I assume it didn't come to blows," Sam said quietly as he stared out the window.

Her laugh came out grim. "It almost *did*, a couple of times. Trust me, if it had, I would have cleaned his clock. I'm much more angry than he is."

Out of the corner of her eye she saw Sam do a double take. "Your father isn't spitting nails over being set up?" he asked.

Holly shook her head. "I explained your theory. He doesn't believe that he's *been* set up. A worst-case scenario for him is if Eden drowned; nothing else matters much. When he actually understood that she might still be alive—who cares under what circumstances—his eyes lit up. I could have killed him on the spot."

"Jesus."

"He's obsessed with her, and it's eating him alive. He's not sorry, he doesn't want to come home, and— my mother's catty friend notwithstanding—he actually enjoyed those public fights with Eden. What kind of man does *that*?"

Sam's voice seemed distant and preoccupied as he said, "A woman like that can get under your skin."

"Oh, bullshit. Eden is pretty, she's clever, she's a flirt—but she's not Cleopatra. I've never understood this *femme fatale* business," she groused. "Maybe it's because I'm not one myself."

If that was an opening, Sam sure didn't take it. "I'd say you're the polar opposite," he maintained. "You're the freckle-faced kid next door. And you know what?" he added, smiling. "There are worse things to be."

"I do not have freckles, Mr. Steadman—as if you'd notice," she added in a dark mutter.

Clinging! She was clinging! Shutupshutupshutup!

"You do have freckles," he argued. "Three tiny ones, on the left side of your nose about half an inch below your eye. And when the wind blows your hair away from your face, you can see two more near your right ear."

She felt a wave of delicious heat roll over her cheekbones. "Oh, I forgot," she said breezily to disguise her pleasure. "You're a photographer."

"That's right. Uh, did your father . . . did he have much to say about Eden?"

Eden again. Holly was learning to hate the sound of the name. She blew frustration through puffed-out cheeks and said, "He thinks it's none of my business."

"Interesting," said Sam. He sounded bemused, almost relieved.

Holly said, "I don't think my father killed Eden—God, I can't believe I'm even saying words like that out loud; they sound so ridiculous. But Sam, he was lying about the blood. I don't know how the boat got blood on it, but it wasn't from Eden cutting herself as she sliced an orange. I know my father. He's a rotten liar. When he explained the blood, he was lying rottenly well."

"How do you think it got there, in that case?"

"I don't know. Not from slicing an orange. And here's another thing that's puzzling me: Eden hurled her cell phone into the sea."

Holly explained the mysterious phone call and Eden's impulsive reaction to it and added that Eden had insisted on staying aboard the boat during the emergency repairs.

Naturally Holly had a theory for all of it. "My guess

is that she stayed on the boat during the repairs just to guard the engraving, and that the person who called later was someone—either Stefan or the actual buyer—making an offer that she considered insulting. She was infuriated by it. Then, after she impulsively threw away her cell phone in a pissy-fit, she became frightened—maybe that's not the right word—*alarmed* because she'd cut off her link to a willing buyer. It can't be easy to fence art that has no known provenance. Y'think?"

In her preoccupation, Holly overshot the drive to the barn. She slammed on the brakes, sending Sam lurching forward, and then threw the truck in reverse, sending his head whiplashing back.

Sam said, "You *do* have a license to drive, right? Sometimes on an island people get casual about niceties like that."

"Very funny. I ferry people around all the time and no one complains."

"Maybe, darlin', but here's some advice: don't quit your day job."

"Okay, smart-boy; next time *you* drive," she said, grinning. She did love the sound of that *darlin'*.

They got out of the car and Sam retrieved his duffel from his latest Corolla. Technically, Holly should have handed him the key to the loft apartment and gone on her way, but . . .

"The T.V. reception is a little quirky; I'd better show you," she said, accompanying him up the outside stairs. "You've got to smack the box a certain way."

She saw him look at her curiously, but she pretended not to notice. She was attaching herself to him like ivy to a tree; she knew it, loathed herself for it, and was helpless to do a damn thing about it.

I want to be with him; only him. It's as simple as that.

But only for comfort and reassurance, she insisted to

herself—which didn't explain why her heart was knocking around so wildly in her chest as she watched him slide the retrieved key into the lock. They stepped inside, and immediately she marched up to the beat-up television and began to babble.

"Okay, here's the thing; you have to turn it on with these pliers because the knob fell off somewhere and it's a little tricky. My mother says someone will electrocute himself, but so far so good. And then you wait until you get this black-and-white snow on the screen—the color comes later—and then you hit it on the side, not too high, though, or the picture just disappears, just hit it down here, like this, and, oh, shit, it's not working, okay, then you have whack it a little harder," she said, giving it a sound and desperate thump. "There! See how eas—?"

She turned around straight into his arms, and he kissed her full on the lips in a way that left her reeling. She hadn't been expecting it—or, rather, she had, which made it all the more surprising—and the sound that came from deep in her throat was one part pleasure, nine parts thrill. She returned the kiss with a passion that equalled his own, and all the while, a single triumphant refrain was scrolling through her mind:

No troopers!
No troopers!
No troopers!

This was between him and her and the barn, and she was, oh, so ready for it to happen.

Sam held her fast.

You want it, you got it, he thought; *I'm here to oblige.* He drove his tongue deeper into her mouth, sucking the sweetness of it, wondering that a creature so fey could have a kiss so fiery. She was intoxicating, an assault on his senses, from the scent of her hair to the softly seductive contours of her breasts. The novel combination of innocence and willingness was irresistible; he kissed her hotly, hungrily, stunned by the depth of his desire for her.

A *femme fatale* she may not have been—but somehow or other Holly Anderson knew exactly how to drive a man crazy. Between kisses, he murmured her name just to thrill himself with the sound of her answering groans; he tipped her head back and sank his mouth in the soft flesh of her shoulder, dragging a hot trail of kisses across her neck, flicking his tongue across the top of her breasts, dragging away her tank top and bra to expose still more flesh, hear still more moans, making himself crazy and taking her along for the spin.

He pulled her against the hardness of him, signalling his readiness. *Is this what you want?* He burrowed into the curve of her shoulder. *Is this what you need? Just say the word, lady, and we'll go for a ride . . . oh, you are sweet . . . sweet Jesus, you taste good*, he thought, reducing her to whimpers that made him wild to have her.

She was so willing, so pliant, so downright *avid*, that he found himself reaching down to the zipper of her shorts and giving it a yank.

"Is this a good idea?" he said on a groan. "Is it?"

"Oh . . . yes . . . absolutely," she said between gasps, dropping the words like cookies before him. "Good . . . great . . . idea . . ."

But Sam was, in fact, talking to himself, addressing the thickheaded moron who seemed fixated on the tricky buttonhole above her zipper.

What the hell was he *doing*?

Seducing the daughter of the man who had taken his wife, that's what. With a wrenching, shuddering effort he made his hands lift up from her hips and onto her shoulders, which he used to brace himself away from her.

"Not a good idea," he said shakily, holding her at arm's length.

"*Why?*"

There was nothing shaky about her protest, that was for sure; she looked like a kid who's just been told there'll be no trip to Disney World this year.

"Y'know, it's just not the best thing. Maybe if we'd met some other way . . . but . . . y'know: Eden. We're coming at this from two different directions . . ."

That craven, roundabout mention of Eden's name was the best that Sam could do. He despised himself for not making a full and abject confession on the spot:

When she left me, I thought I'd die. Worse, I thought she was pregnant. I swear to God: she told me she was sure she was pregnant, and for years and years I wondered if she was hauling my kid around with her, maybe in a shopping cart up and down the streets somewhere as she worked her cons with sometimes more and sometimes less success. That's why I didn't divorce her. But that was before I knew about the visits to my parents, the loans, the engraving. Now I'm sure . . . pretty sure . . . very sure: there is no kid. There never was. But try to convince me back then.

Unless maybe, just maybe, there's a seven-year-old child with her mother's sweet cunning and her father's bitter fatalism, hanging on a street corner in New Bedford or sitting out her life in foster care.

"Sam? Sam—what's wrong with you?" Holly asked. "Your face is white."

She was breathing heavily and was in some pain. He knew before she did that he was digging his fingers into her flesh enough to make her hurt.

"Ah, Jesus! This is *not* a good idea."

"But why?"

"Why, why, who cares why! It's just not." He let go

of her as if her shoulders were hot coals, and she took it as the spurning it was.

"You know what?" she said in a voice thick with hurt. "You're right. This is probably the worst idea I ever had. This is probably right up there with bungee jumping off a bridge in the fog, only with a rubber band instead of a bungee cord."

He sighed and said, "Look . . . Holly . . . I'm sorry. I can't say more than that. I wish I could, but I can't. Maybe someday—"

"Oh, please, *again*?" she said, cutting off his excuse at the knees. "Spare me your maybe-someday speech!"

Sighing, he reached into his pocket to retrieve the much-traded key and held it out to her. "I assume you want me to go?"

"To hell, mister! The faster, the better!"

Sam sat on the edge of the bed, wondering whether to leave or to stay. The honorable thing would be to leave. He was messing with her head by sticking around. But either for effect or by design, Holly had spun on her heel and marched out of the loft without actually taking his key.

There were several reasons to stay. One, Sam had no desire to spend another night in the car. Two, he needed a base of operations. Three, he felt more than ever that Holly might be in some danger. And, of course, four, he still could taste the sweetness of her kiss.

Four to one. Honor lost.

If Holly wants me out of here, she's going to have to pick me up bodily and throw me down the stairs. He smiled at the very idea. She was so obviously the non-violent type.

Weary now of his endless pursuit of Eden, and dampened by a sheen of oppressive sadness, Sam headed for the shower. Maybe a meal and a beer would restore his equilibrium before his next move, which was bound to be awkward and might even be brutal: an attempt at a tête-à-tête with Holly's father.

He showered, he shaved, he couldn't shake the sadness. Triggered by the stinging exchange with Holly, his thoughts seemed determined to seek new and wider avenues of pain. What if Eden *were* dead . . . and what if she *had* given birth to their child? Sam would never know, then, who or where the child was. He would never know if the child had caught a lucky break, a Millie Steadman somewhere, or if his son, his daughter—*his* child!—was being shuffled without hope from one foster home to another.

His child.

And Eden was the mother of his maybe-child: Eden, in whom he had spilled his seed with high hopes and infinite joy. Eden, the maybe-mother of his maybe-child. His heart ached over the whole misbegotten mess.

For years he'd wondered, and followed up leads, and made inquiries about her. As recently as eighteen months ago, he'd thrown an unexpected windfall at yet another private investigator who ran into yet another brick wall. It seemed inconceivable that he, they, *everyone* had completely missed the fact of Eden's visits to the Steadmans—but then, the Steadmans had never had any reason to divulge her visits. Sam had never told them about Eden's apparent pregnancy, so how could they know? Maybe if he hadn't been such a tight-lipped bundle of wounded pride . . .

Missed opportunities: they lay strewn around him like casualties of war.

He gnawed on the distant past and chewed on recent events until evening, when on an impulse he drove out to the west side of the island to watch the sun go down. He felt restless and weary, angry and tender, all at the same time. His emotions were ripping him apart; he needed desperately to center himself.

He hiked out to a bluff in Chilmark and dropped onto a patch of sand in the grassy dunes, carefully choosing his seat from, oh, a thousand perfect perches for the show. The sun was low and blazing, an immortal diva who knew her own worth. Sam plucked a strand of dune grass and wrapped it around itself, forming a ring, he didn't know why.

Tiny green ring; big red sun. It was all the same, really. You went round and round in circles, and every time, you ended up at the same old spot: wondering why, exactly, you were plunked down on earth.

He slipped the grass ring onto his left ring finger, then felt uncomfortable. Wrong vibes, somehow. He pulled the ring apart and stuck it in his mouth to chew on as he pondered the ocean vista before him.

The diva sun was ready to take her bow for the night. Throwing her arms wide in a last dazzle of pink and blue and gold, expecting—demanding—the applause of the world, she blew everyone a last, heartbreaking kiss and then dipped below the deep blue sea, trailing true clouds of glory behind her.

And an awestruck Sam understood, if only briefly, at least one good reason for having been plunked down on earth.

19

When Sam returned home, he saw lights in the studio behind the rolled-shut barn doors: Holly was working late.

Sam had every intention of proceeding up the stairs and to the loft, but his feet had other ideas. He found himself planted in front of the barn door and knocking on it, although he didn't have a clue what he'd say when Holly came to open it.

Through the small square window he saw her look up, recognize him, frown, and go back to her work.

Huh. That didn't sit too well with him. Granted, a cold shoulder from Holly would be the best thing for all concerned, but . . . huh.

He knocked again, louder.

She didn't even bother acknowledging him, but bent over her birdhouse with more purpose than before.

He knocked a third time, pleading with her gently to let him in.

"Holly, goddammit, will you open the goddamn *door*?"

She rolled her eyes and muttered something he was pretty sure had four-letter words in it, but she did relent and unlock the door, sliding it open just enough to let him in.

He looked around at the friendly jumble of broken-down furniture, half-built birdhouses and clutter of old farm tools and wondered how someone like her had ever taken up a career like this. A degree in fine arts, which she'd told him she had, seemed totally irrelevant to the art of making whimsy.

No way was he going to say that out loud, however, so he smiled and said, "Burning the midnight oil, I see. Why don't you leave the door slid open? It's awfully warm in here, no?"

She shrugged and went back to her workbench. "It's the only way I know to keep out a skunk."

"Oh, hey, c'mon," he said, flushing. "Isn't that a little harsh?"

"The furry kind. There's a family living under the shed where I do my woodworking and welding, and one of the litter keeps wandering over here. She must remember the bags of birdseed that I used to store in the corner. I had to relocate all of it to my basement after I came in here one night and found eight babies rummaging through the open bags."

"They sound kind of cute."

"Unless you try to get close," she said, throwing him a dirty look. "Then they turn into *skunks*."

Oka-aay, it was official: he was not forgiven.

"I, ah, thought I'd ask how your mother was faring after her talk downtown." He had heard Holly's truck leave late in the afternoon and had assumed that she'd gone off to see Charlotte. "Is she all right?"

Holly was painting a picket fence on the outside walls of a pale blue birdhouse that was way too fancy ever to hang from a tree. Personally, Sam didn't see the point.

"Why should you care how my mother is?" Holly asked without looking up from her picket.

"I don't know. But I do."

"To paraphrase my father—it's none of your business," she answered, and Sam thought, yep, it was time to say g'night and back out smiling.

But instead he hunkered down and waited, and after an interval she said grudgingly, "As soon as my mother saw the tomatoes, she knew that I'd been to see the Bouchards. But since I hadn't said anything when I dropped the bag off, she assumed that my father wasn't staying there. It was a shock to her when I went back and told her he was."

"I can imagine."

Holly started to say something, then decided against it and went back to her birdhouse. Some of the pickets must have been dry; she was painting hollyhocks through and between them. Like the woman herself, the flowers were lively, straightforward, and unpretentious. They were also amazingly realistic; birds were going to love snacking on the beetles that tried to feed on Holly's hollyhocks.

Sam smiled at the notion; damned if she wasn't drawing him straight into her fantasy.

Which wouldn't be a bad place to be, all things considered. He watched, bemused, as Holly scrunched her brow in concentration and dabbed a rainbow of blossoms on the tall, spiky stems. It was picky work, no doubt about it; but she had a wonderful eye and an unerring hand. This was no mass-produced product, but a charming and original work of art. Suddenly Sam wanted to reach out and stroke her hair, just to connect with the creative process.

Or maybe . . . just to feel the shining strands between

his fingers. It was a maddening thought, when he was doing his best to put her behind him.

Sure you are, pal. Why don't you beat it, if that's the case?

I will. I will. Just . . . not yet.

He stood there transfixed, watching Holly make something from nothing, pictures from thoughts. It seemed much more profound a miracle than his merely sticking a camera in someone's face and pressing a button.

So entranced was he that when she finally did speak, it startled him.

"I've decided," she announced without looking up, "to search my father's boat. I'm just waiting for everyone to bed down for the night. That's why I'm working late."

Are you out of your mind, you crazy, nutty lady?

"Uh-h-h, do you think that's altogether wise?" he asked gingerly. "The same laws apply in the wee hours as they do in the afternoon."

"I don't care anymore. I know your engraving is still aboard the *Vixen* somewhere," she said, leafing here and there with her brush. "I've been thinking about it all day, and I even know where she's hidden it. All I have to do is step aboard the boat and retrieve it."

"I see. Well! You sound pretty confident."

Listen, missy, they won't be letting you take your paintbox to prison.

His smile was inanely upbeat. "On the other hand, we could always just let the authorities find the engraving for us, no? Because they get paid to do stuff like that."

"Obviously they haven't found it, or Chief Cottler would have told us."

"They didn't know they should be looking for it," he

argued. "By now, they may well have gone back and found it."

"And if so, do you assume they're going to just fork it over to you?"

Actually, Sam wasn't assuming anything of the kind. Just the opposite, in fact. His parents couldn't seem to find any documentation proving ownership. It's possible that there *was* no documentation, what with the odd terms of the will and all. He'd been uneasy all along about what would happen to the Durer if it were discovered aboard the boat.

He must have looked it, because she said, "See? You could end up getting really screwed."

That's the *only* way, then, he thought, noting the hostility in her eyes.

It was so at odds with her Joan-of-Arc plan. "I don't get it, Holly. Why stick your neck out to retrieve the engraving for me?"

She dumped a brush into soapy water and began swirling madly. "Simple. The sooner I find you your engraving, the sooner you're out of my—apartment."

"I see. Your apartment. If it's the money that's worrying you, I've written a check for a week in advance—high-season rate, of course." He slapped his hand on his back pocket. "Here, I'll—"

"That's not the *point*, Sam!" she cried, wagging the paint brush at him. "The point is, you go on and on about Eden flouting the law for her own evil ends. Maybe it's time someone flouted the law for the other side once in a while."

"Oh, for—is that what this is about? You want to out-Eden Eden?"

"I didn't say that."

"Sure you did." He grinned and said, "If that's not the dopiest—I'm sorry—the most enterprising plan I've ever heard, I don't know what is."

"Oh, stuff it, would you?" she said wearily. She began wiping her brush dry on a man's undershirt.

While Sam was wondering whose undershirt it was, she said, "I wouldn't have mentioned it at all, except that I don't want you doing anything stupid like sneaking aboard the boat yourself. They'd go harder on you than they would on me."

He laughed louder than he had in a good long while. "You honestly think I'm going to mess up a murder investigation?"

"There *is* no murder; you said so yourself."

"But there *is* an investigation."

She scanned him up and down with contempt and said, "Brother. Is there anyone worse than a reformed offender?"

"Yeah. A bad-girl wannabe."

She scowled. "I don't wannabe anything except free of you. Now will you *please* go? I have four more houses to paint."

And she probably got paid as much for them as men did for doing the people-sized ones. Why was he feeling sorry for her? Why was he feeling anxious, protective, lusty for her? He'd been right in the first place and in the second place: she was just another poor little rich girl.

He took his folded check from his back pocket and slapped it on a broken-down bureau. "Sweet dreams, darlin'," he said caustically, and he let himself out.

Ooh, ooh, four more birdhouses to paint. He snorted. Talk about high-class problems.

Upstairs, aware that she was downstairs, Sam had a hell of a time trying to fall asleep. God, what an irritant she was. Like a burr on his bedsheet, like a torn-back fingernail, she was all he could think about. He tossed and turned for what seemed like hours, mulling everything from the warmth of her breath to the charm of her hollyhocks. It was stupid; he'd got more sleep in the Corolla.

He heard her dragging some pieces of furniture across the floor, and his instinct was to run down and help her, not from a sense of chivalry, but just to get some peace. Then she became quiet again and it was even worse: was she there, or was she not?

He lit his watch: one-freaking-thirty. Where did she get her energy? He dragged himself out of bed and went to the east window to look out. Cool air washed over his bare body: a fog was rolling in. Below him, a rectangle of misty light cut past the mildewing lilac and spilled across the runaway ivy.

Still there. Still working. He shook his head and sighed. If he could, he'd go down there and snap every one of her brushes in two; anything to get her to leave the area.

He had a thought: maybe it was the fact that Eden had slept on the mattress beneath him that was making him so irritable and restless. He reached over for the pillow that had smelled like her that first day and dragged it across his face, inhaling deep. Yep. Eden, all right. He hurled the pillow across the room, knocking over a lamp in the process.

Hell!

Hotfooting gingerly across the floor, he straightened the lamp back up and waited for sounds of an irate landlady storming the stairs. But no; Holly didn't seem to care if he trashed the place or not. Grimly, he lay back down. He'd give it—give her—another half hour. If he wasn't asleep by then, it was back to Chez Toyota.

The threat of the car bed worked. In the next little while, Sam fell asleep. Dreams followed, none of them sweet. Boats going aground, boats being stove in, boats being knocked flat on their sides in squalls and sinking—

the theme was boats and the variation was disaster. The
engraving did not fare well in any of them. In the last
dream, the worst dream, Sam was trying to grab an inch-
thick line dangling from a Coast Guard helicopter so that
he could tie it around the engraving to airlift it from a
sinking *Vixen*.

The engraving did not fare well.

Frustrated, Sam woke himself up and then realized
that it wasn't a helicopter he had been hearing in his
dreams, it was the rotting muffler of Holly's truck.

He looked at his watch—three A.M.—and jumped out
of bed, scrambling for his clothes. The little vixen was
headed for the *Vixen*! He couldn't believe it. He thought
he'd succeeded in embarrassing her out of her wild plan.

He got out of the loft as if it were a burning building
and made a dash for the Corolla through a blanket of
fog that had turned London-thick. Just what she needed:
help from above. There was no sign of Holly's taillights
ahead, but Sam had no doubt where she was bound. The
only question was, how many bunny rabbits scampering
through the fog was he going to run over in his mad
pursuit? He couldn't see a damned thing.

He rolled down the windows for better visibility and
wiped the inside of his windshield with the palm of his
hand, to no avail. It was the kind of night where bad
things happened to good people, and good people went
out and did very bad things.

And yet: if Holly wanted to go aboard her father's
boat, who was Sam to say that she couldn't?

*Why am I bothering? Why not let the little witch do
what she wants?*

Because I don't want her doing it for me.

It all came down to guilt. Sam couldn't stand the
thought of any more of it. It was bad enough that he—
bunny rabbit! He swerved, catching some branches in
his open window and carrying them along for the ride.

It was bad enough that he felt responsible for having put
a skilled con artist in close proximity with the most kind
and trusting couple he knew. But if Holly were arrested
trying to rescue his parents' nest egg, if she were to
suffer fresh hurt and humiliation because of Sam's once
and technically still-current wife—if she were to suffer
the least little smidgen of pain because, in any way, of
Sam . . .

It all came down to guilt.

If I catch up to her, I may just kill her.

He couldn't stand the thought of any more guilt.

He slowed down past the police station, dropped onto
Water Street, and then bore left, pulling off almost immediately at the marina where the *Vixen* lay roped off
from the ordinary world.

Although probably not for long. Sam spotted Holly's
truck and pulled in behind it, effectively blocking her
escape. *Gotcha!* was the single thought that formed in
his brain—but then, it was three A.M. and he wasn't
capable of much more than simple concepts.

He kicked off his deck shoes and left them in the car;
no point in announcing his approach during the long
walk down the length of the dock. In the soupy fog he
could barely see three slips ahead of him as he padded
barefoot over splintery dockboards toward the *Vixen*.
The good news was that there was no dock master
around. The bad news was that Joan of Arc was riding
high.

A distant foghorn *hooooed* ominously, setting the
tone for Sam's mission. His mission was . . . what? To
get Holly out of the boat and back to her house. He was
going to do that . . . how? At the moment, no clue; he
was going to have to show up at the scene and see what
developed.

He paused just before reaching the taped-off sloop.
The dropboards were out and lying on a cockpit seat.

Through the open companionway he could see that the cabin below was dark. Standing in the mist-filled air, damp and chilled in his tee shirt and khakis, he waited for some indication of where she might be. A siren added its forlorn wail to the ominous brooding of the foghorn: be warned . . . be warned.

Down below, Sam saw a small beam of light arcing across the overhead in the main cabin, pinpointing Holly's position. Her back was to the companionway as she scanned a collection of rolled-up charts in an overhead rack, then pulled one out. Ah. Charts. Not a bad place to roll up an engraving—if it were a contemporary piece. But one that was several hundred years old? Hard to believe that it wouldn't crack or crumble.

He took advantage of Holly's preoccupied state to climb aboard the yacht. Stepping down slowly into the cockpit, praying that the teak grate wouldn't knock against the fiberglass sole beneath it, he went forward to the bridge deck, all without her being aware of him. God, she was immersed. No wonder she was so good at her art.

She was in the process of rolling the chart up before slipping it back into the overhead rack when Sam made his move. He dropped down into the pitch-dark cabin and slapped one hand over her mouth before she could scream. During the act he felt her body go rigid with terror in his arms, and the sensation sickened him.

"Shh! Not a sound," he whispered in her ear. "I cannot believe that you're this big a fool. Not a word!" he repeated. "All right . . . I'm going to let go now. *Don't* scream."

Gingerly he took his hand away from her mouth, trusting that she wouldn't put them both in jeopardy.

She turned and kicked him viciously in the shin.

"OW!"

"What're you doing, scaring me half to death like that?" she said in a low hiss.

"This—*this*—is dumber than bungee jumping," he shot back in his own furious hiss.

"So why are *you* here, then?" she whispered.

"Because I don't want you doing an end run around me!"

"Fine. You can look through half the charts; there are twice as many as I remembered."

"You're nuts, you know that?" he muttered in her ear. "What makes you think the cops haven't been through these?"

"They might have been," she admitted as she slid a chart back into the overhead rack, "if they were in fact looking for the engraving. But maybe that's on tomorrow's docket. State police investigators like to go home for supper, too, you know."

She took down the next chart. "Here," she said, slapping him across the chest with it. "Make yourself useful."

So this, apparently, had been Sam's plan: to report to Holly Anderson for lawbreaking duty on the sailing yacht *Vixen* at 0300.

If Millie Steadman could see him now.

He shook his head, wondering how he had managed to get snagged on Holly's spur as she rode hell-bent for perdition, dragging him blithely behind her. "Okay, just . . . fine. Let's get this over with."

He took down a chart and tried to unroll it in the dark—*she* had the flashlight—but his elbow ended up in her breast.

"Hey, watch it!" she hissed.

"You're in my way."

"You're in *my* way!"

"Oh, for God's sake!" Sam snapped. "We need a system. I'll take them down and unroll them; you roll them back up and rack them."

"No, *I'll* unroll them. I want the satisfaction of discovering your precious Durer myself."

Unbelievable. How had he ever considered her either naive or vulnerable? She was a witch! An overconfident, uncontrollable, irrepressible, just-plain-ornery *witch*.

He let her have her way.

They fell into a fairly smooth rhythm of unroll, check, roll and rack. Sam was close enough to catch a whiff of her fragrance, despite the lingering smell of resin from the fiberglass repairs that had been done to the boat. Occasionally their arms brushed. He tried not to notice.

Toward the end, Sam—who had not been able to make himself believe that the engraving was hidden there—began actually to feel sorry for Holly. She was so sure.

He murmured, "Wouldn't there be a risk of your father finding it when he took out a chart to navigate?"

"Not really," said Holly as she pulled down the next-to-last chart. "If they were sailing to Maine, she'd be fairly safe hiding it, say, in a Long Island chart." She added, "There'd be *some* risk, naturally."

"Which doesn't sound like Eden."

"Oh? Did you know her that well?"

Whups, walked right into that one. "I meant, considering how much the engraving is worth."

"In any case, it would hardly matter if my father *had* discovered the theft," Holly said glumly. "He told me he would have been willing to cover its value."

Sam did a double take. "You didn't tell me that."

"No, I suppose I didn't. Well, this is the last one." She took the chart down and unrolled it. Nothing. Her sigh was a feathery whisper of disappointment.

"Okay, that's it. Let's go." Sam was suddenly sick of

the whole escapade. "Once we step onto the dock, we'll be home free."

Meanwhile, of course, he was thinking that his bare feet were leaving much better traces on the boat than any measly old fingerprints could do.

"One more minute. The engraving is on this boat, Sam, I know it. Let's look under all the seat cushions."

"*What*?"

"Shhh!"

"Are you *crazy*?" he whispered. "Eden wouldn't put it somewhere so obvious."

"We have to make sure. If she died suddenly, she had to have left it somewhere on the boat."

"*She's not dead.* Either she's already fenced it—"

"She did not fence it! She stayed with the boat all the way back from New Hampshire. That means it's still here."

Through gritted teeth he muttered, "She has it with her, then, wherever she's gone!"

"I don't think so."

Ignoring him, Holly began lifting every cushion on the boat, from the long settees to the little triangular filler-piece in the forward cabin. Every damned cushion was held in place with Velcro; the sound of the strips being separated from one another roared in Sam's ears, more irritating than a hundred fingernails across a chalkboard.

Holly was focused on their discovering the engraving; Sam was focused on someone discovering them. Undoubtedly that explained why he and not she was able to hear footsteps approaching on the dock. In two strides Sam was alongside her, shushing her and urging her gently down to the cabin sole with a hand to her shoulder.

She dropped low on the spot and they crouched together, waiting for the footsteps and low voices to continue past.

A couple of sport fishermen out before dawn? Sam waited, feeling vaguely ignominious squatting in the dark. If it weren't for the fact that Holly·was thigh-to-thigh with him . . . if it weren't for the fact that he could feel her warm breath on his hand as he held her softly in check . . . if it weren't for the fact that his tired body was springing in predictable ways back to life . . .

Don't do this, he thought as he brought his hand up to her cheek and gently turned her face toward his.

Get a grip, Steadman, he warned as he angled his head and brought his mouth over hers.

This is not the time, the place, the woman, he argued as he let his tongue glide over hers, savoring the sensational sweetness he found there.

His objections skipped across his consciousness like pebbles on a pond, and then they sank without a trace. He gave himself up completely to the blissful joy of the moment, perfectly willing for it never to end. He wanted nothing more, demanded nothing less out of life than that particular kiss, in that particular harbor.

And yet end it must.

With a wrenching effort, he broke off the kiss. He tipped his forehead into hers and murmured softly, "That never happened."

"Yes it did," she whispered.

"No, Holly. It can't happen."

"Yes it can. Watch," she said, dropping the rest of the way to her knees and kissing him with a tenderness that rocked him.

She sat back on her heels and said, "See how easy?"

Strange as it seemed—considering the circumstances—it was much more agonizing for Sam to keep her at arm's length than it had been in the loft. In the loft the issue had seemed so simple: animal desire. Despite the surge of it that Sam had felt, he was a man who knew how to control his basic instincts. It hadn't been easy, it had taken hellish discipline, but he had succeeded. In the loft.

But this . . . ah, this. *This* feeling scared the bejesus out of him.

The sound of a powerboat's engines revving up nearby was the wake-up call that Sam desperately needed. He held Holly firmly by the shoulders and whispered, "Okay . . . they're leaving. I suggest we wait until the boat pulls out and then you and I . . . we . . . ah . . ."

She was tracing the outline of his face in the dark, skimming her fingertips lightly around the shape of his mouth. In his life, Sam had never had a woman touch him that way. It was the touch of an artist, the touch of an angel. The touch of a lover.

With excruciating reluctance, he caught her wrists and held them. "Holly . . . don't," he said, practically groaning the words. "You don't know me . . ."

Her laugh was achingly rueful as she whispered, "One thing I've learned recently: no one knows anyone, when you come right down to it. But . . . I'm more than willing to take a chance."

Though he still held her by her wrists, he saw in the dark that she had opened her hands palms up, in a signal as endearing as it surely was candid.

Please, let's be lovers. That was her plea.

He sighed. "Ah, love . . ."

In the distance he heard the moan of the foghorn: *be warned . . . be warned.*

Was he headed straight for the rocks? Very possibly. But somehow he didn't care anymore. Her song was far more compelling than any Siren's, an irresistible coupling of innocence with ecstasy. He was suddenly desperate to hear it at closer range.

"Holly . . . sweet, unheeding Holly . . ."

Lost in her allure, he released her wrists, then caught the hem of her top in his hands, lifting it up and over her head and tossing it aside. Her shudder of acquiescence thrilled him to the marrow: she truly did want to be his.

Humbled as much as he was emboldened, he lowered his head to her bare breast, sucking and nipping gently, revelling in the sweetness of her surprised gasps, driving them up to the level of moans.

Not enough. He wanted her to beg for more, to cry out his name. He pulled her to her feet and pounded her with kisses, aware that it was madness, aware that they might be caught in a spectacularly compromising position. They could go to jail. Did he care?

Not enough. He groped at her zipper, then—grateful for a looser buttonhole this time—undid the fastener of her jeans. "Here . . . on this berth," he said, easing her onto her back.

Madness.

She said, "I'm not forcing you, am I?" and he laughed out loud, sending her into a fit of answering giggles. Laughing, kissing, hushing one another, they hurried through their disrobing and lay down side by side on the narrow berth. No room for acrobatic loveplay here: Sam relished her breasts, small and firm and cool, up against his chest, but she had to put up with his rock-solid hard-on jamming her stomach. He repositioned himself so that his parts would lay against her parts in the right places, murmuring giddy endearments the whole time to this most endeared of all God's creatures.

She was a delight, hot and coy and easy and teasing at the same time, stroking him lightly, teasing with her tongue, still giggling between kisses, her giggles dissolving into deep, labored moans as he began to work his fingers against the warm, wet flesh at her entry.

Sam had never enjoyed seeing enjoyment so much in

his life. She was bliss to make love to—uninhibited without being histrionic, deeply emotional without being theatrical. The artist in her made everything intense, and the innocent in her made it even more so.

He was in awe of her.

"Come in me now before I die," she murmured in his ear, flicking her tongue in and out of it in prelude.

"Oh, sweetheart—oh, yes," he said, swinging a leg over hers and positioning himself to come in. "I thought you'd never ask."

Another burst of giggles, joyous and giddy and—on the *Vixen*—outrageously dangerous.

"Shh, shh," he begged her. "Sweet, goofy darling . . . *concentrate*."

"Aye, aye, sir," she whispered, and somehow the phrase made her go suddenly all quiet.

She sighed and took a deep breath, and when he slid into her, her moan of pure pleasure took his own breath away. Sam's senses were acutely heightened, and he heard everything around him: the siren at the end of the breakwater, the horn at West Chop, the low gurgle of an outboard as some skiff picked its way through the fog. He heard it all, but what he would remember for the rest of his life, what he would carry in his heart around the world, was the soul-satisfying sound of that moan.

He began a slow move to ecstasy, back and then forward at a controlled pace, straining at the reins of his self-imposed discipline, even as he savored the whimper of her ragged breathing. Her body arched underneath his as she dug her heels into the narrow berth, creating a deeper entry. The sound of his flesh slapping against hers as he stepped up the rhythm made his head spin, impelling him into an ever faster, deeper rush to fulfillment.

Making love to her on her father's impounded boat

was surely the most foolish thing that Sam had ever done, but if they came after him with handcuffs swinging just then, it wouldn't have made any difference: he wanted this woman at this moment in a way he'd never wanted anyone before.

Not even Eden.

He increased the pace to a furious pump, slamming the breath out of her in staccato grunts as she kept pace with him thrust for thrust. Everything about her whipped him on as they raced in tandem to the finish. His mind reeled, his ears rang; he began to see bright colors flashing before his closed eyes.

And then, because he was being so willful, taking Holly on a berth in the *Vixen*; because he was thinking of her and not, for once, of himself; because he didn't want her to dwell for one split second on the possibility of having to make a wrenching choice if this should be her fertile time—because of all those things, and because he cared for her in ways that he couldn't begin to understand: he pulled out of her, a single heartbeat before he came.

"*No-o-o*," Holly cried, and at the exact moment that Sam withdrew from her with a wrenching groan, she felt herself go over the edge in a climax so dizzying that she blacked out, if only for the briefest of eternities.

They lay together in exhausted silence for another, longer eternity, until Holly took a deep, deep breath, letting it out in moan of satisfaction. If they were in a hut in Tonga, she couldn't have felt more spent.

"That was . . . unbelievable," she whispered.

"I'm having a hard time believing it myself," Sam said. He did sound stunned.

"But . . . I wish you hadn't pulled out."

She felt him nod agreement against her. "I didn't

know if you were protected," he said. "We were a little spur of the moment."

"I'm not on the pill," she admitted. There hadn't been much need; her sex life had been depressingly low-key lately.

"Holly, I'm—"

"You're not sorry, are you?" she said quickly. Somehow he sounded as if he was going to be sorry.

He nuzzled the curve of her neck and dropped a light kiss on her damp skin. "I should be, God knows. But right now . . . Holly, right now, the only place on earth I want to be is in your arms."

And if she had her way, he was going to stay there the rest of their lives.

They lay there for a dangerously long time, and then Sam said, "Much as I hate to say it, I don't think we should compound our folly by hanging around."

He smiled at his choice of word. Folly? A folly was a pretty little structure in someone's backyard. What Sam had just indulged in was pure and indulgent madness.

Holly groped around in the dark and came up with some paper towels, which Sam used to wipe up the puddle he'd left on the berth of the *Vixen*. Part of him—the old, ironic, cynical part—thought, *Is this symbolic or what*? But the bigger part, the newly joyful part, stuffed the paper towels in his hip pocket and said to Holly with a grin, "Let's get the hell out of here."

In absurdly comical silence they tiptoed out of the cabin, slid the dropboards back in place, locked the padlock to which Holly had a key—big oversight on someone's part—and stepped off the boat onto the dock. Joyous or not, Sam breathed a sigh of relief; at least they wouldn't be nabbed *en flagrante*.

Holly was ready to make a mad dash, but he pulled

her back and caught her in his arms for a long, delicious kiss.

"Let's go home," he said after he released her.

"Oh, God, yes," she said, sounding tired and happy. She looked up with a shyly wicked smile. "My diaphragm's there."

They began retracing their steps down the long, still-deserted dock. Sam looked out to the east and was convinced that he saw dawn nudging its way through the fog; they had been aboard the *Vixen* for what had seemed like hours. He lit his watch and was amazed to see that it was only three forty-seven.

Morning light would be a long time coming.

20

For the first time in many days, Holly slept without dreaming.

When she woke up, it was in Sam's embrace and to the profoundly satisfying sound of his gentle snoring. She opened her eyes a little, just to be sure. Yes: this was the guy, all right. Straight nose; dark eyebrows and no-nonsense lashes; high-cut cheekbones, shadowed with a day's growth of beard; sandy brown hair, curling under his ears and still damp from their last lovemaking—all part and parcel of Samuel Steadman, the light of her life.

She touched her lips to his temple. "Sam. Are you up?"

"Mnuh-hh," he answered, burrowing more deeply into his pillow.

"Sam? You *are* up, aren't you?" she asked, shaking him gently by the shoulder.

"Mnnph."

"Because if you are—I wish we could make love again."

He opened one eye. "Izzat true?"

She smiled and reached for him under the covers. "I am, if you're up for it, which, after last night, you may not b—ahh, no problem," she said with a sly smile. She loved that he wanted her as much as she needed him.

"You're scaring me, woman," he said, rolling on his back. He pulled her toward him for a wake-up kiss and brought those dark brows down in a comical look of worry. "Is there such a thing as being hooked on fear?"

"Sure," she said, nibbling his upper lip. "Ask Stephen King." She sighed with pleasure, convinced that Sam Steadman had the most perfect mouth, the most perfect everything, she'd ever kissed.

But still. "I've never been like this with anyone before," she felt obliged again to explain. "I'm not exactly the island nymphomaniac; ask anyone. Honest. I don't know what's got into me."

His own laugh was low and still sleepy. "Me, for one thing—after that iffy start."

"Oh, I *know*." It was the one pang of regret she'd had about their wonderful night: that during their first time together, they hadn't climaxed together. At the same time, yes—but not together, him in her, the way it should have been.

She kissed him softly. "I don't want this ever to end, Sam," she confessed.

He smiled a game smile and said, "Okey-dokey; I'll see what I can do."

She loved his answer, loved everything about him. Loved him. But she was impatient, and she wanted more.

Averting her gaze from his, she said, "There's something I should tell you, Sam. It's not the easiest thing for me to say. You may not want to hear it. But I have to get it off my chest; it's killing me not to have you know."

He murmured a surprised kind of *hmp* and cleared his throat. "Funny; I have something I need to tell you, too."

She began tracing an embroidered rose on the hem of his pillowcase. "Let me go first," she said, still not daring to look at him. "Sam, I . . . I love you. I was going to hedge and say that I was just falling in love with you, but it wouldn't be true. Isn't it obvious?" she asked with a tiny shrug at the roses. "I love you. You know how when some of us meet the right one, we know it right off the bat? I'm one of those."

Her confession was at an end. She exhaled loudly and looked at him to discover: an entirely new expression on his face. She had been expecting to see surprise, maybe wariness, hopefully delight. If God were in His heaven, he would have looked thunderstruck and said, "Oh, my darling, you *too*? I feel that way exactly."

The one thing she had not expected to see in Sam's face was agony. Fear, caution, even horror would make some kind of sense. But agony?

Confused and deeply embarrassed, she began to lift herself up. Suddenly it seemed not that right to be naked in bed with him. "See? Told you you weren't going to like it."

"Oh, God, Holly, that's not it. How can you think that?"

He wrapped his arms around her and drew her down across his chest, cradling his hand around the back of her head, kissing her hair softly between whispers of endearments.

"Understand this," he said. "The last few hours with you have been . . . beyond bliss."

That's all that she wanted to hear. "*I* thought so," she murmured contentedly.

"If someone had told me when I arrived on this island that I'd soon be flipping over a fey socialite who was more comfortable with a table saw than I was, and who hung rusty farm tools on her living room walls as art—I would have laughed and asked him what he'd been smoking."

"But you're an artist, too," she argued, instinctively looking for common ground between them both. "We have careers in common, at least."

"I'm just a photojournalist," he said, dismissing the comparison. "And anyway, it's more than that. Our backgrounds, our lifestyles, are completely different. But here's the real kicker, Holly: you don't know a thing about me."

She shook her head. "Not so. I know what's important. I know that you were adopted by two wonderful people who still care about you. I know you love them very much, or you wouldn't have come here in the first place. What more do I need to know than that?"

"Well—one or two things," he said, sounding much too grave.

She didn't want to hear him sounding much too grave. That's how fathers sounded who took off with very young women.

Determined to counter his tone, she said lightly, "Tell me this, Sam: are there any outstanding warrants for your arrest?"

He smiled and said, "Not any more."

"Are you a compulsive drinker, gambler, womanizer?"

"No. No. And you've just ended a pretty long dry spell."

"Any social diseases I should know about?"

"None."

"There you go, then," she said, nervously twisting a couple of hairs on his chest. "I'm giving you a clean bill of health, physically and morally."

. His laugh was soft and low and sad. "It's the latter one that's hanging me up."

She began untwisting the hairs before they hurt him too much. "Oh? Are you a reprobate?"

"Define reprobate."

"*Sam.* If you have something to tell me, then just . . . tell me," she said, reversing herself. It was a measure of how deeply she had fallen in love with him that she found uncertainty more unbearable than possible bad news.

Their gazes met. "It's about Eden," he said.

"Eden? What can Eden have to do with you and me?" she asked, baffled.

"It's a pretty long story. The telling's overdue."

Holly never heard the knock on the kitchen door downstairs. It was only when Sam jerked his head toward the bedroom door that she realized she had a visitor pounding.

Sam scowled and said, "Hell! Can't we just ignore that?"

"Of course we can, and we will. It's too early for— oh my God! What day is it? Say it's not Friday."

"Okay. It's not Friday."

"It *is* Friday! That's my *mother* down there!" she said, scrambling for the clothes that were strewn around the room. She grabbed the first thing handy, Sam's tee shirt, and pulled it over her bare breasts. "We're supposed to meet Ivy and the kids at the ferry dock in five minutes. How could I have forgotten about that?"

"Do *you* have to be there to meet them?" Sam asked, plainly preferring that she didn't. "We were in the middle—"

"Of course I do! It's a yearly ritual, our month by the sea together. She's my *sister*. And this year the month is only two weeks!"

She thrust one leg through her shorts and began hopping to the bedroom door. "Coming, coming!" she yelled into the hall and down the stairs. After dropping one shoe, she dropped its mate, then picked them both up, knocking her head against the eave in her hurry. She swore, then started down the hall before reversing herself and running back into the bedroom. "Shh—not a word," she said, holding a finger to her lips. "I'll see you tonight. Thank God you're renting the apartment; we have an excuse for your car."

Sam was standing naked as a jaybird at the foot of the bed. She scooped up his khakis and tossed them his way. He caught them and said, "You're not planning to tell her we've been together?"

Holly sucked in her breath. "I can't be happy when she's so unhappy. How would that look? Shh! Stay right here. *Coming*," she shouted down the stairs.

Raking her fingers through her hair, she ran down the steps and then opened the door to her mother, the essence of summer in a floral shift and a big straw hat.

"Holly, for pity's sake, we're late already, and look at you. What have you been you doing all morning?"

"Oh, you know. A little of this. A little of that," Holly said as she glanced around for her bag.

"You're not wearing *those*," her mother said, staring at Holly's navy-blue shorts. "Have you been painting? You've got some kind of stain on them," she said, giving the shorts a tentative swipe.

Holly looked down at the cloudy-white stain there. Sperm! Oh no! She jumped out of mothering range. "I'll change! Start the car!"

"It's started. Will you hurry up? Cissy and Sally will be crushed if we're not there to greet them."

"The boat'll be late—fog," Holly yelled over her shoulder as she dashed back up the stairs.

"Where are your eyes? The fog is nearly burned off."

"*I* know that," said Holly, but it could have been raining artichokes; she wouldn't have had a clue.

"And put a nicer top on!" her mother yelled from the foot of the stairs.

By now Sam was dressed and leaning against the deep sill of the gabled window that overlooked the drive, waiting dutifully for them to leave.

Bug-eyed, Holly pointed melodramatically to the stain on her shorts. "Next time—khakis!" she whispered, and burst into nervous laughter that she immediately squelched by slapping her hand over her mouth. Too many jolts; she was becoming unhinged by them.

Off went the shorts for the third time in twelve hours. Holly grabbed another pair out of the drawer, yanked them over her tanned legs, switched tops, and grabbed a tube of lipstick from a crystal bowl on the dressertop. One last sprint across the room for a quick kiss from a bemused Sam, and she was bouncing down the stairs again, dabbing lipstick blindly as she went.

In the car, she and her mother talked of preparations for Ivy's arrival, which her mother clearly was dreading. Everyone knew that the absence of Grampa would hit the children hard. Cissy and Sally had been told that their grandfather had an important case in Providence, but that maybe later in the month he'd be able to come to the Vineyard. If there was wishful thinking involved in the lie, it was that the children would be having so much fun that they wouldn't miss him as the days wore on.

Her mother suddenly asked, "Why was Sam's car parked in front of your house and not at the barn?"

"Oh, that. He's filling in some of the potholes around the studio, and his car was in the way," Holly said easily. *Liar,* liar, pants on fire, went through her mind.

True on both counts.

"What a nice thing to do," said Holly's mother.

"He's very good with his hands."

"But . . . do you really think it's a good idea, having him stay in the loft?" her mother ventured. "I mean, I know you have feelings for him—but he's probably too fixated on this Eden business to reciprocate them right now. I just wouldn't want you to get hurt, honey," she added with a worried glance. "You've been—we've all been—so emotional."

"I suppose, but personally, I'm getting past all that," Holly said ambiguously. "It's time to move on." *Liar, liar, pants on fire.*

Still true. Both counts.

"So he seemed wretched?" her mother asked.

"Yeah, just all of a sudd—oh, you mean Dad. Oh, yes. Dad was flat-out miserable."

"Well—good. Maybe the fever is running its course."

Holly had made a tactical error the day before by telling her mother how terrible her father looked from the ordeal. She had done it to make her mother feel better, but she'd omitted one little detail: that Eric Anderson's misery was because he thought Eden might be dead.

"Look, Mom, we're not too late," she said to distract her. "People are just getting off the boat."

Charlotte Anderson took one glance at the ferry and her face was immediately transformed. Gone was the weariness, gone was the dread: in their place was a radiant, heartening, grandmother's grin.

"Oh, they're here, they really are here! I can't believe it; at *last*—something happy."

"Quick, let's ditch the car," Holly said, hanging out the passenger window and waving wildly. "I think I see the girls on the upper deck. Yep, that's them; they've spotted the angel whirligig. Look at Cissy, swinging her arms like one; what a little devil she is!"

They parked the Volvo and ran it to the foot of the

gangway in time to open their arms in welcome. Cissy, a seven-year-old with her father's charm and fiery red hair, hurled herself at Holly like an Irish setter, nearly knocking her down. Sally, her pretty blond sister, was far too conscious of her French braids, double-pierced ears and decorated fingernails to indulge in such a gauche display in public.

"Oh, my goodness, how you two have grown! How old are you now, Sally? I thought you were nine."

"I *am* nine, Gram."

"Going on fourteen," Ivy muttered in Holly's ear as they hugged. "She's driving me crazy. You don't know how much I need this vacation."

"And look at *you*, Cissy," said her grandmother. "You're so tall! You're catching up to your sister."

Cissy lifted her nose in triumph. "I know I am. I already can run faster and even if my bike isn't as big, I can still beat her."

"Because you cheated, that's why. You said count to three, but you went after *two*."

"Did not."

"Did too."

"Did not."

"Oh, stop; *stop*—or there'll be no beach this afternoon. There's the car; go put my carryall in it," said Ivy.

"I'll do it, Mom!"

"No, *I'll* do it; I'm older."

"Mom, I asked first!"

"Here, Cissy," said their grandmother, whipping off her wide-brimmed hat to distract her. "It's too breezy for this, anyway. Put it in the car for me, would you?"

"Can I try it on?"

"Nuh-uh, you can't, Cissy. It's too big for you and you'd look foolish. Wouldn't she, Aunty Holly?"

"It's not too big, Gram. See?" said Cissy, jamming it

over her head. "It's like being under your beach umbrella."

"You can't *wear* that, Cissy," said an outraged Sally. "Mom, tell her she can't."

"Can too."

"Mom! She always wants to do everything!"

"Oh, good grief . . . give me the hat. Get in the car, both of you, and not another word. You're going to give Gram a headache before you've been on the island five minutes. *Go.*"

Ivy turned to her sister and her mother and said, "This is how it's been, all the way from California. I was ready to open the emergency hatch and shove them out of the plane."

The girls shouldered and nudged one another for a few steps and then burst into a race for the car, and it was true: Cissy *was* faster. She turned to the three women she loved best in the world and pounded her chest in triumph. Sally got in the wagon ahead of her and claimed the seat behind the driver, undoubtedly because it had access to the rearview mirror.

"They'll settle down," Holly said to her sister. "They're just excited, that's all."

Her mother smiled and said, "You know who they remind me of, don't you? You two. Holly was forever trying to beat you at something, and you were forever not letting her."

"Ivy beat me at marriage," said Holly, though she hoped to catch up there, too, before long.

"I *had* to get married," her sister said wryly.

"Not your fault; that was genetic," Holly teased, nudging her mother. "Like mother, like daughter."

"Will you hush," said Charlotte, reddening. "You're both so loud."

"Sorry, Mother," said Holly, linking her arm through Ivy's. "We'll be good."

An hour later Holly and Ivy were sitting in wet bathing suits on the big, raggedy pink blanket that Charlotte kept in a wicker trunk just for trips to the beach. The blanket was worn around the edges now, just like the Anderson family, but it was soft and familiar and almost unbearably comforting. Holly and Ivy had napped on it under a beach umbrella when they were babies, and so had Cissy and Sally. During an outing, no one would think of plopping her fanny anywhere else but on that pink and precious heirloom.

Ivy stretched out on her back and let the sun do the work of a towel. "This just feels great. The Pacific is still as cold as a witch's tit. Three cheers for New England."

Holly nodded toward their mother, shelling with Cissy and Sally at the edge of the gently rolling surf. "Incidentally, I told Mom that I called you late last night, so she knows you know that Dad's staying at the Bouchards."

"Which reminds *me*: what were you doing up at two in the morning?"

"Oh, just . . . foolin' around," Holly said vaguely. "You know how restless I can get when I'm working on something."

She watched as Cissy and Sally began to build a castle at the edge of the water. Foundation first: side-by-side went two inverted buckets of sand.

"Hey, look, a duplex castle," she said to her sister. "And you're worried that they can't get along."

Ivy twisted her head sideways for a view of her daughters and smiled. "They'll be best friends again by the time we leave, and then they'll spend the next eleven months forgetting what it was they liked about each other."

She rolled onto her stomach and turned her cheek to the sun. "If you're going to have kids, you'd better move it along, Hol. They take a ridiculous amount of energy."

Holly smiled and dug her toes into the warm sand at the edge of the blanket. "I'm working on it," she admitted.

Her sister squinted at her. "Oh? And how *are* you coming along with your Mr. Right?"

"He's looking right as rain to me."

"Mom's worried about you ending up hurt."

"I know. She thinks he's too involved in chasing after Eden to notice me."

"No one's found that engraving, I take it?"

"It's not for want of trying."

"Oh, well. The engraving is the least of our problems," said Ivy, reaching for the suntan lotion. "Did you redo the back of Cissy's shoulders?"

"Yep."

"So—are we all caught up now on the family soap?" Ivy asked, sitting up to reapply lotion to her own shoulders. "Dad's deluded, Mom's deluded, and Eden's having the last laugh according to your Sam. Charming. Do my back for me?"

"Sure. There *is* one other thing," Holly said, taking the bottle and squirting a blob into her hand. "Sam and I made love aboard the *Vixen* last night."

"*What?*"

"Mm. It kind of just happened. Stop twisting."

"What were you doing aboard the boat? What was *he* doing aboard the boat?"

"I was looking for the engraving and Sam was looking for me," said Holly, trying to coat her sister's pale skin. "Hold your hair up. Anyway—you know how it is when you and a guy are at each other's throats, and what you really want is sex?"

"It was like that?"

"No—but for a while I thought it was. I was *so* hot for him that I thought, okay, it must be because it's been a few months since I've been to bed with a guy. But when Sam and I finally made love, it wasn't just good sex or even great sex, it was . . . more than that."

"How *much* more?"

Holly handed the suntan lotion to her sister and pivoted from the waist. "It was like, I don't know, finding myself. Completely. In Sam."

"Since when were you lost?"

Scooping up her hair, Holly bent her head down. "You know how it feels when you're looking for your car keys, and you look everywhere, and you get more and more frustrated, and then you finally see them and you think, *ah*, and for that one split second everything comes together? You're complete? It's like that. You still have to get in the car, do your errand, deal with traffic; but for that one fraction of a second, your existence is perfect. That's what it's like when I see Sam."

"You're comparing Sam to a set of car keys?"

"I'm doing a really rotten job of explaining this, aren't I?" Holly said, laughing. "You're the analytical one in the family; *you* try. How was it with you and Jack when you met?"

Ivy gave her sister a querulous look and then shrugged. "Do you know how long ago that was? Jack and I were seniors in college. We were young, we were stupid, we got caught, we got married."

She rubbed the lotion onto Holly's back with the same no-nonsense efficiency she used on her kids. "All in all, we weren't a bad match. There are things—a lot of them—about Jack that I'd love to change."

Her voice seemed to catch as she said it, but she sighed after that and said, "For one thing, I wish we hadn't married so young; we'll always wonder about paths not taken. And I *wish* he wouldn't roll up his socks in his shorts when he throws them in the laundry," she added lightly.

"But if you're asking, is he Mr. Right, then I'd have to say I no longer believe—if I ever believed—in the concept. I think lots of people are suitable for one another. Does that answer your question?" Ivy said, capping the lotion and tossing the bottle in her beach bag.

"Do you have any regrets?"

Smiling, Ivy nodded at her two little castle-builders and said softly, "What do you think?"

"That's great," said Holly, and it *was* great that Ivy had no regrets; that her two children had made her not-bad marriage worthwhile.

Holly gazed at their mother as she knelt with her granddaughters, dripping wet sand down the side of a giant turret on the duplex castle—and she wondered, really for the first time, whether Charlotte Anderson felt the same.

21

The tradition had been carefully established over the years: after the beach came cotton candy and carousel rides on the Flying Horses, and after the carousel rides came cheeseburgers, and after cheeseburgers came ice cream cones at Mad Martha's. This year the cast was smaller, but the play was the same.

Late in the day, five weary females—the middle two with stomachaches—returned to the beautiful Greek Revival on Main Street, where the twin beds under the gabled dormers had been made with special care in sheets splashed all over with pink geraniums, and pillowcases trellised in blue and white.

The children showered up the hall while Charlotte showered down the hall, and Holly and Ivy unpacked the trunk that Ivy had shipped east earlier in the month. After weeks of dreary emptiness, the house was suddenly abuzz with people and movement. Holly could hear the squeaks of excitement in the old wood floors, feel the sighs of relief on her cheek as the seabreeze gusted through newly opened windows in rarely used rooms.

The house was happy again.

To make room for her visitors, Charlotte had moved back into the master bedroom for the first time since learning that her husband no longer wanted to share the big four-poster bed there with her. Holly noticed, when she popped into the bedroom to see how her mother was, that she had bought new sheets of periwinkle blue to replace the white ones trimmed in eyelet that she always used to prefer.

Whatever works, Holly thought as she paused outside the bathroom.

"Mom? You okay in there?"

"Of course I am; why shouldn't I be? *I* didn't eat a double cheeseburger." She opened the door for Holly, then went back to towelling her hair.

"You got some color today," Holly observed.

"I know. My nose is going to peel," her mother said, grimacing at herself in the mirror. "I was so busy running after the girls that I forgot to use the lotion myself."

She turned back to Holly and said, "Is that why you're here? To check on my sunburn?"

Holly returned her wry smile. "You know why I'm here."

"I'm fine. Really, I'm the best I've been so far. The children are a wonderful tonic; I don't know why I was afraid of their coming. The visit's going to work out perfectly. Now beat it," she said, nudging Holly's bare foot with one of her own. "Before you ruin my mood with your constant hovering."

The doorbell rang and Holly yelled that she would get it. Silly thought; she never stood a chance, not with Cissy and Sally in the house. They thundered past her down the stairs, barely glancing back for permission before swinging the door open to their caller.

Parked outside was the van from Beauty and the Beast, a toy shop in Edgartown. Holly's mother had complained during the previous week that she no longer had any up-to-age toys for the girls. She must have gone shopping.

Both girls took in the van, then the festive pink and yellow bows on the shopping bags. They exchanged a quick, sisterly look of understanding—*loot*!—and stepped back with uncharacteristic restraint so that Holly could tip the delivery girl and take the bags.

"Well, well, well—what have we here?" Holly said as she carried them high over her head so that no one could reach the envelope ribboned to the shopping bag handle. "This must be the curling iron and hot rollers I ordered for myself."

Cissy giggled and said, "They're from the toy store, Aunty Holly, and anyway, you already have curls in your hair."

"You can never have too many curls. All right," she said, setting the bags on the sofa. "Let's see now; what could be in the envelope? Directions for the hot rollers?" She pulled the envelope free without letting the children see their names written on it in a calligrapher's hand.

Sally said, "I'll read it!"

Cissy said, "No, let me!"

"No, me!"

"Me!"

Their mother appeared in the doorway, hands braced on hips, and said, "*I'll* read it." Turning to Holly, she said, "Is this your doing? Didn't I say—?"

"Don't look at me; I took you at your word."

Ivy sighed and said, "Obviously Mom did not." She took out the card and scanned its contents, then handed it without comment for Holly to read:

Sorry I can't be there with you girls; have fun with these the next rainy day. Hugs and smooches, Grampa.

"*Oh*, boy," muttered Holly.

"My goodness. What's all this? Presents?"

Everyone turned around. Charlotte Anderson, smiling and pink-nosed and summery in a yellow shift, had come downstairs to see what all the fuss was about.

"We don't know who they're from, Gram," said Cissy. "Mom won't let us see the card. Are they from you?"

"We don't even know who they're *for*," Sally pointed out. "Aunty Holly wouldn't even let us see the envelope."

Charlotte glanced at the store's logo on the shopping bags and said, "Well, I imagine they're for—"

In that instant it became obvious to Holly that her mother had figured out not only whom they were for, but whom they were from.

Her smile ratcheted up a notch and became brave. She said, "I think your mom should let you read the card for yourself. Don't you agree, Ivy, dear?"

A direct order. Reluctantly, Ivy handed the card over to her daughters. Each of them insisted on holding half of it as they read together: sorry, sorry, sorry. Fun, fun, fun. Hugs, hugs, hugs.

"From Grampa!"

Sally attacked the shopping bags; Cissy said, "How did Grampa get these presents if he's in Providence?"

Her older sister rolled her eyes as she began lifting out the first gift-wrapped package. "Did you ever hear of telephones, stupid?"

It was all the excuse that Ivy needed. "Sally! That is *no* way to address your sister. Give me the bags," she said, taking them angrily from her daughters as Holly watched uneasily. "I'm putting them away."

Sally's eyes got huge. "*Mom!* You can't *do* that!"

"Those are for *us!*"

"Not if you're rude. Besides, you read the note: these are for a rainy day. It's not raining. When it rains, we'll think about it. And that's that."

Cissy burst into tears; Sally tried not to.

"That's so unfair! You're so unfair!" cried Sally, and she ran up the stairs with Cissy howling behind her.

Ivy said grimly, "Well, at least they're not on opposite sides, for once," and shoved the bags to the back of the closet in the hall.

Holly was considering how she'd feel if someone had ripped presents out of her hands. Kid or grownup, the answer would be the same: rotten.

"Ivy," she ventured, "wasn't that a little harsh?"

Ivy glanced at their mother, who was hugging herself as she stared out a window overlooking the garden. Seething, she said to her sister, "Don't you get it? He's done it *again*."

"Done what? Tried to reassure his grandkids that he cares about them? That's not despicable behavior, Ivy."

"He's doing this for himself, for his own selfish need. How do you think Mom would feel, having to watch the girls opening the gifts, asking her when Grampa's coming, wondering why they can't at least talk to him on the phone? *How*?"

"He's only trying to connect, for God's sake!"

"Oh, please!" Ivy said, her anger rising. "Trying to connect is what hurts most of all. I'm sure Mom wouldn't feel as bad if he had just ignored the girls altogether. The way it is now, she has to face what might have been if Dad were here himself to give them the presents—*and* deal with the guilt from having the kids run away bawling."

"Guilt! *She* didn't take away their presents; *you* did!"

"For Mom!"

"Bullshit! For *you*! You're angry with Dad and you're using the kids as weapons!"

"Oh-h-h, listen to Daddy's little girl," Ivy taunted. "How typical of you to defend him."

"I'm not defending anyone! All I'm doing is trying to see both sides."

"Both sides? How can he have a side? He sailed off from his entire family just to have sex on the sea, and now that Eden's dead—"

"She's not dead!"

"—he wants to get back in our good graces. *He's* the one who's using the kids!"

"That's twisted! When did you turn so sour on life? Does everything have to have an evil motive with you?"

"And speaking of sex on the sea, just because you're currently looking at life through an orgasmic haze—"

"Shut up, Ivy. Shut up!"

"No, I won't shut up! If you had kids, you'd understand what I was talking about! It's easy to act like a high-court judge when you have no emotional stake in the case."

Holly was outraged. "Of course I have a stake! My God, I *love* the kids . . . and Mom . . . and you—and, yes, Dad, too! You don't stop loving someone just because he screwed up!"

"And that's another thing: you've never been married! Not even close! How would you *know* if a woman stops loving or not?" Ivy cried, driving the knife deep and then twisting. "How would you know?"

"I—wouldn't," Holly said, reeling from the attack. "You're right. I'm *not* married, I *don't* have kids." Furious, she fought back with the only weapon she could lay her hands on, bitter sarcasm. "Obviously I don't deserve to breathe the same rarified air as you and Mom. You're whole! You're complete! You've done it all! Whereas I—my goodness, whatever was I *thinking*?"

She shot her arms out in front of her and bowed low in scorn, then turned and swept out of the hall, breezing past her stunned mother in her flight.

As she unhooked her purse from the back of a kitchen

chair, Holly overheard her mother say in a disapproving voice, "That was cruel, Ivy. She doesn't understand."

Ivy said angrily, "Maybe it's about time she learned! Forewarned is forearmed; there are a lot of Erics and Jacks out there!"

Jack?

Still in a state of roaring adrenalin, Holly slammed the back door behind her and went around to where her car would be if she had come in her car.

Shit. This is what happened when you let your mommy drive you places. Too embarrassed to return and ask for a lift, Holly decided to go home on foot. Her house wasn't that far—and God knew, she had the head of steam to get herself there.

Ironically, the evening was a fine one for walking, dry and clear and with no trace of the bone-chilling fog that had shrouded the island the night before. Tourists strolled and islanders drove, and every last one of them was undoubtedly in a better mood than Holly was.

She loved her sister too much to stay angry; that, she knew. But it was hard not to feel hurt. If something had happened between Ivy and Jack, then why hadn't Holly been told? She was going to have to get married and then pregnant simply to have adequate credentials!

Her pride was smarting big time now, so she resisted the impulse to run back and make up and forced herself to plow ahead until she reached the turn onto the drive that led to the barn. To Sam. Out of all her relationships, hers with Sam was the only one that hadn't been tainted by Eden.

Eden! Holly remembered now. Sam had wanted to tell her something about Eden, but between her mother interrupting them in bed, and the day's nonstop visit immediately after that, Holly had forgotten all about it. Instinctively, she began to drag her steps as she neared the barn. Whatever it was that Sam had to say about

Eden, it was probably unpleasant. Holly wasn't in the mood for unpleasant. What she needed now was someone to tell her that she was right and everyone else was wrong.

As it turned out, Sam wasn't home; his Corolla was gone. Holly actually felt relieved. She was feeling too tired and too wretched to exchange another sorry sentence about Eden.

Maybe after a cup of tea.

The water hadn't yet come to a boil when the phone rang.

Holly ran and snatched it up. "Ivy?"

"Who is this?" a man's voice asked quietly.

"Who is *this*?" Holly challenged. Her heart began to pound like a piston.

"Miss Walker, I want my money."

"*I'm* not Eden. You have the wrong wom—"

The click at the other end sounded, like the caller's voice, lethally calm.

Again Eden! She was everywhere and nowhere, like an island fog. Stefan Koloman obviously didn't believe Holly's claim that Eden was missing and presumed drowned. Where was he, anyway? Watching the house? Watching her?

Oh, God. She hung up and then called her mother, just to hear a friendly voice.

"Ivy left in tears to look for you," Charlotte told her. "The children are still all weepy over no presents. I seem to be the only dry-eyed one around," she said wryly.

Holly said nothing about the hang-up call, preferring not to rattle her mother. Better to wait and tell Sam.

The knock came right after she hung up. Holly peeked through a sidelight before opening the door to her red-eyed sister, who threw her arms around her and said between wails of apology, "It's my fault, it's all my fault—"

"My fault, too," said Holly, hugging her tight. "I was being defensive—"

"No, no, it's *all* my fault; I'm taking Jack out on you—"

"I overheard you in the kitchen. What happened with Jack?"

"Mom didn't tell you?"

"Not a word."

"I thought for sure she would, even though I begged her not to. And when you never said a thing to me—"

"I didn't know! Start from the beginning," Holly said, heading for the kitchen. "We'll have our tea on the swing."

Ivy trailed after her, blowing her nose into a shredded tissue, then tearing off a square of paper towel to finish the job. "You know how Jack often has to fly to customer installations to upgrade their hardware," she said, after a big sigh to compose herself. "Well, sometimes he travels with others from his regional tech support team. One of them is a single woman."

"Uh-oh."

"Yeah. When they first started going off on assignments together, he talked about her a lot. She was good looking *and* she spoke computerese, a killer combination for someone like Jack. I asked him jokingly if I should be jealous, and he honestly laughed it off.

"Anyway, after a while—even though I knew they were still being sent off together occasionally—Jack didn't bring her up at all. Everyone knows what *that* means."

"How did you finally find out?"

Holding the screen door open for her sister, Ivy smiled ruefully and said, "I asked him."

"That's one way of doing it."

In the dim halo of the backyard light, they picked their way over a newly mulched path and took seats opposite one another on a wooden swing that Holly had built herself, over the winter, from a pattern she'd sent away for. It was dark out now, and strangely eerie. The birds had packed in it for the night, leaving the sisters with no other company than an army of crickets.

Holly peered in the direction of the barn, but a stand of scrub oaks and pines baffled sound and blocked all light from there. Was Sam back yet? She couldn't tell. In any case, right now her thoughts had to be for her sister.

Between sips of tea and bites of cookie, Ivy said, "There was no lipstick on Jack's collar to set me off, and he didn't suddenly start coming home late. No hang-up calls, no attempts by him to lose weight—and you know what a pot Jack has. I don't know what made me eventually ask him. Just a routine check, I guess."

"And he actually *told* you?"

Ivy shook her head. "No—but he looked so guilty that I poked him in the middle of a sound sleep and asked him again. This time he snored out a yes."

"Oh, wow. Really?"

"Uh-huh," said Ivy, voice quivering. "It was a Saturday. I managed to hold myself together until I dropped the girls off at a birthday party, and then Jack and I had a knockdown, drag-out fight. He insisted it had been a one-time thing. I don't know why the hell *she* did it, but I know why Jack did: because she asked him to. I was stunned. You expect a fifteen-year-old boy to respond that way, not a man who's supposed to be happily married and has two kids."

"Ivy—I don't know what to say."

"Well, anyway," she said, sipping from the mug, "that's the whole story. He swears it was only the one time. We've been seeing a marriage counselor, but Jack keeps insisting that he has no complaints. He claims he loves me, adores the kids, likes his work . . . But I resent him so much. He was so *stupid*. When I think about it, really think about it, I could kill him still. I don't think I'm making progress at all."

"I can't blame you," said Holly. "But if it was just once . . . if he's sorry . . . if you love him and want to save the marriage . . . won't you have to put it behind you?"

"I don't see how. I really don't. Bastard."

In thoughtful silence, in deepening night, they rocked idly back and forth, making the swing squeak in protest.

"I should get some oil on that," Holly said absent-mindedly.

But she was thinking, what the hell was wrong with the men in her family? Why were they so restless? What were they looking for? A supermom who earned super-money and gave them supersex? What, exactly, was their problem?

Why, she wondered, couldn't they just be like Sam?

The squeak of the swing drowned out the low murmurs of their conversation, but if they had said Eden's name, he would've damn well heard it.

He stepped away from the shadows of the trees, straining to make out their conversation. The tall blond wasn't Eden, a disappointment. But the dark one—Holly Anderson. She was Eden's buddy, her landlord. How could she *not* know where Eden was, for chrissake? Waste of time, asking her nice. More than one way to skin a cat.

He took another step nearer and snapped a twig.

The creaking of the swing stopped.

"What was that?" he heard the one say.

"A deer, maybe?"

"So close?"

"There's a lot of development going on; they're losing habitat here, just as everywhere else."

"I don't like it out here, Holly. I don't know how you can stand the isolation."

"I'm an artist. It lets me think."

"Let's go inside. I have to be getting back, anyway. I left Mom with the kids."

"When did you turn into such a scaredy-cat, Ivy? This is the *Vineyard*, for goodness' sake."

"Blame it on all the traumas. Nothing and no one seems safe anymore."

"Boy. You would've loved my pal Stefan."

22

Eric Anderson looked less old than Sam had imagined him to be, and less miserable than his daughter had described him to be.

Sam found him waiting on the beach side of a wrap-around porch on a house in Chilmark. Yes, it was dark, and yes, Sam had never seen the man before—but no way was this any grieving lover in a near-suicidal depression.

Anderson's handshake was firm and his voice tight with repressed excitement as he said to Sam, "Let's walk along the beach, Steadman. My hosts turn in early and I don't want to wreck their serenity any more than I have already."

His considerateness annoyed Sam, who wanted intensely to dislike the man. Still, Sam was fairly sure that he was going to have the last grim laugh of the evening, so he said, "Fine with me. Let's go."

By the time they dropped down below the tide line where the wet, hard sand was easier to walk on, Sam's eyes had adjusted to the night. A dazzling canopy of stars overhead made him resent his mission all the more. He should be strolling on this beach with Holly, not her old man, and talking about their glorious future, not Sam's misbegotten past.

The low hiss of the sea as it advanced and retreated at their feet seemed to set the stage for what was bound to be a venomous conversation—but Holly's father seemed blissfully unaware of that.

He said genially, "Sorry I couldn't meet with you earlier; I've had a million things to do. So what's on your mind? You said on the phone that you have important information about Eden."

"That I do," Sam said wryly. A wave rolled up a little higher than the rest, washing over one of his deck shoes. He hardly noticed. "It seemed best to handle it face-to—"

"Y'know, I could have saved you the trouble of coming here," Anderson cut in, sounding laughably cocky. "I already know what you have to say. I know pretty much everything there is to know about Eden—now."

"Really. I'm probably wasting your valuable time, in that case," Sam said in a dry voice.

It was obvious that Eden had made contact with Anderson. But even if she *had* told him about Sam and her—which Sam did not believe—it wouldn't have made any difference. Sam was there to make it official before he returned to tell Holly. In his mind there was a definite protocol to a full confession: first you prevented the bigamy; then you went back and dealt a full body blow to your own chances for happiness.

"So Eden got in touch with you," he said.

"Indeed she did," Anderson crowed. "She did not drown. I did not kill her. She did not run off with a Durer engraving."

"That's not what my folks tell me," said Sam, seizing on the one inaccuracy.

"That was all a misunderstanding," Holly's father assured him. He was so clearly eager to explain. "Eden took the engraving to have it appraised, just as she had promised your parents she'd do. She knows how naive they are, and she didn't want them getting fleeced by some unscrupulous dealer."

"Uh-huh," said Sam, studying a brightly lit house down the beach with more interest than he could muster for Eden's excuses. "Unfortunately, I know at least one dealer who's offering a different version of events."

"Stefan Koloman, you mean. Yes, she told me about him, too. A shady, unscrupulous character. He claims that she cut him out of his commission," Anderson acknowledged. "Not so. Technically, Eden found the buyer on her own: she deduced the name of the party from something that Koloman said."

"She stole the name of the party from Koloman's Rolodex."

"Is that what he claims? Why would you believe a man like that instead of Eden?"

"Doesn't it tell you something that I believe a man like that instead of Eden?" Sam asked wearily.

"She was trying to get the most money she could for your parents, Steadman. Can't you understand that?"

"Where's the money, in that case?"

"I didn't ask. It was enough for me to know that she's anxious to give it all to your parents. You ought to feel the same."

There was a shame-on-you quality to his scolding that Sam found infuriating. He said, "Are we to assume that Eden was traveling by windsurfer to the nearest safe-deposit box?"

Anderson's laugh sounded genuinely bemused. "Crazy kid—you wouldn't believe what she was trying to pull off."

"Sure I would," Sam said. "Try me."

"We were in Portsmouth. She took a call on her cell phone that upset her very much. I know—now—that it was from Koloman; he was threatening to kill her for going around him. She didn't know what to do—she didn't want to involve me and put me in harm's way—so she decided to fake her own death. It seemed like the only way to throw Koloman off her trail. That's why she staged the windsurfer accident. Poor thing . . . she had no idea that the police would misinterpret the scene and term it suspicious. She was devastated when she read about that in the papers—devastated."

"I can imagine," said Sam, but the irony eluded Anderson.

Sam knew that Eden wouldn't give a damn if the scene were misinterpreted; she might even prefer it to look like a homicide—although he couldn't imagine why.

No, there were only two possibilities to explain Eden's return. Either the money or the engraving was still on the boat, in which case Holly was right and they should have searched the *Vixen* harder.

Or (and in the circumstances, the second possibility was distinctly relevant):

"Have you offered to marry her yet?"

Anderson's head jerked up—the question was bluntly put—but he declined to answer.

They were abreast of the brightly lit house that had caught Sam's eye. A party of beautiful-people types were enjoying drinks and muted patter on one of its decks, high above the beach. Holly's father maintained a steadfast silence as they passed, and Sam listened instead to the waves rolling in and then out, flat and hissing, dragging shells and stones behind in their wake.

The next few houses were dark—a better backdrop, apparently, for what Anderson had to say.

"You're the second person to ask me that," he said

at last. "It doesn't concern you, but—maybe because you're not family—I think I'll tell you, anyway. The answer is, no, I hadn't spoken of marriage with Eden before she disappeared. But earlier today when she called me—yes. I did."

Sam felt no jealousy, only sadness for Holly and her family as he said dryly, "Presumably Eden is willing."

"She is!" Holly's father blurted, sounding amazed and grateful.

He recovered and said in a more dignified way, "I'm only telling you this because I want everyone to understand that Eden took a huge risk when she re-established contact with me. She had no idea that I'd be willing to forgive her for the embarrassment—the humiliation— I'd endured. You have to realize also that she's opening herself up to the possibility of prosecution by the Coast Guard. At a minimum, they'll likely present a hefty bill for their search effort. The State Police aren't too happy, either."

He made a dismissive gesture with his hand and said, "But that's all behind us now. I told her we'd pay Koloman his outrageous commission, we'd give your parents the full amount of the transaction, we'd make everyone happy."

"Everyone?"

It was a jab to the throat; Anderson's voice became taut. "You know what I mean."

Another wave oozed around their feet as they marched doggedly on in their walk to nowhere. Behind them Sam heard the cocktail chatter become suddenly animated, and then several guests breaking away from it in a shouting, laughing run through the dark for the beach.

Sam wanted out of there. It was time to tell the besotted fool that there was one little detail that Eden, for all her candor, apparently had forgot to mention. Before that, though, Sam had one last question. "Did Eden ever explain the blood on the deck of your boat?"

"Holly told you about that?"

Sam said bluntly, "Your daughter thinks you're making up that story about Eden hurting herself cutting an orange. Although she didn't say so, I assume she believes as I do: that Eden did indeed try to frame you for her murder, and that you're lying to cover for her."

"Well, that's where you're wrong, Steadman!" he said in triumph. "I admit, I didn't know how the blood had got there, and I accounted for it in the most logical way I could envision. But this morning I asked Eden if she had cut herself without my knowing it, and she said yes, absolutely yes. So much for your frame-up theory."

Sam snorted. Eden could have seen this guy coming with her eyes closed and a lead box over her head.

Anderson sounded almost plaintive as he said, "No, I'm telling you: she was staging an accident, not a murder."

Out of patience, Sam stopped where he was, pulling the other man up short. "And I'm telling *you*," he said, "Eden is a liar, a con—and somebody's wife."

"*Wife*? What are you talking about?" Anderson said angrily. "Whose wife?"

"Mine, Mr. Anderson."

He staggered as if Sam had kicked him in the balls. "You're full of shit," he said. "Eden's never been married."

"Oh, yes, sir. At least once. We never divorced. I thought for a while there that she might be legally dead, but what do you know? She lives to wreak her havoc."

"You son of a bitch liar—my family put you up to this!" he cried, taking an awkward swing at Sam.

It was such a contemptible accusation that Sam lashed out with a fist without thinking, landing it, despite the darkness, squarely on Anderson's jaw.

Anderson let out a shocked *uh*—no doubt he'd never been decked before—and then something seemed to snap in him, as well. He came lunging back at Sam with surprising ferocity, catching Sam completely off guard. Down they went, rolling and flailing in the wake of retreating shells and stones, getting soaked, tasting salt, cursing like a couple of kids in a schoolyard brawl.

He thinks we're fighting over Eden, Sam realized as he tried not to hurt him. *For all I know, he's right.* He held Anderson immobile, but he wriggled free of Sam's grip. *Maybe I'm taking her out on him.*

He tried to contain the man, but Anderson continued swinging wildly, a clueless knight on an ignoble mission. And then Sam caught a punch to the ear, ridiculously painful for a creampuff swing, and it infuriated him. The New Bedford street fighter took over and he landed a succession of punches, left, right, left, to Anderson's nose and chin. He wanted to pull back, but there was something about the man—something so stupid and irrational and mirror-image of Sam—that he wanted to destroy it completely.

Anderson tripped and fell. Sam pounced on him. Round and round they rolled, with Holly's father clearly on the run, trying to claw away from Sam and crawl up the beach. Sam wouldn't have it. He grabbed the lawyer's sodden slacks and yanked him back, back to the sea—for all intents and purposes, ready to drown him on the spot.

"You asshole!" he shouted between grunts. "You idiot fathead asshole!" He was sitting on Anderson now, screaming in his face, trying to get through to him, oblivious to the fact that the waves were washing around them, oblivious to the fact that the man was no longer resisting.

In horror he suddenly sat back. *What am I doing? What am I doing?* He rolled off Anderson and began hauling him to his feet. *I'm beating up Holly's father, for pity's sake. What next? Little old ladies at bus stops?*

Sickened by the fact that he'd yielded to such an easy temptation, he said between gasps for breath, "You okay? Are you okay?" He had to support Anderson and was grudgingly impressed by the man's response.

"I'm . . . okay. I started it. I'm okay," he said, weaving in place.

"Good. Well—good," said Sam. He let go tentatively of him.

Anderson was able to stand on his own. "I shouldn't have said that . . . about my family," he said, huffing and wheezing. He reached in his back pocket and pulled out a wet handkerchief, then held it to his face. "I think my . . . ow . . . nose is broken."

Sam shook his head. He knew when and how to break a nose, and when to leave it in one piece. "You'll be fine. Maybe sore."

"Yes. Sore. Black and blue, too."

Yeah, you won't look any younger for her when she shows up for your money, you poor dumb cluck.

"I never should have said that about my family," Anderson repeated as they turned and began staggering back to the Bouchards' house. "They're innocent in all of this."

"Well, gee, ya *think*?" Sam said scathingly. His mind was already racing ahead to part two of the sorry soirée: explaining to Holly that her father wasn't the only sucker in town. He touched a spot above his right eye: swollen. Something else to explain to her. Shit.

They walked along in sullen silence, jeered by the hissing sea. *Idiots! Both of you! Idiots!*

The partiers who had decided to take a dip had dipped and gone—possibly scared from their lark by the sight of two men brawling a little too close to their playground for comfort. Sam prayed that they hadn't called the cops. He picked up the pace.

"You married a long time ago, I take it?" Holly's father asked, almost shyly.

"Eight years. She disappeared after the first one and never came back."

"There had to be a reason."

"Far's I know, it was to stay one step ahead of a warrant. But if you find out there's another reason, by all means tell me. I'd be mildly curious to know."

I love you Sam, please believe that. I'll never love anyone else. I can't stay on to explain; I wish I could. Just know that I love you.

And then the kicker: *We'll meet again.*

During the past seven years Sam had wanted that to happen for so many different reasons: love, lust, a maybe-father's longing; vengeance, curiosity, and recently, plain old-fashioned justice. But the most recent motive, the justice thing, had dropped away like the last petal of a daisy when Eric Anderson promised to make good on the Durer. Eden might have Sam's child—Sam would want that child—but there was no reason in the world for them to meet again, except possibly in court.

Anderson was doing his best to recover from the latest plunge in the roller coaster that had become his life. "Eden never tried to get in touch with you during those seven years?"

"Nope."

"Don't you see? She disappeared because—well, because she didn't want to put you through the trauma of being divorced by her. She knew the marriage was a mistake—"

I'll never love anyone else.

"And she knew that there was no hope of your ever getting together—"

We'll meet again.

"And she meant to let you get used to the idea of living without her, but one year led to another—"

"Good grief," Sam said in disgust. "Is it possible that you were once smart enough to pass a bar exam?"

Stung, Anderson said, "Why the hell didn't you divorce *her*, then?"

Now it was Sam who—despite the wet clothing that clung to him—was feeling the heat. "You want to know why?" he snapped. "Because just before she walked out, she told me she thought she was pregnant."

"Eden has never had a baby," Anderson said flatly.

"This, from the man who thinks Eden simply forgot to divorce me?"

Ignoring the crack, Anderson said, "I'm no Lothario, but I know when a woman's had a baby. Eden has no scar, no stretch marks, no stretched . . . anything. Her body is perfect."

They were on dangerous, dangerous ground, as shifting as the sand beneath their feet. Sam did not—did *not*—want to get into a kiss 'n' tell with a man who by rights should've been a candidate for father-in-law. He gritted his teeth, and Anderson, who seemed to realize that they were a sentence away from renewing their brawl, let the matter drop.

As for Sam, he was appalled that he'd said as much as he had. He'd never mentioned Eden's claim about pregnancy to anyone, not even his parents—and yet here he was, spilling his guts to a man he should hate.

He couldn't quite do it. Sam might have been the better fighter, but he sure as hell couldn't claim to be any smarter.

"Let me ask you this," he said. "What makes a man like you walk away from a thirty-year marriage for someone like Eden? I don't get that."

"I've thought about that question constantly," the older man admitted. "You think it's for the sex—"

"Don't tell me what I think."

"I was going to say, it's not. Sex enters into it, but it's more that Eden is so full of life. She understands that time is short; that we have to live our lives to the fullest and that we can't hang on and drift just out of habit. She's very wise that way. She's told me that Charlotte will get over this if I make it quick and make it clean. So far, I haven't done a very good job of that. Of course, Eden admits that she's made things more complicated than they had to be, and she really feels bad about that."

Somehow, Sam didn't think so. He was very close to throttling Anderson all over again. How could the guy be so damned gullible?

How could Sam ever have been?

"Eden wants to sail around the world with me," Anderson said, sounding more and more eager to present his case. "Whereas my wi—Charlotte—has always got seasick on the *Vixen*."

"So take her on a bigger boat. The *QE II* goes around the world; so do tramp steamers."

"It's not the same," Anderson argued. He sounded almost petulant as he said, "I want adventure. I want to live life stripped to its essence. I want to be scared out of my wits once in a while."

Sam thought, *Cancer, heart disease, stroke—not scary enough for you, pal?*

Shrugging, he said, "Sorry. I still don't get it."

Maybe it was because he had discovered that danger wasn't all it was cracked up to be, and because he had an aching hunger to spend the rest of his life with someone who was bedrock-solid in her loyalties. Someone who was good, not Machiavellian; generous and not greedy. Someone who liked kids and cats and, even better, who was liked by kids and cats. Someone who was oblivious to the power of her beauty, and who had deep ties to her family and couldn't bear to hurt them, and who wanted to be a mother herself, and who looked positively enchanting hopping around a room with one leg in and one leg out of her shorts.

Someone like Holly.

A vision of her rose up before him as he plowed through the lapping seas of the incoming tide: it was of Holly in her shop, her dark hair tumbling across her cheeks as she bent over a birdhouse with her magic brushes, creating a garden where once there was none. In the vision Sam saw clearly—though he had hardly registered it at the time—a real, live black-and-white cat curled up in an upside-down straw hat on an old bureau behind her.

How had he missed the cat in the hat? What else had he missed? Suddenly he became seized by panic: there was a whole *world* of Holly that he didn't know. While Eric Anderson was fixating about crossing a globe covered mostly in water, Sam Steadman wanted nothing more than to explore every last inch and every last laugh of one of its inhabitants.

Is this what love was, then—a feeling of blind panic that what you wanted most might slip through your hands and be lost forever? With Eden, Sam had felt many emotions, but she had never inspired panic in him. When he discovered that she'd taken off, he felt humiliated, depressed, rejected, angry . . . but never in his worst moments had he felt panic.

"I'm gonna have to get going," he said abruptly to Anderson, who was lost in his own set of musings.

"What—? Oh. Sure," said Holly's father. "I'm sorry things got a little—"

Sam never heard the rest of the sentence; he was running across the sand, headed for the Bouchards' house and his rental car parked behind it. His surge of panic had bred more panic: *Don't let Eden have got there be-*

fore me. Don't let her be up to new mischief.

Was Eden on the island? Holly's father hadn't said; but if the hair standing up on the back of Sam's neck was any indication, she must be somewhere near. He drove irrationally fast, convinced that Holly was in danger, convinced that it was his fault.

By taking the State Road, he was able to bypass the inevitable crush of tourists and traffic in Oak Bluffs; he didn't slow down until he fetched up hard at the studio. All the lights were on and the barn door was slid open. Filled with dread, he hopped out of his car and ran inside.

"Holly?"

He went up to her workbench and touched one of the pickets on the birdhouse fence: still wet.

"Holly?"

He began a quick search of the place, checking behind the stacked-up furniture and old broken farm tools, easing his bulk into nooks that were out of the way and out of sight. With every passing second, his anxiety ratcheted higher.

She wasn't in the barn. Outside?

Holly . . . where are you?

"Sam?"

He swung around.

"Sam—is it really you?"

23

W ho'd you think it was?" he asked, grinning with relief. He walked straight up to her and took her in his arms, kissing her as if they'd been apart for twelve years instead of twelve hours.

She tried to say something, but he kissed it away. All he wanted, all he needed, was to know that she was still willing to be held by him.

"Sam, what happened to you? You're all salty," she said, running her tongue lightly over his upper lip. "And soggy—your clothes are soaked. You're hurt!" She touched his eye lightly; it was an effort for him not to wince. "What *happened*?"

"Aw, some dufus and I were arguing politics on the beach and didn't agree. Where'd you go wandering off to?" he asked, trying to get her off the subject.

"I heard a noise upstairs in your apartment and assumed you'd come back. Call me cocky, but I couldn't imagine why you wouldn't have stopped by the studio first to say hi. I was halfway up the stairs before it occurred to me that whoever it was might not be you."

Eden? Koloman?

"Lucky for me, the place was empty when I looked around—"

"You went *inside*?"

"I searched inside and outside. There's no one around. It could have been the wind knocking the screen onto the floor," she said with a shrug.

The hair on the back of Sam's neck was standing again, not a good sign. "Holly, something's going on around here that I should know about. Tell me."

She hesitated, then said, "It's nothing specific, really. My sister was here earlier and we were sitting on the swing in my yard, and she—I have to say, she became really spooked. I tend to be less citified about dark places than Ivy is, so I didn't share her feeling that we were being watched. But . . . *could* it have been Stefan, do you think?" she said, shivering suddenly in Sam's arms.

"If it was, he'll be out of the picture soon," Sam answered cryptically. He resolved to guard Holly around the clock until then, come hell or high water.

And in the meantime: "Look, about the engraving . . ." he said, but he cut off the sentence before it was formed. This wasn't about the engraving at all.

Get it done. He took a deep breath, then corrected himself. "About Eden . . ."

Holly had drifted away to peer through a window at the darkness outside. "Yes?" she said over her shoulder as she scanned for crooks in the night. "What about Eden?"

Ah shit, ah shit.

"She's—back."

Holly whipped her head in his direction. Her beautiful green eyes were wide with amazement. "*Back*? When? How? Where?"

"I can't answer most of that. All I know is that Eden called your father this morning. Long story short, she claims it's all a misunderstanding. She's prepared to give my parents the entire proceeds of the sale of the engraving, and your father is going to pay Koloman his full commission."

Holly looked completely blank for a moment, and then she said, "Oh!"

It was the kind of "oh" you used when you were still working things through, and Sam could see that she was doing just that.

Oddly, her first—no doubt least painful—thought was for the engraving. "So it's not on the boat, after all."

"No, the engraving's gone."

"That's too bad; I would have liked to have seen it," she admitted, sitting back on the narrow sill. A few heartbeats later, she added, "So he's serious about her."

"He appears to be."

"And she's willing to have him, of course."

"He seems to think so."

"Do the police know she's alive and well?"

"I got that impression."

Holly nodded. "Someone should tell Stefan and get him off our backs."

"Consider it done."

She pushed herself off the sill and walked back over to him, then laid her cheek against his still-damp shirt and wrapped her arms around his waist. "I should be thankful that Eden's alive—but I'm not," she murmured. "She's caused so much pain around here."

Her sigh ripped Sam in two. "More to come, I'm afraid."

"I know," she said, and she began a long ramble. "I'm going to have to break this to my mother . . . and my sister . . . and who knows where Eden and my dad will want to live . . . more scandal . . . as if there hasn't been enough already. I hope my mother doesn't decide to move off the island . . . but it's such a small place . . ."

Mute in his guilt, Sam was stroking her hair, touching her with reassurances that he could not speak. He had waited too long, for too many reasons, to tell her about his short-lived but somehow unending marriage to Eden. And now that the stakes were higher than ever, he was less able than ever to make a clean breast of it.

"Holly . . . sweet . . . do you remember Percy Billings?"

"Do I!" she said, laughing softly. "He was really cute, but not very forthright. I like honest Sam Steadman a lot more. A whole lot more."

"Well . . . good," he said, kissing the top of her head. "But getting back to Percy Billings—"

"Hey, I just realized," she said, looking up at him. "When did you see my father, anyway?"

"Just now. Ten minutes ago."

She gasped and said, "*He* was the dufus you fought with? My *father*?"

"Yeah, but don't worry about him," Sam said, brushing aside the distraction. "He's fine. Maybe a black eye, that's all. Some cuts and scrapes. Will you listen to me?"

"But—what were you fighting about? Not politics, surely!"

"It was my fault; he rubbed me the wrong way. Holly—"

"No, you don't understand, Sam. My father's not the least bit violent. He's the kind of person who catches spiders in the house and sets them free. Really, he is *so* non-violent. It's almost a thing with him. He gives to causes against abuse and aggression. He'd *never* have— how did you get him to fight? What on earth did you say?"

"I don't remember. It's not important. Jesus Christ, Holly! Will you let me get this out?"

"Get what out? What are you talking about?"

"Eden! What the hell are we *ever* talking about? Eden! God, I'm so sick of her name!" He took Holly by the shoulders and held her at arm's length, forcing himself to look her square in the eye. "Stop interrupting. Just . . . for one minute *listen* to me, or I'll never get this out," he said in a voice thick with agony. "Eden Walker is still my wife."

Nothing.

Then: "Oh."

Then: "Still?"

Then: "Oh" again.

And then a heartwrenching, shuddering sigh. "Did you say 'still'?"

"Yes. We never divorced."

Her cheeks burned red; her eyes welled with emotion. "Oh. Okay. Because somehow I must not have been listening when you told me you were married to her in the first place."

Her irony cut him down much more effectively than any display of hysteria could. He said in a hoarse whisper, "I'm sorry, Holly. My God . . . I am sorry."

He closed his eyes, shutting out the vision of her hurt, but when he opened them again, she was still hurt. Her look was blank; her breast was lifting and falling rapidly. She reminded him of a bird that's just flown into a window and dropped to the ground. He was afraid to let her go, afraid that, wounded or not, she would fly off, just to get away from him.

She wiggled out of his grasp just the same; but she was too wounded to fly very far.

"Is that why you came to the island?" she asked in the faintest of whispers. "For her?"

Sam started to shake his head in denial. But he wanted Holly's mercy, and there could be no mercy without a full confession. "That was part of it, yes. I'd be lying if—"

"Lying? You?" she said softly.

He felt his own cheek smart from the words so gently lashed. "I deserve that. My only defense—and it stinks— is that I didn't know you then."

"Ah. Now I feel better: you only lie to strangers."

"No, I only withhold information from strangers. Miss Manners says that's permissible," he said with a wan smile.

"Does she? Then I suppose she says it's permissible to abduct a stranger into a waiting seaplane," Holly said with a lift of her chin.

"You weren't a stranger by then," he said, and immediately he wished he hadn't, because he could see where she was leading him.

"And Miss Manners wouldn't have any problem with your making wild, passionate love all night to a stranger, either, would she?"

When he refused to answer, she goaded him. "She wouldn't, would she?"

He wanted her mercy; he said softly, "Obviously by then you weren't—"

"A stranger?" Her eyes blazed, her voice rose. "Then why the *hell* didn't you tell me you were married? To Eden Walker! My God—to Eden Walker! I can't even *begin* to take this in."

She began to pace, but there was no room for that luxury, so she stopped and laid her hands on the corners of a low dresser, probably trying to decide whether she could lift it and hurl it at him.

He took a kind of wild comfort from the fact that she hadn't turned and walked straight out of the barn and out of his life. "It was a long time ago, Holly," he pleaded. "I was young; I was a fool."

"And now you're not?" she cried, whirling around. "Who but a fool would make love to me when he was married to someone else?"

"We aren't married—not in anything but name. She didn't even *take* my name. I had no idea if she was dead or alive. We couldn't have been more separated!"

"Oh, where have I heard *that* one before?"

"It's the truth. I know you don't want to believe a thing I say, but it's the truth."

His mind wasn't thinking straight; he was succumbing to panic at the thought of losing her. He had expected it, dreaded it, deserved it—and yet now that it was happening, he was shutting down completely in denial.

He went scrambling after his wits like a kid with a runaway skateboard. Trying to be scrupulously honest, he said, "Eden and I were whatever it's called when the woman takes off, never to be heard from again."

"Oh, what, you had a tiff a few months ago and I'm supposed to believe it's over between you?"

"Seven years, Holly! She disappeared seven *years* ago!"

It slowed her down, but only just. "Seven years, seven decades, seven centuries! What difference does it make? You never divorced her!"

"True," he agreed. "And here's my politically incorrect response: Up until I met you, I didn't know whether I loved her or not. So shoot me. I didn't know."

"You *still* don't know. You haven't seen her. You still don't know! She's going to walk back into your life with an armful of cash for your parents, and you're going to fall in love all over again! I know it!"

"You're wrong! You couldn't be more wrong!"

He wanted to take her in his arms and reassure her, but when he took a step closer she threw her hands up in front of her as if he were a vampire bat. "No! One woman at a time, please! I've never been keen on the concept of harems."

"Holly, for pity's sake, you're being melodramatic. Eden doesn't mean anything to me."

"Oh? Are you willing to look me in the eye and tell me that during the whole time you were coming on to me, you had no feelings—no feelings at all—for Eden?"

"I—" He took a deep breath and blew it out in massive frustration. "No. I can't do that."

"Oh—damn you," she cried, equally frustrated. "You lie at all the wrong times, you know that?"

Confused now, he said, "You wanted the truth, Holly. Do you know how hard this is for me?"

"As a matter of fact, I do," she shot back. "You've been tight-lipped about everything from the start. It's the kind of man you are. I should have known. I *did* know, and yet . . ."

She closed her eyes against the tears, and when she opened them, her look was unmistakable: complete disdain. Even worse was the unconscious gesture that accompanied it. She wiped her fingertips across the cuffs of her paint-smeared shorts as if she were wiping herself clean of paint stains. Of Sam stains. Wiping herself clean of him.

"You're right," he said, unmanned by the innocence of that gesture. "I should have told you. I have no excuse."

He had plenty of them, but none that mattered. Bottom line, she wasn't inclined to grant him mercy, and he had no right to beg for it.

But, for the first time in his life, beg for it he did. "I'm sorry, Holly," he whispered abjectly. "Will you forgive me?"

She stared at him for a long, long time—trying, he thought, to see into his soul. He studied her face as he had never studied a face before, memorizing it. She was so beautiful. Her dark brows, her deep-sea-green eyes, the smudge of blue paint on her cheekbone, pink on her chin . . . all of it was heartbreakingly endearing. Her eyes as she gazed at him seemed fathomless. And then, just when he felt sure that she recognized the love that he had for her, she sighed, and pressed her lips tightly together, and shook her head.

"No, Sam. I won't forgive you."

She turned away from him and walked out.

24

Holly stumbled in blind anguish down the footpath that cut through the trees between her cottage and the barn.

It must be me. I fought with Ivy, and now I've fought with Sam. It must be me. I'm making mountains out of molehills. Sam didn't do anything. What did he do? Nothing. He didn't lie; he just didn't say. Ivy and Sam in one night, that's impossible. Something is wrong with me. It's my fault.

What had he said exactly?

Eden Walker is still my wife.

Holly tried to brush away a stream of tears. How could it possibly be her fault that Eden Walker was still Sam's wife? It was *his* fault, that bastard, that bastard, it *was* his fault. She let out a moan: she so much wanted it all to be hers.

Blindly, she staggered on. She caught a fallen branch with the toe of her sandal and went sprawling onto the mulched path. Surprised, she lay there picking off pieces of pine bark that were sticking to her right leg and arm;

she was numb with shock, completely out of it. Behind her she heard a twig snap. It got her scrambling to her feet again: she had no desire to repeat the agony with him in the barn. Her barn. Her wonderful red barn. Her studio, her refuge, her art. Ruined. Ruined by a stupid, stupid man. Two stupid men.

They tell you what they think you want to hear. They don't want to hurt you, but they don't want to make hard choices, either. They want it all. Pigs, pigs, all of them. They're all alike, not to be trusted. Ever.

She ran inside her house and locked both doors, spooked not by the fear of bogeymen or Kolomans, but by the thought of having to face Sam again.

I have to talk about this with someone. But Sam was her someone of choice. Who instead?

Not her father, that was for sure. He knew—surely that's what the fight on the beach had been about—and he didn't care. The only choice, the obvious choice, was for Holly to confide in her mother.

She knew that it looked bad for a thirty-one-year-old to be running straight to her mom. But her sixty-year-old mom had come running to Holly not so long ago, and over the same woman at that.

How ironic, thought Holly. *How totally twisted.*

She drove on automatic to the turreted house on Main. It was late when she arrived; the house was dark.

Unless. She skirted around to the side. As she expected, the lights in the master bedroom were on. She crept over to the gnarled old cherry tree that grew alongside the house and began climbing, monkeylike, from lower limbs to upper until she reached the small balcony outside her mother's bedroom.

The French doors were open to the night air, but the screen doors were locked. Her mother was in the bathroom: Holly waited until she emerged and then called softly through the opening. Her mother jumped half a foot.

"Holly, for Pete's sake," she said, tying her robe around her as she approached the screen doors. "You're too old for that. *I'm* too old for that; you're going to give me a heart attack."

Holly put a finger to her lips. "Mom, we have to talk."

"At this hour? About what? I'm exhausted. I want to go to sleep."

"I know, I know." She went directly to the stereo system and put on a New Age CD to drown out their voices.

Her heart was still thumping from the climb; the extra oxygen helped keep her from breaking down. When she turned around, she had a ridiculously amused smile plastered to her face. "You won't believe what I just found out," she said.

That part she got out with no problem. She forced her smile to broaden.

"Eden's back, and . . . it's the funniest thing. She's actually married to—this is so *funny*—Sam."

The thing that undid her was the look of deep and instant sympathy on her mother's face as she rushed to embrace her. Holly knew that mothers understood their daughters' pain. But *this* mother understood *this* pain in an extraordinary way. It was as if a single bullet had gone through both their hearts, leaving both women clutching one another to keep from falling down.

Holly broke down, despite her best efforts. In the next few minutes she related, in bits and tear-stained pieces, the scene that had just taken place in the red barn between Sam and her.

It was harder for Holly to tell her mother that her father had been informed and that her father didn't care; and that he was eager to help straighten out Eden's financial—and presumably her legal—entanglements. But Holly made herself do it, because she believed that not to say anything was to lie.

Her mother accepted the news with eerie resignation: undoubtedly she was too shell-shocked to do much else.

"So now there are *two* men who want her?" she asked when Holly was done.

Holly said, "Sam says no, that she doesn't mean anything to him. How can I believe him? He's lied about everything, including his own name, to me."

Her mother was awash in her own sea of misery. "She's on the boat? She's actually on the boat right now?"

"Yeah, if Sam is right," Holly answered. Too tired to move, she was lying like a rag doll stomach-down over a huge tufted hassock. "What will you do now, Mom?" she asked in a mopey voice. "You won't stay on the island, will you? If you go, I go," she decided.

Her mother had her bare feet perched on the edge of the hassock, pulled up to the wing chair in which she sat. Her head was thrown back, her eyes were closed; her wrists were draped limply over the rolled arms of the chair. She seemed even more weary than Holly; it had been another hell of a long day.

"You're jumping the gun, dear; you always do. No one knows where they'll stay. Maybe they'll sail off into the sunset. That's your father's dream, isn't it?" She sounded bitter and sad and lonely as she said it.

"Eden would never do that," Holly said, flopping over on her back and easing the stretch in her limbs. "She needs more than an adoring audience of one. Just ask Sam."

She threw in the last three words to show how brave she was; but the effort hurt more than she thought possible. How on earth was her mother getting through this?

"Don't go rushing for the ferry yet, Holly," Charlotte

said grimly. "It's not over until it's over. Something could happen. She's reckless. Accidents do happen."

Something in her voice made Holly uneasy. "Mom," she said softly, "I don't like you like that."

"Yes. You're right. Sorry."

Holly went back to thoughts of Sam. "We should form an organization. We'll call ourselves the Man-Haters' Club—East Vineyard Chapter."

"And that would accomplish what?"

Holly spread her arms wide in a martyr's pose. "We could have weekly meetings and eat chocolate and write dreary poems about how pathetic men are."

"I *thought* I heard voices up here," said Ivy, poking her head in the room. "What's this club? I like the sound of it. Who're we hating and why?"

They were women, they were family, they were currently short on pride. It wasn't hard for Holly to relate her tale of woe for the second time that night, this time with fewer sobs and tears.

"So here we are," she said, pulling her knees to her chin. "All in the same boat, all at the same time. I think we would've been better off staggering our traumas," she added glumly. "It would be nice if one of us were emotionally intact."

"Nah," said Ivy. "We'd end up hating her for being that way."

"Ivy, for goodness sake!" her mother admonished. "You're both too young to be so disillusioned."

"Right now I feel old enough for the old folks' home," Holly admitted, yawning. She stretched full-length on her mother's needlepoint rug and closed her eyes. "I think I'll just sleep here tonight."

She was prodded alert by her sister's next remark: "Now that I think about it, Holly, I'm not sure you're as qualified as we are to be in a man-haters' club."

It struck a nerve. Holly had been feeling slightly un-

easy herself; her situation was not the same as the other
two women's.

"Okay, *obviously* there was nothing wrong with his
marrying Eden," she allowed, opening her eyes. "But
there was plenty wrong with not telling me about it."

"Well, you can see why he'd be reluctant to do that
with you, honey," her mother chimed in. "I've told you
before: you want everyone to be too happy. That's another way of saying you hate bad news."

"Mother! Now it's *my* fault?"

"Not at all. But it's been my experience in life that
in most situations, everyone is at least partly to blame."

Holly sat up. "No! I'm not taking any blame in this.
I didn't do anything wrong, damn it! And neither did
you. It's not your fault if you can't sail around the
world."

"No, but even if my stomach were able, I wouldn't
want to do it. For a marriage to work, big dreams have
to be shared; it's only the smaller ones that are optional."

"If it is a dream. If you ask me, I think Dad is just
bored, bored, bored with work. It's not that he really
wants to see the world; it's just that he wants to run
away from his job. There's a huge difference."

"Okay, Dear Abby—what was Jack's problem?"
asked Ivy. "He loves his work."

"Oh, Jack. He was just incredibly stupid."

"And Sam? Why do you think Sam jumped into bed
with you? To get back at Dad?"

"Not at all. If that were the case, he would've slept
with Mom."

"*Holly!*"

Holly shrugged at her mother and said, "Sorry. We're
just theorizing." To her sister, she said, "Frankly, in retrospect I have no idea what Sam saw in me. You haven't
met Eden, but I'm the polar opposite of her. I hate to
play games; she lives to play games—"

"Sam may not *like* to play games."

"There are other things. I'm not coy; she's a flirt. I'm not confident—"

"Earlier this evening, you were brimming," her mother reminded her with a gentle smile.

Holly sighed and said, "That was before I got dumped."

"You didn't get dumped, Holly. *I* got dumped. You found out that Sam once got taken in by Eden's allure, that's all. He was twenty-three; what did you expect? Twenty-three is just a few months older than thirteen."

Holly wasn't comforted by the fact. "If Eden has the power to make Dad throw away a thirty-plus-year marriage, she certainly has the power to reclaim a man who's been carrying the torch for seven years. The only option I have is to wait and see what happens," she said, more to herself than to them.

It was time to go. She stood up. "To be perfectly honest," she added, "I don't think Eden will want Sam. She's ignored him for seven years; that must mean something. Besides, she's going to go where the money is, and Sam doesn't have that much. Not compared to Dad. So. Where does that leave *me*?"

Resting her forearms on her head, she swung left and right, working out the day's kinks. "It leaves me with someone who will—possibly—continue to carry the torch, even if he buries it deep down inside. How would I ever know for sure?"

It was hard to argue with that, and neither Holly's mother nor her sister bothered to try. The three became silent; Holly had just waved her evil wand over the slumber party and turned it into a wake.

Ivy tried to brighten the mood. "Stay over tonight. Stay. Mom will make us breakfast in the morning—won't you, Mom?" she said.

Their mother was unhappy with Ivy's plan and was blunt about it.

"I don't think that's a good idea," she told Holly. "With Ivy and the girls here, there's really no room. I don't want to make up the sofa bed—for pity's sake, you only live a mile away."

Surprised by her mother's resolve, Holly shrugged and said, "Okay by me; I know when I'm not wanted."

"I feel a headache coming on," Charlotte added. She was virtually showing Holly the door.

"With or without a premonition?" Holly murmured, studying her mother curiously.

"Don't be flip, Holly; it's your biggest flaw. Good night. Both of you. Please."

And that was that.

25

A little before six the next morning, Eden Walker snuggled her naked body against her exhausted lover and licked the lobe of his ear. "Mornin', big guy," she said in a sleepy, sultry voice. "Ready for more?"

The response she got was a pleased, delighted groan—but a groan, nevertheless.

Eden laughed and sat up in the berth. "Then what do you say to a warm doughnut instead?"

Eric Anderson rolled onto his back and opened one eye. "I say yes." He closed his eyes. A sleepy, sated smile softened the deep lines of his face. "It's good to have you back aboard."

Eden pulled a denim jumper over her bare body and slid into a pair of espadrilles. "Don't go sailing off without me, now," she teased.

"Oh, my darling," said Eric, doting on every syllable. "Never."

"Good," she said, grabbing her straw carryall. "Be right back!"

Emerging on deck, Eden bent over double and

combed her fingers through her auburn hair, then shook it back as she straightened and took a deep, long breath of salt air. She glanced around at the other boats, but the marina was quiet at that hour. Her step was light and sure as she hopped down to the dock, then walked out toward the road through the shell-strewn parking lot.

She was halfway across the lot when a car shot out from its place among a row of parked automobiles and headed in her direction.

She turned in time to see the wagon swerve toward her, running her down before racing out of the lot.

Sam lucked out: there was a seat available on the Cape Air Cessna for the first flight out to Boston that morning. Arriving early on standby had something to do with nabbing the spot, he knew; but he had chosen to believe that God had simply got tired of the way he was screwing up his quest for justice and had decided to step in and lend a hand.

Immediately after dropping into one of the coveted nine seats, Sam closed his eyes, trying to shut out the string of disasters that had made up his previous day. His thoughts were murderous, and they were aimed at himself. What a jerk, what a fool, what a paranoid ass he'd been. Why couldn't he have just told Holly the truth from the get-go? Instead, these were the cards he had handed her to play:

Hi, my name is Percy Billings. I'm a lawyer. No, wait, I'm a P.I. No, scratch that. I'm actually an idiot. Did I mention that I'm sleeping in my car? And that I'm married? To the same woman who's just destroyed your family?

Who'd want to play a hand like that? Obviously Holly had to fold. It was the only reasonable thing to do when your cards really stank.

Nonetheless, a small part of him fiercely resented the

fact that Holly had refused to believe him when he told her that Eden no longer meant anything to him. He had been telling the truth, damn it. Holly of all people should know truth when she saw it. On the other hand, he hadn't yet told Holly that he loved her. Why not?

Three possibilities came to mind. One, he hadn't been looking to fall in love and in fact preferred *not* to fall in love. Two, he had been too busy insisting that he didn't love Eden to have time to mention, oh, by the way, that he did love Holly. And three, he was so screwed up that he didn't think he'd ever be able to love a woman, any woman, again.

For half an hour Sam got sucked more and more deeply into a spiral of self-doubt, and he didn't come out of it until the Cessna touched down at Logan. Jarred into action, he hopped into yet another rental and headed for the Ironic Curtain, Stefan Koloman's hole-in-the-wall gallery on Huntington Avenue. Sam had made contact with the dealer late the night before (which was grimly reassuring; it meant Koloman wasn't running around the Vineyard stalking innocent women). The men had arranged to meet at the gallery—early, if Sam could catch a flight.

During their phone conversation, Sam had learned that Koloman had not yet heard from Eden, which wasn't surprising; without a doubt, the lady had another con up her sleeve. It was Sam's job to make sure that the art dealer understood he'd be getting his money, and that he was not to approach Holly again, under any circumstances. In the mood he was in, Sam was just itching to have the chance to drive the point home, preferably with his fists.

He arrived at the gallery to find it locked. There was no bell; he banged loudly on the door. Eventually he heard an angry voice overhead. Koloman—unshaven, tank-topped, and half-asleep—was hanging out of an apartment window overhead, pouring down a stream of invective on his early caller.

Recognizing Sam, he said, "Fuck, man. You got no place better to go?" Annoyed, he signalled Sam to come on up.

Sam climbed three flights of a littered, foul-smelling stairwell to the first open door, where Koloman, cigarette stuck to his lower lip, was waiting to usher him inside. The small, shabby apartment reeked of stale smoke, which would have affected the value of the many paintings stacked everywhere—if they had been real. Or even finished.

There was a half-done rendering of what looked to be an early Renoir sitting on an easel next to a museum poster of the real thing, tacked on the nearby wall. "I see you do your own . . . impressions," Sam said ironically.

"Not me; my roommate," said Koloman, jerking his head toward the bedroom. "There's no law against it," he added, his cigarette bobbing up and down as he spoke.

He sat on the edge of the sofa's torn, paint-smeared arm. His shoulders hulked over his thin and hairy chest, giving him the look of a bird of prey. His dark eyes, alight with curiosity, were fixed on Sam. "So. You have good news?"

"In fact, I do." Very briefly, Sam explained that Eden Walker had found herself a wealthy patron of the arts who was willing to pay Koloman the commission that he thought he deserved. The patron would no doubt be getting in touch soon; Sam would see to that. In the meantime, Holly Anderson, the young woman on the Vineyard whom Koloman had threatened, was not to be bothered. For one thing, she was the daughter of the patron in question. For another, Sam would beat the holy shit out of Koloman if he set foot on her property again.

"Do you understand? You're dead. If you go near her, you're dead," he said in a pleasant voice through narrowed eyes when he was done.

Koloman nodded sullenly and flicked off a coil of ash that was lying next to a tomato stain on his ribbed undershirt. "Why do I wanna waste my time going after this Anderson chick?" he said with a shrug. "She ain't got the money."

"Exactly," said Sam. "I'm glad we agree."

Koloman stared at the floor a moment, then looked up. "The deal is, no one gets to know Stefan Koloman got his money, right? No one."

Sam didn't care. He said, "If that's the way you want it."

"That's the way I want it," Koloman answered, scowling.

Sam let it pass. "Just one more thing. Did you ever let Eden know the way you felt about being cut out of the transaction?"

Koloman snorted. "How? The bitch keeps moving."

Sam said, "True enough. Well, Stefan. Thank you for your time. And good luck with the new . . . inventory," he added with a nod to the easel. "I'll let myself out."

At street level, Sam took a deep breath of hot August air which, compared to the stuff in the apartment upstairs, was as refreshing as the Alps in May.

Next stop: Portsmouth, New Hampshire.

The call from Chief Cottler surprised Holly; she thought she was done with all that. As it turned out, he wasn't looking for her. He was looking for Charlotte Anderson.

"I don't think she had any big plans for the day. Why?" Holly wanted to know.

"Thanks very much for your help," said the Chief. He hung up without responding to her question.

Half an hour later, Holly had her answer. Her father called, and he was in a state of holy rage.

"Where's your mother? *Where is your mother?*"

"How am I supposed to know?" Holly said, both anxious and annoyed. "Why does everyone keep asking me that?"

"Because Eden was run down by a white Volvo wagon this morning," he said. He was barely able to sputter the words.

"Oh, my God. Was she hurt?"

"Of course she was hurt! She was shaken up, she's black and blue. She has a possible concussion."

"You can't possibly think it was *Mom's* car."

"What else can I think? Who has a better motive?"

"That's outrageous! Offensive! How can you think that?"

"Eden saw the wagon as it sped off. She wouldn't lie. What could she possibly gain by making it up? When I told her that your mother has a white Volvo, she was shocked. Naturally she didn't want to go to the police. I had to go to them myself to report it."

"*You* did? Dad, how could you?"

"This was a deliberate hit and run, Holly, for God's sake." He added, "What do you care, if it wasn't your mother?"

"I don't care. Do what you want. Do what you damn well want!" She hung up in a state of fury.

It was a coincidence. There were probably half a dozen white Volvo wagons on the island. And yet . . . what had her mother said? *Accidents happen.*

Holly shook off the cold misgivings that washed over her like January breakers and drove straight to her parents' house. She was waiting in the kitchen, nursing a cup of cold tea, when her mother returned.

"Where have you been?" Holly said. "Everyone's looking for you."

Dumping her handbag on the counter, Charlotte said, "Really? I didn't know I was that sought after anymore."

"You weren't with Ivy and the girls; they're off with Bebe and her kids today."

"That's right," her mother said, throwing Holly a sharp look. "I wasn't."

She excused herself and went off to the first floor powder room, leaving Holly to fret over her evasive manner. When she returned, Holly picked up where she'd left off. "Mom—where have you *been* all day?"

"Out. Stop giving me the third degree." She began flipping through the day's mail, dumping flyers in the recycle box, putting aside the first-class mail.

"Consider it a dress rehearsal for Chief Cottler," said Holly with a pounding heart. "He's looking for you."

Her mother looked up. The expression on her face was carefully bland. Holly remembered, not for the first time, that her mother possessed a minor in dramatic art and had acted in community theater.

"Did he say what he wanted?" Charlotte asked.

"No. But Dad did."

"Your father called? Here?"

The bland look crumbled, if only for a moment. In its place was a fearful look of dread and hope.

"Dad called me at my house. Eden's been in an accident."

Her mother looked away. "Well! I can't say I'm surprised."

Holly jumped up and took her mother by the shoulders. "Mom—look at me. A white wagon ran Eden down in the parking lot, and Chief Cottler is looking for you. Is there anything you want to tell me?" she asked, choking on the urgency in her voice.

"I've told you. Eden's reckless; she probably wasn't looking where she was going."

"It was a *white Volvo wagon*, Mom!"

"Oh, for God's sake! Did it have an angel whirligig on it?" her mother snapped, wrenching herself free of Holly's grip.

"Oh! I . . . don't know. No one said."

"Then stop looking at me as if I were Jack the Ripper and leave me alone. This migraine is killing me. I'm going to bed."

She did look riven by pain. Holly murmured something inadequate and watched in misery as her mother dragged herself up the stairs.

Relieved and yet mortified by her lapse of faith, Holly escaped from the house and past her mother's whirligiged wagon. It wasn't until she turned the key to the engine of her truck that a thought occurred to her.

Almost against her will, she climbed down from her truck and walked back to the Volvo. She had to stand on tiptoe to see the center of the roof, but the mark there was clear: a suction-cup imprint, right alongside the actual suction cup holding the whirligig to the roof.

The angel must have fallen off sometime, she told herself as she hurried back to her truck.

It couldn't have been removed.

Sam Steadman had to lean hard on his pal Billy to get him to fly him back to the Vineyard. Twice in high season: it was asking a lot.

"Tell you what," said Billy, banking the seaplane gracefully to the south-southwest. "Give me that old snowblower in your garage and we'll call it even. You never use it, anyway."

"Take it. The thing hates me."

"Deal. So: tell me why I'm spending my afternoon

flying you for free instead of passengers for hire?"

Sam stole a sip of coffee from his friend's thermal mug. "Couldn't get a flight to the Vineyard. You've spoiled me, buddy."

"Not what I mean. What were you looking for in New Hampshire?"

"Anything I could find out about Eden. She spent time aboard the *Vixen* in a marina there. The yardhands told me she was all over them, asking questions about the repairs they were doing. I'm convinced she's into a new scam, but I'm damned if I can figure out what it is. I have a theory or two, but don't ask me to explain them. They're still half-baked."

"Fine by me. Where's your lady friend Holly? I kinda miss getting smacked on the back of the head every two minutes."

" 'Lady friend' is probably going too far," Sam said grimly. "Try 'mortal enemy.' "

"Uh-oh. You told her about Eden?"

"You got it."

Billy muttered one of his more thoughtful profanities and said, "Why the hell you didn't divorce that female years ago is beyond me."

"Let it go, Billy. This one's old."

"I getcha. You finally told your folks, too. Did Millie box your ears?"

"Damn tootin'," Sam said, instinctively scanning for *Vixens* on the water, now awash in shimmering gold from rays of the setting sun. "She's grounding me. For the rest of my life."

Chuckling, Billy said, "Millie brings a whole new scariness to that tough-love thing, don't she?"

"Yeah . . ."

"What's up?" Billy said right away. "Something's eating you big time. Is it Eden, or is it Holly?"

"Damned if I can tell you. I . . . ah . . . well, Holly has hit me hard, no doubt about it. Harder than I ever thought possible. But the photo's out of focus, and I don't know why—I mean, besides for the obvious reason that she hates me now."

Billy snorted and said, "Might the picture be out of focus because, duh, you're still married?"

"What, because a shitty little piece of paper says so?"

"Either that, or it's Eden herself who's holding you back."

"*No*. I can't believe that."

"Why the hell not? She's got you, man. She won't let go. Geez. A vampire has less of a hold on his victims than she has on you."

"That's pure bullshit," Sam snapped. "I told you, I'm done with Eden. Done with her bullshit cons and her bullshit cruelty and her bullshit . . . bullshit," he said, growling to a halt. "She's finally got herself the sugar daddy she's wanted all along. End of story."

"Sugar daddy, my ass. You said the poor sucker's an accountant."

"Lawyer. Real estate."

"Whatever. The point is, do I detect a certain jealousy, Sammy, my friend?"

"Not at all."

Billy sighed and said, "You gotta confront her, man. You gotta find out how you feel about her, one way or the other."

"Not gonna happen," Sam muttered. "My parents are getting their money, and that's all the closure I need."

"Talk about bullshit!"

"Shut up and fly."

26

Charlotte Anderson was a hit-and-run suspect for less than twenty-four hours.

A white Volvo wagon, stolen from a parking lot in Edgartown, was found back in its old spot soon after it was taken, and Chief Cottler himself called Holly's mother to tell her the news and apologize for any inconvenience. Which was all very well, except that Holly's mother was no longer the kind of woman who could see humor in the coincidence.

"He thought I'd done it; I could tell by the way he questioned me," she said to her daughters later.

"That's his job, Mom," Holly reminded her gently. Since she herself had had a dark moment or two of suspicion, she was feeling a lot less indignant than she normally would have.

"But he was so much more sympathetic the first time he interviewed me," Charlotte said. She seemed bewildered by the latest turn of events, and more fragile than ever.

Ivy saw it, too, all that progress from her visit undone. Frustrated, she said, "Too bad Mrs. Slaussen saw you leave the house so early. I never heard you, so I could have sworn to them in all honesty that you'd stayed home. What'd you have to go off and watch a sunrise for, anyway?"

Bristling, her mother became her old self again. "Excuse me? Should I just buy a fainting couch and spend the rest of my life in a swoon? Look, if I was going to go to the trouble of staking out Eden, you can bet that I would have finished the job. I would have flattened her like a pancake."

"Way to go, Mom!" Holly blurted, laughing.

Her mother smiled for the first time in days. "I have to admit, it really was a hell of a coincidence."

If it was a coincidence, thought Sam after hearing from Cottler about the stolen car.

Sam had been tracked down in the loft and questioned hard on the night before, soon after Billy dumped him out of the seaplane. When he'd first heard the news about the hit and run, Sam hadn't been surprised. He figured that Charlotte had been trying to knock Eden back a little, like a pitcher throwing a brush-off ball to a batter crowding home plate.

But the recovered car had a piece of Eden's clothing caught in its trim, which left Charlotte off the hook. She was, in fact, the class act she seemed to be.

So who stole the Volvo and knocked Eden down with it? That was the question Sam pondered as he wandered the streets of Vineyard Haven, looking for a place to eat where the line didn't go out the door.

As for the line of candidates willing to knock down Eden, it could easily match the ones in any of the restaurants tonight. Sam himself was an obvious choice; he wasn't surprised by Chief Cottler's tough grilling. If he hadn't been sitting at the airport at the time of the incident, he had no doubt that he'd be looking around for a lawyer now.

Stefan Koloman was another candidate. It was physically possible—although hard to believe—that he could have pulled it off, however; he'd have needed his own plane to have beat Sam to Boston.

Had Eden duped and infuriated any others on the island? Stupid question. Did Tiffany's have diamonds?

As he waited among the crowd at a deli takeout, Sam considered the possibility that the driver might not have had a grudge against Eden at all, but against Charlotte Anderson. The sex scandal must have been common knowledge on the island by now. It wouldn't have taken a genius—only an opportunist—to swipe an unlocked car and drive it into Eden. Everyone knew that the rich led soap-opera lives. Running down some Other Woman and framing the spurned wife was just the kind of stunt they'd pull.

The timing had to be exquisitely right, of course; but that was true in either scenario. In either scenario, someone had to be watching the players carefully.

And that's what Sam found unnerving.

He paid for his sandwich and chips and carried his booty out of the shop. He was more demoralized than he'd been since the afternoon he learned from his parents that Eden was back in his life big time. What he wanted were fewer complications as one day rolled into the next. What he was getting was a whole lot more of them.

He found a bench and wolfed down the sandwich—mere fuel, something to keep him going as he doggedly pursued his recovery of his parents' nest egg. If only they hadn't waited until their backs were against the wall . . . if only they'd told him about the *Adam and Eve* years ago . . . if only Eden and the *Antiques Roadshow* hadn't shown up together in his parents' lives.

If only he'd met Holly before he'd met Eden.

*   *   *

The phone rang as Holly walked through the door. She expected it to be Ivy. It was her father.

"Hi, honey," he said, sounding guilty and happy at the same time.

His tone infuriated Holly. She wanted to lash out at someone, and Eric Anderson was the second best someone she knew.

"*What*."

Sounding sheepish, her father said, "You heard about the stolen Volvo, of course. Your mother must be relieved."

When Holly didn't bother to answer, he said quickly, "We want to arrange to hand the money over to the Steadmans, and Eden thinks the best way to accomplish that is to give it directly to their son."

The idea absolutely floored Holly. "Sam, you mean. Eden's husband."

"Please, Holly. That's only a formality. I've recommended an attorney to Eden who will handle the divorce."

"And you don't feel threatened by her wanting to see him," said Holly, incredulous.

"No, actually, I don't," her father said in the lawyer's tone that she knew so well. "Obviously Eden can arrange to see Sam any time she likes. I'm not her jailer. Nor could I be if I wanted to."

He added in a gently beseeching way, "Holly, I'd like us—all of us—to act like adults in this. It's been a little rough, a little emotional, but now we have to start mending. It's Eden who's setting the example; she wants to begin the process by setting things right with Sam."

"That should make him very happy," Holly said dryly, but inside she felt as if someone was on the loose and pulling apart her organs.

"After that, Eden would like to sit down with your

mother and just . . . talk, woman to woman. She'd like to see us all be a family again. She'd like, eventually, to be friends. She knows it won't be easy or quick—"

By now Holly was hemorrhaging emotionally; she said faintly, "Are you out of your mind, Dad? Are you completely insane? Eden will never be welcome here. Mom shouldn't—I can't—Ivy won't accept her. Are you completely out of your mind?"

"All right, all right, I'm sorry I brought it up," he said, cutting short her breathless rejection. "It's too soon; I see that now. The reason I called is to find out where Sam is staying on the island. He is still on the island, isn't he?"

Holly glanced at the rental check that Sam had handed her in the barn. It had a smear of blue paint on it now that obscured the numbers in the amount box. She wasn't sure she could cash the check if she wanted to. Was it the numbers or the written words that the bank went by? She couldn't remember.

"I don't know if he's still on the island," she said, staring at Sam's chicken-scratch writing. "He was staying in the barn." She walked over with the phone to a window and looked out in that direction for lights. In the winter, she would know. Not now, with the trees leafed out. She told herself that she didn't care; but if it were winter, she would know.

"Can I ask you just to run out and check?" her father said meekly. "I know there isn't a phone."

"No, Dad. You'll have to go see for yourself."

There was disappointment in his voice as he promised to keep in touch.

Holly hung up in a state more numb than depressed. She felt like a ladybug who's been flitting happily along from flower to flower, minding her own business, and suddenly gets caught in a vast and sticky web of relationships. Family? Friends? Lovers? The words were so tangled that they had no meaning anymore.

All in all, the best thing, the most logical thing, was for her to enter a cloister. Yes. One of those places where you tended the vegetable garden and ate on wood trestles and most of all, never had to converse with another living soul. Because people only told you what they wanted you to know, anyway, and never what *you* wanted to know. So nuts to everyone; it was the cloisters for her.

There was a knock at the door—Ivy, irate. "Where the hell have you been?" she asked, breezing past her sister into the kitchen. "Mom half-convinced me that you'd challenged Eden to a duel."

Holly rolled her eyes. "Life should be that simple. I was in Chilmark all afternoon, fawning at the feet of a new client. I should have blown off the appointment."

"Have you heard from Sam yet?"

"Nope."

"Not to sound picky," Ivy said, "but you're not making this any easier, getting involved with Eden's husband. Or ex-husband. Or whatever he is at this point. I think he shares a little too much history with Eden for Mom's taste."

"Ha. Trust me, Sam's the least of Mom's problems," said Holly. She dropped down on a chair, pulled another one out with her toes, and put up her feet on it. "Dad just called and told me that Eden wants to become best friends with us all."

That took Ivy's breath away. She stood with mouth agape and then, unexpectedly, broke into laughter. It was contagious; Holly laughed, too.

"I have to meet this woman," said Ivy. "She doesn't sound real."

"No problem: Dad can hardly wait to bring her around."

"He's not that dumb!"

"Sure he is."

"*She's* not that dumb."

Holly scrunched her face into a thoughtful squint. "No, there, I'd have to agree with you. Eden has an ulterior motive, I have no doubt."

"Forcing us to seem like the bad guys?"

"There you go," said Holly, raising her water bottle in salute. Wearily, she said, "You know what? I don't want to think about her any more; she makes my head hurt."

"Fine. Let's go over tomorrow: beach in the morning, Bouchards for lunch, and then to the Camp Ground for the festivities. Pray that it doesn't rain; they're talking about pop-up thunderstorms. I feel so bad that we came so late this year. Usually we work up to Illumination Night; this is like having dessert before dinner."

She glanced at her watch and grimaced. "I promised the girls we'd have make-your-own pizza tonight; they must be starving by now."

Holly got up to walk her sister to the door; it was still such a treat to have her around again, and now the visit was almost over. She embraced Ivy in a quick hug and said, "You didn't have to drive over. Why didn't you just call instead?"

"I did. Three times. Check your machine." A kind of grayness passed over Ivy's blue eyes. Her voice sounded clouded, too, as she said, "I can't shake this feeling that something awful is going to happen, I just don't know to whom. Things have been so strange . . . and it doesn't help that I know about Stefan Koloman. Really, Holly, keep that stupid back door locked. I feel better now that I've seen you, but . . . keep it locked, please."

"Yes, big sister," said Holly, hugging her again. "Move east. Then you won't have to worry about me all the time."

"You're too trusting. You always have been."

"Yeah. Look where it's got me."

"I *have* to go," said Ivy, glancing at her watch again.
"Wait! One more thing. Jack?"

"We talked. I haven't decided whether to let him come out next week or not," Ivy said over her shoulder on her way to the Volvo. "See you tomorrow."

An hour later, Holly was showered and no longer hungry, but her heart ached in a way that it hadn't so far. Eden wanted to see Sam. It was as if someone had pulled hard on the barbed wire that had wrapped itself around Holly's heart when Sam finally told her about Eden. Holly could scarcely breathe; it hurt too much when she did.

Not a heart attack, exactly—more an attack of the heart, she decided. It wasn't life-threatening, but her soul was barely limping along, and it frightened her. And all because Eden Walker wanted to reunite with her long-lost husband to give him the money. And to say she was sorry. And—whether her father knew it or not—to check out Sam one last time before throwing in her lot with Eric Anderson. How could her father not see that? But then, he had always been oddly naive; that's what had made him such easy pickings.

She wondered if Sam had already been contacted by Eden, but she couldn't see how. Even Holly didn't know where he was. He might be photographing lighthouses or off on a lark with a Vegas showgirl. As Holly well knew, he wasn't beholden to tell her.

Or how about this? He might be in the apartment above the barn, with Eden. She had a key. He'd paid the rent. Wouldn't *that* be a kick in the teeth.

The thought began as little more than a grain of irritant sand; but by the time Holly turned down the sheets of her bed that night, it had become a full-blown, dark Tahitian pearl of certainty.

It would be just like Eden to pull something like that.

And if she did, it would be all Holly's fault, because she was the one who'd told her father where Sam had been staying.

Holly groaned. She was *so* much dumber than her father.

Angry with Sam, herself, her father, and pretty much the rest of the world, Holly pulled on a pair of shorts under her nightshirt and slipped out the back door to check the barn. She despised herself for being jealous and craven and needy, but there it was: as a sophisticated lover, she more or less stunk.

The night was murky. No moon filtered through the swaying trees, and the rising wind drowned out the usual friendly and familiar nightsounds. Holly waited for her eyes to adjust to the dark and then struck out on the mulched path. She wished her sister hadn't gone on and on about feeling spooked, because now *she* was spooked. She felt an irresistible impulse to run, but, remembering the spill she'd taken on the path the night before, she forced herself to walk.

The trees fell away and Holly's heart soared: lights were on in the apartment above her studio. Her joy levelled off when she saw that no car was parked near the barn. Where was his rental *du jour*?

The lights could be on and Sam could be out, she supposed. But in her new and edgy mood, Holly didn't think so. She stepped back into the shadows of the trees, both to hide and to get a better angle of viewing. Heart thumping and more wary than ever, she stood in the darkness and watched the loft window for signs of an occupant. If her sister's premonitions were right, it could well be Koloman, poking around. But Sam had promised to take care of him, and Holly believed wholeheartedly that he had.

Fool. You believe too much.

A shadow moved across the living room on the way

into the bathroom, which told her nothing: even burglars had to pee once in a while. She backed up a little and stood on a tree stump and waited. The occupant came out of the bathroom, and yes, the good news, the bad news, the only news, was that it was Sam who was up there, not bothering to come and see her.

She saw him disappear from view at the bed end of the room—*to sleep, perchance to dream, but please, please, not to make love with someone already lying there.*

Holly bowed her head, completely, miserably aware that she loved Sam Steadman despite his entanglement, and that nothing would ever change that. She knew that she was going to spend the rest of her life with make-believe cows and cats and cottages and kids, mere painted images of her deepest desires, unless Sam were around to make those dreams reality.

It hurt. Once, her art had been enough to satisfy her. No more.

She climbed down from the stump and turned to go, but it occurred to her that she had to give Sam one last chance. People had been trying to reach her all day long; maybe he had been one of them. She brushed aside the obvious fact that her sister and her father had succeeded where Sam apparently had not, and she made a noisy business of sliding the barn door open and setting up to work in her studio. There was no possibility of her going upstairs, of course; not with Eden remotely in the picture.

But if Eden was there, by God, then Holly was going to make absolutely sure that Sam stayed aware of her all night. If Eden wasn't there, then Holly wanted Sam to have every chance to come downstairs and do something, anything, about the tattered state of their relationship.

Please, God. Anything.

An hour passed, and Sam didn't come down. Another hour. Holly kept banging on metal and slamming drawers and hammering birdhouse walls together, and in between, listening for sounds from upstairs, happy that there were none, crushed that there were none.

The barbed wire tightened; breathing became harder than ever. Her heart seemed to be getting squeezed into two pieces. Sam heard her, she knew; he had to. But he didn't come down.

And Holly didn't go up.

Upstairs, Sam lay in profound misery alone in his rented bed. The homely, workaday sounds of a folk artist at work—which in Holly's case always seemed to involve moving furniture—pounded home to him the fact that the one worth waiting for wasn't off on a yacht somewhere, but working her magic just a few feet below him.

Holly had his heart, no question about that. He could taste her warm mouth, feel her warm flesh so intensely that it took his breath away. Funny; whimsical; sexy; amazingly and infuriatingly frank—Holly was a gift straight from God, pure joy to behold.

But. There was this small, deep puncture wound in the most inner recess of Sam's soul. He thought that it had healed over, scarring him in the process, to be sure, but that it was essentially closed and done with. Now he knew that it was not. He had denied that to his parents and to his best friend, to Holly, and to himself. But tonight—either despite or because of Holly's tantalizing nearness—he realized that he would never really be done with Eden, not until he saw her again. So Billy was right; Sam had to know.

And meanwhile, he lay bitterly alone and in darkness, just a few feet away from sweetness and light.

27

Holly and Ivy stood up to their knees in the ocean, watching Cissy perform aquatic feats and Sally trying to duplicate them.

"I never should have told you about Dad's call, not without warning you to keep it from Mom," Holly told her sister.

Ivy tugged in irritation at the high-cut leg of her new swimsuit and said, "That's not why she didn't come to the beach today, dope. It's cloudy."

Holly was adamant. "I'm sure she's afraid she'll run into Eden with arms extended."

"Ridiculous. The island is surrounded by beaches."

"And this is our favorite. Dad knows that."

"Boy, you're in a mood."

Cissy had been standing on her hands underwater. After flopping on her back, she stood right side up again with her arms stretched wide like Mary Lou Retton: a perfect little ten.

Both women dutifully applauded. Sally shouted, "Watch me, watch me. I can do it for longer." Down into the water she plunged.

"What's wrong, Holly? You look exhausted," said Ivy as they waited for feet to emerge.

"It's Sam. I'm so numb. It really is over, almost before it began."

No feet. Eventually Sally popped up, choking and gasping for breath. Holly felt a stab of sympathy; she knew exactly how her niece felt.

Ivy said, "You're better off without him. I don't understand why he's still in your loft."

Holly shrugged. "It's that or his Corolla."

"Tough! Let him live in his car like any other self-respecting homeless person."

"Cut it out, Ivy; the kids will hear and take you seriously. Actually, he has a home in Westport, on the water," said Holly, cupping a little ocean in her hands and wetting down her thighs in preparation for the Big Plunge.

"Then why isn't he living there?" Ivy persisted.

"You want my theory? I think he's planning to take Dad head-on. I think he's sticking with Eden because his own father walked out on his birth mother, and he doesn't want to be even remotely that kind of man."

"Aren't you kind."

"Okay, and possibly because Eden is gorgeous and hard to get," Holly admitted. "But I really think that with Sam, it's more the trauma of his childhood. It was truly rotten until the Steadmans took him in and adopted him."

"Come on, Holl. He's old enough to have got over that. He has a career, a house, a certain amount of fame and respect."

"I don't think you ever get over something like that. It dogs you your whole life long. Consider your own kids," Holly said as she whistled Cissy from swimming too far out. "Would you want them ever to know about Jack?"

"Of course not! That's different."

"How? Because they're your daughters, and not just some guy you've never met?"

"They'd be devastated! They adore their father."

"Yes. Which is exactly what children are supposed to do. If they can't, who knows how they'll choose to work it out? Maybe some way screwy like Sam. God, I wish Eden had never come into his life."

"I'd like to meet your Sam," said Ivy, dipping to her waist and popping up with a little shiver. "I'd know in a New York minute if he was any good."

"Oh, because you're *so* perceptive," mocked Holly.

"More than you, dollink. Come on; we came here to swim, so let's swim."

"Race you to that kid on the boogie board," Holly said, and she dove right in, leaving her sister to catch up.

The cloudy, breezy day made it easier to coax the girls out of the water for the visit to the Bouchards. It was Ivy's belief—and even her mother agreed—that the Bouchards should not be shunned for being the most forgiving and nonjudgmental people on the island. They had given shelter to a tormented man, and if he had come to a decision that no one liked—well, no one could blame the Bouchards. They were simply too good for that.

So the children gobbled up their peanut butter and jelly sandwiches while their mother and their aunt lunched on chicken salad and on tomato slices the size of dessert plates. The girls played with the cat and went shelling on the beach, and Ivy brought the Bouchards up to date about life on the other side of the country. Before long, it was time to go—because in the summer, on an island, there always seemed to be another treat around the next bend.

Illumination Night was unquestionably the most magical of them. For nearly a century and a half, islanders, cottagers, and lucky day-trippers had gathered at the Camp Ground in Oak Bluffs to say goodbye to one another and to the season. This year, the event was going to be more of a hello-goodbye for Ivy and the children; but there was no drop in the level of excitement in the big house on Main as everyone donned her summer best for the festivity.

Even Cissy, who normally despised wearing dresses, consented to wear one for the occasion: a bright yellow jumper with big white buttons over a knit top printed with wildflowers. She looked wonderfully sweet and charming, but no one dared tell her that. Sally took longer to dress, working her way methodically through every item that her mother had packed before settling on a pale blue shift that set off her blond hair, done up for the evening with an extra-grownup single French braid. She looked pretty and ultra-feminine—and *she* expected everyone to notice out loud.

Ivy, whose lithe, blond figure looked good in anything, threw on a boxy, shapeless sundress that would have made Holly look like a fire hydrant. As for Holly, she wore black, she didn't know why. It wasn't her best color, but it wasn't her worst, and she liked the way the rayon fabric flowed when she moved. It reminded her of the sea.

Charlotte Anderson fussed as well, emerging from her bedroom in a flattering sundress of cream linen printed all over with the outlines of tiny seashells. Her mood was upbeat, and that made everyone glad.

The weather was warm and muggy and iffy enough that Charlotte ran back for umbrellas and threw them in the Volvo before the women set off for Oak Bluffs. Traffic was a predictable nightmare; the fact that Renata Nevin had parking for two cars was itself cause for celebration. Eventually the Volvo was snugged behind the widow's brand-new Volkswagen bug, and six women, no men, gathered under Japanese lanterns hanging from every open piece of gaily painted gingerbread on Mrs. Nevin's Gothic confection.

Painted pink and lavender and ivory and you-would-have-to-call-it purple, Wren House was only a little more exuberant than its neighbor to the right, painted green and blue and mauve and rust, and far less adventurous than its neighbor to the left, whose gingerbread alone was painted three shades of red.

Holly and Ivy left their mother and her old friend to entertain the stream of visitors stopping by, and they went off with the children to the sing-along.

The two big and two little sisters wandered among the milling crowd, enthralled like everyone else by the village of Hansel-and-Gretel cottages built often no more than an arm's length away from what originally had been neighboring tent sites. The Camp Ground was a fairyland of intricate scrollwork highlighting turrets and eaves, teeny balconies and tiny verandas, steep-gabled roofs and fish-scale shingles, all of it a-twinkle with thousands of Japanese lanterns. This was no commercial, made-for-admission Disney fantasy, but century-old enchantment in its original form. Every year, at least once, the Vineyard got it exactly right.

Holly said to her sister, "I feel a little as if we're fairy-people, and this is our magical ground, and the paper lanterns are stars from the sky, and something wonderful is happening here. You feel it, too, the spell."

Smiling, Ivy said, "Yes, I do. Even I."

"*Nothing* bad can happen here; we're enchanted, at least for tonight."

The women strolled serenely while the girls darted in and around them, all of them whispering sisterly secrets and forming bonds that would carry them into their old ages. Strains of "Cruising Down the River" made them linger at the crowd's edge to join in; everyone knew the words to that one.

Ivy spotted an old friend. "I haven't seen Eva in years! Keep an eye on the kids for me, would you? I'll be right back."

The songleader launched another old-fashioned crowd pleaser, "Shine On, Harvest Moon," and Holly and the children stayed to sing those lyrics, too. Holly had her arms around Cissy, snuggled in front of her, as they swayed to the old-fashioned tune. Sally, it was true, seemed more fascinated by two nearby girls wearing midriff tops over low-slung jeans, and bangles that jangled when they fluttered their hands—but even Sally was singing along.

The crowd loved the song. Holly could almost see a little white ball bouncing across the top of the words.

I ain't had no lov-in' . . .

Since August twenty-first around six-thirty A.M., she realized, substituting her own sad version for the lyric.

The simple truth was that there would be no moon tonight—harvest or otherwise. The sky was threatening; there was rain in the air. Still, for the length of the lyrics, the life of the song, Holly truly believed that love was a simple emotion that led, inevitably, to a happy ending.

Sam stood alongside and a little behind her, aware that he should keep moving, unable to do it. She looked so completely lovely, swaying slightly to the song, her hair swept up off her neck, her arms dropped over the shoulders of a young girl, undoubtedly a niece. He could hear Holly clearly above the crowd; she had a beautiful singing voice, something else he hadn't known about her. And she knew the lyrics. They all knew the lyrics. What kind of people *were* these?

For me and my . . . *ga-a-a-l.*

The song ended; it was time to move on. Sam was pushing himself to leave, and she must have noticed the struggle, because she turned to him with surprise and wonder in her face, as if he'd suddenly materialized from another century.

Caught.

Approaching her with a wry smile, he said, "Evenin', ma'am," simply because nothing else occurred to him. At this point, what the hell could he possibly say?

"*Sam* . . . ?" She still didn't believe it.

Sam wasn't sure himself why he'd come, except that he knew that tonight on the island, the Camp Ground was the place to be. He said, "I had some time to kill," and immediately hated himself for saying it that way: the thought seemed unworthy of the fantasy that surrounded them.

"Oh—well, naturally. I can see how . . . how . . ." she said, stammering to a halt.

Holly Anderson, at a loss for words? It was more painful to witness than if she had jammed a knife in his gut and turned it. He could deal with her rage. He just couldn't handle her hurt.

In a desperate diversion, Sam turned to the two young girls who were watching him curiously and gave them a stiffly smiling "Hello."

"Oh, I'm sorry," said Holly. "That's Cissy, my niece, and this is her sister Sally. Girls—"

The little redhead was looking up at her aunt in surprise. "I'm not Sally. I'm Cissy."

Holly gazed at the girl's earnest face and said, "Did I say Sally? I didn't mean that. Sam, this is my niece Sally."

"I'm *Cissy!*"

"I'm sorry. What did I say? Cissy?"

"You said Sally! I'm Cissy! Are you just fooling, Aunty Holly?" she asked, turning suddenly plaintive.

As for Cissy's blond sister, she turned her back on the whole conversational fiasco and simply pretended not to be there.

Despite the tension, Sam probably would have continued to stand there like a moonstruck servant if it weren't for Holly dismissing him. She half-sighed and said, "I hope you enjoy the time you have left to kill, Sam. When you're done with the loft, just leave the key on the dresser." She stuck out her hand and said, "Goodbye."

Not good night; goodbye. No questions asked. Sam was so stunned by the finality of it that he didn't think to take her hand. She shrugged and turned away, flanked by her nieces. The last thing he heard was the little redhead—Cissy or Sally, he still didn't know which—asking, "Is that the man who sleeps in his car?"

He stared at the three until they were joined by a fourth and got swallowed up by the crowd. After that, his world went from color and magic to plain black and white. He didn't see anything except in terms of obstacles to move around as he sought to escape. He circled the huge wrought-iron Tabernacle—historically the stage for so many spiritual revelations and conversions—on his way back to Circuit Avenue. People, trees, the gingerbread houses themselves—all seemed no more than indistinct blurs that got in his way. He wanted out of there; the idea that he was going to find illumination on Illumination Night suddenly seemed laughable.

He bumped into someone walking too slow, excused himself, got caught in a stroller-laden, slow-moving family, couldn't get around them, clipped the mother's shoulder, excused himself again, turned to detour down one of the cottage-lined spokes of the wheel that was Trinity Park, and found himself face-to-face, for the first time in seven unending, gut-gnawing years, with Eden Walker, who had refused to take the name Steadman when they were married at City Hall, sending Sam a signal as loud and clear as an air raid siren, only he had been too damn stupid to see it.

Because she was so beautiful. Her beauty had been blinding then, and it was positively awesome now. She was standing at the end of Tabernacle Avenue, actually a short and narrow lane, and she looked as if on this most magical of nights she had been expecting him. The lanterns hanging from every conceivable perch threw a rainbow of color over her short white dress, a form-fitting thing which reminded him, if he needed reminding, that her legs went on forever and her breasts were high and firm.

He approached. She met him halfway.

He was able to see her face: the high, sculpted cheek-bones, the Brooke Shields eyebrows, the mane of hair that was no longer blond, as Holly had said, but the color he remembered, a rich, dark auburn. It was straight and shining and bounced as she walked, trailing a cloud of confidence behind her.

For years he had been convinced that he'd been ex-aggerating Eden's beauty to himself, but now he knew that he had been wrong. She was all that and more.

28

"Hello, Sam," she said.

He remembered now: for all her sophisticated beauty, her voice had a kind of little-girl pitch to it that he had always found off-putting. Funny how he'd forgotten that.

"Long time, no see," he managed to say.

"I told you I'd come back."

"True," he said, and meanwhile his heart was taking flying leaps at his ribcage. "But you didn't mention that it would be for my parents' engraving."

She laughed and circled him, which made him feel like livestock at auction. He remembered that, too, about her now: that she looked before she bought. He used to enjoy it. Tonight he was comparing it to Holly's straight-ahead enthusiasm, and he wasn't so impressed. This seemed tired, and somehow nasty. He half-circled Eden himself, so that she wouldn't have the advantage of him.

He watched as a corner of her mouth lifted in a querulous smile. She rested her shapely behind on the cap of a low picket fence and let him take her all in. And he did, from the perfectly shaped fingernails, so unlike Holly's shop-torn ones, to the curve of her long neck as she watched him watching her.

"The years have been good to you," he said grudgingly.

She lifted a bare shoulder. "I play to my strengths."

"You have them in spades."

"I—thank you," she said. She cast her gaze downward in a gesture of humility that surprised Sam. She seemed to be waiting out a thought. He decided that he'd wait it out, too. She looked back up at him, and even in the kaleidoscope lighting he could see that her eyes were glazed over with tears.

"I'm sorry, Sam," she said, her voice catching. "It was a huge mistake, leaving you."

His heart took a big jump. *It was a huge mistake*: words he had waited seven long years to hear. He savored them, let them roll back and forth in his consciousness like fine brandy.

And then, amazing himself, he spit them out. All he wanted, he realized now, was the taste of her remorse. He had waited seven endless years to hear her say that she'd made a mistake. The magnitude of his wasted life didn't hit him all at once; it rolled in slowly and in stages, like an incoming tide.

"There was no baby, of course," he said tersely.

"No . . . there was no baby."

"But there *was* a warrant."

"Yes. I cheated an old woman and I'm sorry for that."

"And yet you came back to try to cheat another old woman, and her invalid husband."

She shook her head. "I came back to find out about you, whether you were with anyone. The engraving falling into my hands, that was a detour."

"An irresistible one."

"I won't deny it. But it wasn't what I came for, not what I wanted."

"I don't think you *know* what you want, Eden!" he said in a burst of frustration.

"Yes . . . I do, Sam," she whispered.

He was beginning to feel ill. "Besides money, I mean."

That brought a flash of anger from her. "If it was about money, I'd be with Eric right now."

Seven years! Sam nodded and said, "Where *is* the poor sap, anyway?"

Eden pushed herself off the low fence and said dismissively, "He's showing me how much he trusts me."

He'll get lots of practice at that, Sam thought, but he didn't say it aloud. What was the point?

Seven years! There was only one real sap in this scenario.

"Since we're here," Sam said tiredly, "I suppose I ought to bring up the subject of the money. Sorry," he added, when he saw the look of pained surprise on her face. "I know it's gauche."

She pressed her hands together in a prayerful pose, the index fingers touching her lips. She had beautiful, long fingers, very talented. But not as talented as Holly's. Holly could make bookcases! The thought was a tonic to the dryness Sam felt inside. Just thinking that the woman he loved could perform such a miracle of carpentry, among other miracles . . .

"No . . . no, you're not being gauche," Eden said in a trembly voice. A tear broke loose and rolled down her cheek; she brushed it away with her clasped hands. "I understand, I do, Sam. Why *wouldn't* you be concerned; a hundred and fifty thousand dollars is a lot of money. Your parents must have been frantic all this time."

"You know what, Eden? They were."

Seven years. He was almost dizzy with the thought

of the bouts of melancholy, the evenings spent playing the songs he knew she'd loved. If he never heard Phil Collins again, it was going to be way too soon.

"But Sam, here's the thing," she said with a mournful sigh. "I'm going to have to give it back. All of it."

"Give it—what—back?"

"All of the money that I got for the engraving."

It was like a meltdown at a nuclear power plant: a din of sirens and alarms went off at once, making thought impossible. Sam had to force himself to stay calm. This was Eden he was dealing with; he'd need his wits.

He said cautiously, "And why would you do that?"

She shrugged and gave him a look that he'd have sworn was filled with sympathy. "The engraving was a forgery," she explained with a hapless smile.

"*What*?" he shouted. "A *forgery*! Jesus Christ, what next, Eden?"

"Shh, shh," she said, touching her hand to his lips. "Don't, don't, Sam," she begged.

She looked around her with something like panic and began dragging him away from their fairly conspicuous spot to a slightly less conspicuous one behind a tree. People were milling everywhere; it was impossible to get out of earshot, but she did the best she could.

"I sold the engraving to a fairly rough character," she said. "Don't ask me details; you don't want to know, except that I'm sure he's somewhere on the island, which has me terrified out of my wits."

She sounded nervous enough, but she seemed determined to get out her story. "After your parents gave me the engraving, the first thing I did was track down the lawyer who'd handled their inheritance. I found out that he'd been the gay lover of your parents' bachelor Uncle Henry. I suppose because of the intimacy, the attorney knew that Uncle Henry had been given the engraving by an Allied soldier who'd stolen the painting from a museum in Berlin. I'm assuming that old Uncle Henry had once been lovers with the Allied soldier, but that's neither here nor there."

Sam was mesmerized. "You managed to find all this out about a long-dead uncle and his now-dead lawyer?"

"Oh, come on, Sam. How hard was it? The attorney's secretary is in a nursing home and desperately lonely; she was more than willing to reminisce."

All Sam could think was, *What a waste of smarts.*

"I admit," said Eden, "that I was going to keep half the money and lie to your parents about how much I got. But then I fell in with Eric, and I was pretty much resolved to give your parents all—well, nearly all—of the money, because I figured I wouldn't need it and I know they did. I'm sure you don't believe me—you have no reason to believe me—but that's what I had planned."

"Uh-huh. Keep talking."

"But then, while I was sailing with Eric on his boat, I got a call on my cell phone from this—" She looked around, then lowered her voice. "This brute I sold the engraving to, and he was furious. He told me he'd had the engraving looked at, and an expert had told him that it was a nineteenth century fake. He threatened to kill me, Sam! I could handle one creep coming after me," she said, "but not two. As it turned out, I'd also pissed off a dealer—but you know how middlemen are, Sam; everything pisses *them* off."

"This would be Stefan Koloman."

"Stefan, yes. You met him? So you know he means business. All I can say is, he doesn't mean as much business as Hans."

"And that's why you faked your death to look like a

murder: so that each of the men would think the other had done it."

She looked surprised; surprised and pleased that he was able to keep up. "I've always thought that you and I made the best team, Sam," she said with an irrepressible grin. "Yes, that's what I had planned. I didn't expect poor Eric to be blamed."

Sam, who knew that she'd told Eric only that she had staged the scene to look like an accident to put off Stefan, said, "Did you care that Eric was suspected?"

She shrugged. "Not as much as I cared that Hans and Stefan be convinced I was dead. But when Eric came under suspicion, the state police impounded his boat. That, I *didn't* expect."

"Or you never would have hidden the money there."

"I didn't say that," she said, shaking her head. "Just that I was surprised. Eric had wanted to take me on some voyage or other, so I knew I could talk my way back aboard the boat any time I wanted to. He's having a late-life crisis," she added, sounding utterly bored. "He's obsessed with this dream to sail somewhere far. Which is convenient for me: in the Bahamas or in Bora Bora, no one much cares who you are or where you're from."

Not a bad plan. Sam could see how she'd managed to keep out of jail all these years.

He said, "And yet Eric suspected that you set up the boat to look like a murder had been committed there. He lied about how the blood got on the deck either to cover for you—or because he was too humiliated to admit that he was out of your loop."

Again she shrugged, and Sam had to admit, she had the most eloquent shrug he'd ever seen. "He lied because he loves me."

"Eden, he's such a little fish—hardly worthy of your hook," Sam said softly. "Throw him back to his family. Find someone worthy of your talents."

"How can I, Sam? Maybe if *you* were rich. But I'm giving back all of the money; I'll have *nothing* after this."

Ah, shit: the money. His parents were on the way to being destitute again, if—*if*—Eden was giving back all of the money.

Something in his face tipped her off that he didn't altogether believe her. She became angry; she said, "What does it take to make you believe me? Hans is a *thug*. Do you understand? A murderous thug!"

"But possibly an imaginary one?" Sam asked wryly.

"Oh? Imagine *this*, in that case." She turned away slightly from him and yanked up her already high dress: the backs of her thighs were appallingly black and blue.

"My God," Sam said, his jaw clamping down tight. He touched the massive bruises gingerly, hardly able to believe that someone could punish a woman that way. "Where do I find him?"

"His name is Hans Erlich; he hangs out in South Boston," she murmured, pulling her dress back down. "He's an arms dealer, I'm pretty sure, and a big-time collector of Nazi paraphernalia. I guess he wanted the Durer because he's decided to move into something more mainstream," she quipped. But her voice was quavering as she added, "He said that if I don't bring him his money tomorrow, he was going to . . . to use the next car to kill me. Sam, I am so scared," she said, hugging herself as she stood before him.

He had never seen her afraid before. She was trembling violently as she said, "I'm sorry, I'm sorry, I don't want you to see me like this." She made an effort to pull herself together, but she failed. "I'm sorry, I'm sorry," she kept mumbling.

Sam couldn't bear to see a woman in terror. He took Eden in his arms to reassure her and said softly, "Does Eric know about this?"

She rolled her forehead in a back-and-forth *no* across his shirt. "I didn't tell him I recognized Hans in the Volvo."

"Do you want me to give the money back for you?" he said, holding her a little away and searching her face for some clue what she wanted from him.

"Yes. No. I can't ask you to do that," she said, looking down at the ground. When she raised her head again, tears were flowing down her cheeks. "I can't ask you, even though I know that once you would have gone to the moon and back, if the man in the moon were threatening me. Oh, Sam," she said in a soft wail, "I love you so much. I was such a fool. I've never stopped loving you; I knew I wouldn't, and I never have. We were so good together . . . that's why I never could bring myself to divorce you . . ."

She jerked away from him and made a massive effort to bring herself under control. Wringing her hands desperately, she kept repeating, "I'm sorry, sorry . . . I swore to myself that I wouldn't say anything. I know it's over between us, I know that . . . but we were so *good* together. Oh, Sam, when I heard you were on the island, I—something happened. I don't understand it, I can't explain it, but something terrible and wonderful happened. I fell in love all over again . . . still . . . for the first time. I can't explain it. Sam . . . Sam . . ." she said through her tears. "I *love* you."

It was that last "I love you" that did it for Sam.

Something about it was too insistent, too like Eden wanting her way. Maybe she meant it and maybe she didn't, but the amazing thing, the joyous thing, the absolutely liberating thing, was that Sam didn't care either way. He had given his heart so completely to Holly that he had little room for any emotion for Eden except pity. He did feel genuinely bad for her: her conning ways had finally caught up with her. He'd help her as much as he could, but not out of love.

"Eden, I don't know what to say—"

"Say you love me, then!" she cried. "At least say you'll have me! Just once—for old times' sake." She threw herself at him, and before he could unwrap her clinging arms from around his neck, they were accosted by a scandalized, disillusioned sixty-two-year-old with a shiner.

"*Eden!*"

"Eric! Thank God you're here. It's Sam," she said, backing away from him in sudden horror. "I don't know what came over him; he went into this jealous rage," she said, rushing toward Anderson.

"*Get away from me!*" he cried in a ghastly voice. He raised his arms so quickly that she ran up against them and staggered backward.

"Eric, how could you? You . . . you said you *trusted* me," she said plaintively. Anyone would have thought that poor old Eric had been the one caught cheating.

Sam felt a little like the father of a problematic bride: *Here you go, fella; she's all yours.* "Well," he said, feeling oddly buoyant, "gotta go. Eden, if you want me to deliver that money for you, just call Holly. She'll know where I am."

Tonight, tomorrow, for the rest of their lives. All Sam had to do was convince her that he was, indeed, The Right One for her. She had believed it once. If he had to park on her porch until the island got swept into the sea, he was going to make her believe it again.

"You lied to me!" Eric said in a scandalized croak. "You filthy liar! I heard everything. Lies!"

"I'll leave you two to it," Sam said with a polite smile and a shrug. Then he turned and walked out of the swampy mire of Eden's influence once and for all.

But he didn't know where he was walking *to*. Holly

was in the Camp Ground somewhere, but where? He remembered that she had originally invited him to help her hang lanterns on a cottage whose name had something to do with birds. What was it? Robin's Nest? Chicken Coop? He racked his brain and came up with the owner's name: Renata something. Wren House, yes, that was it; it was a play on her name.

The search began. He went from porch to porch, asking arbitrary guests if they knew where Wren House was and for a while got no for an answer. Finally he hit pay dirt. "Take the next left," said an elderly gentleman.

He turned down the next spoke of the hub that was the park and was lucky enough to spot the Cissy-Sally redhead, getting scolded for standing on the banister of the porch. The scolder was a taller, older version of Holly's other niece. Sam walked up to the woman and said, "Hi; Sam Steadman. Where can I find your sister?"

Ivy looked him up and down from under her lifted eyebrows. "You're Sam Steadman?" she asked, her voice slathered with disbelief.

"You bet. Where can I find your sister?"

His urgency made an impression. She cocked her head and said, "Why?"

"None of—"

Screw it; it *was* her business. It was all of their business. "Because I love her and I want to tell her that."

"Ah. That's a good reason. Are you eligible yet?"

"Soon."

"You'd better be. Because you broke her heart a few minutes ago. She hitched a ride home."

"Thanks. See you."

He dropped down the two steps, waved to Cissy-Sally, and took off at a canter, aware that his car was parked practically on the other side of the island. It was hot and muggy and already he smelled like an overworked pony, but he was in an unbelievable hurry to see

Holly again. He'd just blown seven years clinging to the flotsam of a misguided notion. That had to be why he didn't want to waste even seven minutes without engaging Holly on what was bound to be a long debate over whether he was worthy of her.

He wasn't. He knew that. He tried to chalk up his blunders to his lack of experience. What did he know about women like Holly, really? Nothing. He'd never known someone like her before. The closest he could come to her was . . .

Millie Steadman. Good grief—Millie Steadman! Honest, candid, funny, and good, *those* were the bedrock values that Sam had been looking for in a woman. Throw in a few other attributes—Holly was beautiful, talented, and fantastic in bed—and you had the makings of a world-class, once-in-a-lifetime chance for happiness, which Sam had just blown completely to hell.

No. *Nearly* blown completely to hell. He refused to fall back into his usual defeatist view of women. How could he, when he'd been taken in by Millie Steadman and taken up by Holly Anderson? How many men had that kind of luck? He practically yodelled for joy as he hopped into his Corolla and took off for Holly's place.

Crawled, that is, to Holly's place: Oak Bluffs was gridlocked. Nothing new there; but in his present mood, Sam was ready to tramp across the roofs of stopped cars. Holly, Holly, *Holly*! He could hardly wait to throw himself at her mercy. He had no doubt that she'd point out his stupidity to him (many times), but he could count on her to be kind and clever about it when she did. And when they were well into their old age, and sitting by a fire, and the snow was blowing all around them, she would doubtless remind him again, hopefully not in front of the children, and he would be sheepish and agree.

Him! Sheepish! He positively looked forward to the prospect.

Hey, when you're right, you're right, and when you're wrong, you're wrong.

He was sitting through his third red light, wistfully if anxiously fantasizing, when something that Eden had said hit him with the force of a crowbar across the face: *I'm pretty sure he's somewhere on the island, which has me terrified out of my wits.*

More lies from Eden? But what if they weren't? What if the Nazi-lover really was skulking around, looking for his money before Eden took off with it?

Where would he skulk?

Where else?

Ah, Jesus, ah, hell, Sam thought, washed over by a wave as cold and terrifying as any a mariner faced. *The barn.* Hans had been there before, but he'd taken off when Holly showed up; that was suddenly as clear as a bell. And Holly—Holly, who'd never been on a Mean Street in her life—was undoubtedly working through her emotions where she always did, in her studio, pounding and banging and moving furniture.

Sam felt, literally, as if he were drowning. Breathing was impossible and it was all he could do not to go into a full-bore panic. He took an arbitrary detour, sideswiping the rental on a fire hydrant in the maneuver, and managed to cover two hundred feet before running smack into yet another roadblock, a squad car and two vehicles whose fenders were bent.

Hell! He couldn't back up, so he abandoned the car altogether and headed for the nearest bike rack. Locked, locked, locked, locked, not locked. Out came the steal-able bike; Sam hopped aboard and began pedalling his way out of the traffic jam. On Eastville he began walking the bike with his thumb stuck out for a lift. A pickup pulled over and Sam chucked the bike in a ditch, then told the driver, "Fifty bucks if you take me to Tashmoo."

"Cool," said the long-haired kid in painter's pants. He launched into an endless stream of chat, maybe to earn his dough, but Sam wasn't interested. He was able to manage a grunt or two, but his mind was in overdrive, fearing the worst. *Holly, please, stay out of the barn.*

29

The barn door squealed as Holly slid it open and entered her studio, determined to salvage what she could of her life. Her mother was right. She lacked discipline. She needed to focus. No time like the present. Never put off till tomorrow. Just do it. Today. Now. This minute.

And to hell with Sam Steadman. Seeing him wandering around and killing time—killing time!—at the Camp Ground had been a heart-stopping blow for her. Whether he was waiting to rendezvous with Eden or whether he was just hoping to run into her there, one thing was clear: he hadn't been looking for Holly. If he had, he would have gone straight to Wren House.

To hell with Sam Steadman. Who needed him? She'd rather grind her iron *tuteur*.

Holly was proud of the birthday present she'd created for her mother, a three-foot-high garden structure shaped into a pair of wrens perched on a gnarled branch. Holly had intended it to be a support for a small vining flower, but it was pretty enough to stand alone in a garden. She had painstakingly cut and shaped and welded the wrens, instantly recognizable by their perky tails, and had shaped the branch with a fair amount of horizontal in it. The effect was almost eastern in its simplicity and very pretty, but some of the edges still needed grinding.

Better them than my teeth, was her grim thought as she donned a clear face mask to protect herself from flying particles. She plugged in her grinder and set to work, and if Sam happened to return and the noise happened to keep him awake, so much the better.

Because to hell with Sam Steadman.

Gradually Holly let go of her misery, getting lost instead in the artistic process of making something carefully planned look charmingly spontaneous. No question, grinding was a form of therapy tonight. The loud noise, the play of sparks, the smell of metal heating up under the spinning disk—all of it served to take Holly out of herself and onto another plane. It wasn't exactly a happy place, but at least it wasn't painful.

Until someone came up behind her and gave her a stunning blow to the back of her head.

Sam had three twenties; he threw them on the front seat of the pickup and told the kid to keep the change. The sense that Holly was in danger was overwhelming now; he took off in a sprint down the shell-lined drive, wondering how he had missed the obvious: that at any given time, Eden probably had half the New England underworld hot on her trail.

He saw that the door at the top of the stairs was open and that all the lights were on inside the loft apartment. But the same scenario was being played out in the studio, and that made his blood congeal. He ran inside the shop. There was no sign of Holly, but a buzz-cut hulk in a black tee shirt and slacks was methodically tearing apart Holly's beloved workplace.

"Hans!" Sam shouted. "Over here!"

Hans it was. At the sound of his name, the thug turned and sent a narrow hand-painted drawer flying past Sam's ear as he ducked to the side. Were there any other weapons than drawers? Sam hadn't been thinking of a gun, hadn't been thinking at all except of Holly. His instincts had been two steps behind his emotions, but they were catching up fast. He dropped behind a wardrobe and ducked down low, waiting to see if Hans was dumb enough to have carried a weapon onto the island.

Apparently he was. Sam heard the gun being cocked. The good news was, Hans must not have had occasion to use it yet. The bad news was, where was Holly?

"Move out where I can see you," Hans commanded. "Now. Believe me, no one will hear if I shoot."

"Since you put it *that* way . . ." said Sam. He stepped out from the shadow of the tall, half-painted armoire and dutifully put his hands up.

Hans squinted through steel-blue eyes at him. "We've met?" he asked, almost genially.

"No," said Sam, "but your reputation preceeds you." Where was Holly?

"Which reputation? I'm very talented."

"I've heard. I guess I'm thinking, as a hit-and-run expert."

"Ah. Too bad you know me, period. Sit down—that chair," he said, nodding to a sturdy armchair.

"Where's Holly?" Sam said, wild to know now.

"Who's Holly? Oh, so that was Holly."

"Where's Holly, you bastard?"

"Shut up. Sit down."

Hey. There's Holly!

Sam saw the top of her head as she rose slowly from the floor not far behind Hans. Her face was fierce in concentration as she lifted an iron garden ornament, one he knew she'd been working on for her mother, and positioned it behind and above Hans.

"No need to get testy," said Sam, playing for time. "I'm going. Just . . . stay cool, man."

He was careful not to look anywhere but in Hans's eyes as he made a business of edging around the jammed-up furniture.

Down came the birds-on-a-branch, crashing into Hans's arm and sending the gun flying. It seemed to Sam that Holly fell to the floor after that, but he was too busy jumping Hans and knocking him semi-senseless to know for certain. He recovered Hans's gun and had to resist slamming it against the man's head in retaliation for the blood he saw fresh and wet on Holly's neck as she half staggered to her feet again.

"I'm okay," she said, trying to reassure him.

Sam was anything but reassured. "Sit down, sit down," he begged, dragging over another chair—this one a rocker painted with a mama goose and a trail of goslings—while he kept the gun levelled at Hans, who was sitting on the floor with a dazed look and blood streaming down his face.

Holly sat in the rocker and pulled out a cordless from the flap pocket of her smock. Calmly, she punched in 911 and then handed Sam the phone.

In less than a minute he had the police and an ambulance on the way. He handed back the cordless to her and said, "You okay enough to hold the line open?"

"For Pete's sake, I've been whacked on the back of the head before," said Holly with spirit. "I was captain of the soccer team my senior year."

"I didn't know artists could be coordinated," he said, smiling with relief.

"Folk artists can."

Sam turned his attention to her attacker. "How about filling me in, Hans? We can make it easier for you when the cops get here."

"Yeah, sure."

"I mean it. Look, suppose I get the ball rolling for you. Here's what I know: Eden stole an engraving from my parents—yeah; surprised? But now it turns out the engraving's a fake."

"That's right," said Hans, his eye beginning to swell over a bloody gash on his cheek. "I got that straight from an expert. You want his report?"

"No, I'll take your word for it. I have to say, I'm curious: why would you even *want* a Durer?" Sam asked. "He doesn't seem like your style."

"We're descended."

"Ah. The family tree thing. All right, well, let me give this a shot. You tell me if I'm right or wrong. My guess is that Eden told you that she didn't have your money anymore—that it went to pay the medical bills of her in-laws. Correct?"

Hans nodded.

"And she said she was going to pay you in installments, because she was now engaged to a very wealthy man. Also correct?"

Again Hans nodded. "She gave me her engagement ring as token collateral. Said it was worth a chunk of change."

"Nice touch on her part. Do you have it on you?" Sam was thinking of the marquis diamond, very small, that he'd given her after their elopement.

Hans seemed to consider whether he should answer or not, then shrugged and said, "In my pocket. She said it was worth fifteen grand, and it is. I had someone look at that, too."

"Fifteen!" Obviously not Sam's marquis. "Let's have a look. Nice and easy, please."

Hans reached slowly into his hip pocket and pulled out what was clearly a very old ring filled with gem-stones, chief among them, a startling emerald.

Holly gasped. "That's my *grandmother's* ring. Give me that!" she said, snatching it out of his hand.

"What can I say."

Sam said, "And meanwhile you're crawling all over the island because—why? You didn't believe that Eden had given away the money?"

"Shit, I didn't know what to believe. First I hear she's missing, presumed dead. Then suddenly she's in touch, saying she'll try to get me the money back. Then she says it's already gone to the hospital. Then she says she'll pay it back in installments. Then, a day later, she ships me the ring as a sign of good faith. No addresses during any of this; she's on a boat, she says."

Holly muttered, "How the hell does she keep track of her lies?"

"Meanwhile, I'm doing some checking around," Hans said grimly, "and I find out there's a *Vixen* on the Vineyard, just like the newspaper says, only now it's getting fitted out for a long voyage. Uh-huh. Like she's gonna pay me from Tahiti."

"Very perceptive. Eden's good at playing all ends toward the middle."

Hans shrugged and said, "Makes no difference to me. I'll get my money if I have to go to Tahiti to do it."

"Sam, we have to stop her!"

"Don't worry," said Sam. "Your father won't be taking Eden to the south Pacific or anywhere else. He's finally figured her out."

But that didn't mean that their problems were solved. "Do you have any rope around?" he asked Holly.

Holly perked up. Something to do. "Of course!" she said, completely revived by now.

He had to be careful not to grin like an idiot and to pay attention to the task at hand. When she brought him a sturdy line, he said, "You know how to use a gun?"

"A gun, are you crazy? But I know how to use a rope."

Sam moved in closer, keeping the semiauto aimed at the chest of the luckless collector. Holly had the man bagged and tied to the chair just as sirens began wailing in the distance.

They walked outside to wait for the cops, but by now Sam was wild with impatience to track down Eden. He said, "Explain everything to the police when they arrive. I've got to go after Eden before she takes off with the money again."

"What? And leave me here? I'm going with you."

"No way."

"Yes I am. Get *used* to it, Sam."

Get used to it. Sam loved the idea of getting used to Holly Anderson, but then and there didn't seem like the time and place to say so. So he grunted something that might or might not have been permission, and when the police arrived they gave them a quick rundown and were told to go to the station to fill out a report. Hans was hauled away, and the paramedics cleaned Holly's wound. After trying unsuccessfully to get her to return with them to the hospital for follow-up care, they left with their wagon.

By then Sam had moved Holly's pickup to the front of the barn.

"Let's go," he said, as good as his word. "If I'm right about where the money's hidden, we might still be in time."

"But you said that my father is done with her," said Holly, climbing up to the passenger's seat.

"Yeah, well, I've been wrong before," Sam acknowledged.

"*Have* you," she said with a sly sideways look, and he had his inkling of what was to come in their old age.

It was a wonderful inkling. He got behind the wheel

and was about to put the truck into drive when he thought, *What the hell am I doing?*

He turned to her instead and said urgently, "First things first. I haven't said I love you. I love you, Holly. Madly. Truly. I love you." To the rumble of thunder he leaned over to kiss her—not a long kiss, not a kiss that was going to lead to anything like imminent sex; but a kiss that was meant to reestablish the connection between them. It was a little like plugging in an electric cord. Now he had the power to see.

"I love you," he said again, "and I'm sorry."

"I love *you*," she answered, her breath fanning warm against his lips, "and you're forgiven. Now let's go find your parents' money."

"Technically, it's not their money," he felt bound to say as he took off, spinning shells in the pickup's wake. "The Durer's a fake, after all."

"So *what*?" Holly answered, sounding outraged at his scruples. "You saw Hans. How do you think he made that money? Selling tie-dyed tee shirts on a Boston sidewalk? He's a criminal; he got the money exploiting people. I can't imagine a more just scenario than Hans in jail with a forgery hanging on his cell wall, and your parents having a little security in their old age. Don't you *dare* tell them it was a forgery."

"Okay," Sam agreed, awed by her absolute conviction of right and wrong. "Have you ever considered becoming a federal magistrate?"

"Sure, as soon as I finish med school. Oh—shoot; it's starting to rain. At least it held off for the crowds at the Camp Ground."

After a spatter of raindrops, the skies opened and torrents of rain pounded them, washing over the pickup in blinding sheets and forcing them to slow to a crawl.

"This'll slow Eden down, too, hopefully," Sam said,

wiping the inside of the windshield with the palm of his hand.

"Why are you so convinced she's trying to get aboard the boat if my father's on to her?" Holly asked again.

"I dunno. I guess, because she's Eden. Nothing can stop her. She just keeps going and going and going."

"How *did* my dad figure out her game?"

"He, ah, overheard her proposition me." Among other things.

"Yikes! In the middle of the Camp Ground?"

He was relieved that Holly didn't press on with a third degree, wanting every little detail of the confrontation between Eden and him. It was a sign, the very first sign, that she was prepared to begin trusting him.

"You know what?" he said, reaching over for her hand. "I love you."

"And so does Eden, it sounds like," Holly said ruefully.

"Nah. She needed me to explain to my parents why the money wouldn't be coming, that's all; she had to get me involved in whatever way she could. It was all part of her plan, along with convincing Eric that she had in fact paid my folks the money. She knew Eric would never have insulted her by verifying it. After that, I imagine she planned to squeeze him for some or all of the amount to pay back Hans."

"You're right about my dad not wanting to check with your parents. But how could he not have missed the ring? He's not *that* blind."

Sam said, "She could have told him she'd lost it overboard while they were sailing. He would have believed it. He wanted to believe."

I know how it feels, Sam thought, amazed to realize that he didn't have to cross his fingers and hope for the best anymore.

The squall passed on, leaving them rolling down the

windows in search of a breeze. "My next truck will have air conditioning," promised Holly.

"*Our* next truck," Sam said. It was as close to a proposal as he could come, encumbered as he was. But oh, that *our* tasted sweet on his lips.

They drove through huge puddles, sending sheets of water flying in both directions, and turned off into the marina where the *Vixen* was berthed. The air temperature had dropped maybe five or ten degrees, but the rumble of thunder told them that the evening's fireworks weren't yet over.

"If she's not here, then what?" Holly asked as they parked the car.

"Let's first find out if she is or not."

She wasn't—but then, neither was the *Vixen*.

30

The *Vixen's* slip was empty, though that hadn't been the case a couple of hours earlier. Holly, for one, couldn't believe it.

She stood in the spitting rain and said, "Unless my father was drugged or hypnotized, I don't see how Eden—even Eden—could have talked him into taking the boat out now."

They had heard on the weather radio that a line of severe squalls was going to pound the island for the next couple of hours. Boaters had been advised to seek shelter immediately, and in fact a sailboat was headed—much too fast—directly for the *Vixen's* empty berth even as they stood on the float overlooking it. The man on the bow, wearing a foul-weather jacket and holding a coiled dock line in his hand, was shouting over the wind to his wife on the helm, "Hard astern, hard astern!"

But the boat kept coming forward, bouncing off a piling before heading toward the float where Sam and Holly were standing. They jumped out of the way as the boat slammed directly into it, its bow nudging over the edge like a friendly horse in search of an apple. Sam grabbed the bow rail to steady the vessel, while Holly caught a dockline from the owner and secured it with a half-hitch to the nearest bit.

"Lash it to the bit!" shouted the owner, still issuing orders after the fact.

He jumped down to the float and, with Sam and Holly's help, tied down the boat fore and aft in the darkness, doubling up on the spring lines against the wind, which was now driving walls of on-and-off rain before it.

By the time they were done the squall had passed, leaving Sam and Holly soaked through. The owner of the boat thanked them, blaming his seamanship on his wife, who was below—probably packing a bag before she ran away.

Sam said, "Did you pass any boats going out as you came in?"

The owner laughed and said, "Yeah. A single nutcase, headed on a course for Woods Hole."

"Sailboat, or power?"

"Sail, but moving under power and not getting very far in those choppy seas."

"Size?"

"I don't know—forty, forty-some feet. Why?"

"You didn't see the name on the transom, by any chance?" asked Holly. "Or whether the dodger was a dark color? Or how many people were aboard?"

"At the time, I wasn't paying much attention," the sailor said dryly. "I passed it near the gong off West Chop."

Holly turned to Sam. "Now what? We don't even know if my dad's on board."

In thirty more seconds, they had their answer to that one, at least: Eric Anderson appeared on the dock, just as drenched as they were.

"Dad!" cried Holly as he approached. "Then Eden really is on the boat *alone*?"

"She must be—crazy fool," said her father. "She can't handle the *Vixen* alone on a night like this!" His voice held more agony than outrage, although Holly couldn't tell whether that was for the boat's sake or for Eden's.

Another wave of heavy rain, simultaneous with a roar of wind, drove down on them, making it almost impossible to hear. The owner scrambled back aboard to the comfort of his boat, heedless of the fact that he was a poacher.

With her back to the driving rain, Holly shouted to her father, "Where were you when she was stealing your boat, for God's sake?"

He echoed Holly's posture, presenting his back to the onslaught of weather. "She asked to meet me at the Bouchards," he said, raising his voice over the howl of the wind. "Said she wanted to give me my ring back. I was confused . . . she'd told me she'd lost it . . . But I went out there anyway . . . they hadn't seen her. When I got back here, the boat was gone. I've just got off the radio with the Coast Guard . . . they won't go after it until the weather clears," he said as he staggered off balance under a gust of wind.

"We think she's headed for Woods Hole," said Sam, bowing his head to avert the stinging rain.

"Christ! She'll never be able to take that boat through Woods Hole herself, not against the current; she doesn't know the channel!"

"We need a fast boat," Sam decided, looking around him through squinty eyes. He looked as if he was about to steal the first one he saw.

Holly had a more legal idea. "Dad—do you still have keys to Robby's Robalo?"

Holding his forearm above his eyes as a visor against

the pounding rain, her father nodded and said, "That's where I called the Coast Guard from just now."

"Sam," she said, turning to him. "What do you think?"

"We can find her if she's running with nav lights on."

"What if she's not?"

"We come back and let the big boys go out later on."

Holly turned back to her father. "Dad! We can do it!"

"Nothing doing," he said flatly. "You're not risking your neck for a boat." Even as he said it, the rain began letting up.

"The Robalo's fast and can handle this weather," Holly argued. "Look—the squall's passed over already! And we'll be in open water; I promise we won't chase her into Woods Hole. Dad, please! Let me have the Robalo," she pleaded. "We'll be right back with it."

She sounded as if she were begging for the keys to the van to dash off for ice cream. It was the perfect note to strike, and it helped that it was no longer raining.

"The Petersons are aboard the *Saracen*," father said. "I'll be there, monitoring channel sixty-eight. Make sure you stay in touch. I mean it, Holly. Just because you grew up on boats—"

"Keys, keys!" she said, trying not to jump up and down with impatience.

He fished them out for her and repeated, "I mean it, Holly. You will stay in touch."

"Yes, yes, come on, Sam, let's *go*!"

She was on fire for the chase and she had no idea why. Because of Eden, Sam, her father, her mother? Because she already loved the Steadmans and wanted them to live long and happy lives?

Yes to all of it, but especially because of Eden.

I want to catch her. I don't want to see her get away with this.

It was an unfair world; Holly knew that. But if she

could do anything to tweak the scales of justice to weigh a little more evenly, then by God . . .

"You should see the expression on your face," Sam said as they passed the breakwater and she opened the throttle. "You look like Charles Bronson."

"I do not," said Holly, embarrassed. She altered course for the number four nun. "I was just concentrating, that's all. I think Robby keeps some spare jackets in a locker somewhere," she added. "You want to take the helm while I look?"

"I thought you'd never ask," Sam said, grinning. Holly knew the buoys like the back of her hand—but Sam knew how to ride a fast boat.

The worst of the weather seemed to have passed; visibility was distinctly improved, and the seas were dying down. Holly saw a star or two peep through the scudding clouds overhead. It was exhilarating, being on a boat with Sam at night on the Sound. If he'd ask her to sail to the ends of the earth with him just then, she'd say yes without thinking twice. How unlike her mother she was that way.

I don't care. I'll go with him around the world or around the corner, as long as I can go with him.

"Nice boat," said Sam with a boyish grin. "We'll have to get one of these. You like fishing?"

Or, I'll go fishing. As long as I can go with him.

"Sam, you still haven't told me where she hid the money on the *Vixen*," Holly said after she'd found rain jackets for each of them. "Where could she hide it where my dad wouldn't find it?"

Sam steered with his knees as he zipped up his jacket. "It's just a theory, of course, but the fact that she had to take the whole damn boat away from the marina makes me feel more confident about it. You remember how she stuck to the boat in Portsmouth? I went up there

and found the boatyard that did the repairs. The yardhands all remember her—"

"Gee, I wonder why."

"Not only for the usual reasons. They said she was
fascinated by the fiberglass repairs they were doing to
the engine bed. That amazed them; it's a messy, smelly
job with very little glamor to it. I'm reckoning that before Eric returned to Portsmouth from his trip to Providence, she fiberglassed the money—protected, of
course—to the inside of the hull."

"You're right, you're right! It's obvious to me now.
But—she'll need to chisel or ax it out."

"And if you're trying not to be noticed, the best place
to do that—assuming you have a careful hand—is at
sea."

"Oh, my God; could she actually sink the *Vixen* trying?"

Sam said grimly, "Let's hope not."

The mood became more somber then; Holly couldn't
quite recapture the illusion that they were on a starlight
cruise. In the open runabout, she could feel that the air
had turned damp and chill again. Definitely, the wind
was picking up; the seas were getting choppier. She
zipped up her jacket, then pulled up the hood, then tightened the drawstring around her bottom, all in an esca-
lating effort to keep warm.

The binoculars were good ones. Even in the dark, she
was able to identify a variety of marine traffic, nearly
all of it commercial, plying its way across the Sound:
the last ferry of the night, headed for the Vineyard from
Wood's Hole; a tug, towing a barge; a fishing boat with
booms extended; a luxury yacht steaming for Nantucket.
As for smaller craft, they seemed to have heeded the
marine warning and run for cover; there were none
around.

"Either that, or Eden *is* running without lights."

"Wait, I see—no; it's just a little cabin cruiser," said Holly, disappointed. She let the binoculars hang around her neck as she rubbed her eyes, then scanned the sky overhead. No stars, and lowering visibility. Damn it. She'd been overconfident about the weather. Flashes of lightning to the north and west told her what she didn't want to know: that the squalls, like a gang of marauding bikers, weren't done with them yet.

"Maybe we should think about heading back," she ventured as she returned to scanning the near-empty waters with the glasses.

Sam glanced at her, and she knew he was disappointed. But he said, "No problem. Raise your father on the radio and let him know. He'll feel better."

"Ohmigosh, my father. I forgot all about him." She was touched that Sam had not.

She was about to put down the binoculars when she spied a dim red light close to the water, bobbing up and down. She snapped into a state of high alertness. "Sam," she said.

"*Where?*"

"Head fifteen degrees more west."

He altered direction. She said, "There. A sailboat, dead in the water. Sam, I think it's the *Vixen*. Hold this course," she said, barely able to contain her excitement. "What time is it?"

He punched the light button on his watch. "Eight after eleven,"

She made a mental note of it and said, "Let's kill the nav lights; we'll be okay for a little while."

He did, and they began closing in on the stolen vessel. A few minutes later, Sam slowed down the Robalo, minimizing the noise of its engines as well.

"The dinghy is tied alongside, ready to go," said Holly. Her arms were aching from holding the binoculars so long. "She must be planning to abandon the *Vixen* and head for the nearest shore in the tender after she retrieves the money."

"Then she isn't watching the sky," Sam said. Clearly he was.

Holly couldn't get over Eden's fierce determination to come out of this with cash. "What a risk she took, fiberglassing the money to the hull," she said. "What if she hadn't been able to talk my father into taking her back after the mess she got him into with the state police?"

Sam said wryly, "As you can see, Eden always has a Plan B. Okay, no more talking. Voices carry."

Their approach was slow and wary and, it seemed to Holly, ear-splittingly obvious. (She was convinced that Horatio Hornblower would have swum out from the nearest point of land, breathing through a bamboo reed.)

Still, what could Eden do, once they descended upon her? Holly's greatest fear, her only fear, was that she would hurl the money into the ocean from spite.

They could see the *Vixen* clearly now, even without binoculars. Small bars of light shone through the cabin portholes where the curtains were poorly drawn. Sam cut the engines still more, but there was a look of concern on his face. Holly interpreted it to mean that he was worried that Eden would hear the Robalo pulsing through the water; she was in the bilge, after all.

But that wasn't it. He pointed to the western sky, and it looked, even in the current murky visibility, positively evil. Another squall loomed, and this one had their name on it.

The flashes of light and rumbles of thunder quickly became bolts of lightning and cracks of gunfire, and a gust of wind unlike any other so far rolled over them like a bowling ball, sending their small runabout reeling to starboard. Holly clung to a grab rail while Sam goosed the engine and headed up into the wind, presenting the smallest possible target to the brutalizing force of the squall.

Rain pelted them at a horizontal angle, making hearing and speaking impossible. The horizon, the sky, the sea, the *Vixen*—all gone, lost in the fury of nature at her bitchiest. Holly hung on with wordless trepidation, barely able to open her eyes. There was nothing they could do now but try to ride it out. They had power enough, if Sam had skill enough; and he seemed to know instinctively what to do. They bowed their heads, as much in humble submission to the awesome power of the screaming banshee who ruled over them as to the pounding, biting, savage rain that did her bidding.

The *Vixen*, too, was taking it on the chin. Through the pummelling rain, Holly could see a big bright square of light in the hull, issuing from the cabin below. The boat was lying beam to the wind, being pushed eastward and sliding on its ear in helpless response to the ruthless beating it was enduring. No one was climbing on deck, rushing to the boat's defense; the boat was on its own. Holly waited and wondered how Eden could bear to be below with all hell breaking loose outside.

They were within a hundred yards of the *Vixen* when a figure clad in a white foul-weather jacket popped up in the companionway of the boat, holding the hood from blowing back off her head. As if on cue, the rain began to abate and the wind dropped, if only slightly. The squall was running its course.

"Sam!" said Holly in an urgent undertone. "What should we do? If we let her get in the dinghy and have to follow her, we'll lose the *Vixen*."

Save the money or save the *Vixen*: it never became a full-blown dilemma.

Oblivious to their presence in the darkness nearby, and clutching something silvery to her breast, Eden was making her way forward to the gate in the lifelines, where the dinghy lay tied to the low side of the drifting boat. Light and inflatable, the dinghy was streaming downwind, ahead of the *Vixen* itself. They watched as Eden sat down on the starboard deck with her legs dangling overboard, then tried to haul the dinghy in closer before jumping into it.

By now Holly, who had been taught to sail by a once-cautious man, had a sick and sinking feeling in her stomach: it was insane to take the kind of risk that Eden was taking, all for a suitcase of cash. She wanted to shake Eden, wanted to scream in her face, "It's not worth it! Don't you get it? It's not worth it!"

Eden still did not see the Robalo as it closed on the *Vixen*. That was the wonder of it. She stayed focussed on her foolish, dangerous task.

Unwilling to drop the valise into the dinghy, she attempted the awkward maneuver of dropping down into it while still clutching her cargo. She landed on both feet, all right, but lost her balance and the valise flew out of her hands and into the sea. They heard her cry out in dismay and saw her reach for the money with both arms extended, upsetting her balance even more. She tumbled out of the dinghy just as a sea lifted the *Vixen* and sent the boat rolling to starboard over her before resuming its angled slide downwind.

"Sam, Eden's overboard!" cried Holly, aghast. "We have to save her!"

Sam was ahead of Holly, moving the Robalo almost alongside the *Vixen* and its still-tethered dinghy. "I see her—that patch of white! Take the helm," he shouted, kicking off his deck shoes. "Keep it in neutral as much as you can."

Shaking in fear for Eden's life now, Holly nodded and got behind the wheel of the Robalo just as Sam dove over the side and plunged into the still-churning seas.

He was in a navy jacket and harder to see, and Holly stopped breathing for the entire time it took her to spot his face, bobbing up from below.

But he was alone. Where was Eden? Again Holly lost sight of Sam as he dove below the surface in search of her, with the *Vixen* drifting steadily to the east, and the valise of money who knew where.

Call in a Mayday, a voice told Holly, but another voice said, *Don't take your eyes off him, not for a second*. She listened to the louder instinct—and listened to Sam, putting the Robalo in gear only enough to keep from drifting too far downwind from them. Even so, her stomach tightened at the thought of what a spinning propeller could do to someone in the water.

She heard Sam finally shout in a watered-down cry, "I've got her!"

Thank you, oh, thank you.

Holly's concentration was ferocious as she maneuvered the Robalo into a position downwind of Sam and Eden and then put the boat into neutral. "Hold on, hold on," she cried, dumping a float cushion and an inflatable fender into the water next to Sam for extra insurance.

She grabbed the hood of the unconscious Eden and held her heavy, waterlogged weight, freeing Sam for his hand-over-hand struggle up the dock line she'd thrown over the side. He managed to get aboard without her help, then immediately relieved Holly of the weight of her burden. Between them, and with the help of the sturdily-made, zipped-up jacket that Eden was wearing, they were able to pull her lifeless form aboard.

"CPR," was all Sam said after a quick examination of her on the cockpit sole. "You breathe."

He assumed that Holly would know what to do, and she did, because her father had insisted she learn. Tilting Eden's head back, she began mouth-to-mouth breathing without waiting for Sam. Sam positioned Eden's body for external cardiac massage, counting aloud, cuing Holly to her part in their CPR effort. Holly's mind was absolutely blank as she focussed on one wish only: *Let her live.* If there was a single reason why Eden didn't deserve to be revived, Holly couldn't think of it. *Let her live. Just, please, let her live.*

Sam pumped Eden's heart and Holly supplied Eden's breath until finally Holly felt a breath coming from Eden on her own. "Sam . . . you feel it?"

"There's a beat!" he said, breathing heavily from his efforts so far. "Call the Coast Guard."

Holly radioed for help while Sam kept up CPR on his own. After being grilled by the Coast Guard about their knowledge of the treacherous passage through Woods Hole, and after being informed that the squall line had now passed completely through, Holly and Sam agreed that they should begin ferrying Eden to a dock there.

A Coast Guard cutter came out to intercept them, but they were close enough to their destination that the cutter, lights flashing and sirens wailing, simply blazed a trail in front of them to the dock and waiting ambulance.

Eden was rushed, semi-conscious, to nearby Falmouth Hospital, and Holly found the time at last to contact her father. She had to raise him on the marine radio because, almost inconceivably, she did not know the number of his cell phone. The only person who had that number was now in no position to use it.

Sam returned to the Robalo just as Holly signed off. "How did he react?" he asked as he gave her a hand out of the boat.

"He was devastated for Eden, of course," said Holly, sinking onto the dock's edge in bone-weary exhaustion. "But I think the enormity of the mess he's made has begun to sink in. He sounded scared and alone and more at sea than the *Vixen* right now."

"Speaking of which, how did he take the news that his boat is wandering the Sound without a care in the world?"

"More shock; he's calling a salvage outfit to rescue it. What did the hospital say?"

"They'll keep her under observation awhile, watching for delayed reactions."

"Fluid in the lungs, that kind of thing?" asked Holly, skirting around the big question.

"Mmm. Lung infections, inflammation, cardiac problems . . ." His voice trailed off.

"Sam?" she said timidly. "Did they say anything about . . . about the possibility of brain damage? She was under for what seemed like an eternity."

He shook his head. "They wouldn't; how could they know yet?"

It was a somber moment, the realization that someone so smart, so daring, could end up incapacitated—and possibly die from complications.

Holly was having trouble dealing with it. "It's so overwhelming," she said softly. "I thought I hated her. I was sure of it. And yet when I saw her go overboard . . . well, I don't, that's all. I just don't."

"I know," said Sam. "I know."

They sat side by side in silence, with their legs dangling over the dock, like two kids playing hooky to go fishing.

Only there were no poles. There was no joy. And unlike two kids, they knew that life was finite.

"Sam?"

"Mmm."

"The money's gone. We'll never find it now. If this were a movie, we'd discover the valise—I think it was the kind that floats—tangled in a line hanging overboard on the Robalo."

"Yeah, but you're too good a sailor to leave a line dangling overboard," he teased.

"You know what I mean. No one is going to turn the money in, and even if they did, how could we claim it? Legally, I mean."

"See? This is where thinking like an outlaw got you. Bitter disappointment when your hopes went amuck."

"Because it's not *fair*."

"Life isn't fair. If you hang up on that, you die miserable and unhappy. The money's gone. Assume it's at the bottom of the sea; for all practical purposes, it is. We move on. My ma and pa will be fine. I'll see to that." He added a little wistfully, "It's just that I know how proud they are. They wanted that independence."

"At least now you can tell them the engraving's a fake," Holly realized. "They'll feel better about that after this."

He smiled and put his arm around her and pulled her close. "Now yer talkin'. Come on," he said, standing up. "It's going to feel like a long way back to the Vineyard."

"Oh, Sam, I can't," Holly protested, refusing to be dragged to her feet. "I'm so tired. I'm sick of the ocean, sick of the salt. Let's stay at an inn in Falmouth. We'll have a nice shower, clean sheets. We'll want to go to the hospital first thing in the morning, anyway."

Sam thought about it and suddenly snapped his fingers and dazzled her with a eureka-smile. "Or how about this? We go to my place. I wouldn't mind waking up in my bed with a dish like you. I don't suppose," he added with a boyishly hopeful look, "that you brought your diaphragm along?"

Tired as she was, Holly laughed out loud at the notion. "My thoughts haven't exactly been running that way," she admitted.

But now, suddenly, they were.

"Of course, since you bring it up," she said, "I don't

really see why we should need a diaphragm at all," she said softly. "Don't you agree? Sam?"

Will we be married and have babies and barbecues and go on vacations mostly on land and prune our forsythia and take your dad on walks in the park and fill stockings at Christmas and teach Sally it's okay to get her hands dirty and have more barbecues and try to get my parents together and tell Jack he can't do that ever again and take ballroom dancing and have more barbecues and teach our kids not to lie and take turns cooking and will you do all the cooking and will we love each other no matter what?

"Sam?"

He tipped her chin up and, still smiling, kissed her lightly, lovingly, on her lips. "Yes, Holly. Yes."

Epilogue

June on the Vineyard is a hit-or-miss thing. Sam and Holly's wedding day missed a stretch of perfect weather and hit a cold front going through.

They were married under a tent pitched right on the beach not far from the house because the events planner "just had the most fabulous feeling about it" and knew that the day would be perfect. So the ceremony was marked by—what else?—thunder and lightning and drumming rain, and no one except Sam heard the lovely vow that Holly had written, promising till death did them part. (As for Sam, no one would have heard him rain *or* shine, because he barely whispered the vow that *he'd* written. What did he think, that it was only for her?)

As the ceremony proceeded and the tent sprang leaks, the planner, the photographer, the caterer, and the bride's mother all put their heads together and decided to move the whole shebang to the big house on Main, where, if you asked just about anyone, it should have been held in the first place.

So much for the charm of the beach.

It was coming down hard by the time the wedding party (maid of honor, two flower girls, and one best man who owned a seaplane decked out with a Just-Married sign) piled into the two rented minivans pressed into limo service. Sam drove the women (Cissy sat on Holly's lap and Sally sat on Ivy's, to make room for the flowers), and Billy—still red-eyed from sobbing uncontrollably through the entire ceremony—drove behind them with the cake, the planner, and Charlotte Anderson.

Jim and Millie drove with Eric Anderson. They were too thoroughly intimidated by their first journey offshore and society wedding to go in Charlotte's van, despite her entreaties. It was only after the Steadmans saw the bride and her sister in bedraggled hair and soggy hemlines, laughing and sprinting barefoot behind the flower girls from the van to the house, that they looked at one another and whispered, "Well, maybe this won't be too bad."

They were surprised, in fact, at how many guests were just folks. Ivy's husband Jack from California—*he* was just folks. And Holly's artist friends from the Island, they were all a bit strange but still very friendly. The elderly couple with the French last name were not just folks, but still so easy to talk to.

It was too bad that their son Sam had so few friends of his own, but that was the kind of man he was. Anyway, he had Billy from way back by his side as best man, and the Steadmans were very fond of Billy.

They were supposed to have been in a receiving line or some such; but the rain and the unscheduled move, praise the Lord, had taken care of all that. Holly, sweet thing, made sure that they met each and every guest, introducing them with a new hug each time as her mother-in-law and father-in-law. It was so different from when Sam had brought Eden home from City Hall and then when Eden went to the bathroom, said, "Well?

What do you think?" as if she were a brand-new car.

No, this was a different woman, and this was a different Sam.

Of course, sometimes you couldn't turn them around no matter how hard you tried. They'd had a foster son like that once. He lied, he stole, he drank, he fought with everyone and anyone. Eventually he was killed in a fight when he was only fourteen, and Millie had been devastated and had decided that she was unfit for foster parenting, but then the Good Lord had sent her Sam.

"Look at him, Jim," Millie whispered to her husband as she moved his walker out of the way of traffic. "Don't he look handsome? And don't he just look so in *love* with her? I can't remember him doting on Eden that way."

And Sam's father, never a man of words, nodded wisely and said, "Boy's older now. He's found what to look for." After a moment, he added, "That's something about Eden, no?"

"Yes . . . that Marjory woman does seem to know everything about everyone, don't she? To think that Eden would have ended up married to an oilman! It's just so hard to believe. Where do all those rich Texans come from, anyway?"

"Texas, I expect," said Jim with a wry smile.

"At least he found out her true colors. I wonder how the court fight went."

"One thing's for sure: she'll find somebody else."

"Until she loses that bloom."

"Or runs out of states."

"Oh! Here's Charlotte!"

The mother of the bride arrived with plates of fancy food that she had made up personally for each of the Steadmans, and sat down with them a while.

"We haven't had any time to talk," she complained with a really gentle smile. "Please consider staying the

night here; I can easily send someone to the inn for your
things. I'm upset with your son, you know, for booking
that room instead of bringing you here."

"Oh, don't be, please!" Millie begged, afraid that
she'd wrecked things for Sam. "We're the ones made
him do it."

Charlotte kept asking and Millie came around, by degrees, into agreeing to stay for just the one night. "After
that, it's home to the bungalow, right Jim?"

"It's where we feel best," her husband explained.

"It's settled, then," said Charlotte, and she went off
to make the arrangements.

They watched her leave the room. "She seems
happy," Jim volunteered.

"And why wouldn't she be? She's the mother of the
bride," said Millie, as if that explained everything.

"Well . . . *you* know . . ." murmured her husband as
Eric Anderson caught their eye.

He came over and sat on a folding chair next to the
more comfortable armchair that Holly had found for her
new father-in-law.

He looked tired. Tired and a bit down in the dumps.
But that was natural, thought Millie, him losing his
daughter to another man and all. All fathers went
through it. He hadn't been with Charlotte for almost a
year, so *that* couldn't be it.

Still, Millie was feeling uncomfortable, and when she
was nervous, she babbled. "Charlotte was just here a
minute ago," she said, because for sure he must have
seen her. "She's talked us into staying here for the
night."

"Ah. Lucky you. I haven't had any success that way,
myself," he said with a rueful smile.

Oh, thought Millie, that was putting her foot in it!
Her husband began studying the wallpaper, which just

infuriated her. He never knew what to say at times like these.

"I'm sorry," Millie murmured, because she didn't know what to say, either.

"Oh, don't be sorry!" Eric said. "I didn't mean it the way it sounded." He made the corners of his mouth go up, but Millie wasn't convinced in the least.

He said, "Would you like me to retrieve your luggage from the Stone's Throw Inn?"

Millie pointed in some confusion to Charlotte, who was in the next room talking to someone Eric's age. "I think she's just asking someone—"

"Well! Let's see if I can't take over; they'd recognize me at the inn, since I picked you up there earlier."

He excused himself, and Millie gave Jim a poke for not handling the situation better.

Eric was aware, as he approached the woman from whom he was separated, that he was fighting for his emotional life. Charlotte Anderson had put up a wall between them that he hadn't yet been able to scale. It was a pretty wall, to be sure—all covered with sweet-smelling roses—but that had made it all the more difficult to climb.

If only she'd scream at him, curse him, throw things. But no, she was always unfailingly kind—when *wasn't* she kind?—and polite, but crushingly firm: she wasn't prepared to take him back. He had already spent nearly a year dying a slow and painful death, watching his life-blood slowly ooze from his self-inflicted wounds.

And now she was seeing someone! Carl! That . . . that gigolo! He had to be a good six or seven years younger than Charlotte. Granted, she still looked younger than Carl did—contractors weathered more quickly than most—but for two cents Eric would knock his block off. If he could. Eric felt personally betrayed by the man.

After throwing so much business his way over the years . . .

He went up to his wife in time to see Carl accepting a room key from her and smiling at something she said. She turned to Eric and the smile lingered, and yet something fell away from it. He felt as if he'd just hosed off half the petals from a blooming rose.

He nodded to the guest—who was, after all, *just* a guest, not the father of the bride or even the estranged husband of the bride's mother—and said, "Excuse me, Carl, would you? I'll just steal Charlotte for a minute."

Eric felt pleased with his collegial manner, but when he got Charlotte to the side he wanted desperately to take her in his arms and kiss her. It had been so long. He missed her so much. To lie with her in their old bed tonight—that would be heaven.

"Lotty," he said, feeling entitled to use the pet name on this of all days. "I—you look really beautiful," he said, interrupting himself. How had he ever been oblivious to that? "What a glow you have today."

"Thank you, Eric," she said, smiling. "You look very dapper yourself."

"Our little girl. Can you believe it?"

"I know," her mother said with a half-mournful smile. "They grow up so fast."

He pretended to be in the way of a passing guest and moved in closer to his wife. She stepped aside, too. He ended up no closer.

"Holly's in good hands, right?" he asked, desperate to keep the conversation going.

"Eric! How can you ask?"

"Of course she is," he said quickly. "But you know I want the best for her."

"I do know, Eric," said Charlotte. "You always have."

She recognized that, then; that for most of his life,

he hadn't been a shit. He'd been a good father, a loyal husband. For almost all of his sixty-three years. Heartened, he said, "The house is going to seem emptier." He wanted to say, *even* emptier.

Charlotte said, "Oh, not at all. Those two hang out here all the time; it will be more of the same—only better," she added with a secretive smile.

Guilt didn't work on her; nothing did. Desperate, he said, "I've just been talking with the Steadmans, and they told me they're staying here tonight. I offered to run over for their luggage; the innkeeper saw me pick them up earlier, so at least there wouldn't be any question."

Charlotte's smile broadened, sending his spirits soaring. She *did* appreciate the gesture!

"Eric, that would be *so* nice," she said, even laying her hand on his forearm.

The heat of her touch sizzled through his shirtsleeve. For the hundred-thousandth time in the past year, he flayed himself for being a fool.

"Carl," she said gaily across the room. "Could you give me that key back? Eric's offered to go instead."

Carl flashed a grateful grin and said, "Here you go," and tossed the key underhand to Eric, who dropped it and then scooped it up quickly.

He turned in time to see his wife rejoin Carl and walk into his old study. He smiled to himself: a sad, wistful, melancholy smile. He'd been too smart by half.

On his way out, he detoured past his daughter, just to breathe in her happiness; it might last him through part of the long night ahead. "Hey, punkin, you got your curls back," he said, slipping his arm around her and giving her a peck on the cheek.

"I know," his daughter said. She scrunched her face in disgust. "After all that work blow-drying it straight this morning before the rain."

"You look radiant. Happy?" he murmured.

"Oh, Dad," said Holly, sighing. "More than anyone in the world." Her face lit up, and Eric didn't have to ask why. He turned in time to see his son-in-law and ex-rival coming to reclaim his bride.

"Hey-y-y," he said good-naturedly to Sam. "Give me a break. You'll have her for the rest of your life."

"Not long enough," said Holly's husband, and Eric knew too well it was true.

He was about to say, "Treat her well," but it would be stating the obvious, and besides, he had no right to be giving that advice. Instead he smiled and said, "You're a damn lucky guy, Sam."

He yielded his daughter with more grace than he'd just yielded his wife, and then he went out to his car, slapping the inn key idly against his thigh.

Holly, arm in arm with the man she loved, watched her father leave. "I wish he could be even a tiny fraction as happy as we are," she said, sighing.

"That would be blazingly happy indeed," said Sam, stealing yet another in an endless series of kisses from his new bride.

Holly enjoyed the kiss—she was no fool—and then resumed her train of thought. "At least he's over Eden. Frankly, I didn't think he'd be able to resist her when she tried again. I keep pointing that out to my mother, how he deserves credit for that, but so far she's not impressed."

Sam said, "I dunno. I just saw her talking to him, and she looked pretty happy."

Holly smiled and said, "That's because she knows our secret."

"Holy cats, you told her? When?"

"Just a little while ago. I wanted her to know before we go off on our honeymoon."

"Uh-oh." Sam glanced guiltily around the conservatory and shepherded his wife away from their guests and behind a huge schefflera. "What did she say?"

"She asked me when my due date was."

"Cool."

"Just don't go stealing her station wagon and taking it for a joyride around the island," Holly teased.

Sam grinned and said, "The hell with the Volvo; I have my eye on your dad's new Porsche."

Sighing, Holly murmured, "Yes . . . the Porsche. That didn't help his case with my mother any."

"Holly, if it was meant to be, it will be."

"I know," she said, slipping her arms around his neck. "Sam? *Will* you love me forever?"

His face softened in a look that took her breath away. For an answer, he repeated part of his vow from a few hours before. "You're my sun, my moon, the stars beyond," he whispered. "You are my life."

He kissed her again, a long, tender, utterly devoted kiss, and Holly knew that he meant it forever.

They were discovered by Billy, sweating profusely despite the undone bowtie and rolled-up sleeves. "Hey, you two, let's move it. Daylight's burnin'. Besides," he added to Sam, "I can't get out of this godforsaken monkey suit until you do, man. Have mercy, will ya?"

And so Holly and Sam changed into island wear— shorts and tee shirts—and ran through a hail of rice under brand-new sunshine (which everyone took as an omen), and Jack drove them and Billy to his waiting seaplane, and Billy flew them to Nantucket and their waiting bed.

And Holly and Sam stayed in that bed for the rest of the day and much of the next, without once coming out to say hi to the innkeeper.